THE LAST
ROAD HOME

THE LAST
ROAD HOME

DANNY JOHNSON

KENSINGTON BOOKS
www.kensingtonbooks.com

KENSINGTON BOOKS are published by

Kensington Publishing Corp.
119 West 40th Street
New York, NY 10018

All Kensington titles, imprints, and distributed lines are available at special quantity discounts for bulk purchases for sales promotion, premiums, fund-raising, educational, or institutional use.

Special book excerpts or customized printings can also be created to fit specific needs. For details, write or phone the office of the Kensington Sales Manager: Kensington Publishing Corp., 119 West 40th Street, New York, NY 10018. Attn. Sales Department. Phone: 1-800-221-2647.

Kensington and the K logo Reg. U.S. Pat. & TM Off.

eISBN-13: 978-1-4967-0250-0
eISBN-10: 1-4967-0250-6
First Kensington Electronic Edition: August 2016

ISBN-13: 978-1-4967-0249-4
ISBN-10: 1-4967-0249-2
First Kensington Trade Paperback Printing: August 2016

10 9 8 7 6 5 4 3 2 1

Printed in the United States of America

This novel is dedicated to the person most responsible
for its creation and the person
who will never be able to read it:
My Warrior Brother, James V. "Dot" Dorsey,
KIA 05 Feb 1969,
final homecoming at Arlington National Cemetery,
20 May 2015. RIP

On January 1, 1863, Congress enacted President Lincoln's Emancipation Proclamation. One hundred years later, it was still the law of the land, but in the South it was more theory than reality.

PART 1

Chapter 1

Maybe it wasn't true. "Come on, Junebug, it's all right, don't be afraid." Grandma took my hand. Inside the house, a late-afternoon shadow stretched like a long rectangular arm across the living room carpet. The Coke bottle Daddy used for an ashtray was stuffed with cigarette butts and sat on the coffee table. Momma's rocking chair waited for her; I pushed on the painted wooden arm to hear it squeak.

Two applejacks left over from Friday sat in a plate on the kitchen stove; this time of day the house should smell like fresh-made sweet tea and supper cooking. I looked on the back porch, but nobody was there either. In the bathroom, I touched the last pencil line where Momma marked my height every year on my birthday. In their bedroom, I lay on the pillow to smell her. My head knew they were gone, but my eight-year-old heart didn't yet.

Grandma sat beside me, tears rolling down her face; she'd cried a lot in the last two days. "Let's go find what you want to carry home."

In my room, I got the cigar box from my closet while Grandma packed clothes in paper bags. When her arms were loaded, she stood at the door. "Ready to go?"

"In a minute." I went back to Momma and Daddy's room, looked in her jewelry box and found the silver gum wrapper necklace I'd made for her in school. "Okay." I stopped at the bottom of our steps and picked one of the red roses Momma had planted in the spring.

The next afternoon I sat under a tent in the graveyard, staring at blankets of flowers that covered the tops of two caskets. They smelled like Momma's rose. The preacher patted my head. "It was God's Will," he said. "They'll be waiting for you in heaven."

I blinked back angry tears. "Tell me why God would want to kill my momma and daddy?"

"Shhhh." Grandma squeezed my shoulders.

After the funeral, Granddaddy took me to talk under his woodshed. He sat on a stump used for splitting kindling, and I sat beside him on an upside-down peach basket. He laid his big hand on my shoulder. "Junebug, sometimes things just are, nobody to blame or no way to make sense of it. All a man can do is put one foot in front of the other and keep going. Do you understand?"

What was I supposed to understand? One day you're alive and the next you're dead? I went into the house and the bedroom where I slept when I stayed with them on the farm, the one that would now be mine forever. I pulled the cigar box from underneath the bed. Inside it were baseball cards I'd saved, a picture of Momma holding me when I was a baby, the silver dollar Granddaddy gave me last year for my seventh birthday, and the collar I'd taken off Grady's neck.

Daddy killed Grady on my birthday. We had gone to Grandma's for supper and I'd just blown out the six candles on my coconut birthday cake when we heard Granddaddy's dog start howling like something was killing him. By the time we ran outside, the taillights of a truck were rounding the curve of the road.

Grady lay at the edge of the ditch, whining. Granddaddy knelt beside him. "Back's broke." He gently rubbed Grady's head.

"Be right back," Daddy said. He walked to the car and came back holding his big black pistol. "Y'all back up." He bent over and stuck the barrel close to Grady's head.

I yanked on Granddaddy's pants leg. "What's he going to do?"

He squatted beside me. "Junebug, when an animal is hurt bad like that you can't fix it, so it's better to put it out of its pain. Can you understand?" He laid his big hand against my head. "You don't need to watch."

Instead of turning away, I took off running and fell into the ditch with Grady, covering him with my body, pushing the gun away. "I'll help you, Grady." I lay with my eyes level with Grady, tears trailing across the bridge of my nose. "I'll fix you, don't you worry." Grady's soft brown eyes watched me, and then he reached to lick my face.

"Get out of the way, Junebug. Go in the house with your momma." Daddy grabbed me by the back of my shirt, pulled me up, and half-shoved, half-threw me back toward where Granddaddy stood. "Keep him out of the way."

"Easy, Roy, you ain't got to be so rough." Granddaddy reached down and picked me up.

"Then take him in the house with the women."

My crying had turned to hiccup sobs. "You leave Grady alone! I can take care of him."

Grady whined loud again. Then came the thunderous boom of Daddy's pistol, and Grady made the most awful screaming crying sound I'd ever heard. Then silence.

Granddaddy cussed at him. "Dammit, you could have waited 'til I got the boy in the house."

"Won't hurt him, he needs to understand life ain't always easy."

I hooked Momma's necklace inside Grady's collar, closed the box, and put it back under the bed.

* * *

"Come here a minute, Junebug." Grandma waved me to her. It was a hot August morning three weeks after my parents' funeral. The hard-packed sand on the dirt path in front of Mr. Wilson's barn was cool on my bare feet. We had come to help the neighbors harvest tobacco.

"Junebug, this is Fancy and her twin brother, Lightning. They live on Mr. and Mrs. Wilson's farm."

The girl was a lighter black than her brother. Her hair was bobby-pinned in little curls, and the boy's was cut right down to the skin. They both watched the ground. "Fancy, would you and your brother mind showing Junebug around and playing together while we work?"

The girl didn't look up. "Yes'um." Her brother didn't say anything. We waited in silence until the grown-ups headed to the fields, leaving us alone. Fancy stared at me, and she didn't look happy. She crooked her finger. They led me down a dirt path to the edge of the woods where a bucket of rocks sat alongside a line of tin cans on a log. The three of us stood apart, getting the measure of each other. I wiped sweat off my upper lip with the back of my finger.

Fancy stepped close, put her face up to mine, and balanced her hands on her hips. "How old are you?" She was bony thin, had a big head, and her upper teeth bowed out. The expression on her face was *I ain't scared*. I thought she might punch me if I didn't answer.

"Eight." I wiped again.

She thumbed back at Lightning. "Us too. Where'd you get a name like that?" Her brother watched.

"Momma give it to me."

"Where's your momma at?"

I studied the ground, shying away from her demanding tone. "Dead."

"Sure don't talk much. Ain't off in the head are you? How'd she die?"

"Car wreck."

"Your daddy too?" She moved even closer. If they jumped me, I'd have to try and outrun them.

"Yep." I closed the toes of my bare foot over a rock and tried to pick it up.

Fancy glanced at her brother, like she was asking a question. He shrugged. When she turned back around, her look was different. Her arm came up. I leaned sideways. But instead of punching me, Fancy grabbed my hand. "It'll be all right, June-bug."

Lightning walked over to the bucket and picked out a rock. He sent it flying at the cans and hit one. "Try it," Fancy said, and handed me a rock. I threw and missed everything.

We spent the next few hours trying to hit cans. Lightning showed me how to curve a rock, and Fancy was actually better at it than either of us.

After breakfast on Tuesday morning the following week, Grand-daddy said, "Come on, Junebug, I need to smoke the barn." We stacked some kindling and an ax into a wheelbarrow.

"What do you mean 'smoke' the barn?"

"The Wilsons are coming to help us put in tobacco tomor-row, and the snakes need to be run out before we can hang it." Granddaddy was a big man, arms like posts, and a heavy belly. He was fair-faced with a leathery, sunburned neck, and was never without his wide-brimmed felt hat. At the barn he laid dry pine slabs in the firebox, struck a match to them, then cut down a couple of oak shoots. When the fire was burning good, he added the green leaves and sapling wood. Smoke began to fill the inside of the barn, some leaking from between the logs where the chink mud had come loose.

"How you going to catch the snakes?"

"Ain't. Snakes won't bother you unless you bother them." He started around the side of the barn, looking up to see how much smoke was coming out of the roof. I squatted in front of the fire and tossed in a handful of leaves.

I heard a yell and saw Granddaddy running around, cussing and slapping at his hat. A long black snake flew through the air. He chased and stomped at the snake, but it took off under some leaves.

"What happened?"

"Durn thing fell off the top of the barn square on my head."

I couldn't help laughing at him. "Didn't bother you, did he?"

He got red-faced. "Watch the fire, I need to go to the outhouse for a minute."

I told Grandma the snake story at dinner. She laughed so hard she got tears, and came over to hug my neck. Since the funeral, I'd heard her and Granddaddy whispering a lot at night when they thought I was asleep, and I caught her crying several times. My daddy was their son. I'd stayed with them a lot since the time I was a baby, so it wasn't hard to get used to living with them. It was good to see some happiness slip out from behind her blue eyes.

After dinner Granddaddy and me went back to the barn and used garden hoes to clean away poison ivy that had grown too close to the open shelter. I didn't really know what poison ivy was, but I chopped at anything I thought might need it. A few yards from the barn, I noticed a place the grass was worn down, like a path. "That a deer track?"

He came over to have a look. "Used to be a horse trail a long time ago, way back before anybody had cars or trucks." He pointed through the woods. "Comes out at the Wilson place."

The next morning after the grown-ups headed to the tobacco field, I showed Fancy and Lightning the path, thinking it might be an important contribution to the new friendship. "Granddaddy said it goes all the way to where y'all live." We followed the trail until the woods ended, and discovered it came out at a clover field behind the Wilson farm.

"I never knew this was here," said Lightning. Halfway along the trail, several trees had been cut, leaving good-sized stumps. Immediately, we agreed it was probably where Indians used to camp.

We sat across from each other. "How come you got a name like Junebug?" Fancy asked.

"It was the month I was born. My Christian name is Raeford Earl Hurley. Where'd y'all get the name Fancy and Lightning?"

Fancy stood up, put her hands behind her back, and started pacing like a preacher in a pulpit. "Well, I'll tell you about it. You see"—she imitated a deep voice—"there was this big storm that come over the land the night him and me was born." Fancy waved at the sky with both hands, eyes wide and fearful. "Thunder boomed like shotguns, and the wind howled like witches on Halloween." She pointed at Lightning. "He came first, then me. Daddy named him because of the awful lightning that caused three fires in the community." Her tone changed to sweet and cheerful. "But Momma said she always liked the name Fancy so it's what I got." She went back to the fierce look, dropping her voice low again. "Now, that's the way it was told to me." Fancy gripped her hands behind and went back to pacing, like she was considering. "But . . . after all these years of thinking . . ." She paused again. Lightning and I leaned forward, waiting to see what she was going to say. "I really think Daddy named Lightning Lightning because he knew what a big pain in the ass he'd always be." She ran in a circle pointing at Lightning, cackling.

"Very funny," said Lightning. "Keep it up and you're going to sure enough get struck by Lightning."

I had to hold my stomach from laughing so hard.

The stumps became our secret place.

Tobacco season had ended and school was set to begin in another couple of weeks. Fancy, Lightning, and me sat shooting the breeze. Lightning got to his feet and walked back and forth, like he was irritated. "I'm gone have enough money to do the bossing one of these days. The two of you will be working for me then." He marched around with a swelled chest. "Git in that kitchen and make me some food!" He waved his arm at Fancy like he might smack her.

"Try bossing me and I'll hit you in the head with a hammer when you go to sleep."

Lightning faked another swing, then went back to circle-walking. "I need to get some money before I go back to school, can't get no girlfriend if you ain't carrying no change. I want to go to the store just one time and reach in my pocket to find something other than a hole."

We sat thinking for a bit. "I went with Granddaddy to Markham's store the other day and he took back some empty Coke bottles. He got two cents apiece for them. Y'all got any bottles?"

Lightning stopped. "Heck, yeah. They's laying all over Mr. Wilson's barn shelter. We could take 'em and sell 'em. And I bet we could go around to other farms and ask if we could look; folks might be glad to get rid of 'em. That's a good idea, June-bug." He started counting on his fingers. "If we was to get a thousand bottles at two cents each, what would that come to?"

"Twenty dollars," Fancy said quickly. "How we going to carry that many bottles?"

Lightning smacked her on the head. "Feed sacks, stupid."

Fancy leaped to her feet. "Just touch me again!"

"Y'all quit fussing," I scolded.

Lightning was excited. "Meet here tomorrow early and everybody bring a sack. We'll visit every farm around 'til we fill 'em."

The next morning I rushed through breakfast. "Where you off to in such a hurry?" Granddaddy and Grandma smiled when I told them what we were going to do.

Fancy and me listened while Lightning laid out the plan. "I'll head to Mr. Ferrell's place. You two go the other way toward the Seagrove farm. When everybody gets a sack full, we'll meet back here and count 'em up."

The day started hot and got worse. Fancy and me, barefooted and no hat to keep off the sun, headed down the dirt road that led from in front of our house to Evergreen Baptist Church, which was near the Seagrove place. We had a skipping race for a ways. Fancy was lagging behind, and when I turned around she was gone. "Fancy?" I looked around the bushes. "Fancy, where the heck are you?"

A dirt clod hit me in the shoulder. I heard a giggle from Mr. Riggsbee's tobacco patch on the other side of the road. "Oh, want to play, huh?" I dived in between the rows, bombing her with dirt balls. I accidentally knocked over a tobacco stalk.

Fancy grabbed my hand. "Let's go. Folks don't like somebody tearing down their crop." We ran until we were out of breath.

An hour and a half later, we made it to the church, but it was still another half mile to Mr. Seagrove's farm. It never seemed this far riding in the truck. By the time we got there, both of us were worn out, soaked with dusty sweat, and in a foul mood. "Damn Lightning," Fancy said. "I know it ain't this far to Mr. Ferrell's place."

Fancy stood back in the yard while I walked up to Mr. Seagrove's door and knocked. His wife came to the porch, a big woman, thighs wide as two fat hams and a voice deep as a man's. She sang in the church choir and you could hear her a mile away. "Junebug, what are you doing here? Is your grandma with you?" She looked out at Fancy.

"No'um, she's at home. We're trying to collect some Coca-Cola bottles to sell, and wanted to see if we could look around your place."

"You're welcome to look. I'd try around the tobacco barn if I was you. Just go down that path." She pointed beside the house. "When y'all get through, stop and I'll have some iced tea for you."

When we reached the barn, we took a break in the shade of the overhanging shelter before starting the search. I heard a noise and looked up to see a dog standing in the path watching us. He reminded me of Grady.

"Junebug, if we get a sack load how the heck are we going to tote 'em?"

"Don't know, and right now I wish I'd never brought it up." We rambled in the bushes and briars around the barn, managing to find fifteen bottles that weren't broke and a lot more that were. Fancy came across an empty whiskey bottle, screwed off the top, and stuck her tongue inside to taste. "Aaah, that's nasty." She smacked her mouth in disgust, then pitched it back in the weeds.

I began to understand Granddaddy and Grandma's smile this morning. "I figure we've made about thirty cents."

The best thing we found was a blackberry patch. Each of us picked a couple of handfuls and sat on the dirt floor under the shelter to eat. Dark juice ran down our chins onto our clothes. The flies wanted a taste. We couldn't swat fast enough. Fancy got up. "Come on, I'm ready to go home, had enough of this dumb mess."

We didn't bother to stop at Mrs. Seagrove's house for tea; blackberry juice had quenched our thirst. I carried the half-full sack a ways and Fancy carried it a ways. She talked nonstop most of the walk home, about church or how she was anxious to go back to school so she could be around somebody other than Lightning. With Fancy, life was never lonesome.

Lightning was already sitting at the stumps. I didn't see any bottles and he didn't look happy. "What happened? You couldn't find any?" Fancy showed him ours.

"I went over to Mr. Ferrell's and told him what I wanted to do. He told me to get my black ass away from his house, said he didn't want no niggers nosing around his place." Lightning wouldn't look at me.

My face turned warm and flushed. I held out our bag. "Here, Lightning, you can have my share."

He took the sack and went home.

Fancy got up to follow him. She held her arms out from her sides like she wanted to say she was sorry. " 'Bye, Junebug."

We didn't meet on the path for a long time after that.

CHAPTER 2

"Can I go with you and lend a hand?" It was November and a bitterly cold day. One of our neighbors, Mrs. Luter, fell off her back porch two days before, broke her neck, and died on the spot. She was eighty-six and everybody in the community called her Granny May. Her ninety-year-old husband had to leave her on the ground until he could walk a half mile to get help. Granddaddy loaded his pick and shovel in the truck. He was headed to the church to help dig her grave.

The yard grass crunched with morning frost. "You stay by the fire, ain't enough starch in them fourteen-year-old britches of yours yet to break frozen ground." It took him three tries to get his old Chevy truck cranked. I was too cold to argue.

Grandma had started to cook dinner, the house smelling up with collards and fatback, expecting Granddaddy to be home any minute. The men could usually get a grave dug in three or four hours. I'd just added a couple of oak pieces to the pot-bellied stove when somebody knocked on the screened-in-porch door. I saw Mr. Jackson, Mr. Wilson, and Preacher Mills standing in front of the steps, hats in their hands.

"Morning." I looked out, expecting to see Granddaddy's truck in the yard.

Mr. Jackson said, "Junebug, we need to talk to Miss Rosa Belle."

A knot twisted in my stomach. "Where's my granddaddy?"

Grandma came up behind me. "Come in and get warm." We went to sit in the living room close to the stove. Wood cracked and popped as it burned.

Grandma sat on the couch, and Preacher Mills squatted in front of her. He took her hands in his. "Miss Rosa Belle, we got some bad news." He looked down at the linoleum. When he raised his head, he said, "Ernie fell over a couple of hours ago while the men were digging the grave for Mrs. Luter. By the time the ambulance got to the church, it was too late. The medic suspects he had a heart attack. They just left a little bit ago; they'll carry him by the hospital first, then to Apex Funeral Home. We figured you'd want to go to him."

I couldn't have heard him right. I stood up. "My granddaddy's dead?" I wanted to hit Preacher Mills in the face.

Grandma pulled her hands from the preacher's and grabbed my arm. "I'm grateful to you for coming to tell me. Let me change my clothes." She went into the bathroom. I knew she'd do her crying in private, it was her way.

Nobody talked as Grandma and I rode in the backseat of Mr. Jackson's car. I listened to the whine of rubber tires on the pavement and watched pastures of brittle brown winter grass and fields of sad-looking cornstalks, dried up and bent over like a crowd of cripples, pass by the window.

At the funeral home, heavy gray carpet and whispered conversation made for unsettling quiet. I held Grandma's cold hand while the man in charge guided us to a room in the back of the building. When he opened the door, I could see Granddaddy's body covered in a white sheet on a rolling metal table. I stopped. Grandma tugged on my elbow. "It's all right. We need to say good-bye, Junebug."

I had to make myself look when she pulled back the sheet. His skin was a pale off-white. There was a big purple bruise on his chest and scratches on the side of his face. What struck me the most was the unnatural stillness of him, how it was so different from a person who was just asleep, how strong you could feel the absence of life. Grandma rubbed his head and used her fingers to comb his gray-specked dark curly hair. She stroked his face, her lips moving but making no sound. I gripped his arm, and when I let go, the skin stayed indented.

At his burying, snow mixed with sleet rode on a freezing wind. Sitting beside Grandma in the ice-covered cemetery, I thought about six years before when I watched my parents disappear into this ground. Now I watched Granddaddy's box being lowered into a hole, and heard the preacher say to Grandma it was *"God's Will."* I looked at the dark sky, and bit my tongue. Granddaddy had been the fence post I'd leaned on since Momma and Daddy died. "Junebug," he'd said back then, "when things are hardest, all a man can do is not quit, even though nobody would blame him if he did."

That night I dreamed I saw Jesus standing on a mountain. Lightning bolts flashed around him. He held out a long staff and roared, *"I AM THY GOD AND YOU WILL BOW DOWN."* On the other side of the valley stood the devil, a giant dark being with a river of fire shooting from his hand. He pointed back at Jesus. *"YOU ARE THE GOD OF PROMISES, I AM THE GOD OF TRUTH."* I jerked awake shaking, and lay there until daybreak with the light on.

The following summer, after a morning of helping Mr. Wilson harvest tobacco, I sat at the dinner table with them. Grandma always told me never to take the last of anything when I was eating at somebody else's house, so, as much as I wanted that chicken leg, I laid my fork and knife in my plate. "That was mighty good, Mrs. Wilson."

"Glad you liked it, Junebug." Mrs. Wilson was a frail, fidgety woman with a sharp nose, and hair too white to be natural. She could never be still, constantly getting up to check to see if the coloreds eating at the outside bench needed something, or refilling Mr. Wilson's tea glass.

I pushed away from the table. "Think I'll go sit on the porch swing until it's time to go back to work."

"Good idea, Junebug, everybody needs to rest an hour." Mr. Wilson reached for the chicken leg. His jaws were already full, puffed out like an ugly squirrel's, but that didn't stop him from packing in more. He'd always acted with kindness to Grandma and me, but over time, I'd come to have an inkling of distrust for him, nothing I could put my finger on, but it was there just the same. He'd stopped by the house yesterday to ask if I would help. Since I was broke as usual, the five dollars for a day of priming tobacco would come in good. Mr. Wilson was a short, thick-legged, red-faced man with a floppy face and a full head of straight black hair. He looked like he toted a five-pound sack of flour in his belly, made me wonder how he could see so as not to piss on his shoes.

I put on my hat and went out the side door to the yard. Fancy was eating at the plank table with her momma, daddy, and the other half-dozen coloreds. I was curious why I hadn't seen Lightning this morning at the tobacco field. I gave her the eye before walking around to the rear of the house.

I settled into the wooden swing, shut my eyes, and laid my head against the top rail, pushing back and forth with my toes. A soft breeze stirred through the trees that shaded the yard. Jay-birds squawked at squirrels that chased each other up and down a giant oak, and noisy carpenter bees hunted for dead wood along the eave of the house. It was a good country band.

Footsteps shuffled through the leaves. I pushed up my hat. "Hey, Fancy."

"Hey." She watched the ground as she walked.

"Is Lightning sick?"

"He's sick all right—sick in the head." She had on a red cotton dress frayed at the hem, and wore pigtails tied with yellow strips of cloth. "He's gone."

I stopped the swing. "Gone where?"

Fancy sat down on the bottom step of the gray-painted plank porch, smoothing the dress under her legs. She let out a big sigh and shrugged her shoulders. "Took up with some migrant workers at Old Man Jackson's place last week. They moved on and he went with 'em, said he needed to see something other than Chatham County before he died." She used her big toe to mash piss ants that crawled along the ground.

"What'd your momma and daddy say?" Maybe he'd got one of his mad spells and just decided he'd had enough of white folks.

"What could they say?" Fancy scratched her foot where one of the ants bit her. "Lightning had made his mind up to go, so Daddy gave him a good pocketknife and told him to watch his self. Said he was nigh on a grown man and didn't reckon it would do him harm to learn his way. I could tell it hurt Daddy, but he wouldn't let on. Momma and me cried."

Lightning had always talked about seeing the world, so maybe this was his chance. "Did he say where they were headed?" The three of us had turned fifteen, them in May and me in June. Fifteen was considered adult in farm years.

"Said they'd be working toward Florida by wintertime and out of the cold." She slapped her leg. "Just plain stupid."

I went to sit next to her and mash ants. "Hope he makes out all right. Wish he'd have stopped in and said good-bye. Sure will miss sitting in the woods and shooting the bull."

She clamped her big toe over mine and we foot-wrestled, giggling at each other. "I'm still here."

"Figured you'd be scared to be traipsing around the woods after dark by yourself." I tickled her ribs.

She slapped my hands away. "You won't let nothing happen to me." Fancy turned her face up. "I ain't scared." Her face had lost its baby fat, leaving high, sharp cheekbones and a slender jawline that made her blackberry-sized eyes look bigger. Her teeth still bowed some, but her head had caught up, giving Fancy a smile to warm your heart.

"Won't be the same without Lightning," I said.

She covered her top lip with her bottom one. "Going to be mighty lonesome for me."

Lightning had always been the windbreak between us, that constant reminder there would be no us without him. I wasn't sure how Fancy would handle him being gone. "We'll find something to pass the time." I squeezed her shoulder.

Fancy pushed off the step. "I better get back."

"Tell you what. If Mr. and Mrs. Wilson take me to Apex in the morning, I'll bring you something. Meet me tomorrow night on the path, and we'll sit and talk some."

That got a little smile. "I appreciate that, Junebug."

I shrugged the gallouses off my shoulders and pulled the dirty T-shirt over my head, no longer needing it since the sun had dried the dew from the tobacco. "You like to read?"

That gave her the mad-face. "Read better than you, I bet."

I held up my hand, laughing at the fire in her eyes. "Wait now, I just wanted to be sure not to waste money."

She took a play swipe at my head and grinned. "See you to-morrow night."

I watched her walk away, the stride purposeful, long legs that made her almost as tall as me. She was getting to be a handsome woman, like her momma.

Mr. Wilson came around the house, and I followed him, Fancy's daddy, Roy, and the two other colored men back to the tobacco field. Priming tobacco was a boring job, up one row and down the next, pulling yellow ripe leaves from head-high stalks and dropping them into a tobacco slide dragged along by the mule. The sound of men picking and slapping leaves had a certain rhythm to it, sort of like radio music. I listened to the colored men joke back and forth with each other; it helped pass the time.

Anne Arundel County
Public Library
Glen Burnie
410-222-6270

Library name: NCO

Title: The last road home
Item ID: 31997094587219
Author: Johnson, Danny,
1946-
Date due: 9/11/2018,23:59

To renew your materials:
Go to the Library's
Website at www.aacpl.net,
or call any branch
****
Did you know we offer
free online tutoring
for all ages? Check out
www.aacpl.net/homework

My granddaddy had taught me everything about how to work a tobacco crop, from planting to selling. He also showed me how to fix a window, nail tin on a barn roof, and most other things a man needed to know so he could look after himself. Then he up and died on me last year. I missed him a lot, and thought about him while we sweated beneath a baker's-brick-hot August sun.

There was plenty of daylight left when we finished priming the ten acres, and we headed to the barn to hang the tobacco for curing. Mr. Wilson asked who wanted to go high.

"I will." I liked to prove myself as much a man as the rest. The log barn stood about thirty feet high at the tallest point of the gable roof, and was about twenty feet square. Smooth, round tier poles ran from front to back on each side, four feet apart so the tobacco sticks could hang between. I pulled up on the lower tier poles, stretched my feet across, and waggle-walked to the top. Fancy's daddy came behind. It was hell-hot in the roof.

"Ready?" Roy looked up. He was a powerful but no longer young man, close to Mr. Wilson and Grandma's age I imagined. His black hair didn't start until halfway to the back of his head. I hadn't asked about the situation with Lightning, not sure if he'd appreciate me saying anything in front of the other men.

"Shit." My sweaty foot slipped on the pole. "Whenever you are." By the time the barn was full, water ran off Roy and me like we'd been dunked in a pond. The end of the day was welcome.

Mr. Wilson took me aside and slipped me a ten-dollar bill. I tried to hand the money back. "I ain't got no change."

He pulled the wad of chewing tobacco from his cheek, tossed it away, and spit. "Not looking for any. You ain't scared of hard work. I have an appreciation for that, and the way you're looking after Miss Rosa Belle since your granddaddy died. I got to get these niggers home; expect your supper's waiting. The missus and me are going to town in the morning if you want to ride along."

"I'd appreciate it."

Grandma did have supper on the table. She'd cooked pork chops to go along with boiled potatoes and greens. The chops were in thick slices. Granddaddy always cut them that way, said he liked a little chew to his meat.

Grandma sat and looked at me like she was giving an appraisal. "You're growing into a good-sized man, son. Folks can't ever say I don't feed you good." She sounded pleased with my progress.

I had noticed the growing bulge in my arms, and the ridges that had started to line my stomach. A new mark for the top of my head on the door to my bedroom measured six feet from the floor, and when I used Grandma's weight scale, it showed a hundred and seventy-five pounds. "Don't want to eat us out of house and home."

When Grandma grinned, her nose wrinkled and pushed up the gold-rimmed eyeglasses. "Don't you worry, we've got plenty. Did the Wilsons say if they are going to Apex tomorrow?"

"They're coming by to pick me up in the morning. You need anything from town?"

Grandma got up and started piling dishes in the washbowl. She was broad across the shoulders and wide in the butt, built sort of like a square, a bit heavy but never slow or lazy. There was a picture of her hanging in the living room. She was young then, around sixteen she said, and sat on a buckboard smiling at the world. I was always surprised at how pretty she was in those days.

She gazed out the window over the sink, watching a big orange sun drop lower on the horizon. Maybe she was thinking about Granddaddy too. "Wouldn't mind having some fresh peaches. Haven't made a cobbler since last year."

"I'll check at Salem's."

"Pick up a few if they ain't too expensive. I'll give you money." She looked over her shoulder at me.

"No need. Mr. Wilson paid me a little extra today."

"Oh?" She was curious. "Well, remember to save part of what you get, Junebug. Never know when you might need it."

I didn't tell her how much. Lately I'd taken to keeping little secrets for myself. "What needs doing after supper?"

"We can shell butter beans if you want. We'll see after you're done with the chores." She went back to looking out the window.

After taking care of the animals, the two of us relaxed on the screened-in porch. A late-evening breeze was cool and carried the smell of sweetgrass from the pasture. The hoot owl that lived down by the barn announced he was up looking for mice, and when the moon got bright, bats looped around the corn-crib, snatching weevils from the air. Everything seemed to be in its right place.

"Lightning's gone," I said. "Fancy told me he took up with a bunch of migrant workers over at the Jackson place."

She turned toward me, her mouth open in surprise. "Hate to hear that, Junebug. Nigras running them crews can be mighty mean. Hope he don't get hurt."

"Me too. Grandma, why do you call them 'nigras'? Everybody else calls them 'niggers'."

" 'Nigras' is more respectful." Grandma let out a big yawn.

I got in the shower, scrubbing quickly under the cold water. We'd put the inside toilet in last fall, the last thing I helped Granddaddy do. The house had three bedrooms, a living room, a kitchen, and a screened-in porch. The place was almost a hundred years old and had been built with hand-sawed boards that were tongue-and-grooved together to form the floor, walls, and ceiling. Granddaddy used to say if Grandma wanted to move, we could just roll the house down the road.

Sticking my face up to the mirror over the sink, I combed my sand-colored hair to the side. Grandma kept it cut close to my head, and the sun had turned my face deep brown, making my pale eyes look bluer than they really were. I'd inherited Granddaddy's big ears, so I couldn't decide if I was handsome, but thought I would do.

I almost didn't have time to close my eyes before sleep came. I dreamed about Momma, seeing her pretty blue eyes and the long brown hair that fell across her face. In the next minute she was on fire, her face black, her mouth open to scream, but all that came out was smoke. I reached across the burning car to help her, but Daddy's skeleton hand grabbed my arm and pushed me away.

CHAPTER 3

After chores and breakfast the next morning, I sat on the porch steps and pitched green chinaberry balls at birds, the dream about Momma still on my mind. The climbing sun burned off a layer of low clouds, letting a bright cornflower sky show through.

Grandma came out to sit. "Might get a cloud this evening." She pointed to the maple behind the woodshed. "See the leaves? They'll turn over like that when rain is coming."

"Huh, never knew that before. Grandma, let me show you something."

She followed me to the edge of the dirt road that ran between our house and the stables. I stopped at a spot close to the mailbox post and bent down to run my hand over a piece of board showing under the grass. "What is that? I felt it the other day when I got the mail."

She leaned over and brushed away some dirt. "That's where the first well was dug on the place. Your granddaddy covered the hole with wood and sowed grass over it. I hadn't noticed the ground was worn away like that. We need to lay some more boards, could be dangerous if somebody stepped on it." As she raked, the outline showed.

"How deep is it?"

"Not more than fifty feet or so. At one time a spring ran across here"—she swept her arm toward the woods behind the house—"but over the years it changed direction. After it went dry, we put potatoes and onions in sacks and lowered them down to keep through the winter."

"Why'd you quit?"

"When we built the pack house, we dug a good-sized cellar for storing vegetables and my potting flowers."

I pushed on the edges of the wood. "Reckon there's any water down there now?"

"Don't think so. Them planks are probably rotten by now. You can make another cover for it next week."

I looked up to see the Wilsons turning off the main paved road. Mr. Wilson drove slow in his brand-new '61 Chevy truck, "so as not to wear it out too quick," he said. I fingered the ten-dollar bill, wanting to remember to get something for Fancy.

Grandma and I walked over to greet them. "Morning." Mr. Wilson leaned across his wife. "You doing all right, Rosa Belle?"

"I'm well and I appreciate you asking." Grandma smoothed her bun. "Morning, Lila." Her and Mrs. Wilson were second cousins. I hopped into the back of the pickup and waved as we pulled off. Grandma stood with her hands behind her back, the trees, the house, and the woodshed in the background. It reminded me of a *Saturday Evening Post* magazine I'd seen at the drugstore.

When we got to Apex, Mr. and Mrs. Wilson headed toward Salem General Store, and I walked up the street. I liked the clean smell of the drugstore, and nodded hello to the lady behind the counter. She was tall and thin with dirt-brown hair piled up in a beehive. Big black glasses made her look older than I suspected she was, and were too big for her face.

They kept the comic books against a wall in the back. I stuck one to my nose to sniff the odd scent of the paper. After some mind wrestling, I decided on ten I wanted, and picked up a magazine for Grandma. While the saleslady totaled, I asked her to add in a good-sized bag of Hershey's Kisses. All together it cost three dollars.

I took my time walking down the sidewalk opposite the one I'd come up. On this side of the two-lane street was a café, a jewelry store, a Woolworths, and a doctor's office. In front of Salem General Store, baskets of golden peaches sat on a wooden fruit stand. I sniffed a few, and then filled a paper sack. They cost me two more dollars. I followed Grandma's advice with the five I had left.

I spotted Mr. Wilson coming out of the barbershop across the street. "Got your ears lowered, huh," I said.

"Needed one." He rubbed a hand over his bald spot. "Let's get some ice cream. The missus should be done with her stuff by then." We took our time, looking in windows at this and that. Mr. Wilson stopped in front of the window of Rosen's Jewelry Store. "All jewelry stores are owned by Jews, Junebug. That's why it's called JEWelry. They'll gyp you coming and going; ain't nothing but white niggers."

I stayed quiet. Granddaddy used to say, "Any man that works for what he has and lives in fear of the Lord deserves respect." I thought about Roy and how hard he worked for what little he had. Yet Mr. Wilson treated him like just another mule, figuring as long as he put a few ears of corn in his box once in a while, he pretty well owned him until he died. Roy was a man who deserved more respect than that.

"Mrs. Wilson wears a pretty wedding ring. Where'd you buy it?" I stared in the window, thinking how Fancy might like a pretty ring one of these days.

He hesitated while his face turned red. "Bought it here, but it was a long time ago, when Old Man Rosen ran the place."

"Was he a Jew man? You think he gypped you?"

Mr. Wilson rubbed his heavy jaw. "Son of a bitch probably did."

The door to the jewelry store opened, and an elderly man

stepped out and looked at the blue sky. "What a glorious Sabbath we are blessed with." He extended his hand. "Mr. Wilson, how are you? Your wife's ring, is it still wearing well after all these years?"

"Seems to be." I waited for Mr. Wilson to lay into him, but he just stood red-faced.

"You must bring it by one day, let me clean it for you. No charge." Mr. Rosen smiled and headed down the sidewalk. "Good to see you."

I dropped my head and smiled to myself. Granddaddy also told me talking to a man's back took a lot less bark than talking to his front.

CHAPTER 4

Grandma took the bag of fruit. "Let's set them out here on the porch in the sunshine." We spread them over a towel.

I yawned. "Think I'll go lay down and read my comic books."

She put her arm across my shoulder. "You do that while I see if I can remember how to make a cobbler for our supper." Grandma had a wide face, like somebody had grabbed both cheeks and stretched them. She joked that her wrinkles were a road map of hard times and bad luck.

Hundred-year-old poplars and sweet gums shaded my room and a good breeze came through the window screen. A rumble of thunder sounded. Grandma was right. Outside, limbs bent away from the wind, causing leaves to chase each other in circles along the ground. Snuggling into the feather mattress, I listened as the first drops tapped on the tin roof. To me, rain always signaled a time-out from bad things.

After supper, we sat on the porch and watched an orange sunset color cloud slices until darkness slipped over us like a blanket. The strong smell of wet manure from the mule lot and pigpen rode the breeze toward us. "I'm going to ask Mr. Wilson about letting us use Clemmy and Roy to help pull tobacco Wednesday."

"That's a good idea, it'll need priming by then." Grandma got up and changed the flypaper hanging by the screen door. She yawned. "Stay up long as you want. I'm going to bed."

I waited a few minutes after her bedroom door closed before getting the candy for Fancy, then slipped quietly out the back. A heavy yellow moon lay low in the east, shining through the tree-tops like a giant headlight. The walking was quiet in the damp leaves and pine straw. I got to the stumps and plopped down, figuring to eat a chocolate.

"Boo!"

I jumped, tripped over my feet, and threw up one arm to pro-tect myself.

Fancy started laughing so hard she was bent over. "I didn't know a white boy could get whiter." She reached out to help me up with one hand and tried to stop laughing by covering her mouth with the other.

I slapped it away and brushed at my britches. "Smart-ass. Here." I handed her the bag of candy.

"Thanks . . ." She snuffled to try and stop her giggles. "How was your trip to Apex?"

"It was okay, good to get away for a little while. Hear any-thing from Lightning?"

She peeled wrappers and stuffed kisses in her mouth. "Don't expect to any time soon."

I sat beside her and stretched my legs out. "You ain't going to be running off, are you?"

"Heck no. I'm fine right at home. Besides, Momma said them menfolk with the migrants ain't particular how old a girl is." Her jaws were full of chocolate, and she kept wiping her teeth with her tongue.

"Would hate to see you get involved in such mess." Lightning had given us the lowdown about sex. By thirteen, he'd found a steady girlfriend at school, and we hardly saw him, said he was practicing what he preached. I looked at Fancy. "You ain't had sex yet, have you?" Immediately I felt embarrassed asking such a question.

Her head jerked around. "Don't make me pop you one. Have you?"

The only experience I'd had was in my head. "Nope."

"Seen my Daddy's business by accident once, and it was a lot bigger than Lightning's." She stared innocently, the moonlight catching the whites of her eyes. "How big is yours?" Fancy looked at me like she was expecting an answer.

"What kind of question is that?" I looked the other way, heat running up my neck.

"Ain't ever seen a white one." She leaned closer, giggling again.

"Well, you ain't going to see this one neither."

"You're funny, Junebug." She punched me on the shoulder. "Going back to school this fall?"

"Maybe. Can't see much need in it, though. I already know how to farm. You?"

"Heck, yeah. I like school, seeing pictures of all those far-off places like France and England and Spain, hoping you'll go visit them one of these days. Besides, you need to be educated for when you're grown so you can do for yourself."

"I can look after myself now." We sat listening to tree frogs and thicket crickets, eating chocolates, and pitching little balls of silver wrappers into the bushes.

"That's true, you seem right smart for a white boy." She got up and walked around the clearing, looking up through openings between the trees. "Do you reckon that's heaven, Junebug?"

I got up to stand beside her. "Most folks hope it is, but I don't know for sure."

"Wonder how a person gets there?" She hooked her arm through mine and studied the sky, like she hoped to catch a glimpse of somebody headed up at that particular moment. "Preacher says we ride on angel backs, fly until we get to the road of gold where we won't have these burdens of earth no more."

"Maybe."

Fancy cut her eyes up, then soft-slapped me on the chest. "Don't be a man of doubt, Junebug, God's got a plan for all of us." She leaned her head against my arm. "You know I'm going to be depending on you now that Lightning's gone."

The shine of her brown skin reminded me of the top of a chocolate pudding. "Why?" I had about all I could handle already, but it made me feel good she felt that way.

"Who else do I have to talk to? And who'll protect me from the bogeymen in these woods?" She poked me in the ribs with her finger.

It was my turn to laugh at her. "The only haints around here are in your imagination."

A gust of wind blew through the trees. Something heavy suddenly thumped the top of my head and rolled down my neck. I dodged in a circle, slapping and swinging. "Shit, oh shit. Is it a snake, Fancy?"

That set her off again, laughing loud enough to wake the dead. "It's a pinecone." She jumped at me, arms out. "Boo! I swear, Junebug, you are going to make me pee in my britches."

I was disgusted at myself. "Ain't it time for you to go home?"

"Don't suppose you'd walk with me part of the way?" She held my hand with both of hers.

I strongly considered saying *hell no,* then circling around to scare the piss out of her. But I liked holding her hand. We started walking, as usual Fancy talking up a storm about anything that came to mind. In a few minutes we were at the edge of the woods and the clover field. I held to her fingers for a minute. "You all right from here?"

"Will you wait there until I get to the yard?"

"Okay."

"'Bye, Junebug. And thanks for the candy." She gave me a quick hug I didn't expect. I watched her hurry across, turning to wave when she reached her house.

On the way home, I decided I liked being alone with Fancy.

CHAPTER 5

Roy, Clemmy, and Fancy showed up at daybreak on Wednesday. The women went to the barn to get ready for looping tobacco, and Roy and me headed to the four-acre field that sat between our side yard and the main paved road. The morning sky was a light blue summer color, and the early air felt cool while it waited on the sun.

"Roy, you doing all right?" I got Sally Mule headed between the first and second rows. I had a comfort with Roy, respect for the good man I felt him to be. Since Granddaddy died he'd taught me some things, always patient with what I didn't know. It took him two hours one morning before I could understand the right way to change blades on the disking machine.

He shoved the back end of the tobacco slide around so it was straight. The yellowish leaves were two hands wide with big ribs, heavy, and coated with dew. "Fair to middling, I reckon. You?"

"Be glad to get tobacco season over and make some money, like everybody, I guess."

"Won't be much longer." Roy was shorter than me, broad-shouldered with a thick neck. "Junebug, I seen the candy Fancy said you give her. What do I owe you?"

Had he found Fancy coming back in the house last night? I took a second to answer. "Nothing, just wanted to help her feelings since Lightning run off." I ducked down to roll the cuff on my overalls. "Hope it was all right with you."

When I stood back up, Roy was waiting, looking at me like he had something to say. "I've knowed you most of your life and feel like we can talk some." He stopped and wiped his forehead with a sleeve, giving me a good look at his arm muscles. "Now that her brother's gone, I worry about Fancy; she's at the age menfolk are starting to notice, and I don't want nobody sniffing around like some hound dog. She needs to stay like she is 'til a man comes along who'll marry and take care of her. You understand I have to keep my eye out."

I bent over and snapped leaves with extra force. "I can understand that, Roy. Lightning, Fancy, and me been friends a long time, and I sure don't want harm to come to either one." I knew what he was edging around, but in no way was I going to act like I did.

"I had a man-talk with Lightning a while back, but I think he got to messing around with them migrant women. Probably why he run off."

"Well, don't you worry. Now that he's gone, I'll keep an eye on Fancy and make sure nothing happens."

"Expect enough's said, and you take whatever the candy cost out of my pay today."

I figured if he'd found out Fancy and me met in the woods last night, he would have said it direct. "Roy, it was for Fancy as a present because she's my friend. If for some reason you don't want us to be friends, I'll respect your word."

"Not that at all, Junebug." He kept walking and picking leaves. "I know having to work like a man at your age ain't easy. When a boy gets to be your and Lightning's age, his jisim starts backing up and he gets to having urges. If your granddaddy was here, I expect he'd be having this talk with you. Hope you'll take it as meant."

I'd never worried with Lightning around, but it was plain that Fancy and me meeting by ourselves could be a different story. "Let's get this field done."

In the middle of the morning we took a break in the shade, sharing water from a mason jar. We sat without talking for a few minutes. Roy stuck out his hand. "I appreciate you being a friend to Fancy."

I shook with him. "It can be mighty lonesome living here, and I've always been grateful to have Lightning and Fancy around."

Roy and me finished the field in a few hours, then went to help the women. I made sure to keep any talking directed at Roy. By the time Grandma yelled for dinner, we were almost done.

Roy, Clemmy, and Fancy sat to eat under the tree outside at the homemade bench, while Grandma and me stayed in the kitchen. After dinner I threw an old quilt and pillow on the floor to doze and give my back some relief. Everybody rested an hour to let the food settle. Grandma shook me awake.

Outside, Roy was walking around the garden to check what was growing, and Fancy picked through fallen pears under the tree to see if any might be ripe enough to eat. Clemmy helped Grandma clean up the plank table and carry the dishes. I listened while they laughed and talked like any two longtime friends. Both had known nothing but tough times, making do with a life that only offered more of the same, yet by luck of color, one was judged better off than the other.

We had the sticks in the barn and hung by the middle of the evening. Grandma paid them for a full day's work even though we were done by three o'clock. I filled an empty slide with pieces of thin dry pine slabs from the woodshed and used Sally Mule to drag it to the barn, preparing for a long night tending the fire to start the curing process. When Roy, Clemmy, and Fancy passed the barn headed up the horse path home, Fancy looked back and pointed her finger down.

* * *

With Granddaddy gone, the tobacco curing fell to me. I'd sat with him many nights and knew how to make sure the drying temperature was right, when to throw in a bucket of water to add some wet to the heat, and, most of all, not to be careless and let the barn catch fire. Many a family had lost everything to a tobacco barn fire that didn't stop with the barn.

After supper and chores, I put a couple of cold ham biscuits and a few comic books in a paper sack, then filled the lantern with kerosene before heading to the barn. Once the pine pieces were burning good in the brick firebox, I added some bigger chunks of hardwood, not too much, just enough to keep the heat low for the first night.

Crickets and tree frogs started up as daylight disappeared. Grandma came to sit awhile, warning me again not to burn up the place. "Sure do miss Granddaddy," I said.

Even after him and Momma and Daddy died, Grandma still believed God hadn't forsaken us. I was pretty convinced by this time there wasn't any such thing as "*God's Will,*" that most of what the preacher spouted on Sundays was just stuff to scare little kids and give grown-ups a day to promise they'd quit cussing or drinking or treating other folks the way they did.

"What do you think happens after we die, Grandma?"

"Why in the world would you be thinking about that?" She took hold of my hand and squeezed it. "It's a question folks been pondering for thousands of years. I believe when the time comes, and if we've been faithful, our spirit lifts out, and we go to live with God." Grandma reached her finger to turn my chin toward her. "Remember this, Junebug, a lot of people might choose different ideas, and some don't have faith at all. But the one thing everybody wants, no matter how un-alike they might be, is a happy ending."

"What does that mean, Grandma?"

"It means nobody wants to think this is all there is."

I lit the lantern, set it in the middle of the packed dirt floor, and lay down on the bench, resting my head on a tote sack filled with dried cornhusk. Maybe Momma and Granddaddy had gone to heaven, if there was one, but I had doubts about my daddy after what he did to Grady.

I heard a rustle in the leaves at the side of the barn, and picked up the lantern. A possum would hiss and grin but usually run. I eased around the corner and leaned the light into the darkness.

Fancy suddenly stepped from behind a tree, scaring the mess out of me. I tripped, my big toe hitting the side of the barn wall, pain shot up my leg, and I dropped the lantern. "Goddammit, Fancy!"

"I swear you is the scaredest man I ever saw." She tried to sound sympathetic and not laugh, but couldn't. "Are you hurt?"

I bounced on one foot to the bench. "What the hell do you think? And what the hell are you doing out here? Your daddy finds you, he'll beat the skin off your ass and mine too."

She waved her hand in dismissal of such a possibility. "He's just edgy because of Lightning. Is your toe bleeding?" She'd tied her hair into a short ponytail that stuck up on the top of her head like a woodpecker's knot. "Want me to rub it?"

I stuck my foot in her lap. "How do you manage to sneak out without anybody knowing?"

Fancy massaged until the pain eased. "Daddy built on an extra room in the back when Lightning and me got too old to sleep together, and that's where my bed is. I just open my window and hop out. Besides, he goes to bed as soon as it gets dark and snores so loud the wall could fall down and they wouldn't know it." She moved my foot from her lap and played with her ponytail. "Junebug, what do you think about my hair like this?"

"Better than pigtails, more grown-up looking. Why?"

"I don't know. Ever since I got my monthlies, seems I feel different about a lot of things, that's all."

"God dang it, Fancy. Why you talking about such stuff?"

She hopped off the bench and spread her arms wide. "Who the hell else am I going to talk to? The only time I get to see anybody other than your ugly face is on Sundays at church or when school is in. Look around, Junebug, ain't no other kids living out this far in the sticks except us."

"If it's woman things, you need to be talking to a woman."

"Never mine. I'll keep my mouth shut and be the dumb-ass little nigger you think I am." She threw a stick at me.

I bounced off the bench and hobbled after her. When I caught up, I held her by the arms. "Sorry, wasn't trying to hurt your feelings." We stood close, eyes locked.

She broke the gaze and peeped out at the dark woods. "You ever get scared being out here by yourself?"

"Nah, nothing out here at night except critters."

"We could cast up a spell." She grabbed my hand. Fancy's eyes opened wide as silver dollars when she was up to mischief.

"What kind of spell?"

"I hid and watched them island migrants once. They drew a circle in the dirt, made swirly lines, and started dancing around talking this crazy stuff. All of a sudden, *whack,* they chopped off a chicken's head and poured blood over the middle." She lifted her arms in my face. "Whoooeee. That's scary, ain't it?"

"Stupid is more like it."

"Might be, but some folks swear it works." She grabbed the stick and drew in the sand. "Heebie jeebie, heebie hoo, yah yah hey, make all the haints go away." Fancy started making a war dance around the circle.

She was a funny sight. "Wait a minute and I'll run get you a chicken."

"What you better do is get in here and help me, never know what might be crawling in these bushes." We held hands and danced 'round and 'round, hooting like little kids. I'd almost forgot what it was like to let go and just laugh. After a few minutes, we calmed down and went to sit.

"You miss your momma and daddy, Junebug?"

I got up and poked the fire. "Miss my momma." I'd clung so close to Momma I didn't know where she ended and I began. At bedtime, she'd sit in her rocking chair, me on her lap, and count the spaces between my knuckles to quiet my mind. If I'd had a bad day she would say, "Junebug, days are like Christmas presents, you get to open a new one every morning." Good days were hard to come by after she died. I looked at Fancy. "People are always saying time heals everything, but that's just bullshit."

Fancy came to stand beside me, leaning against my arm. "How can you not be sad and lonesome all the time?"

I stared at the red coals. "A man has got to keep putting one foot in front of the other. Grandma helps, and Sally Mule and me have long talks when we're working."

"Well, I'm here if you need somebody to talk to, Junebug. I can listen good as a mule."

I grinned. "That's true, but the mule don't talk back." I managed to dodge the swing at my head.

She walked off, shoving my hand when I tried to pull her back. I managed to grab hold and tickle, eventually getting her to smile. "You know I'm just playing."

Fancy put her arms around my neck. It scared me. The moon had moved to the right and lower. "You need to get on back. Your daddy catches us out here, you'll need one of them spells to heal the welts on your butt."

"Okay. You better stay and mind the fire." She let go.

"Holler real loud if you need me."

"Oh, don't worry. People in the next county will hear if a haint tries to grab me."

"I'll keep an ear out for you."

She faded into the darkness. Twigs and dry leaves tracked her as she walked. I went a few steps up the trail, listening as far as possible, then crept quietly behind, stopping at the clover field, keeping watch as she ran to her house.

CHAPTER 6

August brought hot days and hard work. Since there was just Grandma and me, it was pretty much sunup to sundown. Her stamina made me embarrassed to feel tired. The only time we got to rest was Sundays or when it rained. Saturday night's meeting with Fancy got to be regular. A couple of hours alone with her made life more tolerable.

On Labor Day, the Wilsons invited the community to their house for a pig picking. The menfolk in the crowd stood in one group and the women in another. I walked over to join the men. They sipped shine whiskey from glass jars. Mr. Burley Mason said to the group, "How can a nigger tell when she's pregnant?" Somebody asked how. "When she pulls out her tampon and the cotton's already been picked." That got a big laugh all around. Arthur Mills started another one, but I moved away. They were loud enough I knew Roy and Clemmy could hear. I'd listened to that kind of talk all my life at corn-shuckin' parties, hog killings, even standing around the churchyard. It was hard to understand how they could hate the people not a one of them could make a living without. Or maybe understanding that was why they did hate them. I glanced at Roy, but he sat with his head down studying his cooking fire. Clemmy busied herself with table chores, and Fancy stood way at the edge of the yard. Made me wish I could protect them, but all I could do was keep my mouth shut, pass and repass.

Roy had been up all night smoking the hog over hot wood coals in a pit dug in the ground. The pig was ready by sundown, and everybody helped themselves. I took a plateful around to sit in the swing on the porch, sick of listening to foulmouthed farmers with their guts full of liquor.

Fancy followed and sat on the steps. "This is good, ain't it, Junebug?"

My mouth was full of pig and potato salad. "Your daddy sure knows how to cook a hog." By the time we went for seconds, the stars were out bright and a breeze stirred the humid air enough to keep mosquitoes away.

Fancy finished her plate and sat staring up at a bottom-lip moon. "What's your dream, Junebug?" Crickets scratched loud and lizards darted through the grass searching for them.

"About what?" I was so full I was miserable.

"I don't know, the rest of your life. What do you want to be?"

"Never thought much about it. I'm not much for rules, so that don't figure to work out any better with a public job than it does in a public school. I like farming pretty good, don't have to be beholden to other folks. What's yours?"

She hugged her knees and bent her head to rest her chin on her arms. "Like to see something of this world, wear pretty clothes, be something other than some house nigger walking around with babies on my hip, bowing and scraping for white folks. Don't know how it'd ever happen, though. Sometimes my life don't feel any different than them slaves I read about in school."

The hurt in her voice was plain. I realized I had no idea what it was like to see the world through her eyes. I moved to sit on the steps. "If a person can't dream, how can they ever have any hope, Junebug?" She squeezed my wrist. "I like that I'm able to talk to you." When Fancy turned her face up, tears filled the corners of her eyes.

"If any person could make a dream come true, Fancy, it would be you." I wanted to tell her it would be all right, but I didn't know if it would be the truth.

Early on a Friday morning three weeks after Labor Day, Grandma and me packed the truck bed with sticks of cured tobacco, covered them with a wide piece of burlap, and headed to Durham. The crop had turned out good, the leaves golden and pliable. We expected to get a decent price.

Grandma pulled the truck into the wide double doors of the Liberty Warehouse, and we unloaded. The smell of piles of dried tobacco made my nose burn. Selling began about noon. An auctioneer moved down the aisles, shouting in a rapid singsong voice, saying words I couldn't catch. Buyers walked behind and bid on the stacks. When it was over, Grandma went to the cashier to get a check for almost a thousand dollars. "We'll go to town tomorrow so I can pay what we owe."

At King's Hot Dog Stand across from the Durham Bulls Park, we celebrated by buying two hot dogs apiece and Cokes to wash them down.

The next morning after breakfast we started to Apex. When we passed the Wilson place, Fancy was out by the road playing hopscotch in the dirt. I touched Grandma's arm. "Can we take Fancy with us? She never gets to go anywhere."

She slowed and stopped in front of the driveway. Fancy stood back. Grandma leaned across me to talk out the passenger window. "Fancy, you want to ride to Apex with me and Junebug?"

She broke out in a big grin. "Yes'um, I sure would."

"Go ask Clemmy and Roy. Tell 'em we'll be back before too long, and see if they want anything while we're in town." Fancy took off running.

"Thanks, Grandma, feels good to do things for other folks, don't it?"

She smiled patiently.

Fancy came back, changed into a clean dress and some shoes. "They said it would be fine if y'all didn't mind. And Momma sent a dollar for a five-pound bag of sugar, if it's not too much trouble."

"Get on in. Junebug, why don't you sit by the door and let Fancy in the middle?"

Down on Highway 64, Grandma stopped at a Gulf station. Fancy and I stayed in the truck while the man pumped gas. "Junebug, can we go in the store?" she asked.

I looked at the five or six oversized farm boys standing outside the front door. "We need to be going so Grandma can get to Apex."

In town, Grandma was feeling generous, and gave Fancy and me a dollar each to spend. We headed up the street, leaving nose prints on glass windows. I started in the drugstore door, but Fancy stopped. "Junebug, I don't think I'm supposed to go in this way. Have they got a colored door?"

It hadn't occurred to me. I went around the side and checked. "This is the only way in. Come on. This lady knows me and I think she'll be all right. Won't nobody say anything."

I nodded to the woman behind the counter. She gave a hard eye at Fancy. Fancy stared at the floor. I decided on three comics and an ice cream cone. Fancy thought she would get her momma a small tube of red lipstick and a cone for herself.

The schoolteacher-faced lady leaned over the counter and frowned. "Son, I can sell you the ice cream, but not her. You buy 'em and take them outside if you want to."

Fancy flushed, handed me her dollar, and left. I could feel the red burn up my face. I was embarrassed for Fancy.

Outside, we walked a little ways, then sat down on the concrete curb to eat the ice cream before it melted. Fancy wouldn't look at me, and when she spoke her voice was aimed at the pavement. "Why white folks hate black folks?"

I studied the bank across the street.

"I sure do get tired of it, Junebug."

"I don't think it's really hate, they just do what's expected." It pissed me off that I was making up such shit. I should have thrown the ice cream at the woman's face. "Things will change one of these days, Fancy."

The muscles in her jaw were clenching and releasing, like she was chewing a mouthful of disgust. "Been like this a long time before we was born."

Cars passed up and down the street in front of us. Nobody lifted a hand.

"I can't wait to get back to school. Get to see some of my friends." She put a little extra on the "my."

Maybe Fancy was tired of being around white folks. I tried to change the subject. "Got a boyfriend in school?"

"Oh, some boys are always playing and teasing, but I don't pay them no heed. I might get a boyfriend this year, though. Did you have a girlfriend last year?"

"Most girls act too stupid."

White cream was all over her mouth. "Well, I'm a girl and I damn sure ain't stupid."

"You're different."

"Because I'm colored?"

"No, because we're like brother and sister, almost family."

She pulled her head back, giving me a look that said she didn't believe me. "Well, Junebug Hurley, you really feel that way?"

"Sure."

"Then you can call me sister." Her red tongue licked the stickiness from around her lips.

"I'm going to call you Fancy like always. Let's get down to Salem's. Grandma is probably ready to go."

She hopped to her feet and grabbed my hand. "Let's go, brother."

I jerked my hand back. "You can't do that out here in public!"

Fancy stood staring. A crooked smile worked its way bit by bit across her lips. "Why, Junebug, you got more than them two faces I see?" She slowly lifted the ice cream cone and slammed it into the gutter.

I yelled after her, "Don't be stupid, you know what I mean." She walked with her nose up like she smelled shit, refusing to turn around. When Fancy was pissed, she could ignore a person like nobody's business.

I slapped myself on the leg, "Okay, *sister,* you got me." I didn't have the courage to stand up to my words and she knew it. I trailed behind like a whipped dog, head down, hands stuffed in my pockets, moping. I doubted another bag of candy would make up for this. We spent the entire ride home with her making sure we didn't touch each other.

CHAPTER 7

"What do you think about me not going back to school this year?" I'd decided to get it out of the way at supper. We were already eating dessert.

Grandma looked down at the peach pie on her plate and fiddled with her fork. She folded her hands in her lap. I couldn't tell if it was determination or disappointment in her eyes. "June-bug, you're fifteen years old, and the only way you're ever going to be able to do anything other than ruin your back and be old before your time is to get an education."

Granddaddy said he'd only got through the third grade, but I knew Grandma graduated from high school. She even taught for a year before they got married. "Granddaddy told me one time if you took another man's money, you had to eat his shit. I don't think I'd like the taste of that." I waited and watched.

She put her elbows, rough and discolored by too many years of bending to work a dirt farm, on the table. "You keep the cussing to yourself. And don't take everything your granddaddy said to heart; times are different now. If you got land and are able to plant and pick, you won't starve to death, but you need to think about ten years from now. If you get hurt and can't farm, how will you provide if you got kids and a wife to look after?"

I knew she was making a point about our situation and the things that worried her. "Grandma, if you'll be upset, I'll respect your wishes and go to school, but with all that needs doing here, I don't see any sense in it."

Her eyes narrowed, and chilled to the color of steel. "I can manage; been doing it a long time before you were born." She leaned back in her chair. "You're almost a man now, and can reason with your own mind. I wish you would consider school because you'll understand the value of it one day, but I'm not going to make that decision." She picked up her knife and raked food scraps onto her dinner plate. "Your daddy was hard-headed about school too. Maybe if he hadn't been, he'd still be here."

Daddy had been a part-time mechanic, part-time dirt-track race car driver, and full-time bootlegger. I scooped the last of the pie. "Fancy's going back; she likes school."

Grandma blew out a deep breath, letting her shoulders and the stern look on her face relax. "Good, I'm glad. She's a smart girl. Hopefully, one of these days she'll find a man to treat her kind and be a good husband."

I put my fork down and slid the empty plate forward. "Grandma, you don't hate Roy or Clemmy, do you?"

"Why on earth would you think that?"

"Fancy asked me the other day why white folks hate black folks. I didn't know how to answer something like that. Do you think people really feel that way?"

She stacked the plates, and then rested her backside against the sink, folding her arms across her chest. "Junebug, you need to understand something. Cruelty and memory have been married together a long time in the South. My grandpa was sixteen when he went to the Civil War, and twenty-one when he came home with one leg and a belly full of bitterness. He died in 1915 when I was sixteen. All those years growing up I listened to his stories and watched his resentment. He was convinced the South fought and died for honor, and he blamed black folks for his suffering. It's a way of thinking that's been passed down since, like blue eyes or red hair or family land." She turned back to the plates in the sink. "I know you don't think things you see are right, and I'm proud of you for that." Grandma's words surprised me. I wanted to ask more, but could tell she was done talking about it.

I went to lean on the counter beside her. "Oh, I didn't tell you. Roy and me had a talk. He's on the lookout for anybody sniffing around Fancy, said he thought Lightning had got urges around some of the migrant women and that's why he run off. Wanted to give me advice like he thought Granddaddy would if he was here." I got a case of the red-face repeating Roy's words.

Grandma smiled. "It's good to have another man to learn from about growing-up matters. He just wants what's best for Fancy." She looked over her shoulder at me. "You ain't give Roy a reason to worry, have you?"

I headed for the porch. "I promised I'd keep an eye on her now that Lightning's gone."

Grandma went back to drying and putting up dishes. "Why don't you go get your evening chores done while I clean up?"

After Grandma went to bed, I got a pouch of smoking tobacco and rolling papers I'd found in Granddaddy's old coat and headed out to meet Fancy. The night carried some clouds, but they were thin and let a lopsided moon make some light. I considered what Grandma said about school. After everybody in my life dying except her, I knew I might not live long enough to get old and unable to work, and I couldn't get a picture of things ten years down the road. Besides, school bored me. I didn't have big dreams of being a rich person or anything. A person with a place to call his own and make do for himself should be satisfied.

Fancy was already waiting. "Hey, Junebug, thought maybe you won't going to show up."

I took the tobacco pouch out, and tried to roll a cigarette without spilling more than I got on the paper. "Only ain't coming if it's raining."

Fancy watched me strike a kitchen match. "When did you start smoking?"

I coughed from the harshness in my throat. "Lightning and me used to sneak a few times."

"Gimme a puff. How do you do it?"

"Suck on it a little so it goes down your throat, then blow it out." My head was spinning some.

She took a long pull and got to hacking and spitting. "That taste like shit."

"Mostly a man thing, women usually dip snuff."

She wiped her mouth with the back of her hand. "My old granny dipped, spitting that nasty mess all over the place."

The moist air was warm and the tree leaves lay still, like they were waiting. "Talked to Grandma about school today."

"What'd she say?"

"That it was up to me to decide what to do."

"Well?" She'd brought the bag of candy and popped one in her mouth, then shoved the bag toward me.

A heavy odor of rotting leaves under our feet mixed with the sharp woodsy smell of pine. "Don't think I'm going back."

"Might wish you had one of these days. If you want to have a big farm like Mr. Wilson, learning would do you some good. Every time I go over to help Mrs. Wilson with the cleaning, I wish we had such a house."

"Too much to keep up. He gets the thing painted every other year, and Mrs. Wilson has to spend a lot of time working on those nice wood floors and cleaning all the time."

"You might have a wife and some babies to take care of one of these days and need a big place."

"Reckon I'll have to cross that creek when it shows up."

She leaned way over, acting like she was trying to see through the trees, the sky suddenly of interest to her. "I might consider marrying you."

A picture of us in front of the pulpit at the church flashed through my mind. "We'd be dead before we got to 'I do'."

"That's true. Plus, I wouldn't want to find you hanging from a sweet gum tree one of these nights."

I picked up a pinecone lying at my feet and pitched it into the bushes. "I got a shotgun. They might get me, but there'd be some of them riding to hell too."

"A gun won't do you no good if they burn your house down. With you in it."

"I ain't scared of a bunch of Boo Boys."

"Momma said they hung one of her uncles some years back. Got to messing with a white woman. They took a rope and strung him up down by the Neuse River. Nobody found him before he rotted; body fell right off his neck. Said it was the worst thing she ever saw, only his head still swinging."

"You're so full of shit." My hand went to my neck. "His body fell completely off?"

"That's the way she told it. Said animals had about eat all the rest of him."

Raindrops started to hit the leaves, must have been what the trees were waiting for. "You need to head on back before you get wet."

"You going to walk with me?"

"I guess." We got up and Fancy grabbed my hand. The inside of her palm was calloused and rough, hands like mine.

By the time Fancy took off across the field to her house, the rain came hard. Limbs of the big trees overhead shed most of the downpour, sounding like the roar of a train. I sat under the tobacco shelter until it eased, thinking about how Fancy and me were much more alike than different. And I thought about Grandma saying how all the things I didn't think were right weren't. But I knew there wasn't a damn thing I could do to change it.

CHAPTER 8

After a hard frost in late October, I hitched the wagon and pulled corn. Being out in the field let me talk loud and not worry about anybody hearing. "Sally Mule, Grandma ain't none too happy with me right now." I walked beside the wagon yanking ears of corn off dry stalks and tossing them in the wagon. "She's real disappointed I'm not going back to school, and it makes me feel bad. It's the first time I ever went against her wishes. What do you think?" Sally lifted her tail and farted three or four times, meaning either she didn't care, or she was trying to choke me to death.

On Thanksgiving morning, Grandma asked me to build a fire under the black iron wash pot in the backyard while she went to get a chicken for our dinner. Gray clouds rushed across the sky like they had a storm to get to. She came back holding one by the legs, the chicken squawking to beat the band, pretty sure nothing good was fixing to happen. The hen figured right; one whack from Grandma's hatchet left her head on the chopping block while her legs ran in circles until she flopped over. "How the heck you think a chicken can keep running around without its head? Seems like you'd need a brain to know where you were going."

Grandma laughed, picked up the bird by the feet, and dunked its body in the steaming hot water.

"Whew," I said. "That stink could spoil a buzzard's appetite." We sat on a couple of weathered hickory wood stools and pulled feathers, trying to ignore the nasty odor. I watched Grandma's practiced hands. "How many chickens you reckon you've plucked?"

That got a grin. "Let's say I could stuff a lot of pillows." She glanced at the darkening sky. "I remember the first time Momma made me help, must have been six or seven. I'd named all the biddies and played with them from the time they were little, especially a favorite hen I called Big Red. She wasn't nothing but a pet. One Christmas Big Red was the one Momma picked to eat, made me sit while she chopped off her head and plucked her. Reckon she did it to show me that on a farm, animals were just food. I cried so bad over Big Red it was pitiful, and wouldn't eat a bite."

Grandma stopped and looked out across the field. In spite of the story, I wondered if maybe she'd been happier then. Like mine, her childhood seemed to have started out good, but things hadn't worked out the way she expected. I felt the same loneliness in her that I did in myself. We could both maybe identify with that headless chicken.

In the middle of December, we took the truck to Apex to buy fertilizer, tobacco seeds, and other supplies we would need for spring planting. All the store windows on the street had decorations, some with angels or a Santa Claus, and the streetlight posts had big stars on top. The sound of Christmas music played every time one of the shop doors opened, happy tunes like "Santa Claus Is Coming to Town" or "Rudolph the Red Nosed Reindeer." People crowded the sidewalk, laughing and talking and shopping.

Over the summer I'd saved up seventeen dollars, and was determined to get Grandma something for Christmas. A little ways down the block was Miss Adam's Dress Shoppe, and I spotted a pretty blue Sunday frock in the window. The walls inside were painted in bright blues and whites, and it smelled of fresh pine from a decorated Christmas tree. The lady working behind the counter looked up. "Good morning, young man. Can I help you?"

I pointed to the window. "Wanted to ask how much that dress might cost; looking to buy something for my grandma."

She walked over to lift the price tag. "Who's your grandma?" The lady was dressed like she'd stepped out of a hatbox, prim and proper, not a working woman at all, and still had her good looks.

"Mrs. Rosa Belle Hurley."

The lady's shoulder-length brown hair fell across her face in a way that reminded me of my mother. She had a bright smile outlined with red lipstick, and fingernails painted to match. "Oh, I know Miss Rosa Belle. Is she doing well? Real sorry to hear when your granddaddy passed. I'm sure it's been hard on y'all trying to farm shorthanded."

"Yes'um. We're getting along pretty good."

"Let's see." She studied the tag. "Says here this dress is ten dollars even."

I stepped to get a closer look and rubbed a sleeve against my cheek. "Since you know her, do you think this might be something she would like?"

"I believe she would be real pleased." She gave me a big smile and a pat on the shoulder. "And, unless she's changed a lot, should be about the right size."

"Okay, I'd like to buy it then."

"Let me wrap it for you." She folded the dress and put red-and-white-striped paper all around the box, then added a green bow. I started imagining the look on Grandma's face when she opened the present.

It was a day to let my troubles go. I hadn't been to the drug-store since the lady wouldn't sell Fancy an ice cream cone. I ignored the lady behind the counter. They had lots of perfumes and lotions, and I sniffed several. One smelled like vanilla and that stirred another memory of my momma.

Momma had always been happy at Christmas, but then she'd been happy at birthdays or Easter, or when we would enjoy a quiet morning sitting together on the porch steps watching a bright sky and feeling a gentle breeze. Momma's blue eyes would get that particular sparkle and a person couldn't help but feel better. I remembered one day she was playing the radio loud while she cleaned the house, and when I walked in from outside, she grabbed my hand. "Come on, Junebug, let's dance!" We laughed, jumping around and making fools of ourselves, until we had to sit down on the floor. Her happiness would flow out like a circling wind and wrap me up, pulling me into her joy, letting me know it was okay to be alive and be silly. Daddy was the only one I ever saw who could make Momma's eyes water. I think he would sometimes be mean to her on purpose just to show us life was serious and hard, and not to be wasted being childish. My momma was too gentle to die.

On a shelf in the back I spotted a silver cross and chain in a nice box. The label said three dollars, and I thought it would suit Fancy. After picking out ten comic books, I carried everything to the lady in the front.

"You know, for a quarter more, I can engrave a name on the cross," she said.

I could spare a quarter. "That would be good."

"What name would you like?"

"Fancy." I stared right at her. I knew she knew, but if she made one bad remark, I'd let her have it. She didn't have any comment, just used her machine and added the name. "Could you wrap it for me, please?" The lady refused to look at me until it was finished.

Grandma was waiting on the sidewalk. "Gracious, Junebug. You've been spending money."

"Had a little bit saved." She had a couple of big bags herself. "Looks like you bought stuff too."

"Just things we might need." She hooked her arm through my elbow. "You ready to go?"

"Yep. Wanna let me drive?"

"I'm old, not dumb. You'll get your chance next year."

A few days before Christmas, Grandma cooked a big ham, a whopping bowl of collards, a plate full of hot-water corn bread, and three pies. We took them to church on Christmas Eve to share in a community get-together to celebrate the Lord's birthday.

I woke up before sunrise Christmas Day, and shivered in the cold like I was wearing iron underwear. I added more wood to the potbelly. A couple of wrapped packages were on the couch. I got Grandma's dress and laid it beside the others before going to do my chores. A crisp cap of frost lay over the grass, and when I breathed, the frigid air made it look like my mouth was on fire. The morning horizon was bright, colored that deep blue you only see in winter. I opened the gates so Sally Mule and the cow could get to pasture, fed the pigs, and promised the chickens nobody would lose their head today so they should rest easy. Since it was a Saturday I wondered if Fancy would show up tonight.

When I got back to the house, Grandma was dressed in her wool sleeping gown and standing at the stove. "Looks like Santa Claus did find us out here in the sticks." She hugged me, her silver hair falling down around her shoulders. "Merry Christmas, Junebug." The smell of biscuits, ham, and bacon cooking made my stomach growl.

After breakfast, Grandma washed and I dried before we went to sit in the living room. The oak wood burning in the stove gave off just the right comfort. "You go ahead and open yours," said Grandma. She pulled up her favorite rocking chair, the same one she'd rocked me in the night Momma and Daddy died.

In the first box were two pairs of Roebuck jeans, a new pair of bib overalls, and a flannel shirt. I held them up. "Thanks, Grandma, these clothes will look real good."

"Well, I hope they work with what's in that other box." She leaned forward in her chair.

I tore off the Christmas paper. Inside was a new pair of brown brogans with thick soles and treads on the bottom. "Gosh, Grandma, you spent too much money." I ran my hands over the leather shoes, quickly pulling off my old ones that had two holes in the toe. "You shouldn't have done all this."

"Glad you like them. Should be one more thing in there." I turned the box upside down. Something plunked on the floor. It was a big buck knife. Each pull made a strong *click* when I popped the blade up and down. Every working man needed one. It fit comfortable in my pocket. "Grandma, I don't know what to say. Thank you, thank you." I got up and squeezed her around the neck.

"You're welcome. Should last you a long time if you don't lose it."

"Don't worry about that." I picked up the last box. "This is for you." My hands were shaky. It was the first present I'd ever bought with my own money.

She looked surprised. "You ought not to have done this." Grandma carefully removed the paper. "I can save this pretty wrapping for next year." She lifted the dress out. "Oh, Junebug, it's so beautiful. This is the first store-bought dress I've had in years." She stood to measure the size to the front of herself. "It looks like it will fit just fine." Her grin was wide as a river. "Reckon what I'll be wearing to church tomorrow?"

"The lady at Miss Adam's Dress Shoppe said to tell you hello."

"I'll stop in and visit Susan the next time we go to town." Grandma searched around in her bedroom bureau until she found the old Brownie camera, and took some pictures of me. "Merry Christmas, Junebug; this is one of the best I can remember."

I leaned my head into her shoulder and wrapped my arms around her back. "Wasn't for you, I'd be in an orphanage somewhere. You should know how much I appreciate everything you do for me."

She held me. "Don't you fret, we're going to have lots of Christmases together."

Later in the afternoon, Mr. and Mrs. Wilson stopped by to visit. Right after they got there, Mr. and Mrs. Jackson came for a few minutes and brought Grandma the prettiest poinsettia I'd ever seen. It made the house really feel like Christmas. After that, the preacher and his family visited, and we had a houseful of folks. They stayed and talked for a couple of hours.

It had been a wonderful day, and I was tired by the time everyone left. "Grandma, I'm going to lay down."

"Junebug, you better get up and see what Santa Claus brought you." I heard my daddy's voice and knew I was dreaming, but I couldn't, and didn't want to wake up.

CHAPTER 9

Grandma went to bed not long after supper. I eased out the back door and headed to the stumps. A white winter moon was bright as a bulb and had a halo around it, which meant snow if you believed the old wives' tale. Crusty leaves and frozen twigs snapped underfoot. I picked a seat, pulled my coat closer, and tried to roll a cigarette with cold fingers. It being Christmas, Fancy might not show, but Saturday was our time, so I waited. Swaying winter-bare limbs raked and cracked against each other like hands clapping.

I heard traipsing through the brush. "Merry Christmas, Junebug." Fancy sidled up on the same stump and gave me a little hug. "Cold as a gravestone, ain't it?" She wore brogan shoes, blue jeans, a heavy coat, and a knit hat to cover her head. "Did you have a good Christmas?"

"Real good. You?" A cold breeze rustled the dry leaves and blew a chill down my collar. I sucked on the homemade cigarette, getting a few puffs before it burned my fingers.

"We did. All my aunts and uncles and cousins came to the house and we had a big old time. The men got to sipping and telling funny stories." Fancy leaned forward with hands in her side pockets, crossed her legs, and pulled the front of her coat tighter. "We had chicken dumplings and collards and sweet potatoes and corn bread for dinner. Good eating, and plenty of it."

She smelled of wood smoke. "Old Santa find you?"

"Momma made me a new dress for going to school, and Daddy found an old bicycle in Miss May's barn he fixed up so I can ride instead of walk everywhere."

"Be good when the weather gets warm."

She stuck her arm through the crook of my elbow, and folded her hand back into her pocket, snuggling. The softness of her was warm. "What did you get?"

I pulled out the buck knife.

"Dang, Junebug." She snapped the powerful blade open and shut. "Wanna play mumblety-peg?" The bright moon made her white teeth shine in the dark.

"Hell, no, you'd probably stab me in the foot. But we can do this." I pulled her to follow me to a poplar tree close by, and started carving.

Fancy looked over my shoulder. "What are you doing?"

"Cutting our initials so when folks a long time from now come by, they'll know we were here." After some grunting and hard scraping, I finally got a big *F* and *J* skinned out.

She admired the work. "Ought to put an *L* too, in honor of Lightning."

"Have you heard anything from him?" Cutting the *L* proved easier than the other two.

"Not a dang word; you'd a thought he could have at least sent a letter by now." She ran her hands over the letters. "Nice work, Junebug." The blustery wind picked up, sharpened to a freezing edge. Fancy exaggerated a shiver. We went back to sit.

"Got something for you." I pulled the box from my coat pocket.

Fancy rolled the package in her hand. "What's in here, Junebug?"

"Open it and see."

"Now I feel bad that I ain't got nothing to give you."

"Didn't expect anything. Had a little extra and just wanted to."

Fancy took her time removing the wrapping, like Grandma saving the paper from the dress box. Her hands fumbled trying to tear the tape so I snipped it with my knife. The silver of the necklace flashed in the moonlight. I struck a match. "See, it's got your name spelled out right there."

Fancy put one hand across her eyes. Tears started to spill down. She turned and put her arms around my neck. "Hey, now, I won't trying to make you cry."

"Will you help me?" She handed me the chain and turned her back. "I don't know how to thank you, Junebug. I'm going to wear this to church tomorrow."

"Don't let your daddy see it and get the wrong idea. I had enough trouble with him over that candy."

"Then I'll keep it hid and only wear it when I'm coming to see you." She clutched it against her chest.

I would have bought her ten necklaces to get that smile.

Fancy turned her face close to mine. "Junebug?"

"What?"

"Can I kiss you?"

I'd sometimes imagined what it would be like to kiss Fancy, but thinking it and doing it were a long ways apart, which made what came out of my mouth seem crazy. "If you want to."

We faced each other, our noses almost touching. "You ever kissed a girl before?"

My knee started to bounce. "No." Her breath smelled like sweet potatoes. "But I'm willing to start."

She laid her hand on my leg to quiet it. "We could try it if you want to, and see what happens."

I got a vision of Roy walking up while we had our lips stuck together. Maybe it would be worth the pain of an ass beating. "Okay."

Fancy edged closer. "All right, you ready?" She seemed way too calm.

My brain was screaming, *Stop!* but my mouth wouldn't listen. "If you are." An owl hooted. I considered running like hell.

Fancy folded her arms around my neck, and then pulled mine up to do the same on her. "Now close your eyes."

The soft touch of her mouth startled me.

She pulled back. "You all right?"

"Sorry, couldn't see it coming."

Fancy unzipped our coats and we stuck our arms inside each other's jackets. "This time you'll know what to expect."

Our lips lay stiff as a day-old biscuit at first, but then we began to move them around. I pulled my head back. "Are you sticking your tongue out?"

"Lightning told me that's the way you're supposed to kiss. Come on, let's try it." The feeling of our tongues mixing together was weird at first, but got warm in a hurry. We explored, hands squeezing and moving inside each other's jackets, legs stretching and sliding until we almost fell off the stump. My God, could Christmas get any better?

Finally, we pulled apart and zipped up our jackets.

"Well?" Fancy asked.

I sucked in the cold air, wore slam-out from holding my breath. "Well, what?"

"Did you like it?"

"Did you?" If she said no, I would go straight to the woodshed and kill myself with an ax.

"I think we could get real good at it with a little practice."

I was thinking home run and she acted like it was only a single. But I was all for a little more practice.

"It's getting late. You going to walk with me?" Fancy took my hand and we started slowly toward her house. "I might come visit you tomorrow on my bicycle, if it would be all right with your grandma."

Despite the cold, beads of sweat rolled down my neck. "Can't think why it wouldn't be." I was pretty sure what we did was sinful; I'd heard the preacher say mixing races was a road straight to hell. And I knew without a doubt it was dangerous; there wouldn't be forgiveness if anybody, black or white, found out.

When we got to the edge of the woods, Fancy pecked me on the lips. I watched until she made it across.

Walking back through the woods, I tried to pee. The last drops drained and I had a familiar urge. In a minute, jisim shot out, and my knees wanted to buckle. I used to practice behind the barn a lot, but fear made me quit. Lightning told me he'd heard a man could go blind doing it.

In the quiet of my bedroom I worried I'd wake up not able to see shit, having to walk around with a cane and dark glasses the rest of my life. I repeated the Lord's Prayer until I fell asleep.

Daylight came, and I thanked God I could see the ceiling. I put on the new jeans, flannel shirt, and brogans, anxious to get to church and do some praying.

CHAPTER 10

That ring around the moon thing must have been true. Six inches of snow fell right after New Year's. A few days after the ice melted, Grandma said, "We need to get to killing hogs, Junebug. I'll go up tomorrow and ask Clyde Wilson about helping us. You need to get the scalding-vat from the barn."

That night I fed the two pigs one last time, and scratched their ears while they grunted and slurped from the wooden trough. I rubbed the pecan-sized knot on Bumpy's head. She'd always followed me around when I needed to get in the pen, sticking her nose under my legs, curious. "You've been a good girl. I'm going to miss you." She looked up from the trough. If a pig could smile, she was doing it.

At sunup the next morning a crusty layer of heavy frost covered the ground. I dragged the scalding-vat from the barn, filled it with water, and set about building a fire underneath it. By the time Mr. Wilson, Roy, Clemmy, and Fancy got there, steam rolled off the water.

I watched Fancy head toward the house to help Grandma, and noticed how her and Clemmy had the same gait when they walked. I thought about the touch of her mouth and my cheeks burned.

"Mr. Wilson, I never done this by myself." The three of us stood close together, stomping our feet, blowing clouds of smoke, and warming our hands from the heat off the boiling water.

"Nothing to worry about." He got busy hanging a pulley over the mule lot gate. I paid attention to everything he did. "First is to keep the water as hot as can be, so keep loading wood underneath when it gets low. Then we pick us a pig. You want to do the shooting since these are your hogs?"

I figured it wouldn't be very manly if I didn't. "I'll do it."

Bumpy was standing by the fence watching, her snout twitching. Roy went in and she gave him a friendly sniff, but when he grabbed her by the hind legs, Bumpy started squealing. I laid the barrel of the twenty-two between her eyes, and she stared straight at me, like she was pleading. I squeezed the trigger. She made one grunt and hit the ground. I felt sick. Roy slashed her neck to bleed her out.

Mr. Wilson gripped my shoulder. "You all right, Junebug? You seem a mite weak-eyed." Him and Roy had a good laugh.

Once we slid Bumpy into the vat, each of us took a sharp-edged tin-can lid and scraped off the rough black hair. After that we hooked her to the pulley and hung her upside down. Roy cut open her belly and raked the guts into a washtub. I carried them to the house, where the women would clean them and make sausage casings and chitlins.

The other pig smelled the rusty iron stink of blood and went running to take cover at the back of the lot. Mr. Wilson laughed. "Rest easy, pig, we'll be along for you in a minute."

Roy and Mr. Wilson showed me how to butcher the meat proper so nothing was wasted from the "snoot to the poot," as Mr. Wilson said. Within a couple of hours, the only thing left to recognize Bumpy was her head, then damned if Roy didn't cut off her jowls, saying they'd be good for seasoning a pot of greens.

When Roy went after the other pig, she took off around the fifty-foot-long pen, down to the muddy wallow and back again.

"Get her, Roy, get her." Mr. Wilson laughed and hollered en-couragement. Finally Roy tackled the pig and I managed to shoot without killing him. They showed me how to salt and store hams, shoulders, and bacon in the smokehouse. It took most of the day to finish.

I stunk of blood, mud, and pig shit. The shower water wouldn't get hot, so I lathered my face, arms, and hands with lye soap while I shivered, scrubbing hard to get off the stink. I took the washcloth and dug inside my ears, trying to drown out Bumpy. Grandma had laid out some fresh clothes on my bed.

She was busy at the stove cooking parts of Bumpy for supper. "Everything go right today?"

All I could picture was Bumpy's eyes. "Know I ain't going to get too friendly with the next pigs; reckon it was sort of like you and Big Red." I sat at the kitchen table playing with an old penny I'd found, spinning it by holding the top and thumping with my finger. Whenever my mind got sad like it had today watching Bumpy, I thought about Momma, and wished I could hold her hand. I could hear her saying, "Tomorrow your pack-age will be better." Some days seemed too hard to be a man. Every bite of the pork wanted to stick in my throat.

After supper, I emptied the vat and made sure any hot coals were snuffed. Bumpy's squealing was still in my head. By the time I got the scalding-vat stored in the barn, wet snow began to fall, big flakes, like dogwood petals floating out of the sky. It was coming down heavy, and I lifted my head to catch pieces in my mouth.

Grandma and me sat on the porch and watched the fields and yard turn from brown to white. Not a bird, not a cricket made a sound. The snow slowly smothered the world in quiet. "The Lord sure has blessed us with a pretty sight," Grandma said. She had a smile on her face, and her gray head nodded like she might be listening to something. She looked as peaceful as the snow.

"Grandma, do you think everything that happens is *God's Will?*"

She gave me a surprised look. "Why, Junebug, what in the world brought that up?"

"Just thinking about what Granddaddy told me after Momma and Daddy died; he thought it must be God's plan. But if that's true, and everything is already decided, why should a person worry about right or wrong, what's the difference if we cuss or steal or even kill somebody? If it's all *God's Will,* seems don't none of them things matter."

She studied her hands, rubbing them together. "First of all, understand you're at the age when you begin to question things you've always been taught, and that's natural. Here's the way I think about it: When we're born God has a path for us, and, if we obey and live by His Word, we'll find the peace He promised. That's *God's Will.* But each person has his or her own free will. Some people choose to follow another way and give in to sin and temptation, or they're driven by anger or jealousy and have the idea God has abandoned them. In the Bible, Paul says *I can will what is right, but I cannot do it.* He's teaching that we're all weak, and the struggle against sin and evil is forever. When somebody says it was *God's Will,* they really mean they hope the person has lived in a way that God will give him the promised peace."

It was a lot to take in. I wondered if having sexual thoughts about Fancy was sinful, because I knew for sure it was temptation. Grandma and I watched the snow until it got too dark to see. Before going inside, I stepped outside to the ground and looked up. "Bumpy, you check around for Granddaddy up there, he'll help you along."

When I went to bed, I tried to push the battle between doubt and trust from my mind, but couldn't.

CHAPTER 11

By Friday the snow had mostly melted, leaving frozen piles here and there in the early morning cold. Saturday night, despite the weather, I went to the clearing on the chance Fancy would come. Snow patches in the woods caught light from a clear sky, and I could spot deer tracks in places.

She was already there, munching from a paper sack of pork cracklings. "Hey, Junebug."

"Where'd you get the rinds?"

She stuffed more in. "Mrs. Wilson made 'em."

I took a handful. "How does she fix them?"

"Cuts up hog skins, boils to get the fat off, and deep fries them crispy. I helped her, ain't that hard."

"What else you been doing?"

"Nothing. Too cold and messy to ride my bike, but when it warms up I'm going to come visit and see what you think."

"I never rode one."

"You thought anymore about us kissing?" She brought it up right out of the blue.

"Some." What a lie—I'd ended up with sticky underwear more than once.

"I don't think we should do it anymore for a while. Lightning used to say when his jisim backed up, it would make his balls hurt something awful." She sat there like a chipmunk with full jaws. "Yours hurt?"

I felt my face flush. "No."

"So what do you think?"

"About what?"

"About kissing, stupid. Ain't you listening to anything I say?" She munched and talked at the same time.

"I heard you. You're right, ain't proper anyway."

"Why? 'Cause I'm colored and you're white?"

"Do you always have to say that? I mean it ain't right for a boy and girl our age to be out here in the woods kissing."

"Who's going to find out? I ain't told anyone."

My arms went out in exasperation. "I don't know."

"Sometimes you get on my nerves, Junebug." She turned her head away. "You didn't like kissing me, and now you're making up excuses not to do it."

"I am not! You're the one who just said we shouldn't do it anymore."

"Well, kiss me to prove it." She leaned her head over, daring.

"I'm not kissing you with a mouthful of cracklings."

Fancy ran her finger around her mouth and then spit out the chewed-up pieces. "Satisfied?"

"Okay, if it's what you want to do."

Fancy's eyes narrowed. She stood up, fist on her hip. "Hold on just one damn minute. What do you mean, 'if it's what I want to do'? You didn't seem to mind last time. Now I ain't good enough for you? You better consider how you talk to me, Junebug Hurley. I can whup a boy's ass as quick as a girl's."

I got up and put my nose to hers. "Is that so?" We circled. Fancy leaped to get me in a headlock, but I grabbed her, one arm under her legs, the other under her back, and swung her around. We glared at each other.

She slid her arms around my neck and mine went around her back. A piece of straw couldn't have squeezed between our bodies. It set my insides on fire when our lips touched.

We pulled back. "That was some better, don't you think?" Fancy said.

"Pretty good, I thought."

"But that's the last time for a while. We agreed?" Fancy watched my eyes.

If there was a time I knew another person would punch me in the face if I said yes, this was it. "No." I pulled her down to sit.

Fancy took a few rinds from the bag, stuck two in her mouth and one in mine. The hint of a grin showed. "I could feel your business on my leg, don't want you having a heart attack."

I pushed her sideways. "A man ain't going to have a heart attack because of that."

"How you know?"

"'Cause if it did, every man would be dead."

Fancy play-slapped me on the head. "Just messing with you, Junebug. Come on and walk me home." At the field, she took off running, then bent over, crunched a handful of leftover snow into a ball, and threw it at me. "You dream about me, Junebug."

CHAPTER 12

Red maple trees started to bud and spotted salamanders sneaked from their burrows in the pond bank by the end of February. I managed to get the plant bed ready for sowing tobacco seeds by burning off weeds to get some ash into the soil. March sunshine coaxed the smell of moist dirt from the ground as winter's grip started to relax. April would be on us soon, and the real work of farming would begin.

On the last Sunday in March, I got back from morning chores expecting breakfast, but Grandma wasn't up. She should have been getting dressed for church by now. I called through her bedroom door. "Grandma, you okay?"

"Be out in a minute." Her voice sounded sort of weak and feeble. When she came into the living room she was wearing a heavy housecoat. "If you don't mind, we're going to skip church this morning. I ain't feeling too good." Her face was pale, and her blue eyes looked watery.

"What's the matter?"

"Must be a touch of a cold coming on, didn't sleep much and

everything aches." She gave me a look. "Thought I heard you up sort of late."

I'd been with Fancy. "Had a bit of an upset stomach, probably all them collards I ate for supper."

"Mix some vinegar and water if you need it."

"Just a passing thing. Want me to cook you some eggs?"

"Do for yourself. I'm going to lay back down, probably feel better after a while." I watched at the door while she got in bed. "Will you bring me another cover?" I got one of the homemade quilts from the closet. I'd seen her with cut hands, hurt knees, and her back so bad she could hardly walk, but I'd never seen her sick. She slept through the morning.

I was on the porch enjoying the early afternoon sunshine when I glanced toward the road and saw Fancy riding her bicycle. I stepped out to the yard. She had on a pair of bib overalls cut off at the knees. The bike slid to a stop in front of me. "Told you I might come see you one of these days. Got home from church and decided to ride over."

"That's a mighty nice bicycle." Roy had given it a coat of shiny red paint and used a clothespin to attach a playing card in the spokes to make a chatter.

She hopped off. "Want to ride?"

"I'll try." It was hard getting the thing to go straight at first, but I soon got the idea and rode up and down the dirt road. I tried to make a sliding stop the way Fancy had and fell off. "Man, that's fun."

"Keeps a person from having to walk. How was church?" She straddled the bike while we talked.

I squatted, pulled a new grass sprout, and twirled it in my mouth. "Grandma was feeling bad so we stayed home. She ain't got up all day, said she might be getting a cold."

"Does she have a fever?"

"Don't know, but she sure don't feel good."

Fancy pushed the kickstand down. "Can I go see? I can tell."

I knocked on the bedroom door. "Grandma, Fancy's come by

to show me her bicycle, and wants to check if you got a fever. Is that all right?"

"Bring her in." Her voice sounded weak.

Fancy went ahead of me. "Junebug says you ain't feeling good, Miz Hurley." She gently laid her palm on Grandma's head, then the back of her hand to her temple and neck. "Seems real warm to me. You keep anything for a cold?"

"There's some liniment in a green bottle in the kitchen cupboard. Show her, Junebug."

We found the medicine. Grandma had a coughing spell, dry-heaving a little. "Junebug, go out for a minute so Fancy can rub it on my chest real good."

Fancy came out and closed the door behind her. She didn't say anything, but concern showed on her face. "I'm going to fix some soup so your grandma can eat something. She needs to keep her strength. Show me the canned vegetables and pots and such, and I'll fix enough for supper while I'm doing." We found jars of tomatoes, okra, butter beans, and got a little piece of salt pork from the refrigerator.

"You sure know your way around a stove."

"Shoot, Momma's been showing me how to cook since I could walk." She stirred the soup, tasting before adding salt, pepper, and butter. "We need to let the flavors melt for a few minutes." We sat while the pot boiled. "You keep an eye on her, Junebug. She's got some fever and I don't like the sound of that cough." Fancy stirred and tasted one more time, then held up a big spoon to me. "What do you think?"

"Taste good to me." She filled a small bowl and let it cool.

Fancy fixed the pillows so Grandma could sit up, and managed to get her to eat about half of it. "That hit the spot, Fancy. Your momma taught you good." She pulled the quilt back around her neck.

"Oh, wasn't no trouble. Plenty left in that pot for you and Junebug to have for supper. Be glad to come tomorrow and rub on more of that medicine?"

Grandma squeezed Fancy's hand. "I appreciate it, but expect I'll be better by then. Your folks probably got other things for you to do."

"If you don't feel better, send Junebug and I'll bring some of the potions my momma keeps for sickness. They work real good."

Out in the yard, Fancy cautioned, "Come and get me if you need to."

CHAPTER 13

At supper, Grandma wouldn't eat, and when I felt, her skin was hot. I wet a washcloth with cold water and laid it across her forehead. It was getting to be bedtime when I checked again. Not only was her head and face hot, but she was also breathing real heavy and sweating. I didn't know what to do, but knew I needed to do something. I shook her shoulder. "Grandma, I'm going to get Mrs. Wilson."

She managed to open her eyes. "I feel mighty bad, Junebug."

"I'll be right back." I got the truck and went flying to the Wilson place, pounding on the door. Mr. Wilson came. "What's the matter, Junebug? It's the middle of the night." In his long nightshirt, he looked like a barrel with two legs. Did he think I'd show up like this for no reason?

"Grandma's real sick."

To his credit, he didn't hesitate. "Lila," he hollered, "get up. It's Rosa Belle."

She called from the bedroom. "Is she sick?"

"Junebug says she's bad off." He turned back to me. "Go

to the house and wait with your grandma, we'll be there in a minute."

I put another cold rag across Grandma's head. "They're on the way." I should be smarter about what to do, but my brain wouldn't work right. I was scared.

The porch door slammed, and Mrs. Wilson came hurrying to Grandma's bed. "Hey, Rosa Belle. Junebug says you're right smart sick." Her voice was unruffled and soothing, not her usual nervous flitting. She touched Grandma's head and neck and listened to her raspy breathing.

"Hated to bother you, Lila, but it's been a long time since I've felt this poor." Grandma's voice was shaky.

"Well, I'm here. Have you been vomiting?"

"No," Grandma wheezed, "but I'm having a hard time breathing."

"Get me a glass, Junebug."

When Grandma had another coughing episode, Mrs. Wilson made her spit into the glass. She came in the living room, rolled the phlegm around, and inspected it under the light. "There's blood in this, and she's burning up with fever. I think its pneumonia." She was very matter-of-fact. "We need to get to the hospital." Mrs. Wilson put warm clothes on Grandma, then we all helped her to the truck.

"Ain't enough room up here, Junebug," Mr. Wilson said, "and you'll freeze in the back. You might ought to stay home."

"I'm going." I climbed into the bed of the truck. We headed to Durham. Through the back window, I could see Mrs. Wilson wrap her arm around Grandma. All I could do was sit and shiver from worry and the cold wind.

It took about thirty minutes to get to Watts Hospital. At the emergency entrance, nurses came out and put Grandma in a wheelchair. She was slumped over, holding her head in her hands. Mrs. Wilson followed them while Mr. Wilson and me found a seat in the waiting room. The white plastic chairs were stiff and hard.

"Grandma don't look good, does she?" My knee wouldn't stay still.

He had his elbows on his knees and held his hat in his hand. "They can probably give her medicine to get the fever down; just got to trust the doctors."

"I should have come get you sooner." I couldn't sit still and prowled around, looking in the vending machines and reading the signs. Despite the bright orange and blue walls, the place had a sense of misery. A strong smell of turpentine and vomit came from the end of a hall where a janitor was mopping the floor. I wondered how many people died in this hospital every day.

A round wall clock read two fifteen when I spotted Mrs. Wilson coming through the double doors where she had followed the nurses. She forced a smile. "She's mighty sick, Junebug. They're going to keep her tonight and probably a few more. It's definitely pneumonia. All we can do is go home and come back tomorrow."

"Will they let me see her?"

"Not right now. They're giving her oxygen to get her breathing better, and medicine through a tube in her arm. They said she'll probably sleep and that's what she needs most. We'll come back in the morning."

I stared at the white tiled floor. I didn't want to leave Grandma with strange people. Mr. Wilson gripped my shoulder. "Only help we can be is to go home and say some prayers. She's got good folks looking after her."

"Why don't you stay with us tonight?" Mrs. Wilson put her hand on my arm.

"Appreciate it, but I'll be all right. Besides, I got to take care of the animals in the morning."

She didn't argue. "If that's what you want to do, we'll be after you right after breakfast." She gave me a sideways hug.

At the house, I didn't bother to turn on any lights. Strange how you don't miss noise until there is none. I pulled my feet up on the couch, gripped around my middle, and pressed everything tight. "Lord, if you let Grandma get well, I'll go to church more, anything. Just make her better." I rocked back and forth.

The screen door slammed. "Junebug, you here?"

It startled me. "Fancy? It's three in the morning. What the heck are you doing here?" It came out harder than was meant.

She stopped. "I came to make sure you were okay. But if it makes you mad, I'll go home."

I waved her in. "No, it's fine; you just surprised me, that's all. Wasn't trying to be ugly."

"I heard the Wilsons come home and got up to see what was wrong. Mrs. Wilson said they had to take your granny to the hospital." She sat on the couch beside me. "I told Momma I was coming to check up on you."

I leaned my elbows on my knees and scrubbed my face up and down. "She's really sick with the pneumonia, Fancy. What if something bad happens?"

"The first thing is trusting the Lord will take care of things. It'll be okay, Junebug." She leaned her head against mine and rubbed my back.

"You know some prayers, don't you, Fancy?"

"Sure I do. Come on, let's get on our knees so He'll take us serious." Both of us knelt on the floor. She started with the Lord's Prayer and I joined in. "*Our Father who art in heaven . . .*" We prayed to God for Grandma to get well, and I repeated my bargain about changing for the better if He'd help her. Fancy threw in plenty of "*Praise Gods*" and we used up about all the religious words we knew.

Fancy stood up. "You got any coffee?"

"In the kitchen."

Fancy found a pot and the can of coffee. "It'll be ready in a bit."

"I'm grateful you came; I didn't mean to be cross with you."

"What's a sister for anyway? We got to take care of each other when we can."

It was hard not to believe I had a black cloud over me. "Do you think maybe I'm just bad luck?"

"Junebug, you hush." She squatted in front and pushed her face close to mine, her eyes squinted and angry. "Stop being foolish enough to think you got that kind of power. God's got more to worry about than just you."

The clock chimed four. "You need to go on home. It'll be time for your school bus soon. I need to feed the animals before Mr. and Mrs. Wilson get here."

Fancy walked over to a small silver-framed mirror hanging on the wall near Grandma's bedroom door. She took a cloth doily off the sewing machine and covered the glass. "Old folks say this keeps bad spirits away."

I walked her to the door.

She turned and pecked me on the cheek. "You give that to your grandma for me." I watched the bouncing of her flashlight beam until it faded.

CHAPTER 14

When we got to the hospital, I expected Grandma to be better. The sight of her stopped me in my tracks. Tubes hooked to a plastic bag above her head ran to a needle sticking in her arm. Another line fed from a round tank tied to the bed to a mask over her nose and mouth. The sign read OXYGEN—NO SMOKING. Her face was pasty, and red veins ran like a grapevine across her cheeks. Grandma looked as if she'd aged twenty years in a day. The silver hair that was always tight and neat lay spread across her pillow, strands sticking up at angles. It was scary seeing such a strong woman looking so frail. I took her hand. "Hey, Grandma."

When she opened her eyes, they were weak and glassy as flat water. She tried to speak, but the mask muffled her words.

Mrs. Wilson came to stand beside me. "Don't try to talk, Rosa Belle, you rest." She patted Grandma's arm and smiled. Grandma nodded her head and closed her eyes.

I dragged a couple of extra plastic chairs from the hall into the light-yellow painted-concrete block room. A nurse came by to check on Grandma's temperature and listen to her chest. She said the doctor should be around before lunch.

The room across the way was crowded with women, each one trying to talk louder than the others, while three little kids ran up and down the hall raising hell. I figured the sick lady must be their momma, because every once in a while she would yell at the younguns to shut up. It looked like the room was on fire from all the cigarette smoke.

"Them children need a good ass whooping," Mr. Wilson said. Mrs. Wilson slapped his arm for cussing. The clock on the wall read eleven when an older, very tall doctor stooped through the door. His black hair was gray at the temples and he wore heavy brown glasses. He introduced himself as Dr. Murray and listened to Grandma's chest and back, made some notes on the chart at the foot of the bed, and then motioned for us to step outside.

"Mrs. Hurley is a very sick lady. She's got a bad case of pneumonia, and our best chance is the antibiotics we're giving her." He was kind, but all business. "She's a strong woman and that is in her favor. If she can hang on for another twenty-four to forty-eight hours, her odds will go up."

I stared at him. He was saying Grandma might die. Mrs. Wilson put her arm across my shoulders.

He looked down at me. "Do you have any questions, son?"

"I need my grandma to get well. She's all I got."

"We're going to do our best." He stuck out his hand and we shook. "If there's anything you need, ask the nurse to call me."

The hours stretched long as we waited through the afternoon, taking turns walking up and down the hall to stretch our legs. The visitors across the hall finally left, dragging the kids crying and hollering with them. A nurse's aide brought Grandma soup and Jell-O for dinner, but Mrs. Wilson couldn't rouse her enough to eat, so Mr. Wilson ate the Jell-O. "No use wasting it," he said.

It was getting toward five o'clock. Mr. Wilson said, "We need to start home so I can get the animals fed and shut up before dark."

"Mr. Wilson, y'all think you'll come tomorrow?"

"Sure, Junebug, we'll be back in the morning."

"Then I'm staying the night."

Mr. Wilson looked a little irritated. "Junebug, these doctors and nurses will make sure she's looked after. Miss Rosa Belle will be all right."

"I want to be here every time she opens her eyes so she knows she ain't alone." I hoped my tone let them know there wasn't going to be any arguing.

Mrs. Wilson spoke up. "I understand. Come on, Clyde, he'll be fine."

"Anything need doing at the house?" Mr. Wilson asked.

"No. Fancy is going to take care of milking the cow and see to the other things for me."

He pulled out his wallet and handed me a five-dollar bill. "When did you talk to her?"

"She stopped by real early this morning before she went to school." Hell of a place to tell a lie.

"You take this so you can eat something."

I took the money. "Pay you back soon as I get home."

He headed toward the door. "All in due time, Junebug."

After they left, a pretty blond nurse came in the room, made notes, and checked the medicine bags. She had a nice smile. "Is Mrs. Hurley your only family?"

I nodded. "Do you think she will be all right?"

"We'll take care of her real good, don't you worry." The name on her tag said Nurse Freymuth. An hour later, she came rolling in a big easy chair. "Thought you could use something more comfortable in case you want to get a little sleep." She showed me how to use the handle to make the back go down so I could stretch out. "The cafeteria is down on the first floor and opens in a little while if you want some supper."

I sat and listened to Grandma's breathing. I was exhausted, and nodded on and off. Once I caught Grandma watching me. She smiled, then drifted off again.

It was getting dark outside the room window, and I went

hunting for that cafeteria. A plate of spaghetti cost a dollar and a carton of milk was twenty cents. It turned out I wasn't very hungry. A cigarette machine was against the wall in the hallway. They were expensive at forty cents a pack, but figured I needed the smokes worse than the money. I decided to take a break from the hospital stink, and stopped the elevator at the main floor. Stone benches sat along the brightly lit sidewalk outside, and the night air felt good. A few other people came along, and we smoked and chatted for a while.

After two cigarettes' worth of conversation, I went back to Grandma's room. Her hand felt chilly so I tried to warm it in both of mine. She opened her eyes. Her hand reached to move the mask to one side. "Junebug, I need to talk to you." She seemed stronger, and her eyes looked clearer.

"Grandma, you shouldn't be taking that thing off." I got up to help her, but she pushed against my hand.

"Hush and listen." She sounded cross. "There's things you need to know in case the Lord calls me home."

I shook my head. "No need. You're going to be well in a few weeks and up and around."

"Junebug, I know I'm bad off, and should've had this talk with you before now." Her voice trembled like a person would if they were cold. "Out in the pack house cellar there's money the family has been keeping a real long time. It's hidden in mason jars. When you go in the door, they're buried in the rear left hand corner under an old barrel." She stopped and coughed hard.

I put the mask back over her face; she took some deep breaths and removed it again. "I got a plot at the church beside your granddaddy already spoke for." Grandma talked fast, like she needed to get everything said. "My will and the deed to the farm are at Lawyer Stern's office in Apex." She struggled for air. I started to say something, but she moved her finger to my mouth. "You guard that money, Junebug, but use it if you need to. The farm is free and clear, so as long as you keep it, you've got somewhere to live and be able to fend for yourself." She started coughing bad and had to stop. I held a cup for her to spit in, but didn't look at it. "Use that Hurley hardheadedness, and you'll make out. You know I love you and I know you're man enough."

Her face was pale as a daylight moon. I couldn't shake the dread that came over me. "Junebug, there comes a time the Lord sees fit for us to take new reins and go in a different direction." She held my eyes with the tears in hers. "Life don't always play out the way we think it should. If it's my time, I'm not afraid and don't want you to be either. Whatever plan God has, I'm willing to accept it."

My voice choked. "Grandma, you're going to get out of this bed and come home. I'm not ready to be done having you around yet. I don't think I can do the lonesome."

Eye water soaked her cheeks. "I'm proud of you, Junebug, always have been. You keep believing in yourself, that how you see the world is right."

I lifted her hand to my face. "Whatever I am, I got it from you."

I put her mask back on, and in a few minutes, she was asleep again. I went to stand at the window and whispered, "Lord, if You're up there, I've listened to the preacher, and Fancy, and Grandma say all things are according to Your Plan. I've swallowed everything You've dished out up 'til now, but You know Grandma's all I got left, and I've about had a belly full of Your plans."

I sat down beside Grandma. The lines and wrinkles of hard times were etched into her face like a sharp knife on bread dough. I tried to remember a time when she didn't look old. I had no idea what I would do without her if she died, how I would live, or if I even wanted to. But she would consider giving up a sin just as bad as stealing or lying or using the Lord's name in vain. Grandma was my only ally, understanding I struggled with conflictions about God, about how I didn't think things I saw were right, and especially Fancy. I needed to believe her spirit would stay with me, and all I could hope was for it to be enough.

CHAPTER 15

The big chair slid easy on the linoleum floor, and I moved it closer to keep in reach of Grandma. Sleep snuck up on me. I was dreaming Grandma was talking about going to Apex. I jerked awake. She was sitting upright in bed. When I tried to put the oxygen mask over her face, she slapped my hand away.

"Stop it!" She pointed. "Don't you see them? They're standing right there. They're asking me to come." She smiled and waved and mumbled things I couldn't understand.

I searched the room. "Who are you talking about?"

I took her shoulders to push her down, but she wrestled with me. "Leave me alone!" I decided to run and get the nurse.

Grandma suddenly stopped and got quiet. When she turned to face me, chill bumps rose on my arms and neck. Her face wasn't old anymore. It was that girl of sixteen in the picture on the wall at home, sitting on the buckboard, the deep blue eyes staring out at the world. She pulled my hand to her chest, and slowly sank back on the pillow. I felt a whisper of air across my face, and an overpowering sense of Granddaddy surrounded me. Grandma's wide-open eyes stared at the ceiling. The only sound was the shushing of oxygen.

"Grandma?" I shook her shoulder. "Grandma, don't you leave me alone!" But she lay fixed in that awful stillness. The machine above the bed began to buzz.

The blond nurse rushed in and pushed me out of the way. She put fingers to Grandma's neck and wrist, and started shoving up and down on her chest, forcing a breath, then two more, then nothing. Another nurse, and a doctor I didn't know, ran in. The doctor gave instructions as they worked. I stood at the doorway. The top of my head tingled. I could feel Grandma in the room, like she was watching.

In a few minutes the doctor stopped. "Time of death, two twenty-three a.m." The nurse wrote on the chart.

His words slapped me in the face. I shoved past to her bed. "She's still here!" I managed to get my hands on Grandma's chest before the doctor grabbed my arms. We wrestled.

The blond nurse pushed between us, wrapped me in a bear hug, and walked me backward. She stopped in the middle of the room, holding on. I let my forehead drop on her shoulder. She rubbed my back. "I'm sorry."

Everything had gone from fast to slow and back to fast again. There should be some kind of gap between living and dying, give a person time to get ready. I squatted against the wall and held my head. The reality of being alone the rest of my life overpowered me. I looked at the ceiling and whispered, "I need you to come back, Grandma. I don't want to be here by myself." But there was only silence, the bitter quiet of feeling alone, something I'd tasted before.

A couple of aides came in with a rolling bed and asked me to wait outside. As they passed, I pulled the sheet back and kissed her cheek. Other patients woken by the clamor stood at their doors along the hall, fascinated by what they were afraid to watch, but unable not to.

I walked back into the room and stood at the window, staring at the blackness. I pressed my forehead against the wall and hit the concrete until my knuckles bled, needing to hurt somebody real bad.

The blond nurse came through the door. "Are you all right? Anyone you want me to call?" She put a hand on my shoulder.

I was angry. "Yeah, God, and tell Him to send my grandma back."

She stepped backward. "If you need me, come to the nurses' station."

I watched as the red rim of the sun began to show over a line of clouds on the eastern horizon. The only thing left was the silence.

Mr. and Mrs. Wilson came through the door about nine o'clock. They stopped when they saw the empty bed. I just stared at them. Mrs. Wilson put a hand to her mouth. She came and laid her arm around me and started crying. "Oh, Junebug."

"I don't know what to tell the people in charge to do."

She pointed at the door. "Clyde, go find out." She looked up at me. "You're going to be fine, we'll be right here with you."

I bit my tongue; I was never going to be "fine" again.

Mr. Wilson was back in a few minutes. "They're going to send her to Apex Funeral Home."

Mrs. Wilson held on to me. "Come on, Junebug, let's go home."

Walking out of that room felt like giving up, the weight of sadness so heavy I could barely move. I had no idea how to deal with this thing that seemed to want to beat the life out of me. I had nothing else left to give.

While we rode, I stared out the window, picturing the emptiness of Grandma's blue eyes, seeing the love she passed to me before the light in them went out. One minute a person was alive and the next they were dead. In my head, I spoke to my granddaddy, "*I guess I finally understand.*"

Mrs. Wilson said I was staying that night with them and she wouldn't hear any argument. We dropped her at their house, and continued over to the parsonage. The preacher's wife answered the door and Mr. Wilson told her why we were there.

She invited us in to sit in the parlor. He hurried into the room. "This is awful news about Mrs. Hurley. What happened?" He paid attention and let me talk as long as I wanted. When I was finished, he said, "Your grandma has been one of our most loyal members for a long time, and we're going to miss her very much. When are you thinking about having the service?"

Mr. Wilson suggested Saturday. The preacher said a prayer, asking the Lord to be with me in this time of grief. I didn't close my eyes. I'd had all of God's shit I could take and didn't need His sympathy. If he said it was *"God's Will,"* I might choke him.

By the time we got back to Mr. Wilson's house, Mrs. Wilson was busy cooking supper. I went around to the porch swing and pushed back and forth, resting my head against the top. I hoped Grandma was at peace. The sense of Granddaddy in the room was something I'd have to think about.

Fancy came around the side of the house, walking slow, like she was hesitant to come near me. The setting sun was to her back, and the light glowed over her face. "Mrs. Wilson told me about your granny. I'm so sorry I don't know what to do." She came up the steps, and took a chair near the swing, reaching out to offer her hand. "Momma and Daddy said to tell you they was real sorry, and if there's anything they can do, just ask. Wish I had went and got my momma when I seen how sick she was."

"Tell both of them I'm grateful. Grandma told me I knew most things a man needs in order to look after himself. Right now, though, I don't feel like I know shit. I'll probably need to call on them some."

Fancy leaned forward, eyes wide. "Miz Hurley knowed she was dying?"

"She told me some stuff, trying to get me ready in case she did. At the end she started seeing people, talking to them, reaching out like they were in the room."

Fancy's hand went to her mouth. "Was you scared?"

"Scared the hell out of me."

She shook her head. "Old folks say it happens."

"I know I never want to see it again."

"Did any of the angels speak? I've heard tell of folks hearing them."

"No." We sat quiet and held hands until Mr. Wilson yelled around the house for supper.

"Fancy, can I have a hug?" We put our arms around each other and stood that way for a minute.

Her head came to my ear. "You're going to get through this, Junebug. I'll see to it."

CHAPTER 16

I dabbled with the food as long as I could. "That was a really good supper, Mrs. Wilson. I'm going to walk to the house and look after the animals." Mrs. Wilson was a good person, and I appreciated the way she helped with Grandma. Unlike Mr. Wilson, I never felt she had anything but true kindness in her heart.

She touched my hand. "You come on back before dark so we don't worry."

I walked across the clover field and cut through the woods. Seemed every tree branch and bush reached out a hand, like long-dead family spirits offering sympathy. I was flooded with memories, talking with Granddaddy under the woodshed, sitting at the supper table listening to the grown-ups talk and feeling safe in my world. They made the sense of loneliness harder. I stopped to sit on the plank bench at the tobacco barn where Grandma and I had talked about what happened after we died. Her words came back: *Everybody wants a happy ending.* I wondered if she thought her ending was happy.

The house had a lifeless silence, like it was holding its breath waiting for Grandma to come back. The fire in the stove had gone out, and the air was chilly. I sat on Grandma's bed and lifted her pillow to my face, letting my mind go blank. I could smell her. Against one wall in the room was a black-stained wardrobe with tall doors and a large mirror on the front. It had belonged to her daddy, and she used it for keeping Sunday dresses. On another wall was an old-fashioned picture of Granddaddy's folks, Grandpa John and his wife, whom everybody called Miss Minnie. The oval glass had a crack, and the image seemed to get darker every year. I pulled the bedsheets together and smoothed the quilt, then clicked on the bedside lamp.

I stopped at the barn, scratched Sally Mule's ears, and leaned my head against her long nose. "Grandma won't be coming back, girl. We're going to have to try to get through this together." She nibbled at my ear.

On the way back to the Wilsons, I walked backward as far as the curve in the road so I could watch the light in Grandma's window. I imagined her propped on her pillows, reading a book she'd borrowed from the bookmobile. When the light disappeared, the full weight of how alone I was slammed down.

It seemed I'd been alone most of my life, Momma and Daddy dying, then Granddaddy, now Grandma, even Grady, and all I had left was a stupid shoe box. I stopped and squatted down, trying to let the grief ease off a bit. My heart had been broke so much I wanted to seal it in its own casket, bury it deep enough nobody else could dig it up, and put a marker on its grave that said, "Don't touch unless you're tired of living."

Folks would probably say, "But they left you the farm." Well, what the hell am I going to do with it? I'm frigging fifteen years old, for God's sake. Who will I have to talk to about stuff? Who will make sure I don't do something stupid and burn the place down? If I mess up the tobacco crop and don't make any money, what will I do about paying the bills? Maybe I should just sell the place and go live in an orphanage until I am grown. I got up, brushed myself off, and headed to the Wilsons.

Mrs. Wilson had made up the bed in a spare room. It was clean and smelled fresh, but I couldn't sleep. In the morning, she cooked a large breakfast, but her effort to be cheerful made me feel worse. She had been family to Grandma, and I regretted not being able to show her more kindness. "I'm going to head back and straighten up in case folks stop by. I'm grateful for all you've done."

At home, I decided to have a look for the money. Rusty hinges on the pack house cellar door squeaked loud. The windowless cellar was clammy and had the strong smell of dirt that hadn't seen the sun in a lot of years. I had to move flowerpots and sacks of potatoes and onions to get to the barrel. A short shovel sat along the wall. After a few scoops in the loose sand, lids of gallon mason jars showed. All were packed with tens, twenties, fives, and silver dollars. I sat in the grass outside and counted. The total was over five thousand. It must have taken a lot of years, going far back from Granddaddy and Grandma, to save so much money. I put five twenties, a ten, and a five in my pocket and reburied everything else.

For the next two hours I used the old straw broom and a dust rag to clean the house. In Grandma's black wardrobe, I found the blue dress I'd given her for Christmas. It should make a suitable burying outfit. I held it to my face and thought about her smile on Christmas morning. I couldn't decide whether to take undergarments, but figured Grandma would never be caught dead without underwear. I caught myself on the "dead" part, but figured she would get a laugh from it. I put everything in the Christmas box she'd saved.

Mr. Wilson came by early afternoon, and we rode to the funeral home. When he rounded the curve leading into the city limits of Apex, I remembered the redbrick building on the corner. The sickly sweet odor inside smelled like flowers had soaked into the furniture and carpet. Church hymns played softly in the background. The sense of death in this place made the hair on the back of my neck stand up.

Mr. Ashley was a neat-dressed, formal, aloof kind of man. I guessed dealing with dead folks every day didn't leave much for emotions. He invited Mr. Wilson and me into his office. It had expensive-looking brown leather chairs, deep gray carpet, and pictures of Jesus. The burying business must be pretty good. He told me how sorry he was for my loss and began to ask questions about taking care of Grandma, surprising me when he said she'd already paid for her casket.

I handed him the box. "Here are clothes for her to be buried in." He thanked me and asked about the viewing. Mr. Wilson told him the church service was set for Saturday and reckoned we would have the wake Friday night. Mr. Ashley made a note in his book before he went over the cost. Since Grandma had already taken care of the biggest part, renting their viewing room, embalming, having somebody come in and do her hair and makeup, and getting Grandma to the church on Saturday would run three hundred and fifty dollars. When everything was decided and agreed to, he asked if we would like to visit Grandma.

I struggled with the thought of having to share the moment with Mr. Wilson. "I've already said good-bye."

When we got to the truck, Mr. Wilson looked over. "You holding up all right?"

"As well as can be, I reckon." I couldn't stop my hands from shaking.

"You have enough money to take care of Miss Rosa Belle?"

"Yes."

He looked surprised. "Well, if you need help, just ask."

I reached in my pocket. "That reminds me, here's the five dollars you lent me at the hospital."

"Wasn't lending, was giving."

"I'd feel a lot better if you'd take it, might be another time I'll need to borrow."

He stuck the five-dollar bill in his pocket. "Today is Wednesday, and now that word is out, you're going to get a lot of neighbors dropping by the house. Be nice to them because they just want you to know how much they thought of Miss Rosa Belle."

How did he think I would treat folks? We were almost out of the city when I remembered. "I need clothes to wear to the funeral. You mind stopping to let me buy something?"

"Sure. The store is just down the street a ways. I'd lend you a suit, but don't reckon it would fit." He laughed at his stupid joke.

It was just a short distance to Sharp's Clothing. Suits and jackets hung on racks along the walls, and folded shirts, ties, and belts lay on tables down the center of the room. It was darker inside than Miss Adam's Dress Shoppe, more reserved, like church. Mr. Wilson led me over to where a bunch of suits hung along the wall. "Should be able to find one here." He started checking the size tags.

A salesman came over. "Can I help you?"

"The boy is looking for a suit for a funeral."

"Let's see what size he needs." He pulled out a cloth measuring tape and stretched it across my shoulders, then down my arms. When finished, he stood me in front of a section. "Anything in this rack should fit you. Were you thinking of a black suit?"

Mr. Wilson edged between us and started flipping through, looking at price tags. "No use paying a whole lot since you won't wear it much."

Red came up my cheeks. "Don't mean any harm, Mr. Wilson, but let me look for myself." He backed away and went to stand in the front of the store, pissed off. The salesman had a grin on his face.

I did pick out a black one and tried it on. "Mr. Wilson, you think the pant cuffs are too short? I asked.

He hardly looked. "Folks won't be looking at the bottom of your pants."

At home, I hung up the suit and a white cotton shirt in the closet. I decided to make soup for supper the way Fancy had, pulling vegetables out of the pantry and wild onions from the yard. It tasted like shit so I threw it out.

When dark fell, I went to sit on the porch. It was a pitch-black moonless night. I went out the screened door and down to the field behind the feed barn. The trees were heavy green with new leaves that looked black in the dark, full of water sucked from roots a hundred years deep. The moist smell of old ground was strong. At first the woods were silent, but as soon as I got still, night things started to rustle in the brush. I sat against a tree. "I'm missing you awful bad, Grandma. If you want to come visit, I'm not afraid."

I imagined myself becoming invisible, closing my eyes, and pretending to watch the world from a secret place. I liked it there. The night sounds soothed my mind. I fell asleep against the oak.

Mr. Wilson had been right. By eleven o'clock the next day, people started coming to the house, bringing food, and quickly filling the kitchen table. Mr. Jackson brought a big cooler full of ice and cups for the gallons of sweet tea. Mrs. Seagrove took over and served everybody a plate. I was overwhelmed by how they pitched in, not letting me do anything. The story of what happened to Grandma got retold and retold. Mrs. Wilson stayed close to me, making sure I spoke to each person, introducing me to those I didn't know.

The ladies fawned over me right smart, and the men wanted to shake my hand. The house filled and people spilled out onto the porch. One elderly lady, Mrs. Beula Sands, said she taught my daddy when he was in grade school. "He was a good boy, but hardheaded as a goat." It felt okay to laugh with her.

At sundown the last folks had long gone home when somebody pushed open the porch door. It was Fancy, a wrapped bowl in her hands. "My momma fixed this sweet potato casserole for you."

I took the still-warm dish. "She didn't have to, you can tell we got plenty. Get something."

Fancy lifted different aluminum-foiled plates. "I believe I will have a piece of this chicken. Want me to fix you something?"

"I'll sit with you and eat a piece or two myself." I got cold buttermilk out of the refrigerator and poured us each a glass.

We talked while we ate. "Why do you think your grandma was seeing the angels at the end, Junebug?"

"I don't know. Maybe those already gone come back to help a soul cross over."

She poked the air with a chicken leg. "What if all them you knew had been mean and would surely be living in hell?"

I chewed on a thigh. "What if there ain't any hell, Fancy, or no heaven either; what if our spirit simply floats around out of sight?" I watched her face.

Fancy's eyes narrowed. "Junebug Hurley, don't you go to being blasphemous. God's promises are true. Just because we don't always understand His reasons don't give us a right to question them."

We discussed the pros and cons while we finished off a bowl of potato salad. When it got toward eight, she got up to go. "Will you be okay by yourself?"

"It's sure different with nobody in the house."

"Don't worry if your grandma comes, she won't mean you harm. She might just want to make sure you're not suffering."

I hadn't thought about it like that before. "In a way, I hope she does come."

Fancy cut a sideways look. "You want me to stay with you?"

"Well, sure. I been wanting an ass-kicking from your daddy for a while." Although it might be worth it to sleep next to her, have the comfort of another soul.

"Don't be a smart-ass. Rest some if you can. The wake tomorrow night?"

"Yeah. Something else I ain't anxious to do."

"We'd come, but they don't let coloreds in the funeral home. Daddy promised we could go to the services Saturday, though. You know I'll be thinking about you."

I watched the bouncing light as far as the curve. In the dark of my bedroom, eyes wide open, I replayed everything from the night Grandma got sick, and tried to think of what I could have done different.

CHAPTER 17

Birds made love calls to one another and squirrels stretched in the spring sun. The day was warm and pleasant, a good day to be alive, exactly the kind of day Grandma would have said, "God sure has given us a blessing this morning." The last place I wanted to go was to see her in a death box.

I stopped inside the door of the viewing room. Grandma was laid out in her casket. She looked natural in the blue dress, like she ought to be able to get up and walk. I wanted this to be some bad dream, but it wasn't. The reality that I'd never see her smile or feel her hugs or walk into the kitchen to find her busy at the stove again, hit me hard.

Mrs. Wilson took me by the arm and we walked closer to the coffin. "She looks mighty good, Junebug."

Up close her skin looked waxy, nothing natural about her, like one of the fake women in Miss Adam's Dress Shoppe. "Wish they'd fixed her hair in a bun."

Folks began arriving at the funeral home around six, and I took my position beside the casket. Mrs. Wilson stood close in case I needed her. Everybody stopped to shake hands and say something nice. The room was soon full, and the noise of conversation made it feel more like a reunion than a wake. Grandma always enjoyed a good gathering of friends.

After an hour, it became harder to hold the smiles. Mr. Jackson offered to take a break with me. We went around the building and I lit a smoke. He reached in his coat pocket, pulled out his flask, and offered me a drink. The whiskey bit hard going down my throat, but the alcohol settled me. Back inside, Mrs. Wilson suggested it would be proper to mingle with the visitors. I made a point to thank every one of them again.

The wide tile-floored hall outside the viewing room was empty by eight thirty, and I was alone with Grandma. When I bent down close, the inside of the casket had an odd, unpleasant perfume smell. I nervously touched her hair and straightened the collar of her blue dress. I whispered, "You'll always be in my heart, Grandma, even if my mind gets to the place I can't see you. I hope that was Granddaddy in the room and you're with him now. When it's my time, I hope you'll come." I turned to leave, then stopped and went back. I reached into the casket, took Grandma's gold-rimmed glasses off and put them in my pocket.

That night I felt like an old shirt somebody forgot, left behind flapping on a clothesline at a deserted house. I found myself at the edge of the field again. I disappeared into the darkness, looking for something, but didn't know what.

On Saturday, I stood in the yard and gazed at a bright blue sky dotted with cotton balls, and thought about a particular Sunday when I was a kid. The preacher had talked loud and long on how Jesus would soon return. All the way home I watched out the truck window, hoping to spot Him riding down on a cloud.

When Mr. and Mrs. Wilson and I got to the church, the single bell in the steeple was ringing. At the door, Mrs. Wilson put her arm around my shoulder. "You ready?"

I tugged on the suit coat. "No, but reckon I'm willing."

There wasn't an empty pew inside; the casket was open in

front of the pulpit and a few people stood over it and talked quietly to each other. I wondered what would happen if Grandma's hand suddenly jerked up. Fancy said she'd heard of such things. The deacons closed the lid and placed the flower cover over it. Like every funeral I'd been to, the choir led off with "Amazing Grace" to get as many folks crying as possible. The preacher quoted a lot from the Good Book, said he'd talked to Grandma often about her favorite passages. I thought about the long Sunday afternoons she spent reading her Bible in front of the living room window.

Under the tent-covered gravesite, I chewed on the inside of my lip until blood ran. I hated the idea of being left to rot underground like a bushel of potatoes. I refused to shed tears in public. I had no more family and nobody to share them with.

When it was over, folks stopped to speak as they headed to their cars and trucks. I saw Roy, Clemmy, and Fancy standing at the back of the crowd and went to them. I hugged Clemmy and Fancy. "Grandma would surely appreciate y'all coming."

"Your grandma was a fine person," Clemmy said, "and we thought a lot of her."

"Sure is going to be hard." I looked at Roy. He reached out his hand, and when we shook I could feel the kindness and sympathy. "Anything you need, you ask."

A strong breeze blew across the graveyard, unleashing a flurry of whirligigs from maple trees that surrounded the cemetery. It looked like a brown snowstorm. " 'Bye, Grandma," I whispered.

When Mr. Wilson pulled up in the front yard, I said, "I'm really grateful for all the help."

Mrs. Wilson smiled. "You're very welcome, Junebug. We're going to be right here if you need anything."

That night, I got out a piece of paper and started making a list. There was so much to remember, like being sure I knew how to pay the bill for the electric, and a dozen other things I'd never had to do. How would I ever get along by myself?

CHAPTER 18

Mr. Wilson stopped by the house after church the next day. We sat on the porch, discussing the farm. He wanted to make sure I knew what to do and when. "You want to ride to Pittsboro tomorrow and get yourself a couple of pigs?"

At the auction, I bid on two Berkshires Mr. Wilson recommended, and got them for twelve dollars each. He bought four for himself, and we loaded the baby sows into the pen on the back of his truck. When we got home, I opened the gate to the wire box, grabbed one by the hind legs, and pulled her out. She hollered like I was killing her until she dropped over the fence. I hefted the other one, and they got busy investigating their new home.

Mr. Wilson and me leaned on the gate. "You patch the hog lot so they won't get out?"

"Took care of it a month ago." His bossing tone didn't set well with me. "Hope I'll be able to drive myself places one of these days soon."

"I'll take you to get a license in June."

"I'd appreciate that."

* * *

A little after dark, Fancy stepped inside the porch, wearing a brown homemade dress and a man's hat curled up in the front.

"What 'cha doing?" She poked her head around mine, nudging her chin up and down on my collarbone.

"Figured I'd eat what's left of this chicken and such. Don't suppose you could make some biscuits."

Fancy turned her back and sashayed around the kitchen. "Could if I wanted to."

I pleaded a little. "Help me out here."

She put one hand on her hip. "What are you going to do for me?"

I grabbed her waist, picking her up off the floor. "I'm going to beat your butt if you don't."

She squealed and pulled at my arms. I let her down and slapped her on the backside. She punched me on the arm. I went for her again. She tripped into the cupboard, and we ended up nose to nose. She quit laughing. Her arms went around my neck; mine went around her back, and our mouths slammed together, tongues searching and bodies pressing. I knew she could feel me against her.

We broke and backed away. "What was that, Junebug?"

"I don't know."

Her black eyes rolled up and down. "I reckon it was your jisim talking. I told you it was going to back up. Does your balls hurt?" She looked down at the front of my overalls.

My face turned red. "No, and I'd appreciate it if you quit worrying about them."

We went at it again. Sweat popped out on my forehead. I pulled my head away. "What do we do now?"

She moved me backward with one finger, grinning. "Don't know about you, but I'm fixing to make some biscuits."

After cleaning up the dishes, we went to sit on the living room couch. I didn't know what to say, so I lay my head back and silently counted pine knots in the wood ceiling. Fancy picked at a loose string on one of the sofa cushions. We sat and listened to the clock tick.

She broke the silence. "Okay, Junebug, what about these feelings we're having for each other?" Her face was natural except for a bit of faint red lipstick.

It was embarrassing to look her in the eye. "I know it ain't right, but I can't seem to help myself around you."

She pulled my chin up. "We're both getting old enough to have urges, Junebug. I ain't against them. I've started to develop feelings for you that are more than just friends, like I can't wait to see you from one time to the next. Do you think the same way about me?"

I swallowed hard. "Yes. So what do we do?"

She sat back against the couch cushion. "We can consider it some more. One of these days, when we're ready, the Lord will send us the answer."

I laid my head against the top. "Hope He don't wait long."

We kissed some more. "Mrs. Wilson said you were going to show me how to churn butter."

Fancy pushed the tip of her nose against mine, our eyelashes almost touching. "Bet she didn't have in mind churning like this."

I let my hands drift lower on her back. She talked softly into my mouth. "Soon as you've saved up enough cream, it won't take long to make." Her teeth bit down on my lip. "I'll come over Monday after school if you want me to teach you."

"You could stay for supper."

She whispered in my ear. "What are we having?"

My insides were about to bust. "What you best be doing is getting home, wouldn't want any bogeymen chasing you."

"How about you drive me?" Fancy folded her arms around my neck.

"You know I ain't got a license."

"Then you need the practice." We rode, Fancy snuggled against me, my arm around her.

I shut off the lights before reaching the Wilsons' driveway and stopped. The kissing and moving against each other got intense again. Finally, she pushed open the door. "You think about me tonight, Junebug." Fancy slammed the truck door and took off running.

CHAPTER 19

I paced the house and yard all day, trying to find something to keep myself busy, abandoning each thing because my mind wasn't on it. I'd cleaned the wooden churn twice, and debated about where to place it, then decided on the kitchen floor between two chairs.

Fancy showed up after school Monday afternoon. She was wearing a clingy blue cotton dress that showed the outline of her underwear. Her hair was pulled straight back and tied with a rubber band. "Hey"—she smiled—"ready to do some churning?" She wiped the palms of her hands down her dress three or four times.

"I reckon."

Fancy skimmed off the cream in the milk bucket, arranged the dasher stick in the churn, and fit the stick through the hole in the lid. She sat down and started moving the plunger up and down slowly as the liquid began to turn solid. We took turns. I watched Fancy's breasts while she worked the plunger. She cut her eyes at me a couple of times, making me blush. After one last push, she stopped. "I think it's done."

I stood close behind and pretended to watch while she put the fresh butter in a cloth and slowly twisted the bundle, squeezing out the liquid, relaxed her grip, and squeezed it twice more, each time gently rounding the ball.

Fancy glanced over her shoulder, and I could see her cheeks were flushed. She opened the pouch, pinched off a small piece, and turned around. Holding my eyes with hers, she reached out with her finger and slowly rubbed the butter over my mouth. Blood began to pound in my ears. Fancy lightly touched her lips to mine, tasting the salty cream with her tongue. We'd been playing with this fire and now it was burning us up. I pushed her against the counter.

"Wait." Fancy put a hand against my chest, her eyes asking a question. "You really want to do this?"

"Do you?" I knew my answer but didn't say it.

Her black eyes glistened like shiny coal. She stared at me, then gripped my arm. "Come on." There was determination on her face.

In the bedroom, Fancy pulled back the covers and unbuttoned her dress, dropping it to the floor. She waited. "I ain't going to stand here naked by myself."

I was spellbound by how light through the window made a contrast of shadows on her body. She was beautiful. I swallowed like a thirsty camel at a water hole. I'd fantasized about this moment so many times, and now I prayed not to be awful at it.

We lay down on the bed facing each other. I kissed her as softly as I could, trying to not be anxious, to go slow until I could figure out how this was going to work. When I ran my tongue over the tip of her breast, Fancy gripped the hair on the back of my head and twisted. I threw the going-slow stuff out like an old pair of underwear, pretty sure I wouldn't make it through a long warm-up. I moved my hand down her body, over her belly, and below. Her hips flexed when my finger found the right spot. "Ahh." She sucked in a sharp breath, and arched her back.

Whatever was going to happen needed to happen now. I moved between her legs and Fancy's hips rose to meet me. After some fumbling we connected. I was enveloped in warmth and sensation unlike any I'd ever been able to imagine. We lay still for a minute, then began an awkward search for a rhythm. Slow went to urgency, then thrashing and bucking in a flurry of arms and legs, mouths glued together. I felt my stomach tighten. The fierceness of the release left me gasping for breath. "God, Fancy." It was all I could say. I couldn't move. Those trips behind the barn were never anything like this.

Fancy's arms were locked around my neck; her legs stretched over mine and her heels forced their way into my calves. "Junebug"—her voice choked—"for the rest of our lives this belongs just to us." We clung to each other in a silence that wasn't awkward or embarrassing, unwilling to turn loose. Eventually we shifted to lie face-to-face, kissing easily and lovingly.

"I see now why folks are always talking about sex," I said.

Fancy giggled, ran her fingernail down my stomach and beneath my belly button.

"Want to try it again?"

"Don't think I'm able to right now." I nuzzled at her neck, pulled her leg over my hip, and eased into her again. "But we can try."

Fancy arched her back. We found a slower, deeper place than before. The end took longer to reach, but it was just as desperate, trying to drain every drop of pleasure possible.

When it was over, our bodies snuggled so tight we could have been glued together. "Thank you, Junebug." Fancy's voice was soft.

"For what?"

"For being gentle and kind, the way I thought you'd be, not making me feel like some kind of whore."

I put my finger to her lips, "You hush. Don't ever think that way about yourself." I traced around her eyes, down her nose, and circled her mouth. "Fancy, you're so beautiful. I don't know why you even want to be with a dumb hick like me."

She looked deep in my eyes and stroked the side of my face. "You know, Junebug . . . I wonder the same thing." She rolled on top of me, wrestling and tickling and laughing.

We teased and explored and played until it was time for her to get home. Both of us knew we had stepped over a line that had no U-turn. Maybe it was fear of the secret we'd have to keep, or understanding of the commitment pledged; all I knew for sure was our world had now become a completely different place.

CHAPTER 20

I walked up to Mr. Wilson's the next morning, and found him with the hood up on his truck. "Ain't having troubles with the engine, are you?" The freshness of mid-April sunshine made for near-perfect weather.

He stuck the dipstick back in. "Just piddling. What you up to?"

"Wanted to ask about letting Roy, Clemmy, and Fancy help me plant tobacco this week." I leaned my elbows against the fender.

He pushed down on the hood to be sure it was locked. "Reckon I can spare them Saturday. Roy's in the low ground if you want to ask him."

The field was behind a stand of woods below Mr. Wilson's house. Roy was busy plowing. I waited for him to finish the end of the row. "How you doing, Roy?" After last night, I was nervous being this close to him.

"I'm all right, Junebug, you?" He squatted and picked up a fistful of the dark sandy soil, letting it sift between his fingers.

"Trying to keep up with things. Come by to ask about you,

Clemmy, and Fancy helping me plant my tobacco field on Saturday."

Roy pulled off his straw hat and wiped his head on his sleeve. "Reckon we can do that. How come you need three of us?"

"Fancy suggested maybe her, me, and you could work the field while Clemmy fixed dinner. She came to the house yesterday to help me make some butter so I could stop wasting so much milk."

He surveyed the bright sky. "Then I guess we'll be there Saturday morning." Roy turned back to me. "You making out all right staying by yourself?"

I sat on the ground beside him. "Gets to be lonesome, but I know things take time. Wish I'd learned to cook better." I gave him a grin. *Lonesome as long as I ain't doing it with your daughter* lay on my tongue, which I figured was probably forked by now.

He smiled back. "Clemmy or Fancy can help you with that. Fancy is about as good a cook as her momma."

"When she came over yesterday she fixed some biscuits and dang if they wouldn't compare to Grandma's." *And then we got in the bed and had sex.*

He grinned with a daddy's pride. "That gal sure can make a biscuit."

Roy, Fancy, and Clemmy showed up early on Saturday morning. Low clouds had come across early, but had kept going toward the south. I finished hooking Sally Mule to the wagon. A big barrel filled with water and fertilizer was already loaded, and the plants were stacked in the back. Roy took the reins and headed to the field while I showed Clemmy around the kitchen. Fancy pointed out the canned vegetables in the pantry and the butter and milk in the refrigerator. "I helped Junebug make the butter yesterday." Clemmy eyed the two of us. From her look, I considered maybe it wasn't Roy I needed to worry about.

In the field, I hand-pegged the holes, Fancy dropped in the plants, and Roy came last with the water. Once we got a rhythm, we made good time, not a lot of talking. Our shadows had started to stretch when Roy looked at the sun. "I'm guessing it's about dinnertime."

I unhooked Sally Mule from the wagon, and she trotted straight to the barn and waited for me. I dropped a couple of ears of corn and a handful of hay in her stable box, staying a while to scratch her nose. While she munched, Sally watched me with her soft brown eyes, contented to have a rest and a meal. I wondered, if she could talk, what would she say?

"Are you lonesome, girl? I bet you miss Granddaddy and Grandma as much as me, don't you? If you won't so dang big, I'd let you come stay in the house." I laughed out loud, imagining Sally in the bed and eating at the table. "One question I've always wanted to ask you, Sally. What do you have to live for? The only future you got is working pulling a plow or a wagon until you drop dead. That don't seem fair to me." It was sad to think about.

She moved her head up and down, shook her ears, and tried to bite my fingers that were in the stable box beside the last ear of corn. "Sore subject, huh?" I scraped my fingernails up her neck and patted her with gentle slaps. Sally went back to eating and I headed to the house, my own stomach growling for lack of food. I could smell collard greens cooking all the way out to the yard.

I stepped inside the screen porch and started to wash my hands at the water bowl. "Smells mighty good, Clemmy. Where's Fancy and Roy?"

She spooned food into bowls. "They're outside setting up the table for us to eat."

"Clemmy, don't you believe it's silly for me to sit in here by myself and y'all out there? We ain't strangers."

She stopped, a hint of a smile on her face. "What in the world would folks think?"

"We're the only folks here, and the only ones that matter."

She gave me a look that was like a patient momma with a foolish child. "You want to come outside with us?"

"Wherever you say."

Clemmy studied me. "Then why don't you help me tote this food and we can enjoy the sunshine." She was a woman who walked with her head up and looked a person in the eye when she talked. I figured Fancy got her gumption from her momma.

"I'll bring the buttermilk Fancy helped me make the other day." I felt I'd won a little battle.

Roy gave Clemmy a stare when he saw us coming, and Fancy's eyes got wide. "Move your plate over, Roy. Junebug, sit beside Fancy." We got busy on the food, the only sounds were spoons and forks scraping.

Roy smacked his lips. "Clemmy, you make this buttermilk?"

"Junebug said Fancy made it."

"It don't taste right." Roy turned his head and spit out what was in his mouth. "Fancy, did you put any fat-curd in the buttermilk?"

She stopped the fork of food on the way to her mouth. "I didn't put anything in it."

"You didn't put fat-curd in to take out the poison?"

"What are you talking about?" Fancy set the fork on her plate.

Roy grabbed his throat, hacking and coughing. "Oh Lord, she's killed us."

Fancy grabbed my glass and threw it on the ground, then reached for Clemmy's. "Momma, you never told me nothing about that!"

Roy poured another glassful from the jar and drank it down, leaving a big ring of white over his upper lip.

Fancy stood staring, her cheeks turning red. She grabbed a piece of corn bread and threw it at him. "Kiss my butt." The laughter felt like family.

By midafternoon the work was done. I took fifteen dollars from my pocket and handed the money to Roy.

"You know you ain't got to pay us, Junebug. I said when your grandma died I'd help you with anything I could, so I figure we're just being neighborly."

"To me a day's work gets a day's pay, so I'm asking you to take it." White neighbors helped each other because it was expected they would get help in return. No colored folks had their own farms so it was only right to pay with money.

"I'd like to ask you something, Roy. It's a lot harder than I thought taking care of all the things Grandma did, like keeping the house up, washing clothes, and cooking. Maybe you would consider, on the days you don't need her, if Fancy might come and help. She could earn some extra money and it would be a big relief to me."

Fancy got busy with some bug in the grass. Roy looked at Clemmy. "Reckon I'll allow she can come every couple of days after school. But you remember the talk we had, Junebug?"

"Yep."

"Ain't nothing changed."

"Won't no harm come to her as long as I'm around." I wanted Fancy, and was determined to do whatever it took to keep her.

CHAPTER 21

Fancy didn't show up and I worried she might have gotten in some trouble. It was way after dark the following night when I heard the porch door open. "Hey. Sorry, I couldn't come yesterday." She looked mighty good in her shorts and old T-shirt.

"You shouldn't be here at all."

She stopped and parked her hands on her hips. "You tired of me this quick?"

"Shut up. I mean, what if your momma and daddy wake up one night and you ain't home?"

"Unless he's sipping, Daddy is in bed right after the sun's down good, and sleeps like a log. Besides, Momma and me sat down last night and had a long talk about how boys and girls our age have a natural curiosity. She doesn't want me messing around and end up with a baby in my stomach."

That's something that never occurred to me. I'd been too busy walking around like a bantam rooster who'd serviced his hen. "A baby? Fancy, don't talk about shit like that!" I slumped back on the couch. "Well, that's the end. No more. No way we can risk such a thing."

"You're right. I guess we'll have to go back to just being friends." She pulled a loose string on her sleeve and stared out the window. Silence lay between us like two pouting kids.

"Momma did tell me how to keep from it if the time was to come, though."

"How's that?"

Fancy made circles with her finger on the couch cushion, like she was deciding whether or not to let me in on the secret. Then she reached into her back pocket and pulled out a little foil package. "Just need to make sure to use one of these."

I recognized it. Back when I went to school, some of the boys toted one around in their wallet, always bragging. What could Clemmy be thinking to give Fancy such a thing?

She held it by the corner and flapped it like a flag. "Momma says you can buy them at the drugstore, or sometimes they have machines in gas station bathrooms."

I waved my hand to dismiss that idea. "You can bet your ass I ain't going to ask that woman at the drugstore." In spite of myself, I started to consider how far the nearest gas station was that had a bathroom, and how long it would take me to walk.

"Momma said it was for in case I ever lost my head."

"Well, I reckon it's too late for that. How does a person know it fits?"

Fancy looked irked. "What'd you want me to do, tell Momma how big your business was and ask her if it was the right size?"

We stared at each other for a minute before we fell over laughing. I had to wipe the tears from my eyes. "Well, we won't be doing it again." I held it between two fingertips, like something might rub off. "Here, you keep it."

Fancy pulled me up from the couch. "You got any more of them store-bought cigarettes?" We sat on the porch and smoked. The night air was soft and still. "Daddy says he don't think you're going to make it trying to farm by yourself, said it'd be too much work for a man, much less a boy."

I got up from the chair, kicking it backward with my foot. I figured a lot of the folks in the community probably thought the same way. "I ain't scared."

"You got some guts, Junebug. I wouldn't want to think about living by myself."

I snorted. "That's because you're a girl. My boy time is over."

"Don't bite my head off. I didn't say it."

"Fancy, when a person has his whole life pretty much come apart, he don't need somebody questioning if he's man enough to handle himself."

She got up and wrapped her arms around me from behind. "I wasn't trying to hurt your feelings. You're man enough for me."

I opened the screen door and flicked the butt into the yard. "You getting cool?"

We settled on the couch. "Want to thumb-wrestle?" Fancy asked.

"What's that?"

"Give me your right hand." She hooked our four fingers together, put our thumbs on top, and when she yelled, "go," one would try to hold the other's thumb down. Fancy caught me every time.

I finally managed to win one, then made the mistake of looking her in the eyes. I moved my face close. Her tongue flicked out. We teased each other, playing and kissing. I moved my fingers to the tips of her breasts. She closed her eyes as I stroked. "You got that thing in your pocket?"

Fancy nipped at my earlobe. "You fixing to try it?"

"Either that or I'm going to bust wide open."

In the bedroom, I pulled Fancy's T-shirt over her head. We stood kissing and running our hands over each other. Electricity went between us like our fingers were stuck in a socket.

There was less confusion and more of a rush to get to the place we wanted to go. Sex was a new puzzle, not yet understanding how to take what we needed and give to the other at the same time. It was thrashing and grunting and driving of bodies against each other, desperate to make it last as long as possible.

"God almighty." I pulled Fancy across me. "Just shoot me now. Life can't get any better than this."

"Damn, Junebug, you're going to make me crazy." Fancy rolled to straddle my stomach, bending down to run her tongue over my lips. "When you going to Apex?"

"Why?" My fingers tickled up her back.

She arched her back. "Because you need to practice what you're going to say to the lady in the drugstore."

"We got to be crazy." I rubbed the back of my finger from her pelvis up to her belly button.

She sucked in a sharp breath, then reached back and ran her fingernails along the inside of my thigh. "Call it whatever you want, but when we're loving I don't care if the whole world knows."

I cupped her breasts. They were firm and swollen. "Can you use one of those things twice?"

She used her tongue to trace the ridges down my stomach, then gripped me, pulled off the condom, and threw it on the floor. Fancy eased down until I was inside her. She closed her eyes and began to rock back and forth, pulling up and settling back down. It was slow and amazing.

When it was over, Fancy collapsed on top of me. We were soaked with sweat. "I don't want to go home."

I rubbed her back. "There was some blood on my sheets last time. Were you hurt?"

"A little." She raised her head and flashed that smile. "But this time you tried to kill me."

We finally dragged ourselves out of bed and started getting dressed. I picked the condom up off the floor. "What am I supposed to do with this?"

She pulled up her shorts. "Keep it as a souvenir, because if you don't find some more, it'll be your last trip down this road." She dodged my slap at her butt.

I dropped it in an empty tin can in the kitchen trash. She leaned under my arm as I drove.

Back home, I coasted to a stop in front of the house and sat in the truck, enjoying a cool breeze through the open window, watching a full white moon give life to dancing shadows of treetops playing a game of tag across the yard. I lit a cigarette, laid my head back, and thought about Fancy. She made my life so much better. Fancy had replaced a heart full of pain with hope, helping to push away the darkness that seemed to trail me like a hellhound.

Sally stood at the fence of the mule lot watching me. I opened the truck door and walked across the yard; she blew air through her lips and blubbered a greeting. I reached through the rails to rub her nose and scratch her neck. "Can't sleep either, huh?" Sally shook her head up and down and took a playful nip at my fingers. I popped her on the forehead. "Mighty late to be feeling so frisky."

I opened the fence gate, grabbed her harness off the hook, slid the bit into her mouth, and held on to her mane while I jumped on her back. "I'm feeling a little frolicsome myself. Let's go for a walk."

We made an easy pace down the dirt road, going nowhere in particular, the night silence broken only by the gentle plops of her feet. "Sally-Girl, I'm in need of a woman's point of view." I pulled back on the reins and stopped. "What comes after two people have sex? Does it mean you have to get married?" A few clouds eased by the moon. "I reckon I could marry Fancy if it come down to it; be nice cuddling up in bed every night. You ever had sex, Sally? If you ain't, I'm here to tell you it's the greatest thing I've ever experienced, makes you want to holler like Tarzan." I looked at the stars, turning my head as far around as I could to appreciate the way they lay over the world like a round roof. "I know my feelings are mighty strong for Fancy. It's just I ain't quite sure where it might lead, feels like it goes against everything I'm supposed to live by, you know, her being black and all." I scratched Sally's ears. "Grandma could see it coming." My heels nudged her forward. "You think God really cares about such things, Sally?" She perked up her tail and dropped a load of stinking apples on the road. I threw my head back and laughed. "You could'a just shook your head yes or no."

By then we were half a mile from the house. I pulled on the bit and turned to head back. I was feeling crazy. I bent my head back and howled at the moon like a lovesick tomcat, just because I felt like it. I slapped Sally's haunches with the leather and she took off in a run toward the barn, me yelling and laughing at the top of my lungs, "I love Fancy Stroud, and I don't give a dang who does or don't like it, especially a fat, lazy mule. You can all kiss my ass."

If anybody had seen us out there in the dark, they would have been pretty sure I'd lost my mind. And maybe I had.

PART 2

Chapter 22

My head barely hit the pillow before Fancy showed up in my dreams. The two of us were sitting on a hill looking at the moon. In the next instant we were floating, lifting up, soaring among the stars.

A board squeaked somewhere toward the front of the house. My eyes jerked open. The house always creaked when the wind blew, or if it was heating up or cooling down, but the floor only made sounds when somebody was walking. I heard the noise again. My first thought was Fancy had come back. But she wouldn't do something that stupid. Maybe an animal had gotten in the house. I lay still, listening.

When a chair leg scraped, I reached under the bed, got a grip on my twenty-gauge pump shotgun, and clicked off the safety. I slid my feet quietly along the floor to the open door leading to the living room. I peeked out. Nothing. A thief would have to be stupid to rob the poorest house in the neighborhood.

Like a snake stalking a rat, I slipped past the couch and eased my head around the entrance to the kitchen. The man's outline was backlit from light coming through the window over the sink. He put something in his mouth. Who the hell would break into somebody's house and sit down to eat? My hands shook as I stepped into the opening, the shotgun pointed. "You move and I'll blow your head off."

He slowly lowered the food back on the plate and raised his hands. "Now, Junebug, don't let your finger slip on that cockhair trigger."

I hadn't heard that voice in a year. I lowered the barrel and flipped on the ceiling light. "Lightning?" I leaned over to keep my knees from folding. "What the hell are you doing in my house in the dark? You about got yourself killed!"

He got up and came around the table. "Junebug." He laughed. "Man, I'm glad to see you." We hugged and slapped each other on the back. "Didn't mean to scare you. I was going to wait until daylight to let you know I was around, but damn, if I weren't starving."

I pushed him to arm's length, still not believing it was Lightning. He had an ugly, welted scar running from his left ear to the corner of his lip. He smelled like sweat and dirty clothes and was a lot skinnier since I'd seen him last. "What the hell happened to your face?" It was like looking at a stranger.

He put his hand to his cheek. "Had a little trouble down in Georgia."

"Appears like more than a little to me."

Lightning's face was drawn and shallow below his cheekbones. His hair was scruffy and in bad need of cutting. "Some truth to that," he said.

"Here. Sit down and eat. Ain't much, but you're welcome to it." I took a jar of milk from the refrigerator and set it in front of him. "Let me go put on some pants."

Lightning was eating leftover biscuits and ham when I got back. He talked while he chewed. "Stopped in Apex and my cousin told me about your grandma passing. I'm real sorry. She always treated me kind."

I took a chair across the table from him. "Thanks, she was a kind person. Now, tell me why you're slipping around in the dark?" I couldn't keep my eyes off the scar. "Thought you were picking cotton, not fighting with tigers."

His eyes looked lifeless, the color of used coffee grounds. He looked a lot older than he should. "White man tried to kill me."

I tore off a piece of ham and chewed on it. "How come?"

"When we hit lower Georgia last July, the boss man on the migrant bus dropped three of us off with this old white farmer." He drained the glass of milk. "He put us way deep in the woods to work until the fall. One of the old men with me had stayed the year before and knew what to do. Wasn't hard, just keep these plants watered and looked after." Lightning leaned the kitchen chair back to rest on two legs. "It was all right, nobody to mess with us."

I noticed several cuts on his forearms that were scabbed over. "Were you growing tobacco?" The first weak light of day was beginning to show through the window.

"Reminded me of it some." Lightning used his hands when he talked, like he was trying to twist what he said to get it right. "The stalks got as tall, but the leaves were small and bushy, nothing like tobacco. I heard the old farmer telling the migrant man how during the big war, the government gave out hemp seeds for free and paid farmers to grow the crop; said they used the plants to make ropes for the army and navy. He said when the war ended, the government quit wanting the hemp, putting a bad hurt on farmers. Then this man from Florida came along and showed him how to grow a crop that was just as easy, and one he could sell and make a hell of a lot of money. Farmer said he'd been growing it ever since."

"What the heck was it?" I was still finding it hard to believe he was sitting at my table.

"It's a kind of smoking tobacco, but different. The old migrant man called it marjeewana, but the African with us said it was marijuana, said he'd smoked plenty of it in his time. Along about the end of September, the old man came one night and we pulled up the plants, loaded them on his truck, and hauled them back to the farm."

"Why in the dark?"

"Stuff is against the law, like moonshine. Anyway, we hauled about two hundred stalks to a tobacco barn, strung twine across the tier poles, and hung them upside down to dry."

"That's mighty curious. Did you cure it?"

"Nope, just let it dry out. The plants stayed in the barn about a month. We worked cleaning cow stables and plowing his fields in the meantime."

"What'd you do then, store it in a pack house?"

"Naw, we cut off the stems and buds and stuffed them in gallon mason jars." Lightning sat back and locked his hands behind his head, like he was trying to remember everything. "The old nigger in charge said the farmer sold the jars to them folks from Florida; said the old cracker made a killing."

"Why would people come that far to buy the stuff? How do they use it?"

"Crumble it up fine and smoke it, no different than rolling a cigarette. I smoked some. I'm telling you, Junebug, that shit will make you forget all your troubles. You'll be sitting around laughing your ass off until it wears down. And don't hurt you none, not the way drinking shine licker will. The next morning you don't even have a headache."

"Wonder why it's against the law when smoking cigarettes ain't?"

Lightning lifted his hands, palms up. "Ain't paying no taxes, same as white liquor."

"I guess that makes sense. So how'd you catch up with the rest of your crew when you were done?"

"Never did. When time come to settle up, the other two migrants with me got two hundred dollars apiece. The old man tried to say I was too young to have done the same work and he only give me a hundred. I told him I'd worked as hard as the rest and wanted my money. We got to fussing and cussing at each other, him yelling he didn't take shit from niggers. That's when he pulled out a hawk-bill and sliced me, said he'd hang me out there in them goddamn woods." Lightning's hand rubbed down his scar.

"What was I supposed to do? Blood was running down my face, he'd cut me good. Junebug, he meant to kill me right there. I got hold of the knife Daddy gave me, and went to stabbing on him. 'Fore I knew it, he was on the ground squealing and bleeding like a stuck hog. Everybody was hollering to stop. Then his wife come out the back door of the house, seen what was going on, and let fly with a shotgun, yelling she was going to kill all of us. I jerked the billfold out of his pocket, took the money, and we ran to the woods." He finished the milk and wiped his mouth with his sleeve. "I had to tie my shirt around my head to stop the bleeding. My face swelled so bad, it felt like I had two heads."

This story was better than a comic book. "How'd you get back here?"

"The other two migrants and me kept moving, and finally run up on some colored sharecroppers like Momma and Daddy. They hid us out. The woman doctored my face good and sewed it up." He stopped for a minute and swallowed hard, getting emotional thinking about what happened. "Hadn't been for her, I probably would've died. We finally got to Atlanta, split the money, and everybody went their own way. It took me a long time, hopping trains from one place to another before I hobo'd one to Raleigh. I figured once I got close, I'd walk home, and that's what I did."

I lit a cigarette and offered him one. "Why'd you come here instead of your house?"

He took it, and I held the match. "I considered if that old farmer died, the sheriff could be looking for me. I didn't want that burden on Momma and Daddy." He kept his eyes on his plate.

I suspected Lightning might know if the man was dead or not. "So, you come to put the burden on me?" If the law had already got in touch with Roy and Clemmy, Fancy had done a good job of keeping it a secret.

His eyes drooped like a puppy dog's. "Nobody will know I'm here if you don't tell them. I was hoping you'd let me stay, at least until I know for sure."

This was the person, along with Fancy, who'd been there for me when I needed a friend most. I could never forget that. Lightning had always been given to sulking and being angry if he got on his mind somebody wronged him, but now there was a different edge to him, sharper, colder. "How long you talking about?"

"Guess we should know in a month or so." He reached into his coat pocket, took out a paper sack, and set it on the table. He smiled at me. "I got a plan, Junebug."

"What?"

"These are seeds."

"What kind of seeds?"

"Seeds for growing that marijuana I been telling you about. The old migrant worker told me how to plant them, so I kept some from the field, thinking I might come home one of these days and see if I could grow it. Just happened sooner than I thought."

I looked in the bag. "You said that shit is against the law."

"Only if you get caught. If you still got that plant bed out in the woods, all we have to do is go out there where nobody will see us, or be likely to come across it, and plant them." He stretched his hands across the table. "By September, we pull them up and do the same thing that old cracker was doing. We can make a lot of money, Junebug, and nobody will be the wiser."

I considered him for a minute. It was probably another one of his stupid ideas, like the time he tried to convince me we could wait for some of the neighbors to leave home, then sneak into their house. I stayed away from him for a long time after that, figuring if he was that desperate something bad was going to happen. As far as I knew, he never did it. "Tell you what. You can stay here a while, give yourself time to find out if the law is looking for you." I pushed up from the table.

"Appreciate it, Junebug. I'll do my getting outside after dark. Won't nobody know I'm here, and don't worry, I won't do you wrong."

I hoped to hell I wasn't making a mistake. "You want anything else to go with the ham and milk?"

"I'm good, just so tired of running and hiding; scared to death some white bastard would catch me and I'd be swinging from a limb."

It occurred to me Lightning showed up at just the wrong time. What would I do when Fancy and me wanted to be together?

He kept yawning. I went to the bedroom and found an old pair of bib overalls, a clean shirt, and drawers. "What you got on stinks. Chuck 'em in the trash barrel and we'll burn them with the other stuff. A bath wouldn't hurt you none either."

"Sure is good to see you, Junebug." He shook my hand again. "There were times I thought I never would."

I got a glimpse of the old brightness in Lightning's eyes, but still couldn't shake the cold feeling. "I'll get you a quilt and a pillow."

He turned his head toward Grandma's bedroom. "I could sleep in there."

"That's my grandma's bed."

He slapped himself on the forehead. "Sorry, wasn't thinking, and I don't blame you. That quilt and pillow will do good right here on this couch."

I brought them and went to crawl in my bed. All of his story couldn't be true. But I decided I'd help him, for now.

CHAPTER 23

Lightning was still asleep on the couch when I went to do chores. He woke up when I came in the porch. "Damned if that won't the best sleep I've had in a long time." He rolled his feet to the floor. The scar looked worse in the daylight.

After sleeping on it, it seemed foolish to trust Lightning. If somebody found out he was staying with me, it might mean trouble I didn't need. "I'm going to walk up and see if Mr. Wilson will take me to Apex. You going to be all right?"

"Oh yeah. Junebug, you can't imagine how good it felt to close my eyes without worrying."

"Anybody comes to the door, don't answer. Go in the back room until they leave."

"I'll be careful. You think any more about them seeds?"

"Nope."

"That bag's holding a lot of money, Junebug. From listening to the old farmer brag, I figure you might get around five hundred dollars a plant. All we got to do is the work, and it's easier than growing tobacco."

My eyebrows shot up. "Bullshit. Ain't nothing worth that kind of money."

He pointed his finger the same way the preacher did when he wanted to convince the congregation. "I'm telling you, Junebug, this stuff is."

"Lightning, if all you're saying was true, every farmer would be growing it."

"Here's the hitch, Junebug. Even if they could figure out the how, you got to know where to sell it."

I sat on the couch, pulling on my shoes. "How the hell you know who to sell it to?" I tied the laces extra tight.

Lightning sat down in the rocking chair directly in front of me, leaning forward, elbows on his knees so he was closer to my face. "'Cause I'm colored and I promise somebody in Durham is selling it to other coloreds. All I need to do is find him."

I listened, but didn't answer. "See you after a while."

He followed me through the kitchen. "Okay if I fix myself some breakfast?"

I showed him where everything was. "There's a clean towel in the bathroom and plenty of soap. You could use a good scrubbing." On the walk through the woods, I worried some about Lightning rambling around my house, but couldn't think of anything I had that was worth much.

Mrs. Wilson answered my knock. "Morning, Junebug. What brings you out this early?"

"Morning. Wanted to ask Mr. Wilson if he might run me to Apex to talk to Lawyer Stern. I need to get straight about the farm."

"Come on in. He's finishing his breakfast. Have you eat?" She held my arm as we walked.

She would have fixed for me, but I didn't want to waste the time. "Had something earlier."

Mr. Wilson dropped me off in front of a redbrick building on Main Street in Apex. He pointed to some stairs on the side, and said he'd meet me at the truck when I was finished. At the top of the metal steps was a heavy wood door with a glass insert, lettered J. STERN, ATTORNEY AT LAW. I turned the knob and a cowbell clanked when the door pushed open. A gentleman dressed in a gray sports coat and black tie came out of the back office. He reminded me of Mr. Wilson some, short and heavy in the belly, except he was bald as a peach, wore glasses, and had intense green eyes that seemed to look through me. "Mr. Stern?"

"Yes. Who might you be?"

"Raeford Hurley, Mrs. Rosa Belle Hurley's grandson."

He warmed up at once, and came to shake my hand. "Good to meet you, Raeford. I've heard a lot about what a fine young man you are." He had a deep, not unpleasant voice, and when he smiled the wrinkles in his face were plentiful. "I'm glad you came by, been wanting to get in touch and go over some things. Sorry to have missed the funeral, but we were visiting my wife's folks in Virginia. Your grandmother was a fine person." While he talked, I knew he was taking the measure of me.

"Appreciate it. Before she died, Grandma told me to speak to you about the farm."

"Come on in and we'll do some talking."

His office had the smell of old leather, and was outfitted with a couple of fat brown cowhide chairs on one side of the desk and a big black chair on his side. The green carpet had been there awhile and wasn't as expensive-looking as the carpet at the funeral home. I guessed there wasn't as much call for lawyer work as there was for burying. Pictures of presidents and the state capitol hung behind him, and important-looking leather-bound books filled the sidewall shelves. He poked around in a head-high metal cabinet beside his desk and finally pulled out a stack of papers wrapped in a rubber band. I could see Grandma's name printed on the outside of a tan folder.

"What did your grandma tell you, Raeford?"

"Said you had the deed to the farm and to do whatever you say to make sure things got looked after."

"I got a copy of her will right here." He offered the paper. "You want to read it?"

"Just as soon you explain it to me." I sat straight in the chair so he could see I was paying attention, and hoped he wouldn't say words I didn't know.

"What it boils down to, Raeford, is the farm is yours and everything that goes with it, including the animals and machinery. But until you're eighteen, I'm what's called a trustee, which simply means I have the responsibility to be sure the taxes are paid and to look out for your well-being. You can run the farm any way you want, but you can't sell it unless I agree or until you come of age. Afterward you can do as you wish. You understand?"

I'd heard folks say how some lawyers were worse than a crook. I watched his eyes and tried to get a fix on him. "Sounds like I pay whatever money you need and you take care of things."

"That's the cut of it. Legal stuff can be confusing sometimes, so I want to be sure to answer your questions about any of this. My job is to carry out your grandma's wishes."

Seemed simple enough. "Need me to pay you anything now?"

"Did Miss Rosa Belle leave any money in banks? If she did, we'll need to file a motion in court so you have access to it."

"Not as I know of." What was in the jars didn't concern anybody but me.

"Then we settle up in the fall the way we've always done." Mr. Stern folded his hands on top of the desk. "You going to try and farm by yourself?" He appeared concerned, like a good friend or a kindly uncle would be.

"The neighbors offered to help me, so I'm going to try to work through this year the same as always. Mr. Jackson offered to rent the tobacco acreage, and if it gets to be more than I can handle by myself, I'll come get your ideas. But I'm keeping the farm for sure."

"How old are you again?"

"Be sixteen in a couple of months."

Mr. Stern leaned back in his chair, clasping his hands over his ample stomach. "I swear I hear your granddaddy's voice in you. Takes a lot of courage to do what you're fixing to try, Raeford, but I imagine you inherited a big dose of that from him."

I started to feel a good comfort level with Mr. Stern. "Got no option to do anything else if I want to eat and live."

"What did you say they call you?"

"Junebug, because I was born in June."

He got up and reached across the desk. "Well, I'm going to shake your hand and tell you to come to see me anytime you might need help. I'll file whatever paperwork needs doing, so don't worry about any of that."

"Good to have somebody on my side."

He pumped my hand a little extra, and gripped my elbow with his other hand. "Don't you worry, son. I'll talk to you in the fall if not before."

At the drugstore, I spent some time checking all the shelves and corners before going to the counter with ten comics. Behind the saleslady, I spotted what I'd been looking for. They were in a glass case against the wall. "Sir. Sir?" I reached out my hand for the change. There was no way I could bring myself to ask for a pack of Trojans.

Mr. Wilson was sitting on a stack of fertilizer bags outside Salem's, talking to some men. They were all chewing tobacco and spitting across the curb. "You done, Junebug?"

"Yessir."

He turned to the others. "This here is Miss Rosa Belle's grandson."

There were five of them. A great big man stood up. A wad of bright red hair stuck from under the sweat-stained John Deere hat on his head. "I'm Luther; knowed your grandma and granddaddy about all my life." I shook hands with him. He had crazy eyes; one went to the right and one to the left. It was hard to tell which one he was looking at me with. I also noticed he had a tattoo of a cross in a circle with a blood drop in the middle, the symbol of the KKK.

On the ride home, we neared the gas station on Highway 64. "Mr. Wilson, can we stop for a minute? I need to pee something awful."

"All right. I'll get some gas while you go."

I hurried around to the bathroom. It stunk like an outhouse in July. Sure enough, just to the left of the sink, on the peeling painted concrete wall, hung a couple of machines. One said "French Tickler" and the other said "Extra Lubricated." Since I didn't know what French Tickler meant, I dropped a quarter in the other one. I pulled the handle and out it plopped at the bottom. It appeared to be the same as the one Fancy had. I stuck in two more quarters and got some extra. I was so happy I forgot to pee, and by the time we pulled up at Mr. Wilson's I was about to bust.

As soon as I reached the woods on the way home, I leaned against a tree and watered the ground. I thought about the men with Mr. Wilson in Apex. It was no secret in the community that most of the menfolk either were members or supporters of the Klan. The men sitting with Mr. Wilson looked like they might fit under a white sheet. Lightning better damn sure not pop his head up if he did kill that man. Those old boys didn't play.

CHAPTER 24

Lightning sat at the kitchen table counting the pile of seeds in front of him. "We got well over a hundred and fifty, Junebug."

I rubbed a few of them in my hand. "Every one going to make a plant?" They didn't look like much.

"From what I understand, you lose a lot of them from bugs or bad weather, and some just won't grow. The migrant man said you need plenty of extra."

I didn't believe everything Lightning said, but just enough that I was curious. The place in the woods lay fallow, so maybe it wouldn't hurt to see what happened. "Toward dark we'll slip over there." I dropped the seeds back in the bag.

Lightning smiled like he knew I'd come around. "Your meeting go all right?" He had a new gold front tooth.

"It went fine. Is that tooth real or just covering the outside of an old one?"

He reached his finger to touch it. "The African did it, said it would make me look like a warrior."

"That's one man's opinion."

"So, what did the lawyer say?"

"Said the place is mine, except I couldn't sell it until I turned eighteen."

We sat around the rest of the afternoon, Lightning telling me how the migrant workers weren't much more than slaves, that the boss would end up stealing most of their money by saying he "provided" for them. Lightning bragged he got familiar with most of the women on the bus, so there was some fun to go with the work.

"How come you didn't light out once you figured what was going on?"

"Had no idea where in hell we were most of the time, all through the backcountry of South Carolina and Georgia. Plus I didn't have any money, so how was I supposed to get home?"

I decided to test him one more time. "You sure you killed that white man because he tried to kill you, that you weren't trying to rob him?"

He took an attitude. "Junebug, you've known me near 'bout all my life. You know I wouldn't hurt somebody on purpose." I noticed he didn't correct me on the "killing" part.

I was dozing in a porch chair when the noise of Fancy leaning her bike against the side of the house woke me. Lightning was on the couch reading one of my comic books. "Go in the bedroom. Your sister's here."

He scrambled, grabbing his shoes.

Fancy came up the steps. "Hey, Junebug." She wore cutoff jeans and a white T-shirt that was long enough to cover her behind.

"How was school?" I patted my legs.

She sat on my lap and gave me a peck on the lips. "It was good. We're studying about the Civil War. A bunch of folks were killed in that thing. I learned there were even some colored soldiers in the fight."

"Granddaddy told me all the menfolk in our family went, but not many came back." I tickled her ribs. "Ain't found a boyfriend at school, have you?"

She wiggled to move my hands. "Shut up."

"Got something to show you." I lifted her from my lap, reached in my back pocket, and pulled out the Trojans.

Her eyes flew wide. "Where'd you get these?"

"Gas station; a quarter apiece. Here, take one in case your momma wants to check."

"Thanks, Junebug." She sat back on my lap and started running her fingernails up and down my chest. "You want to go try one now?"

"What's wrong with you, girl? Not even dark yet."

She stuck out her bottom lip. "I might not be in the mood when it gets dark."

"Then we'll have to wait 'til you are. Got another surprise for you." I led her to the living room. "Come on out."

Lightning eased from the bedroom. Fancy stood frozen at the sight of him, then let out a yell and ran to grab him around the neck. "Where have you been? I can't believe you're home." Tears ran down both their faces. She pulled Lightning to the couch, and reached up to rub the welt on his face. "How did you get that?"

The two of them still resembled each other enough to be family, but it would be hard for a person who didn't know to see them as twins. Lightning choked up as he told her the story. "That son of a bitch ruined my face for life, Fancy." He spent the next hour telling her pretty much the same story I'd already heard. So near the same it made me wonder.

"When are you going to let Momma and Daddy know you're back?" She spread her hands over her face, looking through the fingers. "Do you think you killed that white man? What will happen if you did?" Fancy started to cry. "Damn it, Lightning, why couldn't you have just stayed home?"

"Wish to hell I had. I'll let them know when I'm sure the sheriff ain't looking for me, when it's safe for them to know." He pulled Fancy's hands from her face. "Everything will work out fine. You quit worrying."

While Fancy cooked supper, Lightning and me sat at the table, rehashing old stories and laughing about stuff we did as kids, remembering how we used to scare Fancy with tales of haints in the woods at night. It started to feel like old times, joking and teasing each other. Lightning's conversation got easy and comfortable. He sounded more like my old friend.

It was close to dark by the time we finished eating. "Lightning, let's walk off supper while Fancy is doing the dishes." I grabbed a flashlight from the cabinet. We found the wide wagon path that led from the cornfield behind the stable to the plant bed deep in the woods.

"I thought I remembered it this way." Lightning knelt down and picked up a handful of dirt. "This would do fine, Junebug. If I recollect, a little creek runs below that tree line."

"You remember right. Don't have a lot of water, but it's still there."

"I bet if we dug it out, we'd have all the water we need." Lightning studied the cleared field. "Take a harrow and run over the ground, and we could plant." He waved his hand. "Got plenty of room for what we need."

"I ain't coming out here in the dark to work." I hadn't decided if I was coming at all.

"Don't have to. Hook up the mule and come during the day. Nobody would question you."

"So you want to leave me all the work?"

"Let's pretend I'm the boss and you're the nigger for a change."

"You wish."

We started toward the house. I put my hand on his arm to stop him. "Lightning, I need to talk to you."

"About what?"

Things quieted, like all the night creatures wanted to listen. "I want you to know Fancy and me has come to being more than friends."

The muscle down his jaw twitched. He lowered his voice, making it plain he was serious. "I sort of figured as much watching the two of you. The only thing I say, Junebug, is you remember she's my sister. Don't ever mistreat her. If you do, I ain't going to take it well."

"Wouldn't expect nothing else."

"So long as we understand each other." He stuck out his hand. "You do realize that hell will come to visit if anybody finds out?"

"I know, and don't think I'm not careful."

Fancy was done cleaning up the kitchen by the time we got back. She picked up the paper bag. "Y'all going to plant flowers?"

Lightning grinned. "You could call it that. But they're going to be some we can make a lot of money growing."

Fancy looked at me. I nodded at Lightning to let him explain.

She kept glancing at me until he finished. "You okay with this? You willing to risk what you got?"

Until that moment I hadn't decided. I rubbed my forehead. "Fancy, I've given this some thought and decided Lightning won't ever be able to get on his feet unless he gets some money. He can't live here if that old man died, because sooner or later, somebody will find out. Plus, what if the tobacco crop fails or I break my leg, how would I survive? But I want to listen to what you got to say." I was making excuses to say yes, trying to maneuver her into the idea. The notion of the money had started working on me. Maybe I had some of my daddy in me after all.

Lightning stared. "Why's she have any say?"

I considered Fancy and me to be on the same footing, she'd watch out for me and I'd watch out for her. "Because she does. We all lose if we decide to do this and something bad happens." And maybe I wanted to test her.

Fancy studied our faces. "Okay. I'll agree so Lightning can get on his feet and you can put some money back." I could tell she was pleased to be a part of the decision, even if she wasn't pleased with the decision. "But I tell both of you, I don't have a good feeling."

CHAPTER 25

"Since it looks like you're going to be here awhile, Lightning, why don't you take my bed and I'll sleep in Grandma's."

He smiled big and broad. "That's real good of you, Junebug. Sure I won't be putting you out?"

"Well, sure you are, but go ahead anyway."

"Enough said. I'm hitting the hay." He got up and kissed Fancy on the cheek.

We waited for him to close the door and get settled before I got up and motioned to Fancy. We lay down on Grandma's bed, her head resting on my chest. On the bedside table was a picture of Grandma. I turned it facedown. "What do you honestly think about all this, Fancy?"

"I don't know, Junebug. One thing I do know is I don't want to see you go to jail."

I ran my fingers up and down the side of her face. "Lightning's changed, like what he's saying might not be all he's thinking. You reckon we can trust him?"

She snuggled tighter to me. "I see flashes of Lightning's old self, but he does seem different somehow."

"Expect killing a man would change a person."

"Why'd he think he had to run off like some crazy person? He's always thought he was meant for something better, but nothing ever seems to work out for him."

"With all I got to deal with already, farming enough to stay alive, you and me having to sneak around like a couple of night crooks, it feels like my life's sprung a lot of leaks, and I'm running out of fingers."

Fancy lifted her hand and spread her fingers wide. "I got ten too, Junebug, you remember that."

The wind blew through the trees and rattled the windows, like it had been listening. "Guess you better be getting back."

She reached up and kissed me. "Things will work out." Fancy had a powerful way of making me feel like a man, confident I would protect and take care of her.

I stood at the edge of the woods until she crossed the clearing to her house. My strong feelings for Fancy made me afraid. I stopped at the stumps and sat down. Lately, my mind felt like it was crazy circling from one thing to another, then going back and starting over. Something was nagging at me and I couldn't figure out what. It felt like I was walking into a windmill and hoping to dodge the blades.

The next morning I hooked up Sally Mule, went to the plant bed field, and cut it up with the harrow.

"How'd it go?" Lightning asked when I got back to the house.

"It's done."

Just before sundown, Lightning hurried across the road to the woods.

Fancy stood at the sink washing dishes. "Junebug, what do you think about quitting this thing right now?"

I could hear the fearfulness in her voice. "That what you want to do? I'll put a stop to it if it is."

She banged a pot on the counter. "Don't put all that burden on me. We have to decide together."

I went and put my arms around her. "And we will. Let's play it out a while longer. Anytime we feel things are going wrong, we'll quit. Okay?"

She turned, laying her head against my chest. "I trust you and I'll go along with whatever you decide. I just get scared thinking about it."

It was full dark before I spotted Lightning coming back across the road. "Well?"

"Looks fine, just got one more thing to do."

"Now what?"

"Need to put something around the field to keep critters out, don't want deer and coons getting in once the plants start growing."

"There's a big roll of chicken wire in the barn."

"That'll work. We can drive tobacco sticks in the ground and make a good fence. You take it over there in the wagon and I'll fix the rest."

Putting up that fence would pretty much commit me to ride this thing to the end. The hitch in the giddy-up would be if somebody out hunting ran across the field and got curious about what I was planting that needed protecting. "I can do that to-morrow."

Saturday came up cloudy, spitting showers of rain on and off. I loaded the chicken wire and tobacco sticks in the wagon and dropped them off at the field. I was sitting on the porch watching it rain when a car rounded the curve up the road. It was a sheriff's car. When it slowed, I spoke through the door to Lightning. "Get in the bedroom and don't make a sound."

A knot formed in my gut. When the car turned in, I recognized Ernest Lee Jones's daddy. I'd beat up Ernest Lee once at school and worried for days his daddy would come put me in jail. I stepped into the yard and walked to the car. "How you doing, Mr. Jones?" The round brim of the sheriff's hat tilted low over his eyes. His nickname was "Bull."

"Real good, Junebug. You making out all right since your

grandma died?" He was the one who'd come to the house to give the news the night my momma and daddy had been killed in the car wreck.

"Yessir. Guess I got her and Granddaddy to thank for teaching me how to do things. How's Ernest Lee?"

He grunted getting out of the car and rested his back against the door. "He's doing good. Mentioned to me you weren't in school this year." He kept looking around the place the whole time he talked. He was a great big man with a roll of fat over his belt. I could sense he was nobody to be fooling with.

I hooked my thumbs on my back pockets. "Just had too much to do to keep the farm going."

"Education is something you'd be glad for one of these days."

Let him preach to his own son. "What brings you out this way?"

"Just up at the Wilson place. Seems that boy of Roy and Clemmy's killed some white man in Georgia. They think he might be headed home."

I forced surprise on my face. "You talking about Lightning? Hard to believe he'd do something like that."

"We got a call from a Georgia sheriff, said they'd caught the other two that was with him. Both of them pointed the finger at Lightning as the one what done the killing. Said he knifed the man up real bad. They're anxious to get their hands on that boy."

I shook my head and rubbed my chin. "Ump. Had a bad feeling when he took off with them migrants."

He gave me a long stare. "You ain't seen nothing of him, have you? Clyde said y'all used to be friends."

I managed to look him straight in the eye. "Naw, last time I saw Lightning was before he run off. Did you ask his momma and daddy?"

"Stopped over there. You know them niggers, though; they wouldn't tell you if they had. And the Wilsons said they ain't seen him either."

I kicked at some chinaberries lying on the ground. "How you reckon he'd get back here from Georgia?"

"What they said was he not only killed the white man, but robbed him too. Got right at a thousand dollars. I expect he could find his way with that kind of money."

I let out a long whistle. "Did they say what happened?"

"Didn't get into a whole lot of detail, so I suspect there might be something they ain't telling, only that the man's wife saw the boy killing her husband and stealing his wallet. It did occur to me as to why a man would be walking around with that kind of cash money." He reached behind and opened the car door. When he got seated, he looked out at me. "I wish you good luck on the farm, Junebug. If you see that boy, you get word to me. And keep in mind"—he paused—"anybody that helps him is guilty of a crime too." He locked on my eyes.

"I'll do that, Mr. Jones. Think I'll make sure my shotgun is loaded."

"If you go killing a nigger, try to get the right one, hard to tell 'em apart." He let out a belly laugh and backed out of the yard. The falling rain went from a drizzle to a steady shower, beating a regular rhythm on the big oak leaves. Ordinarily, it would have been soothing.

CHAPTER 26

The back door opened and Lightning walked in. "I told you to stay in the bedroom."

"I figured if he came in the house wouldn't be nowhere to run. I was watching."

A silence fell between us. Lightning had a look of impatience on his face and stood as if he was in charge of this situation. I didn't like it. "If you were listening as well as watching, you know the old man you knifed is dead. He said they caught the other two and they made you out to be the killer." I stared at him. He'd lied to me all along.

Lightning wouldn't look me in the eye. "I was hoping they wouldn't find out where I was from. If I'd killed a colored instead of a white man, nobody would even bother."

"You know if they get hold of you, they're going to kill you."

He sat down in a kitchen chair. "I wish Daddy had beat my ass and made me stay home."

"Too late for that now. What you got to make sure of is nobody finds out you're here. He said if anybody was hiding you, they'd go to prison too, and I don't feel inclined to end up that way."

Lightning's eyes were flat and cold. He picked up a knife and played with it. "Don't expect you to go to jail for me. When we sell this stuff in the fall, I'm taking my part and going as far away from here as possible. You and Fancy can have Chatham County."

"That's right smart thinking." I went back on the porch and rolled another smoke.

I glanced up the road in time to see Mr. Wilson's truck. "God damn it!" What the hell did that fat bastard want? My temples started to throb. I'd about had a bellyful of this shit for one day. I went to the yard and stood under the oak to avoid the drizzle.

He pulled his truck close.

"Get a visit from Bull Jones?"

"Just left, surprised you didn't pass him."

Mr. Wilson opened his door. "He must have gone the other way. Let's get out of this rain."

"Come on in."

He stuck his head in the open door to the kitchen. "Appears you're doing a pretty good job keeping the house up."

"Fancy's been coming help me do stuff and make sure I don't burn the place trying to cook. I never realized what a hard job Grandma had."

He cut me a sideways look. "Been noticing that gal heading this way right smart. Let me give you a little bit of advice, June-bug. Don't you go to corn holing that black stuff, might ruin you for a proper white woman when the time comes. Besides, you don't ever know what kind of disease they might be carrying."

My face got hot. "Ain't got to worry, Mr. Wilson."

"I know a boy your age has always got a hard-on, but you save it for a decent girl. Did the sheriff tell you Roy's boy killed a white man in Georgia?"

I forced myself to stay calm. "He did? Hard to believe."

"Need to keep your eye on 'em all the time, never know what

they're thinking. They find out you got some money, they're liable to do anything."

I let out a chuckle. "He'd be shit out of luck around here."

"That boy shows up, you let me know. Your gun loaded?"

"Always." Which reminded me, I had left my shotgun under the bed where Lightning was sleeping. I rubbed the back of my neck to ease the pain shooting down from my head. "Don't suppose Lightning would cause us harm even if he did make it back home, do you?"

"Like I said, you never know what they're thinking. We don't need trouble around this community. I aspect if anybody catches a glimpse, they'll save the Georgia folks the cost of a trial."

"You're probably right."

He pushed up off the chair. "Okay then, want us to pick you up for church tomorrow?"

"Believe I will go with you." It would let me keep tabs on what Mr. Wilson might be thinking. I stood in the porch and watched him drive off.

Lightning came in the back door. "What did he want?"

"To ask if the sheriff had come by. This sure ain't what I bargained for." If I kicked Lightning out and he got killed, I didn't know if Fancy would forgive me.

He might have sensed what I was thinking. "All we got to do is make it a few months."

The muscles down the back of my neck throbbed. "I'm just fretting about them months in between."

I wondered if Daddy thought the shiny new Ford he bought with moonshine money was worth it when the fire was burning him alive. Was I playing with that same fire? I walked around the yard, stopped to look around and remind myself I was just a hick farm kid who had no idea what the hell he was messing in with something like this. These trees, this land, these buildings were mine, so what was I doing? And I was wore slam out with folks acting like they were in charge of me.

When I went back into the house, Lightning's expression had gone back to what I now understood to be his bullshit side, easy to come out when he wanted something from another person. "Junebug, you're all right for a white boy. You've grown balls. Ain't shy like you used to be. But just 'cause you're growing them muscles, don't think I can't still kick your ass."

"Don't jump on no horse you can't ride."

Fancy came late in the afternoon. After Lightning went to the plant field, I reached under the bed for my shotgun, wiped it down good with a little oil, ejected the shells, reloaded, and put it under Grandma's bed.

Fancy watched. "You ain't planning on killing somebody, are you?"

I told her about the sheriff. "Don't ever tell anybody about Lightning or what we're doing in that field. And most of all don't let on to anyone about us."

"Why do you think I would?"

"Can't think of a reason right now, but don't mean one might not come up." I rubbed my palms up and down my face. "Wish I'd never let Lightning stay here."

Her eyes narrowed to slits. "And what are you wishing about me?"

I leaned my head against hers. "Wishing we were sitting by an ocean someplace where nobody gave a damn about what color a person is."

She pulled my face down. "Junebug, you have faith. We don't understand it yet, but His plan will be clear one of these days."

I kissed the top of her head.

CHAPTER 27

Fancy cooked peas, cabbage, bacon, and biscuits for supper. "After you go to church tomorrow, I'm going to take the shovel and dig out the creek so we'll have plenty of water," Lightning said.

I stirred my fork around in the food, not having much of an appetite. "All the tools are under the woodshed."

"Sure would be nice to see Momma and Daddy," Lightning said to Fancy. "They doing all right, ain't they?"

"Sounds like it from the bed squeaking all the time. You ever do it with any of them migrant women?"

"Let's put it this way, everybody shared on the bus. If a man and a woman had an itch, they'd scratch it."

I'd never had a sister or brother, so maybe this kind of talk was normal. "How'd you keep them from getting pregnant?"

Lightning took on like a teacher, giving the benefit of his worldly experience. "Truth is, if they did, they did. The boss man said the kids would be a free hand when they got big enough to work." He looked at his sister. "You ain't pregnant, are you?"

Fancy slapped at his head with a dish towel.

* * *

It was sticky hot in the kitchen; no cross breeze at all came through the open window. "I'm going on the porch."

Lightning was right behind me. "You got any more cigarettes?"

Why not put a sign on my back that said, EVERYTHING'S FREE AT JUNEBUG'S?

Lightning relaxed. "Sure is mighty peaceful."

My headache began to ease while the three of us sat and talked. Lightning was full of jokes and stories, teasing Fancy about things from when they were kids. He stood up and stretched. "My bed's calling. Y'all behave now."

As soon as we couldn't hear him anymore, Fancy and me went into Grandma's bedroom. "When Lightning's like that, seems he ain't really gone anywhere." Fancy cuddled against me. "He went through some bad stuff, but maybe, with enough time, he'll get back to his old self."

"It's them other times that worry me." I closed my arms around her, needing to feel better about what was happening.

"I'm sleepy," Fancy whispered.

"Be right embarrassing if Mr. and Mrs. Wilson found us like this in the morning."

"Mr. Wilson would just be jealous. He's always watching me out the side of his eye."

I propped up on one elbow. "Get the hell out of here. Mr. Wilson?"

"A man is a man, Junebug, he's got needs."

The conversation between Mr. Wilson and me about not getting involved with Fancy came back. *Why, you old bastard.* "That's what Mrs. Wilson is for." Maybe all those community men sitting in the church pews every Sunday spouting about loving their neighbors might have a whole other meaning.

"Every old cracker man thinks a young colored gal can't wait to turn up her behind to him. He'll come around to me one of these days."

"What'll you do if he does?"

Fancy hugged her chest, then rolled away from me. "Depends on whether he makes me or not."

"You mean beat on you?"

"He wouldn't have to do that. He could just say I go along with him or he'll kick my folks off his farm." She sounded angry at my stupidity. "What do you think I can do then? How you think all them high-yellows got that way?"

"You ain't thinking of us like that, are you?" How cruel was it a person had to live waiting for a devil to come out of the shadows, helpless to fight back?

"Of course not." Her voice softened. "I'm here because I want to be. We're just a man and a woman to each other. Either one of us can walk away any time we want."

"Why would we?"

Fancy pulled the sheet up to her neck and yawned. "Some folks just do, I reckon. Don't want to be together no more."

"I'd never walk away from you, Fancy, never."

Wide awake there in the darkness, feeling the gentle movement of Fancy's body against me with each even breath of sleep, I considered how so much of dealing with life stuff wasn't about what a person knew, but what they didn't know. What Fancy said about the power Mr. Wilson had over her made a knot in the pit of my stomach. I'd seen him staring at Fancy when she walked. How could I have been so stupid not to understand?

My eyes began to close in spite of the tension in my mind. I jerked awake, reaching to make sure Fancy was still beside me. I buried my face into her hair and reached to cover her with my arms, kissing her shoulder, neck, and cheek, letting the touch, smell, and taste of her chase away the nightmare. When I ran my hand over her stomach Fancy stretched and yawned like a big cat. "You best quit that, Junebug, unless you can back it up." She rolled to face me, at the same time sliding her leg over my hip, connecting us in the warmth of slow, easy, loving sex. As Fancy arched her back to absorb me completely, I whispered to her, "I'll kill him if he ever touches you."

CHAPTER 28

In June, Mr. Wilson took me to the highway patrol station to get my driver's license. I was nervous as an old woman, but passed with no problem. Fancy was at the house when I got home. I showed her my shiny new license. "Come on, let's go for a ride." We drove to Apex, stopped at the gas station on Highway 64, and even rode by Fancy's school so I could see it. The freedom to come and go as I pleased was a breath of air I needed.

By the middle of July, everybody was cleaning out barns, fixing up slides, and getting ready for the start of tobacco priming season. Gardens needed to be picked, and between that and other fieldwork, workdays were long; it was hard, but satisfying to know I was looking after myself.

Fancy and me had spent a long day pinching tobacco worms off leaves in the field, and sat on the porch after a supper of leftovers, hoping for a breeze to cool us. Even after dark, the humid, damp air lay heavy.

Lightning came out to sit with us. "Junebug, you need to take me to Durham."

"What for?"

"Need to find somebody who can buy that marijuana when it's ready."

I leaned my chair back against the wall, lit a cigarette, and watched smoke float toward the wire screen. "How you going to do that?"

"I can stay a night or two with my auntie in Hayti. Don't expect it'll take long to locate the right person."

Fancy put her hand over his. "Don't you let the police catch you running around up there."

"So many coloreds in that place, Fancy, nobody's going to notice one more. Besides, it'll give me some getaway time."

Maybe he would get away for good. "When you aiming to go?"

"We can do it tonight if you want to."

I glanced at Fancy. "You want to ride with us?"

"Yep. Don't know the last time I went to Durham."

We hopped in the truck and headed to town. Hayti wasn't any problem to find, just drive through the center of Durham and turn left across the railroad tracks. It was like entering another world. It felt different; the smell of barbecue and fried fish floated along the street, and there was electricity in the air. Music blasted from open doors of juke joints, and the sidewalks were crowded with colored folks talking and laughing; everybody celebrated the week's end. We rattled over the rough rails and stopped at a red light. "Let me off right here," said Lightning. "Pick me up at this same spot Sunday about six."

Fancy kissed his cheek. "Be careful."

I eased the truck around the corner, catching a lot of stares, a cracker boy riding with a colored girl. On the way out of town we spotted a Dairy Queen and stopped for ice cream. There were just as many hard looks from the crowd of white folks. I got the cones to go.

The ice cream was melting so fast we stopped on the side of the road to finish it. "You want me to go ahead and drop you off?"

"Trying to get rid of me?"

"Thought since it was getting late, you might need to get home."

She slid her hand up and down my thigh. "Not going home."

"What are you talking about?"

"Daddy's cousin picked them up this afternoon. They're going to a wake for Aunt Emma down in Kinston, and won't be back until tomorrow."

"You mean, you can stay all night?"

"That's what I mean, white boy."

CHAPTER 29

Sunlight peeping through the window curtains woke me. Fancy was already awake. "Morning," she said, eyes wide open.

I slid my arm beneath her head. "And top of the day to you. Did you sleep good?"

"I kept watching the ceiling, wondering if your grandma might visit." She draped her leg over mine. The odor of sex floated up when the covers moved.

"Can I tell you something, Fancy?"

The sheet slipped down, exposing her breasts. She didn't move to cover them. "As long as it's not something bad."

"When Grandma died at the hospital, I felt her spirit lift out."

Fancy sat up straight, eyes wide. "What? What do you mean, you felt her spirit?"

"It was strange. I felt this stir of air, soft, like the brush of a bird's wing, and I knew it was her. Granddaddy was there too. I've been thinking about it a long time, trying to make sure it wasn't my imagination in that hospital room."

She looked me hard in the eyes. "You ain't messing with me, are you, Junebug?"

"I never would over something like that."

Fancy lay back and pulled the sheet up to her neck. "What do you think it means?"

"I took it to mean that this ain't the end, that maybe we float around in the air, invisible to folks still living."

"I always thought you'd just close your eyes, then be in heaven."

"Just didn't want you to worry about Grandma visiting."

"Let's don't talk about it no more, okay." She moved the sheet and rolled to face me.

"I ain't going to let nothing happen to you." I lifted her leg over my hip, feeling myself getting excited.

Fancy put her nose to mine, staring me in the eyes, whispering. "You know, you're right pretty for a white boy. Got them crazy blue eyes from your grandma."

"How many white boys you been this close to?" I pulled our middles together.

She lifted and raked herself against me. "You'll make one." I could feel her wetness.

When I slipped into her, she sucked in a sharp breath. "Keep it like that.

"What about when you find a white girl?" We started to move slowly.

"Ain't looking."

Fancy closed her eyes, and began to flex her hips. "Don't worry . . . they'll come for you." She stuttered between words. "That feels so good."

I moved faster, enjoying feeling in control. "Mr. Wilson said you'd ruin me for any proper white woman."

"Am I?" Her hips moved more urgently.

"I hope so." I rolled Fancy to her back, gripped my hands underneath her butt, and forced harder. She came back at me with a fury. It became a battle, a war of passion, fighting and clawing and demanding, the slapping sound of the sex making me crazy. When she felt the end coming, Fancy pulled my face down, kissing and grabbing my bottom lip with her teeth. We slammed together like two trains crashing head-on.

Fancy lay back on the pillow, holding me in place. "Damn you, Junebug."

"I know."

After church Sunday morning, I loafed around the house most of the day. When five o'clock came and Fancy hadn't showed, I got an uneasy feeling. I made myself get in the truck and ride to Durham, turning the radio loud, trying to drown out my worry.

Lightning waited in the same place we'd dropped him off. "Where's Fancy?"

I shut off the country music. "She never showed up today."

"Did you go by the house?"

"Hell no! Are you crazy? If she's got in trouble over something, I wasn't about to make it worse."

"Damn it. I wish I could go home. Daddy can start sipping that shine once in a while and sometimes he'll get mean."

"You don't think he'd hurt Fancy, do you?"

"He's liable to slap her around some, like he does Momma. I don't know what makes him get like that. Momma says to let it pass, says it's the inside hurt of a black man always having to bow down to white folks. She said he ain't got anywhere else to let it out."

I'd never heard that about Roy before.

"We'll find out soon enough. By Monday, Daddy has to have his self back right so he can go to work. Fancy will be around tomorrow."

I picked up the street leading out of town. "Did you find anybody to buy the stuff?" A giant sign above the Wachovia Bank building blinked seven o'clock and eighty-three degrees.

"Oh yeah. I asked around until I got hold of this man called Twin. He used to have a twin brother, but some white policeman killed him a few years back. Now he's meaner than a nodick dog, generally don't like white folks, and hates police. He's the biggest dope dealer in Hayti, which means he's got the money. I spoke to him, and he said he would look at a sample when we were finished."

"You didn't tell him where, did you?"

"Do I look stupid?" Lightning looped his arm across the back of the seat, sounding important. "All I told him is when we're done this fall, I'd come to visit him."

The highway got very dark as we pulled away from the city lights. "You talk price?"

"No use worrying about that until he gets a sample. He's not going to pay much for rag, but he will for good stuff."

"How will we know what ours is?"

He smacked the dashboard. "I told you I smoked some back in Georgia, Junebug."

"Sure hope you know what you're doing."

"I got it under control."

Lightning's attitude wore on my nerves, acting all-important, like he was our savior. I'd give him his due for growing the crop, but it was on "my" land, with "my" equipment, and all the while I was hiding him in "my" house so those good old boys wouldn't have a chance to make him an oak-tree necktie.

The next afternoon Fancy did show up. Her right eye was swollen almost shut.

I gripped her by the shoulders. "What happened to you?"

She tried to wave me off. "Ain't nothing, Junebug, don't worry yourself." Fancy twisted away and went into the kitchen.

"Don't tell me what to worry about." I followed her.

Lightning walked in. "What the heck are y'all hollering about? I could hear you in the yard."

Fancy turned her back so he couldn't see. Lightning walked in front of her. He reached up to touch her eye. "Daddy do this to you?"

She stared at the floor.

"What for?" His voice was loud and demanding.

"Let it go, Lightning. I'm all right."

I edged between them. "Was it anything to do with me?"

"He was drinking and I reckon he had you and me on his mind, so he made sure I understood I better not be messing around." Fancy pulled out a kitchen chair, sat down, and put her head in her hands.

I headed to the bedroom. When I came back to the kitchen with the truck keys, Fancy got in front of me and grabbed my arm. "No, you ain't! You are not leaving this house. I told you I'm all right."

"Nobody is going to beat on you, Fancy, not for any reason, and for sure not because of me."

Lightning came beside us. "Fancy's speaking the truth. This is between a daddy and his child. You got no rights."

I looked down, heat boiling up from my feet to my head. I let my finger trace the red checks in the tablecloth. The room got quiet. I looked him in the eyes. "Lightning, don't ever again tell me what I can and can't do."

"Junebug, stop it!" Fancy shoved me backward.

I went into the bedroom, slamming the door. I could take my shotgun and solve this shit right now. Seemed like I was the odd man out lately. Nobody was going to push me around in my own house. There was a deep-down angry fire inside me I'd never felt before. I didn't know if my hands shook because I was mad or if I was scared of how mad I was.

I could hear Fancy's voice from the kitchen. "You best quit pushing Junebug; he's got enough to deal with."

"He needs to mind his own business."

"I am his business, so you need to get over it or get gone."

The porch door slammed. Fancy came in where I was and put her arms around me. "I appreciate you wanting to look after me, Junebug, but some things a person has to let pass. My daddy loves me. He doesn't mean to hurt me or Momma, just sometimes he can't take it no more."

I pushed her to arm's length. "I understand your daddy's

toted his burdens a lot of years. But Lightning is where he is by his own hand, and he ain't going to run my life."

"Hush. Enough about all that." Fancy pushed me back on the bed. "Come here." She started to undo my belt.

"What about Lightning?"

She laughed as she took off her dress. "Let him find his own woman."

CHAPTER 30

High humidity made the scorching days of August suffocating. The tobacco stalks grew heavy and full, and the leaves ripened. I helped the Wilsons, and they helped me with the priming and barning. Mr. Wilson sounded a little too friendly whenever he was around Fancy, or maybe I noticed it more after what she told me. He was getting on my nerves worse and worse. I even looked at Roy differently, trying to imagine him so angry he would punch his own daughter. I didn't feel the same respect for him. There were days I didn't like my world very much. When you shucked the outside layer of people, a lot of the corn was rotten.

Lightning managed to stay out of sight. He sat up with me the first night minding the fire and curing the leaves. Since the incident in the kitchen, we had steered clear of each other as much as possible. "Lightning, I'm sorry if I got carried away. It seems since Grandma died, everybody wants to tell me this or that, like I'm stupid or something."

"I understand, Junebug. If I thought Daddy was really trying to hurt Fancy, I'd go up there and face him." He stuck out his hand. "No hard feelings."

Fancy and Lightning helped me store the tobacco crop in the pack house so it could turn soft and color out. By the first of October, we'd had a frost and the brisk nights began to color the maples fire red and the oaks brownish yellow. I hauled loads to Durham and sold the tobacco. It turned out not to be a big season for price, but I made enough to pay off my bill at Salem's Store and to Lawyer Stern. With what was left, I bought supplies for next year, kept some money in the house for gas and food, and added the rest to the jars buried in the pack house cellar. I made sure to do that when Lightning was in the marijuana field, but I did show the stash to Fancy.

"What are you going to do with all that money, Junebug?" She sat with me on the dirt floor, like two kids playing with toys.

I screwed the ring top on the last jar. "This is for when I need it or get old and can't work. Don't ever tell anybody what's here, but if anything happens to me, you know where it is. Take the money and go visit some of them places you read about in your schoolbooks."

Fancy leaned over and put two hands on my face. "Better not anything happen to you. Maybe one of these days we could visit those places together."

We went to lay on our backs in the grass outside the pack house and talk while we watched the daylight fade and a quarter moon find its place in the night sky. "I used to go sit in the woods at night after Grandma died. Somehow, it seemed to make me feel closer to her."

"Church didn't help? Or praying?"

"Not much. Something about the dark makes me feel better."

Lightning came into the house late one afternoon a couple of weeks later. "Can you come with me in the morning? Them plants are ready for pulling and I want you to see how to tell when it's time."

"I can do that." I hadn't been to the field in a couple of months.

We went out early. It was obvious Lightning had done a right smart amount of work. The plants had reached head high and looked healthy.

Lightning pushed out his chest a little. "This crop looks better than that old farmer's in Georgia. Let me show you what I was talking about." He took a magnifying glass and pointed out the brownish hairs on the buds. "That's when it's ready."

I was impressed he had stuck it out to the end. His name hadn't always fit his ambition. "So what do we do now?"

"Saturday night, we'll move the wagon over here, pull 'em up, and take them to the barn." Lightning did a dance in the soft dirt. "Boy, we're getting near to making some serious money."

"How soon?"

"Soon as I can get a sample to take to that guy Twin. Then we'll know what's coming."

"And you're sure you got all this under control?"

"All we got to do is keep our mouths shut and take care of business."

It was beginning to feel real, making me have even more doubts this kind of money could be so easy. "You reckon you can trust this man?"

"No further than I could throw him. But he needs us as bad as we need him, especially if we got good stuff. That would let him charge more."

I didn't figure I could throw Lightning very far either. "I'm trusting you."

He chatted away as we walked back to the house. "Don't worry, son, I got this." Two nights later, we pulled the plants and strung them up in the barn.

On Wednesday morning, Sheriff Bull Jones made another visit. He stepped out of his car and walked around the yard to stretch his legs. I wasn't surprised to see him since Mr. Wilson said they were still looking for Lightning, but at that moment all I could think about was that marijuana hanging in the tobacco barn, a two-minute walk from the house. If he headed that way,

I had no idea what I would do. But he only stayed a few minutes.

Lightning showed me how to break down the buds, and then we rolled and smoked some. "Suck it in your chest good, hold it for a few seconds, then blow it out." I hacked and coughed like a sick person before getting the hang of it. After that, I could understand why folks would buy it. The next time Fancy came, we took her to the barn and let her try. We sat around laughing like three idiots, then went to the house and ate everything in sight.

I had to make one run to Apex and another to Durham in order to get enough mason jars and not cause suspicion buying too many in one place. The next few days we spent a lot of time cutting off the buds. We filled up a hundred small jars and fifty half-gallon sizes.

"How much you going to charge for these, Lightning?" We were sitting at the kitchen table while Fancy cooked chicken stew.

"I figure seventy-five dollars each for the little jars and three hundred for the big ones. We might could get more, but I don't want to push too hard."

After quick multiplying on a piece of paper, I looked at Lightning. "You know that's twenty-two thousand five hundred dollars?"

He couldn't quit grinning. "I told you, Junebug."

I'd never heard of anybody having that much money. "This one man is going to come up with that much cash?"

"That's why I picked him; takes somebody big-time to afford it."

The time was here when the wheat and the chaff were going to get separated. With that kind of money, there was no telling what we might do. I kept envisioning a stack of green hundred-dollar bills on the kitchen table. Fancy was watching me from the stove. When we caught each other's eye, both of us broke out laughing.

That Friday afternoon, Lightning was ready to go meet with the guy, Twin. "Time for us to get paid," he said.

We dropped Lightning at the same place. When we got home, Fancy and me lay on the bed talking. "Junebug, you think this is going to work?"

"I'll wait until I see the money. But it seems Lightning might have finally got something right."

We lay with our noses touching. "I can't help thinking about all that money. What are we going to do if we get it?"

I grinned. "I might buy me a new truck. Heck, I might buy you and me a new truck."

She started giggling, stuck her arms in the air, and wiggled her butt. "I want some fancy dresses, be Miss Somebody, be such a fine lady I might not even talk to a hick like you." Fancy got somber for a minute, that logic mind of hers working. "If we go to buying stuff, folks are going to wonder where all the money came from. I guess we better hide it and just spend a little along, keep the rest."

Here we were about to have all this money, yet Fancy and me couldn't even walk down the street together. I brushed a strand of hair from her face. "It's going to get harder not letting anybody find out about you and me."

"I know. Don't worry so much. Momma is keeping Daddy from the shine jug so he don't get crazy." She laid her forehead against mine. "I'll be seventeen next summer and done with school. Then I can live on my own."

"Where you going to live?"

"Why don't I come stay with you? We can tell folks I'm your live-in housekeeper." She squeezed closer. "Or we could move somewhere we don't have to worry about what other people think."

I pushed my hand under her dress and felt her wetness. "We could just buy a tent and live out in the woods."

Her legs parted. "And what would we do all day?" Fancy covered my mouth with hers, reaching for my zipper.

"We'd think of something." She lifted so I could pull down her underwear. Her insides were on fire. We buried our worries and concerns and made love until sweat ran between our bellies.

CHAPTER 31

Lightning waited on the corner. "How'd everything go?" I asked him.

He rubbed his hands against his pants several times. "Good, just got one little thing we need to do first."

A sour feeling hit me. "What?"

"Twin said he needed to know who he's dealing with." Lightning stared out the window. "He wants to meet you."

"Why?"

"Like I said, he's suspicious about folks, especially white folks."

"How does he know I'm white? Dammit, Lightning, why can't you keep your mouth shut?"

"Just came out when we were talking. You'll be fine. It's business, Junebug, nobody's going to start any ruckus. Turn left at the next street."

We drove deeper into the heart of Hayti. Houses along the streets were run-down, white-painted wood that had faded to a dusty chalk. Most had a shaded front stoop, and folks sat outside taking in the night air, watching traffic pass. I felt like every eye was on me.

Lightning pointed to a house that sat above the street. "Pull up right there."

No light was visible from outside. "Don't look like anybody's home."

"They're here, the windows got heavy curtains." Lightning got out of the truck.

Fancy started to follow. Lightning turned and put his hand on her shoulder. "You might ought to stay here."

"I'm going." The tone of her voice didn't leave it up for question.

"Suit yourself." We climbed the cement steps that ran from the street up to a long wooden porch. Lightning knocked.

The curtain moved slightly before the lock rattled. A colored man built like a hickory stump opened the screen door and motioned us in. "Put your hands on the wall." He wasn't asking. He patted me down from shoulders to feet. "Go on in," he growled.

The run-down condition of the outside didn't match the inside. Thick red carpet covered the floor. There was nice furniture, music coming from a long console against the wall, and a couple of crazy-looking lamps with blobs floating up and down. Lightning motioned me to stand beside him. "This is Twin."

A fat, bald-headed man sat on a white leather couch, smoking a cigar, except it didn't smell like cigar. He didn't bother to get up. "So you're Lightning's partner?"

"Reckon so."

He pulled himself up off the couch. "Hell, y'all ain't nothing but a couple of punk-ass kids." Twin towered over me by at least four inches, weighed about three hundred pounds, and had the biggest hands I'd ever seen. His face was pocked bad and a lot of yellow showed in his eyes. He bent down and put his broad nose real close to mine, like he was sniffing my scent.

He moved from me to Fancy. "Now, this is something I can use." He lifted her chin, pushed her around so he could see her behind, then used his first finger to lift one of her breasts.

Fancy jerked away. Her fists balled up. I moved between them. "She ain't for sale."

Twin was startled. He leaned down to me again. "Let me tell you something, you white-bread motherfucker, I'll take whatever I want." His breath stunk like my pigpen.

"Like I said, she ain't for sale." I swelled up the best I could, staring back. He had a fearsome sneer. His man started laughing.

Twin straightened, then suddenly reached down and grabbed me by my privates, jerking up. "I like a man what's got some balls, boy, but don't talk like that to me again. I'll put your ass in a place nobody will ever find all your parts."

The sudden severe pain made me suck air. Out of the corner of my eye, I saw Fancy start to move. I put my elbow against her chest. "She's got no part in this." My tone had a higher pitch than usual due to the grip Twin had on my nuts.

He turned loose. I cut an eye at Lightning, but he just stared straight ahead. He was either scared shitless or more worried about the money than about his sister.

"Oh, I get it now," Twin said. "You done got a taste of this chocolate stuff and you like it. You think this nigger cunt is your girlfriend? Boy, you got a lot to learn about women. But, like I said, I respect a man that's got backbone."

He stepped back and settled on the couch. "Y'all sit down and let's talk business. I have to admit this shit Lightning brought is pretty good. How much you got?"

Lightning talked while Fancy and I sat close together, staying quiet. "A hundred jars like I brought you, and fifty half-gallon ones."

"When can you deliver?"

"Anytime you want."

Twin puffed on his cigar while he glanced at the ceiling. "Okay, let's set up for this coming Wednesday; y'all can get it here?"

Lightning started to agree before I stopped him. "No offense, Mr. Twin, but we ain't bringing it here. We'll meet you somewhere private so we can make the trade."

He pushed to his feet again, his expression pissed off and serious. Then he began to laugh. "What we got here is a junior

John Dillinger." He looked at the other man standing behind us. "What's the matter, boy, you scared of coming to black folks country?"

Maybe I should just agree, and never show up. "I just don't trust you to have our well-being in mind." I watched the blobs float up and down.

That really got him going. He slapped me on the shoulder. "I'm starting to like you, boy. What'd you say your name was?"

"Folks call me Junebug."

He leaned down in my face again. "That's about the dumbest name I ever heard, right behind Lightning." He wasn't smiling when he straightened up. "All right, where you want to meet?"

I was surprised he agreed so quickly. I waited to see if Lightning had any ideas. He just stood there like he had a post up his ass.

I felt like the idiot in the room, putting myself in a place I was scared we wouldn't get out alive, but didn't see anything to do except keep talking. "There's a bridge just past the county line on Highway 751 where it crosses over Northeast Creek. Right before the bridge is a pull-off place people use to go down to the water and fish. We'll meet you there at ten o'clock Wednesday night."

Twin stared at me, rubbing his jaw with a massive right hand. He glanced at his man. "You know the place?"

The man nodded.

"Okay, I'll be there. Make sure you bring all the stuff."

"No disrespect, but it comes to some over twenty-two thousand dollars, as I figure it."

"Don't you worry about the money, boy, I can count. But worry about this: If anybody jumps out of the bushes, know I'll kill you first." He scratched the side of his jaw. "I'm already wondering how two dumb-asses like you could come to have that much reefer." He wasn't loud and he didn't push his face in front of mine, but he wasn't playing. "Try setting me up and I'll bury you and everybody in your family."

I could tell he meant every word. "Mister, all we're trying to do is make some money and not have any trouble." Fancy and I got to our feet.

"You best hope that's all you're trying to do. Now haul your ass out of here." He looked Fancy up and down again. "Unless you want to stay, little girl."

She grabbed my hand and pulled me toward the door.

"Well, ain't that cute, white bread's got him a farm nigger. You be careful, that stuff can mess up your head." They were still laughing as we pulled the door shut behind us.

As soon as I got the truck turned around, I lit into Lightning. "Who the hell have you got us messing with? They could have killed us in there!"

Lightning sounded irritated and impatient with my ignorance. "Junebug, who the hell did you think you would deal with? Ain't no choirboys selling dope."

Fancy tried to ease the situation. "Junebug, I'm okay. It didn't mean anything. It's like Lightning says, he was just trying to scare us."

"He damn sure did me. What if they decide to rob us when we do the trade? I don't want somebody to find my body floating in Northeast Creek."

Lightning made a feeble attempt at putting my worries to rest. "You're getting all worked up for nothing. He said he was starting to like you."

"He can kiss my ass is what he can do. I can't believe you're actually stupid enough to trust that bastard. Telling me I'll be the first one dead, shit, he better be worried about his self." We rode the rest of the way in silence.

CHAPTER 32

Lightning went into the house and right to bed. Fancy and me closed the door to Grandma's bedroom, leaving the light on. I lay on my back, counting knots in the wood ceiling, thinking. "Do you have any idea if Lightning would double-cross us?"

She let out an exhausted sigh. "There was a time I'd say no. Maybe that cut in his face runs a lot deeper than the scar." I felt the shiver in her arms and pulled her close.

"When this is over, we're done with this shit." We could stop now, give Lightning the marijuana, tell him to leave and make the deal however he wanted. But Fancy and me had come too far to walk away with nothing.

"That Twin is creepy, Junebug. He just might want to get rid of us and take what we got. I can't even believe I'm saying that. None of this seems real."

"I won't let anything happen to you, Fancy, but when it's finished, Lightning's got to go."

She sat up, holding her knees. "Life gets crazy sometimes, don't it? Once in a while when the old freight train goes by the school, I feel like I want to hop on and never come back."

I heard the hoot owl down by the barn.

* * *

A loud pounding sounded from the porch, like a hammer hitting wood. Fancy and me hit the floor. "Junebug. Junebug, you come to this door!" It was Roy.

"Shit." Fancy hid in the closet. I reached under the bed for my shotgun. When I went through the living room, I could see Lightning standing in the shadow of the other bedroom and waved him back.

I flipped on the porch light. "What do you want, Roy?"

"I told you, Junebug. I warned you." He stood outside the screen door, his face pressed against the wire. "Tell Fancy to get her ass out here."

I stood close enough to smell the moonshine liquor on him. "You're drinking and it's got your head messed up. Go on home."

"Don't lie to me, boy. She's in there. Get her out here or I'll come in and drag her out." He pushed on the door.

I stuck the barrel of the shotgun to the screen. There was no way I could handle him man to man if he got to me. "You ain't coming in my house unless I say so." He stopped; spit drooled down the corner of his mouth. I waited, hoping all his years of understanding that a colored man didn't challenge a white man, even a younger one like me, would be stronger than his rage.

"Here I am, Daddy." Fancy startled both of us.

Roy's face clouded like a thunderhead. "Look at yourself. I didn't raise you to be some white man's whore. I ought to beat the hell out of both of you."

Her voice choked. "I ain't a whore, Daddy."

Red showed in the whites of Roy's eyes. "What the hell do you call it? Next you'll be having bastard children somebody else will have to raise. Who's going to marry you then?"

Fancy's voice trembled. "I ain't going to be having any babies."

After a minute of the standoff, I decided to get it over with. I hoped to be able to calm him down. "Roy, I'm going to open the door so we can do some talking, but there won't be any hitting or cussing. You agree to that?" He looked down, forced to accept something he didn't want. I helped him up when he stumbled over the casing.

In the living room, I sat between Fancy and her daddy. "Go ahead and say your piece, Roy."

His words slurred, and his neck was rubbery. "I always tried to protect you, Fancy, favored you as much as I knowed how. You're growing up to be a handsome woman, one with a chance to find a good man and have a decent life, not have to settle for some no-account nigger like me." He rambled and blubbered about losing Lightning, and now all he had left to hope for was Fancy to make something out of herself. Drunken tears ran down his face.

Fancy got up and went to kneel beside him. Loud knocking came from the back door. The room hushed. I signaled Roy and Fancy with a finger to my lips and hoped Lightning was paying attention. My first thought went to Mr. Wilson or Bull Jones.

I walked through the kitchen and peeped through the curtain. I was so overcome with relief I had to hold on to the casing for support. It was Clemmy. I opened the door. "Junebug, I'm sorry. Roy got to drinking and found out Fancy wasn't home. I figured he might come here."

She had a big bruise on her face. "He's in the living room."

"Momma?" Fancy grabbed her shoulder, touching her bruised eye before balling her fist and turning back to her daddy. "God damn you, why you always got to be taking out your hatefulness on Momma and me? We're the only people you got! Why don't you pick on somebody who can fight back?"

Clemmy pushed Fancy to the couch. "Fancy, you hush. Sit your ass down and let me deal with this." She took a chair beside Roy. "It's okay." She talked easy to him.

Roy got weepy-eyed again. "I'm sorry, Clemmy. You know I didn't mean nothing by it."

The floor creaked in the bedroom. Everybody turned toward the noise.

Roy fell out of his chair backward, knocking it over. "God

almighty!" His eyes squinted to make sure he was seeing right. "Lightning?"

He stepped into the light. "Hey, Daddy. Hey, Momma."

Roy rushed him, lifting him off the ground. Clemmy doubled over, holding her stomach. "Oh Jesus. Thank You, Jesus, You brought him home." The three of them fell into each other, crying, laughing, and hugging.

"Boy, what are you doing here?" Roy held his son at arm's length.

"Been here staying with Junebug for a while. I knew the sheriff was trying to find me."

"Is what he said true, son? Did you kill that white man?"

"Had to, Daddy. He was for sure intent on killing me."

Clemmy touched the scar running down her son's face. "He did this to you?" As hard as she had tried to guard her children, the evil in the world had gotten to her son.

Lightning sat down between Roy and Clemmy on the couch. They insisted Lightning tell them what had happened and how he got home.

I went on the porch and smoked, letting them catch up in private. I was thumping my second cigarette to the yard when Roy came out. "I owe you an apology, Junebug. You've been looking after Lightning all this time."

"You'd do it for me."

Roy stuck out his hand. "I reckon I would."

I fixed my eyes on Roy while I shook with him. "We still got some talking to do."

"Well, let's get to it." He waited for me to lead the way.

I sat down beside Fancy. Things went dead silent when I reached and took her hand. She hesitated at first. "Roy, Clemmy, we want to tell you Fancy and me has developed feelings for each other. We understand it's not right in the face of the world and didn't intend for things to turn out this way, but it happened and we don't see nothing changing."

The room was midnight quiet except for the ticking of the

wall clock. Lightning turned his head toward the window. Finally her momma spoke. "Fancy." Clemmy's light brown face folded in rows from her eyes down to her chin. "I never thought you'd go this far. You may think you know this world, but you don't by a long shot. And Junebug, you can't imagine what danger you're putting her in."

Fancy took a deep breath. "I know how things are, Momma; I'm not stupid. We're not looking to cause trouble, all we're asking you is to let us decide. Y'all are all I got, and I don't want hard feelings, but there comes a time to loosen the rope some, let me figure out things for myself."

Roy's eyes had cleared some, but his voice now sounded hurt, not angry. "Fancy, your momma and me have sheltered you the best we could. You don't know what meanness is out there in the world. There's folks who will hurt you just because of your black skin, others would kill you for living in sin with a white man. And they won't stop with you." He let his last words sink in.

I put my hand to Fancy's shoulder to stop her from answering, and moved my eyes from one face to another. I didn't see any sympathy. "Roy, I know them people, sit with them in the church pews. They can pray to God on Sunday, then put on white sheets Monday. That kind of hate is bred deep down over a lot of years, and I know it ain't going away just 'cause we hope it will. But I read about stuff happening across the country. Folks are starting to speak up. Grandma told me once she was proud I didn't like the things I see, and I don't believe I'm the only one. I ain't stupid enough to think they can't harm us, but you and Clemmy should know I'll draw my last breath if anybody tries to hurt Fancy."

The look in Clemmy's eyes was frightful. "I'm not agreeing to this," she said. "Junebug, this would never have happened if Miss Rosa Belle was alive. I can't let you think what you're doing is right, or real, or is anything more than two kids caught up in some fairy tale you think is going to have a happy ending. It's not. If you go flaunting yourselves, y'all are going to see what an ugly face the devil has. I hear what you're saying, Junebug, and I pray change will come, but this is still the South and we're still niggers, to be tolerated only as long as we keep our place. That's the reality, and all your high-minded feelings ain't going to change it."

Clemmy stood up. "We need to get home, Roy." She grabbed her son's hand. "Lightning, you got to stay absolutely out of sight. We'll sneak off down here once in a while. I'm just happy to know you're alive, and can touch you." She turned back to me. "Junebug, I'm grateful and won't forget what you're doing for Lightning."

Lightning hugged Clemmy. "I'll be careful, Momma. You can't believe how good it is to see you and Daddy. I've been suffering from the loneliness for a long time." Lightning hadn't said anything during the conversation about Fancy and me.

As I watched them fade into the dark, I didn't know how I felt at that moment. The look on Clemmy's face had cut me to the quick. I'd been considering myself like some comic-book hero who could right the wrongs I saw, and she'd tolerated me. Now I knew she'd just been playing along with my foolish games. Who the hell did I think I was?

CHAPTER 33

At dinner the next day, I went to the mailbox and got the newspaper. "Come look at this, Fancy." She put her head alongside mine. There were pictures of police dragging colored people by feet and shirt collars.

The story was about ongoing civil unrest, showing photos of folks on a hunger strike at the post office in Chapel Hill, and protesting in front of the Howard Johnson hotel in Durham. There were pictures of police using clubs on anybody who didn't move. "We talked about how things would change one of these days, Fancy. I think it's coming fast."

She read over my shoulder. "I don't know if I would be as brave as them."

"It's 1963, Fancy. Ten years ago, them police would have been shooting instead of clubbing. And the Boo Boys would be out there helping them."

CHAPTER 34

"Fancy still in bed?" Lightning came wandering into the kitchen while I was frying bacon and fixing eggs. The morning brought a chilly rain, and I'd made a fire in the potbelly to keep off some of the dampness.

"You can wake her up if you want to, breakfast is about ready." My attitude had changed when it came to Fancy. It felt like I'd fought for her and now she belonged to me. I'd prove Clemmy wrong if it was the last thing I did.

I scratched pieces of egg around on my plate. "Lightning, what's the plan for this thing tonight?"

"Nothing to plan. We show up with our stuff, they bring the money, and everybody goes home."

"You know they'll be toting guns."

"So, take your gun." He put down his fork and looked at me hard. "They ain't going to mess up a business that makes them money, Junebug. It would be stupid, and I don't think Twin's a stupid man. Ugly, yes, but stupid, no."

I broke open a biscuit and soaked the halves with molasses. "Tell me something." I cut the coated bread with my fork. "You ain't by chance made a separate deal with Twin that don't include me and Fancy, have you?"

He kept crunching bacon and looking down at his plate. "What are you talking about?"

"I didn't stutter. Just so you understand, I'm going to take my gun and if any funny business happens, I'm going to start shooting. If you have any thoughts about hanging us out to dry, don't."

He pushed his plate away. "Listen, Junebug, I've carried you this far because you've helped me while I'm in this mess. It's hurtful you think I'd do something behind your back like that."

"Lightning, you ain't carried me anywhere except to a place that could get me killed or put in prison."

He slammed down his hand, pushed back from the table, and stomped out the back door.

I walked down to the road, stood, and gazed out at the woods. Clemmy was right saying this would never have happened if Grandma were here. Maybe I should just stop this whole thing. I stewed about it all afternoon, but in the end, figured I was in too deep to quit now.

After dark, I pulled the truck down to the tobacco barn. We packed the mason jars in the bed and covered them with a tarp. At nine thirty, I laid my hand on Fancy's shoulder. "Why don't you stay here?"

She pushed my hand off. "I'm riding with you." She got in the truck.

Lightning shrugged and got in beside her.

"If anything messes up, stay in the truck. I don't want you in the way or getting hurt."

"If I need advice, my momma lives up the road," she snapped. We were all uptight.

Fifteen minutes later, we were crossing the highway bridge. I spotted the cutoff between some chest-high bulrushes leading down to the water. The rear tires bounced hard when I turned off the paved road. "Easy, Junebug, don't break the jars," Lightning said. Thick fog rolled up from the creek, making the bare limbs on the trees along the bank look like black witch's arms.

Twin stood beside a long dark Cadillac, smoking a cigar. I drove around him and pointed the nose of the truck back toward the main road, leaving about twenty yards between us. His Cadillac idled and its lights were on. I set the hand brake, put the truck in Neutral, and left it running. "Wonder where the other one is?" It felt like a belt was cinched across my chest.

Lightning craned his neck both ways. "Maybe he didn't come." He got out.

I eased open the door, pulled the shotgun from behind the seat, and rested it in the crook of my arm. The other man was here somewhere; Twin wouldn't have come without him. I stopped at the rear fender, close enough to hear and watch.

Twin puffed on his cigar and I could smell the marijuana. "About to give you boys up. Dark out here in the sticks."

"No way we'd stand you up, nothing to worry over. You by yourself?" Lightning asked Twin.

It was dark as pitch every place the headlights on his car and my truck didn't touch. "You be careful, Lightning."

"Don't see anybody else, do you? You got the stuff?"

"Yep. You got your part?"

Twin reached in the back door of the Caddy and pulled out two grocery bags. He handed them to Lightning. "You want to count it?"

"Nah, I trust you."

"I don't." I stepped away from the truck and made sure Twin could see the shotgun.

"Well, if it ain't John Dillinger Jr. Sure you can count that high, boy?"

"She can." I nodded to Fancy in the cab of the truck. Lightning handed me the two paper sacks, and I pushed them inside, whispering to her, "Don't worry about counting, just make sure ain't nothing in there but money."

Fancy nodded.

"You want to count yours?" I asked Twin.

He yanked the tarp, turned a flashlight on the jars, and fingered each one. "Seems to be right, but if it's not, I'll be coming to visit you. You boys want to help me?"

Lightning let down the tailgate. He and Twin started carrying jars. I stayed put, not willing to lay down the gun, keeping an eye on the edge of the tree line. The rank smell of stale creek water drifted on the clammy breeze. It took a good twenty minutes to transfer the jars. Twin pulled a quilt from the backseat and covered them before he slammed the trunk shut. "Your little chocolate sugar through counting?"

I backed up to the window. Fancy nodded. "Yep, guess we need to get moving." All we had to do was leave.

Twin pitched the stub of his cigar and reached inside his coat pocket. "Pleasure doing business with you boys. How about a cigar to celebrate?" When his hand came out, he was holding a pistol.

I knew Lightning was a dead man. "Watch out!"

Lightning dived to the ground. Twin's first shot missed me and went through the back window of the cab. Fancy screamed. The next bullet kicked up mud near where Lightning crawled like a cockroach. "Help me, Junebug!"

I fired at Twin and missed, pumped in another shell and hit him in the left arm before he could duck behind the Cadillac. He ripped off pistol shots that went over my head or into the tailgate. His man came running out of the fog near the creek. Bullets were flying, Lightning was yelling and clawing the mud, and Fancy was hollering my name. I ducked down, put my hand over one ear, and slammed the other ear into the fender. The noise was overpowering. "I told you, Lightning, you stupid bastard," I yelled.

When I came up again, the second man had almost reached Twin. I heard Twin, "Kill that bastard!" The man changed directions, running straight at me. I propped the shotgun barrel on the fender, and the double-ought buckshot caught him full in the face. He went down, clawing at his head.

Twin growled like a dog. His left arm hung limp as he came

toward the truck. Spurts of flame leaped from his right hand as fast as he could pull the trigger. I ducked, but one of his bullets slammed off the fender and I felt a sharp pain in my head. I chambered another round, edged low around the tailgate, and knocked him backward with a round to the chest. Suddenly everything went still.

A song played softly on the truck radio, Marty Robbins singing something about having the blues. Lightning was whimpering and Fancy was crying. I jerked open the truck door. Fancy lay crumpled on the seat, holding her shoulder. Blood was everywhere. "Fancy! Where are you hurt?"

She opened her eyes, moved her hand, and showed me the bloody hole. "Junebug, help me. It hurts awful bad." She fainted.

I went behind the truck and dragged Lightning up by the collar. "Are you shot?"

He grabbed my shoulder for support. "I thought I was a dead man, Junebug."

"You should be, I ought to kill you myself. Get in the truck. We got to help your sister."

"Your head's bleeding," said Lightning.

"I'll deal with it when we get home."

He looked back. "What about them?"

"I'll take care of that, you just do something for your sister for once in your sorry-ass life." I took off my shirt. "Hold this tight to where she's bleeding."

I went back to where the bodies lay while my head throbbed like a drum. I had to stop and squat down for a minute to let my vision clear. When I reached Twin's man whom I'd shot in the face, he had no pulse. I reached Twin and knelt down. The throbbing had turned to pounding. Twin raised his big hand and gripped my ankle. "You got to help me." Blood soaked the front of his shirt. His head fell back, his eyes closed, and he went silent.

"Are you dead?" I waited. When he didn't say anything, I tapped his face with the toe of my shoe. "I said, are you dead?"

Twin's fat tongue rolled out of his mouth. "No." His voice

sounded like something was choking him. I stood up and looked around, trying to figure out what to do. If I left him and he lived it would be a death sentence for all of us; there would be nowhere we could run.

"You bastard, why couldn't you just do the deal like we agreed? Now I got to kill you." It was different standing over a live helpless man; this way seemed more like cold-blooded murder. The Bible says, "Thou shalt not kill." I'd already broken that commandment and was getting ready to add some baggage for my trip to hell. Sweat ran down my face. I shifted my weight from one foot to the other. I could hear Fancy crying in the truck. I needed to get her some help.

With the amount of blood soaking Twin's chest, I didn't see any way he would live. But could I risk it? I looked down and Twin opened his eyes again. He lifted his head and tried to spit at me, but only succeeded in dribbling mucus and blood on his chin. "You ain't got the guts, White Boy."

I pulled the trigger of the shotgun again.

Twin's head blew apart and the strong iron smell of blood made my nose burn. Wind off the water brought the heavy sour stink of creek mud. I sucked air into my lungs to keep from vomiting.

At the truck I laid the shotgun in the bed, then bent over and pressed my head against the coolness of the fender, trying to think of anything that would show we'd been here. I couldn't. I got under the steering wheel.

Lightning leaned around Fancy and looked over at me. "You want to get the dope back?"

I grabbed his throat, slamming his head back against the passenger window. "Say one more word and I'll leave your stupid ass lying here with them." I took off, sliding and spinning wheels on the slick ground before hitting pavement. In a few minutes, we were at the house.

"Help me carry her to the bed." Fancy moaned with every step. We struggled to the bedroom. I handed Lightning a clean towel. "Keep that pressed down hard until I get back."

CHAPTER 35

I drove the truck down near the tobacco barn and parked it where it would be out of sight, then rushed up the path as fast as I could manage in the dark. At the clover field, clouds blocked the moon. I ran to the side of Fancy's house and tapped loud on the window.

Roy pushed up the sash. "What's wrong, Junebug?"

"Fancy's hurt bad. We need Clemmy to bring her medicine." Clemmy appeared beside Roy. "What happened?"

"I'll explain later. Come as fast as you can. I'll meet you there."

They came in the back door just a few minutes after I did. "She's in Grandma's bedroom."

Clemmy flew in. When she saw Fancy, she yelled out, "Fancy! Fancy, what happened to you?" Blood covered one side of Fancy's face, still wet in her hair, and soaked the front of her dress. "I been shot, Momma," she whimpered.

Roy stood at the foot of the bed, his face twisted in a fierceness I'd never seen. "Who the hell did this? I warned you about what could happen, Junebug." He wanted to hurt somebody real bad, and I figured it was me. "Lightning! Boy, bring your ass in here."

Clemmy got hold of herself. "Don't you come in here now," she called out to Lightning. "And you get out, Roy, so I can find how bad she's hurt." She tore Fancy's dress back to expose the wound. "Junebug, bring me a sheet and heat up plenty of water."

"Yes, ma'am." I got a clean sheet from the closet. When I crossed the living room, Roy and Lightning were sitting nose to nose. Lightning looked at me like he needed some help. I hoped his daddy would beat the shit out of him and save me the trouble.

I put a cast-iron pot of water on the stove to boil. When it started to bubble, I dipped a pan full and carried it to the bedroom. Clemmy had cut strips out of the sheet. She laid her palm on Fancy's cheek. "I need to see if the bullet's stuck in you. It's going to hurt, but it'll only last a minute." As easy as possible, we rolled her to one side. Fancy moaned and cried.

Clemmy looked closely at the wound. She let out a breath and wiped her forehead. "It's good, Junebug, the bullet went all the way through." She washed blood from Fancy's face and neck. "I don't see she's hurt anywhere else."

"Am I going to die, Momma?"

"No, my sweet baby, I'll see to it." She went to work cleaning the wound with the hot water. The damage was in the meaty part above her armpit and below the shoulder. "The bullet didn't hit any bone." Clemmy talked to Fancy in a reassuring voice. Of course, after all that soothing talk Grandma's doctor did, she still died.

Clemmy got a dark bottle from her bag. "Fancy, this Mercurochrome is going to burn." She coated the red, torn flesh with the liquid, then topped it with salve and made a bandage around the shoulder. "Junebug, get me some vinegar and baking soda."

Clemmy mixed them together and held it to Fancy's lips for her to drink. Grandma had used the same remedy when one of us was hurting. Next she reached in her cloth sack for a bottle of paregoric and a small bag of white powder. "This white dirt will help absorb any poisons and keep her from being sick or having diarrhea." We leaned Fancy up enough not to choke while she swallowed. After several minutes she started to close her eyes. Clemmy covered her good. "That's all we can do for now. Let her sleep."

In the living room, Clemmy and me pulled up two rocking chairs and Roy moved to sit on the couch next to Lightning. The two of them stared at Lightning and me, the only sound coming from the clock on the mantel. Every muscle in Roy's neck and arms bulged. I wouldn't have been surprised to see steam when he opened his mouth. "Tell your momma what you been telling me, Lightning."

Lightning cut his eyes in my direction. "Junebug took me to Durham a few times, and I stayed with Aunt Pearl. I got to messing around with this girl, and her boyfriend didn't like it."

I came partway out of the chair. "Shut up! Ain't going to be no more lying around here!" I should have killed him at the creek. "Tell 'em."

Roy came off the couch, fist clenched. Lightning put up his hands in defense.

"Sit down!" Clemmy pushed Roy back. "Sit down! Everybody stop!" She waited while Roy sat. Lightning put his head in his hands. "Tell us what happened, Junebug. I want the straight truth."

I told the whole story, except I didn't mention we took the money, just that they tried to rob and kill us. If Lightning wanted to tell about the money, let him do it.

"How the hell would two idiots like you even know where to get that stuff?" Roy grabbed Lightning by the neck of his shirt and yanked him. "You better answer me, boy, or you'll wish you were laying dead up there with them other niggers."

Lightning grabbed Roy's wrist, eyes on fire. "Why you jumping all over me? Junebug was there just like I was! Why ain't you grabbing him? Or are you so used to kissing white folks' ass, you ain't got the guts?" He got to his feet. I slid my chair to be out of the way.

Clemmy forced herself between them, staring down Lightning. "Boy, you better not raise your hand to your daddy." She looked at her husband. "Roy, just stop and let them tell us." Lightning sat back on the couch. Clemmy pointed at him. "Start talking."

Lightning sulked at first, but then slowly admitted how he brought the seeds from Georgia, and had talked me into planting a crop. "I never thought it would turn out like this, I swear I didn't."

"Lightning, you've always thought somebody owed you something, that there must be an easy way to fill your pockets. Now look at you. You're probably going to prison, if you don't get hung from a tree. I'm regretting you ever came back," Roy said.

Lightning looked like he'd been whipped with a knotted rope.

Clemmy sat with her head in her hands. "Them folks you shot, are they still laying dead up there?" She looked up at me.

I nodded. "This stuff is way over my head. I don't know what to do."

Roy shook a finger in my face. "What you're going to do is not one damn thing but keep your mouth shut. If there ain't nothing to tie you to them, I can't see how anybody would have any idea who did it. If they find out, they might arrest you, Junebug, but Lightning wouldn't live to get to the courthouse."

"You think Fancy needs to go to a hospital?" I asked Clemmy.

She shook her head. "I'll come down here every night to clean and rebandage her shoulder. If she does turn bad off, we won't have a choice."

Lightning had not mentioned the money. "You got anything else to put in?" I asked him.

When he lifted his head, his eyes were deep black, lifeless, and scary. "Don't guess so."

An awkward silence fell over the room. These old walls had heard a lot of stories over the years, but I guessed none as wild as this one. Clemmy looked up. "It's three o'clock. Roy, you go back to the house. I'll stay here with Fancy and be home before sunup. What are we going to tell Mr. and Mrs. Wilson if they get to asking about Fancy?"

Roy rubbed his hand back and forth over the top of his head. "We'll say she's gone to visit your sister in Fuquay, that your sister's sick and Fancy's going to stay with her until she gets better. How long you figure it'll take her to get well?"

"At least a month, maybe more. I can make up the cleaning Fancy's been helping with at the big house." Clemmy closed her eyes. "We'll go on like nothing has happened, and pray she don't get an infection. You keep her out of sight, Junebug."

Roy stood to leave and I walked him to the back door. "Junebug, I can't believe you let yourself and Lightning get mixed up in such shit."

I let out a breath. "You're right, Roy, you're absolutely right." What I didn't say to him was that the only reason Lightning was still alive was because Fancy was. She was the only thing that mattered to me, and I would not have hesitated to kill Lightning and leave him in the mud with Twin.

"Come here, Junebug. Let me put something on that cut." Clemmy wiped the blood and dabbed on some salve. "That should do it. I'll sit with her. You boys get some rest."

Lightning went to the bedroom and I stretched out on the couch. "*Why?*" kept circling in my mind. Why did I need to kill Twin like that? I could have done something other than blowing his brains out, maybe used my shirt and smothered him, or dragged him to the lake, dumped him in, and let God decide how he died.

But there was something else, something hard to admit. When I crooked my finger around that trigger, it was as if a voice began to whisper in my head, "*Go ahead and shoot him, he deserves it, see what it feels like.*"

CHAPTER 36

Clemmy left before daybreak. Fancy seemed to be sleeping evenly, not wheezing the way Grandma had. I sat in a chair and laid my head beside her arm, dozing. I saw Twin's head blown to pieces and myself running around to pick up the parts, trying to put them back together. Then Grandma showed up, asking me if I was getting too hot plowing the garden.

Lightning walking around in the living room woke me. He poked his head in the door. "How's she doing?"

"Still sleeping."

"Want me to make some breakfast?" He was calm, even friendly-sounding.

"Maybe fix coffee and we can put in a lot of sugar and milk and try to get her to sip a little."

Fancy groaned and shifted. Her eyes blinked a few times. She searched the room, trying to get a fix on where she was.

"Hey, Fancy, how you feeling?" Her hair was still matted and pasted to her head. There was no brightness in her eyes.

She winced from the pain when she tried to move. "You all right?"

I rubbed her arm. "I'm okay."

She moved her left hand to the bandaged shoulder. "Guess it wasn't a dream, huh?"

"No, but you're going to be fine. Your momma patched you up real good."

She gripped my fingers and closed her eyes. "I love you, Junebug."

My breath caught halfway down my throat. I'd thought it, felt it, even dreamed it. I squeezed Fancy's hand. We'd crossed every line but that one, and at this moment I wanted to say it back, even formed the words in my mouth, but it scared me. When I was little, Momma would say, "Keep your dreams to yourself, Junebug, 'cause if you tell them they might not come true." What a horrible thing to tell a kid. I had loved her, Grandma, Granddaddy, Grady, and each time I wanted to tell them I stopped, but they died anyway. Afterward I wished I had. "Think you're able to drink a little coffee?"

She shifted again. "Maybe." Fat tears ran down her cheeks.

"Just rest easy. You're going to have some pain, but it'll go away in time. Stay still and I'll be right back."

"Is Lightning okay?"

"He's fine."

I blew on the coffee to cool it, and Fancy took small sips. I mixed the vinegar and soda, got her to drink that, and then poured tonic in a spoon. "Take this medicine and you can sleep as much as you want." In a few minutes she was breathing heavy.

I went back to where Lightning sat at the kitchen table. "You stay with her while I go clean the blood out of the truck and see what I can do with the rest."

When I started for the back door, I could feel Lightning's eyes on my back. "What'd you do with the money?"

I ran my fingers through my hair, pulling until it hurt, and turned around. "It's put up right now."

"I never thought things would happen that way, Junebug, you got to believe me." He put on a face like a scolded puppy, but his eyes were as blank as a clean blackboard.

"What I believe is this was exactly what I told you might happen." I slammed my hand down on the kitchen table. Dishes and cups bounced to the floor. "Your sister is lucky to be alive and so are we. And what do you think we're going to do if the sheriff finds out we were involved? Instead of the money, you better be concerned how a noose is going to feel around your neck when they swing your ass off a tree limb."

Lightning recoiled and a flash of fear replaced the coldness. "It's not like that, Junebug."

I held my hand up. "I don't want to hear anymore, Lightning. Let it lay." I forced myself to calm down. "I'll be back in a little while. You look after your sister."

I found another sheet, got some bleach and lye soap from the pantry, and carried them and a bucket of water to the truck. In the light of day it looked worse than I thought. Fancy's blood was splattered on the paper bags and cloth seats, glass was everywhere, several holes were in the tailgate, the back window was broken, and the windshield had red smears. Stuck in the dashboard was the stub of the bullet that must have gone through Fancy. I dropped the bloody sacks of money in the barrel in the pack house cellar, and scrubbed most of two hours to get the inside of the cab reasonably clean. By the time I finished, the five-gallon bucket of water had turned red. I would never get all the blood out of the old seats, but they were dark from dirt and age anyway, so the stains should blend in and not be noticeable. The windshield and vinyl cleaned up easily.

I walked around the outside of the truck trying to figure a way to somehow try and cover the bullet holes in the tailgate. Since they were pretty close together, a sledgehammer we kept for splitting wood might do the trick. A few swings with the heavy maul meshed them into one big dent. With a couple more whacks, it was hard to tell where the bullets had hit. At the feed barn was a five-gallon bucket of silver-gray paint Granddaddy kept to coat the tin roof of the house. I soaked the sheet in the thick liquid and wiped the tailgate real heavy, making it appear to have been bumped hard and the paint was to keep it from rusting. There was no disguising the broken back window, so I knocked out the glass and used plastic and black tape to seal it until I could get it fixed.

I surveyed my handiwork. It looked like shit. I cussed myself out, then got a wrench and just unbolted the tailgate and hid it under the woodshed. I slid down in the grass and leaned against the rear wheel, tired enough to pass out.

When I went back into the house, Lightning was sitting with Fancy.

"She wake up anymore?" I asked.

"Ain't moved since you left. You didn't give her too much medicine, did you?"

"Same as your momma gave last night." I listened to her breathing and put my hand to Fancy's head like I'd seen her do to Grandma. Everything seemed okay. We went to the living room and sat down.

"Lightning, nobody else in Durham knows about us and would come looking, is there?" I was so exhausted I had to hold my face in my hands and look through my fingers.

He studied the ceiling for a minute. "Can't think of anybody. The only time I spent around Twin was at his house, and the only person I ever seen with him was the one at the creek. I know I can't show my face in Durham anymore. He's bound to have friends."

I pulled my hands down, staring at him. "You just said nobody had ever seen you but them."

Lightning looked irritated. "That don't mean he didn't tell somebody."

"Shit. You think they would have any idea how to find you?"

"The folks who know Aunt Pearl would know my name, and if she was scared enough, she might tell them where Momma and Daddy live."

"Then we need to warn them."

Lightning shook his head. "Even if they did find out about

me, it would take a lot to be riding down here making any trouble. All coloreds know that Chatham County is Klan country."

I thought for a minute. "That makes sense. All we can do is make sure not to put our heads above ground. Christmas will be here in another month, and folks will have their minds on other things."

CHAPTER 37

Fancy began to rest a little better, less fits and starts, and stay awake longer over the next few days. Clemmy told me to ease back on the paregoric. Sometimes she would dream and holler out, but as soon as I touched her, she calmed down.

The following Sunday, not wanting to prompt any unwanted visits from Mr. and Mrs. Wilson, I went to church. When the service ended, I walked out with them. Mr. Wilson put his hand against my chest to slow down and let Mrs. Wilson go on ahead. "You hear about the nigger killings up by the creek?"

I stuck my hands inside my pockets. "Killings? What happened?"

"Nobody rightly knows for sure. Bull Jones told Frank May it looked like a nigger drug deal that broke out in a gunfight. Two were lying dead beside a Cadillac, and the car had a trunk full of something called marywanna. You ever heard tell of it before?"

We reached his truck. "Can't say as I have. What is it?"

"Bull told Frank it's dope niggers use. When they smoke it, makes 'em go wild. Bull said what didn't make sense was whoever killed them left all the drugs. At first he thought it might have been somebody in the community, but nobody is taking credit for it."

I leaned my butt against the front fender. "Dang." Maybe we should have thrown the marijuana in the creek. "They have any idea who killed them?"

"Bull figures other niggers; said he weren't going to worry over it too much."

"That's crazy stuff." I started to walk off.

"You ain't seen nothing of Lightning, have you?"

I turned around. "Haven't seen too much of anybody here lately."

At home, I was surprised to find Clemmy in the kitchen setting out dinner. "I fixed enough for y'all this morning. Thought you needed a decent meal."

"Appreciate it. It's for sure neither one of us can cook worth a dang." I took a chair opposite Lightning. "How do you think Fancy is doing?"

"So far, so good. I'm going to chop up a little bit of these potatoes and greens and try to get her to eat something solid. She needs to get her bowels moving so we're sure everything is working proper." Clemmy went in with Fancy and shut the door.

I watched Lightning while I chewed on a chicken leg. "Talked to Mr. Wilson after church this morning. He told me the sheriff found Twin and his man."

Lightning kept his head down. "Yeah, what'd he have to say?"

I gnawed slowly on the gristle of the leg bone, wanting him to feel as uncomfortable as possible. "Mr. Wilson said he didn't think Bull Jones was going to waste a lot of time on it, but he sure would like to find you."

Lightning wouldn't look up; he pushed the food around on his plate. "That so?"

I scooped up the rest of the peas with my spoon, enjoying twisting the knife in Lightning's gut.

* * *

On Tuesday, I was busy splitting kindling in the woodshed when Bull Jones drove in the yard. "Morning, Junebug." He let go a mouthful of brown spit.

I squatted down eye-level with the letters CHATHAM COUNTY SHERIFF painted on the door. "Sheriff. What brings you out this way?"

"Hear about the killings over at Northeast Creek?"

"Mr. Wilson got to telling me about it Sunday."

He kept looking toward the stable and at the house. "You ain't seen nothing of Roy's boy, have you?"

"Nope." I stood up and leaned my hands against the top of the car. "You figure he might be mixed up in it?"

He pushed his hat back and scratched his head. "What I know is all of a sudden I got too many nigger problems, and I don't like it. Takes up time I need to be doing something else."

"If I see him, I'll sure get word to Mr. Wilson."

He laughed, spraying bits of tobacco juice. "If you see him, shoot the sumbitch and I'll come pick him up. By the way, you got a gun, don't you?"

"Yep."

"What kind?"

"Twelve-gauge my granddaddy left me." As far as I could remember, nobody had ever seen the twenty-gauge I got for Christmas when I was thirteen.

"That's right, long-barreled shotgun. I remember that thing; he sure won a lot of turkey shoots with it. If it wouldn't be too much trouble, go get it and let me look at it." Bull eyed me like he wanted to see what I might do, but maybe it was my imagination.

My bladder suddenly needed emptying. "No problem, be right back." I didn't over-hurry but didn't waste time either.

Lightning peeped around the door of the bedroom. "What's going on?"

"Squat down and slip out the back door. If he comes in the house, we're screwed."

I found Granddaddy's old gun. When I reached the car, Bull got out and looked it over, sighted, then broke the barrel down and sniffed. "Don't seem like you've used this much. Ain't been hunting lately?"

I stood back from him, arms clasped behind. "Never seem to have the time."

"That's a mighty fine shotgun. Don't see many with a barrel that long." He handed it back. "All right, Junebug. You got plenty of shells, don't you?"

"Couple of boxes."

He started backing the car out. "You take care now." I stood until he disappeared around the curve, then went onto the porch and kept watching.

"Junebug," Fancy called from the bedroom, "what did the sheriff want?"

I walked in beside her bed. "I took care of it."

She reached her hand out for me. "You're a good man for looking after me." She hadn't mentioned the love stuff anymore, so I'd put it off to the paregoric making her mind a little mixed up. But then maybe she hadn't said it again because I hadn't said it back. Now I didn't know any way to approach it without it sounding stupid. I needed to tell Fancy how much I loved her, because I surely did. "Fancy, I . . ."

She slid over in the bed. "Will you lay down with me?" I pulled off my shoes and stretched out beside her. Fancy turned on her good side and we lay nose to nose. "What were you going to say?"

"Just wondering if it would be okay if I slept in here with you tonight and got off that couch." What a chickenshit I was. My face warmed with flush.

"Sure you can." Fancy took my hand. "I want you to, been a while since I felt your body against mine."

"Ain't going to be none of that, there's no way you're up to it."

That night I lay awake a long time. I never wanted anything to come between Fancy and me, but sometimes I wished I'd never started down this road. Nothing seemed clear now. The one thing I'd never wanted to be was an embarrassment to Grandma. The image of a newspaper appeared in my head. It had a picture of me on the front page being led to jail in handcuffs. The headline read: "Local boy gone bad: dope dealer, murderer, and having relations with a Negro." So, yeah, right now I'd settle for normal again.

CHAPTER 38

Six weeks passed, and churchyard talk about the killings on Northeast Creek died down. Fancy's arm was stiff and sore, but seemed to get stronger every day. She began to ramble around the house, doing her best to fix meals for the three of us. Clemmy was worn out, her face sagged, she'd lost weight, and I was glad she could rest some now. It had gotten so each time she came to the house, she would give me a hug. I believed she understood I truly loved Fancy and would do whatever it took to protect her. Occasionally, I would catch Clemmy watching Lightning, like she was trying to recognize the child he used to be. Her eyes would turn soft, and her shoulders would sink.

The small house got to be suffocating, all of us under each other's armpit. I heard Lightning up some nights walking the floor or going out the back door. He'd asked me on two or three more occasions about the money, and I told him it was safe, that we needed to let more time pass, not be in a hurry. I assured him he would have his money after the first of the year. Roy and Clemmy being able to come visit some nights made being house-bound a little easier on him and me.

The week before Christmas, I drove to Apex to talk to Lawyer Stern.

"What's on your mind, Raeford?"

"Well, sir, I got to thinking. I'm the only one that's left of my family, and wondered what would happen to the farm should something happen to me?"

"Certainly hope nothing happens, but if it did and you didn't have a will, the state would step in and take control, probably sell everything off in an auction."

"Then I guess I'm needing to make a will."

"You got in mind who you want to leave it to? You have other family?"

"No more family, but I have somebody in mind."

"Who would that be?"

I leaned forward. "First, I want to be sure whatever you and me talk about is only between us."

He lifted his palms up and shook them. "Absolutely. It's called lawyer-client relationship, Raeford, and I can never repeat anything we discuss in private. It's a rule I take very seriously."

I studied his face, knowing I needed to trust him, but also knowing what could happen if I was wrong. "I want to leave everything to Fancy Stroud if I die."

"Stroud?" He scratched his head. "The only Strouds I know of are the coloreds who sharecrop with Clyde Wilson."

"That would be her."

He had a coughing spell, then pushed back in his chair and folded his hands over his stomach. "If you don't mind me asking, why?" He searched me with those Superman eyes that seemed to pick your brain.

"Fancy and me have been friends since we were little, and I consider her almost family. Don't intend to sell the place, but if something happened to me, I can't think of nobody better to have it."

He fidgeted with misgivings. "If that's what you want, I'm obligated to carry out your wishes. But keep in mind it can always be changed later. Say you get married and want to leave it to your wife and kids, you can do that."

"And I expect that's what I would do. But for right now, I'd rather leave it to who I want and know it would do them some good."

"Do you think your grandma would approve of this?"

"She ain't here."

He began making notes, holding the pen between his middle and ring finger. "Raeford, I wouldn't be letting your neighbors know anything about this."

We shook hands when he finished. "I appreciate your help."

Storefronts and lampposts on Main Street were decorated for the season, looked like the same stars and angels from last Christmas. Could it only have been a year ago I shopped for Grandma? Be nice to turn the clock back, just be a farm kid again. At the drugstore, I scanned the magazine rack and picked one that had a lot of what they called fashions. Inside I found a card to fill out so it would come every month to the house, giving Fancy something to read all year. I added a bottle of perfume for her, and aftershave for Lightning. I didn't buy any comics. At Salem's General Store I bought a grocery bag of fruit and different kinds of nuts, then checked the meat case and paid for a big beef roast.

Roy and Clemmy decided enough time had passed, and that it was safe to let Fancy come home for Christmas. Fancy cooked the roast the day before, and we had a little early celebration.

After supper, I walked her to the wood's edge. "Going to miss you," she said. "I'll be back the day after Christmas." I leaned against a pine tree at the wood's edge and watched Fancy cross the clearing. I dreaded spending the next couple of days alone with Lightning. We had settled into tolerance, avoiding each other as much as possible.

When I turned to head back, the hair at the nape of my neck stood up. I froze in place, then slowly rotated my head in both directions. Was somebody watching? The air became still, and ice cold. The presence of Grandma was overpowering, and it felt threatening. I talked out loud. "What's wrong, Grandma?"

I sensed violent pain. Did she want to hurt me? I stuck out my hand to push her back. Then, suddenly as she came, she was gone. I stood shivering in the dark blackness of the woods. Was she angry with me, or warning me?

I dreamed about Grandma that night. Every time I called out for her, Twin's face appeared, begging for help just before I killed him.

In the gray early morning light of Christmas Day, I went to the black iron pot behind the house, filled it with water, heaped wood around it, and lit a fire. At the chicken house I grabbed a hen by the legs, carried her to the block, brought down the hatchet, and watched her run with blood squirting from her neck. I still couldn't shake the image of Grandma.

"When you figuring on leaving?" Lightning and me were eating the chicken at dinner.

"Don't know, but it's going to be soon. It's time, Junebug."

I watched his expression. "Where you heading?"

Instead of looking at me, he acted interested in something out the back door. "Thought I might catch a bus and head west. I should have enough money to keep me going until I can land a job somewhere."

"Fancy will be mighty sad when you leave."

"I'll write when I get settled."

I poured the salty pot liquor from the collard greens into a cup and sipped. "I'll take you to the bus station when you're ready."

"Appreciate that."

Lightning seemed unusually nervous all day, but I put it off to not being able to see Roy and Clemmy for Christmas.

After tossing and turning and sleeping in fits and starts all night, I got up before dawn to pee. I got dressed and went outside to have a smoke since it was too early to do the chores. A ceiling of bright stars flickered like fireflies in the clear, cold night sky. Dark spots made a smile on the white moon's full face. I leaned against the pear tree and thought back to a time Granddaddy and me stood here taking a pee before we went to bed. I was about twelve years old. *"How many folks you figure have peed around this old tree?"* Granddaddy had looked down with a grin. *"I don't know, but you ain't ever seen me eat a pear, have you?"* I smiled thinking about when that happened. He always had a good sense of humor when you could get him to talk.

I followed the horizon around toward the faint glow to the west that was Durham, then glanced down toward the chicken house and pack house. My gaze moved to the woods beyond, then jerked back to the pack house. A light showed through the open door of the cellar. All the money I had was in there. I bent over and crept down the path, stopping every few steps to listen. At the edge of the building I squatted and put my head close to the bottom of the open door. Pots of flowers were pushed over on the floor. The dark figure holding the lantern turned toward me. I stood up. "Lightning, what the hell are you doing?"

He stumbled backward. "God damn, Junebug, you scared the shit out of me."

The bloodstained paper sacks I'd hidden in the barrel were in his hand. "You taking the money, Lightning?"

His voice dropped low, like the growl of a dog that's fixing to bite you. "It's to make sure I get far enough away so nobody would find me. I'm only taking what I figure is mine." He set the lantern on the floor.

"Why didn't you just ask?" I blocked the door. "And how do you figure all of it's yours?"

Orange light from the lantern reflected off his red shirt and made a cruel glow in his eyes. "I'm tired of asking white folks for stuff. If it wasn't for me, there wouldn't be any money."

Anger shot up quick. "And if it wasn't for me, you'd have been laying dead like the rest of them. You ain't taking what's mine and Fancy's."

He set the bags down. "How you intend to stop me? I don't see your shotgun." Lightning reached and I heard the click of his knife.

"So now you going to cut me?" I always carried the buck

knife Grandma gave me for Christmas. I stuck my hand in my pocket and closed my fingers around it.

"I told you, Junebug, I know I owe you some for letting me stay here. But I figure my sister for the money makes us even. Just back the hell off and let me leave in peace."

"She's not yours to give. You can go, Lightning, but you ain't taking our part of that money."

He stepped toward me. My buck knife made a sharp *pop* when it opened.

Lightning stopped.

My head started to throb. "You can take your part and leave."

There was a hateful sneer on his face. "You think you can hurt me, white boy? I done killed one man with this thing, and for a lot less money. I'll cut you up like a pork chop."

The cramped cellar space felt like a coffin. The damp dirt and old wood smell was what I figured it would be like buried in one. "So you did kill the old man on purpose."

He stepped toward me and took a swinging cut. "You bet your ass I did. And if I'd had time, I would have give his ugly-ass wife something to remember too." When I didn't move, he crouched, gripping the knife in his fist, the blade toward me.

I wanted this to stop. I held up my hand. "What the hell happened to you? We don't have to do this. We've been friends all our lives, no sense in ruining that over money."

"Friends?" He laughed loud. "We ain't never been friends, Junebug, or should I say Massa Hurley. You ain't no different than the rest of these white bastards around here, always acting like you're better than us. To make it worse, you take what little self-respect Momma and Daddy had left by screwing my sister. Why didn't you just spit in my face while you were at it?"

It felt like we were eight again, and his bottle bag was empty. "I never meant it like that, Lightning. If you feel that way, take my part and leave what belongs to Fancy."

"Oh, I'm going to take your part, Junebug, because you won't be needing it." Lightning charged. His blade came from low to high and ripped the bib part of my overalls, narrowly missing my chin. I slashed down and caught him across the forearm.

He grabbed at the pain. "Aaaah! You son of a bitch!" He lunged, snarling like a wild animal, slicing across, going for my neck.

I dodged left. The flash of the steel went by my face, the pointed tip nicking me below the eye. The force of his charge turned him sideways. I jabbed upward toward his chest, pulled back, and stabbed him again before he could recover.

Lightning fell against me and made a coughing sound. Blood spurted from his mouth, gushing onto my neck. The knife dropped from his hand and he latched on to my shoulder. The weight of his body pulled me over.

"Lightning?" I laid him down. My knife was stuck to the hilt just below his breastbone. I pushed on his chest like I'd seen the doctor do with Grandma, but blood mixed with air bubbled from his mouth. He wouldn't breathe any more. The last moment of shock was frozen on his face. "Lightning, what did you do?" I sat with his head in my lap until early light began to push away the darkness.

I had to figure out what to do. I considered going to get Fancy, Roy, and Clemmy, explain what happened, and let them decide. But I couldn't. They would never forgive me. No matter how disappointed or angry they were with him, he was their son and brother. I thought about digging a hole and burying him in the woods, but that would risk somebody finding him sometime. I couldn't chance that someone being Fancy.

I backed the truck up to the door, dragged Lightning's body from the cellar, shoved it into the bed, and drove to the front of the house. I scraped the grass off the boards and opened the top. He went into the well headfirst. The only sound was a dull heavy *thump* when he hit bottom. At the barn I got a fifty-pound bag of lime we kept for the garden and dumped it in behind him. After covering everything back, I stomped and pushed down until the outline of the boards disappeared. I squatted on one knee. "You always were a stupid bastard." I didn't know if I was talking to him or me.

I moved the truck back around to the pack house and found a rake to smooth the dirt in the cellar and cover the blood. Grandma's money was still buried, and I decided to leave it like that. I carried the drug money to the house, and hid it deep in Grandma's closet under some clothes. There was five thousand dollars buried in the cellar and another twenty thousand hidden in the house. By the time I finished, the sun was coming up. Bloodred strands of clouds, like stretched fingers of a wounded hand, extended across the eastern horizon.

I sat on the porch and tried to get myself under control, hoping to find somebody other than me to blame. I pounded my leg, pinched the skin on my arms, anything to bring me pain. Why didn't I let Lightning go, just let him take the money and the evil attached to it, and get the hell out of my life? He was certainly more valuable than money to Fancy and Roy and Clemmy. Why wasn't he more valuable to me? I remembered as little kids how he taught me to curve a rock and took me as his friend. He was a value to me then. Maybe the Coke bottle incident should have been my first clue.

I know he changed while he was gone, but was I any better? After killing three men, including my childhood best friend, I was pretty sure I wasn't. Pain began to shoot up my arms, and I looked down to realize my fists were gripped together so tight my palms were turning blue. I shook them out, and struggled to calm down so I could think like a God-fearing man. I never set out to hurt anybody; all I did was protect my life. That was bound to hold reason; didn't David kill Goliath, and doesn't good always win over evil? Wasn't I a good person?

Morning birds began to sing to give thanks for making it through the darkness. I remembered one summer when times were really bad, no rain for over a month, crops burning up in the fields and the garden beginning to die, all pointing toward a lean, tough winter. I heard Granddaddy get up in the early dark one morning and found him in the yard. "Why you sitting out here in the grass?"

He put his arm around me and pulled me to sit close. "Waiting to catch first light, son. A new day brings new hope. If the good Lord can lift that sun up this morning, surely we can do better today than we did yesterday."

The sun did come up that morning, and that afternoon I'll be damned if it didn't start to rain, and it rained two days straight. So, on this morning I determined I'd try to make it through this darkness.

When Fancy hadn't shown up by eleven that night, I was relieved not to have to face her. Eventually I slept, and dreamed. Lightning laughed at me from a pool of hellfire. Blood spurted from his chest, and it choked in my mouth and throat.

Whatever hopes I'd had about living a normal life were gone. My suitcase had been stuffed with all manner of things I would never be able to unpack again: the innocence of being a kid, the security of believing I knew what was going to happen next in my life, and the notion that everything would always work out for the best.

CHAPTER 39

At sundown I went to do the evening chores. I got back to the house and Fancy was in the kitchen. "When did you get here?" Pots were sitting on the stove.

She poked her head from behind the icebox door, a smile on her face. "A few minutes ago. Saw you down by the barn, so figured to start a little supper. Where's Lightning?" She came over to kiss me on the cheek.

I had to get this right. "He's gone."

Her smile disappeared. "Where did he go?"

"Said yesterday he was ready to leave, wanted to head west, get as far away from here as possible."

Her face clouded like a thunderstorm. She turned her back to me, and started chopping turnips, punishing them with the blade. She stopped and twisted around, the knife in her hand. "How did he go?" The muscles in her face twitched.

I forced myself not to look away. "I drove him to the bus station."

She jabbed the air with the knife. "Did something happen, Junebug? Did y'all have another fight?" Her bottom lip quivered. "He couldn't wait and say good-bye to me and Momma and Daddy?"

"Nothing happened, Fancy. He waited last night, but when you didn't come, he decided it was time. I took him early this morning. He said to tell all of you he loved you and would write soon as he could."

"Did he take his money?" She spit out questions like darts. "Is our part safe? Or did we do all this for nothing?" She slammed the knife on the counter.

I flung my hat against the wall. "Quit acting like it's my fault. You know how anxious and nervous he'd gotten to be. I tried to convince him not to do it, but he didn't want to hear what I had to say." At least that part was true.

Fancy put her hand to her forehead and rubbed. "I knew I should have come yesterday, but my shoulder hurt something awful after all that hugging and carrying on Christmas Day. Momma gave me some medicine before supper last night, and the next thing I knew it was this afternoon."

"Lightning figured there was a reason." This was the path I'd chosen and would have to stick to. "Just so you understand, I'm glad he's gone, because one of us wasn't going to last much longer living like this."

She started slamming pots around. "Momma and Daddy will be so hurt." She was close to crying.

I got up and took her in my arms. "He was sorry not to be able to tell you 'bye."

Fancy squeezed tight to me. She looked up. "What happened to your cheek?"

I put a finger to the cut. "Caught an old nail at the barn."

"You need to put some Mercurochrome on it so it doesn't get infected." She got the bottle and dabbed it.

"Thanks," I said. "I'm real sorry about Lightning leaving the way he did. I didn't make him or cause it to happen. I want you to understand that." I touched my tongue to my finger to see if it was forked.

She leaned on the back of a kitchen chair, lowered her head, and sounded resigned. "It's not your fault, Junebug. I guess I shouldn't expect anything different from him."

That night in the bedroom, I lay awake until the sky began to lighten. How could I keep such a secret? When I was little and had to watch things between Momma and Daddy I didn't want to see, I'd retreat to the little room in my head, close the door, and never speak or think about what I knew again. Doing that didn't make anything different, but as long as I kept my mouth shut I could pretend.

The next morning, Fancy went home to break the news to her folks about Lightning. Roy and Clemmy walked back with her that night, and we sat in the living room. "Did Lightning say where he might head?" Clemmy asked.

"All he said was he was going west."

"Didn't you see his ticket?" Roy questioned.

"I don't know if he had one, at least I never saw it. I did wait and watch as the buses loaded, and saw Lightning get on one. I couldn't see the sign on the front that tells where it's headed, but I followed it a ways and it got on Highway 55 going west."

"Maybe he's going to California," said Fancy. "He was always talking about how things were better out there for colored folks."

I jumped right on that. "You know, Fancy, I bet you're right. He always was talking about seeing what it was like in California, live by the ocean. Lightning told me one time he'd seen pictures of it and the place looked like a whole other world from here."

CHAPTER 40

By spring Fancy's shoulder had pretty much healed, a scar the only physical reminder. In April we got the tobacco plants in the field and started on the garden. We planted squash on a sunny afternoon after a morning rain. The air was steamy as the sun sucked back moisture the clouds had dropped earlier in the day. I was bent over going down one row and Fancy walked the one beside me.

She rose up, swatting around her face. "Damn gnats! They're about to drive me crazy."

I didn't raise up, just kept walking. "Take off your britches."

Fancy spit out one that had gotten in her mouth. "What the heck are you talking about, Junebug?"

"If you take off your britches, they won't bother your face no more." She stood still for a minute, then hopped over the row and tried to tackle me. We rolled around laughing and throwing dirt clods at each other. I'd never been this happy. Our relationship had become as natural as sunrise.

Occasionally Lightning would show up in my dreams saying, "She's going to find you out." There were days I was barely able to get out of bed, not wanting to face the day, not feeling like doing anything but stare at nothing. Even when Fancy was around, I'd find myself watching her and the guilt over Lightning would make me want to go hide my face in shame. But eventually I would convince myself I hadn't had any other choice. If he'd killed me and couldn't persuade Fancy that blood was thicker than water, would he have killed her too? No, there was no other way it could have turned out. Now what I had to do was just keep putting one foot in front of the other until it passed.

Fancy and me had our seventeenth birthdays, hers in May, mine in June. In another year the rest of the world should consider us adults to do as we pleased. But that was bullshit. We would only ever be able to do as the community pleased.

"Junebug, I got to talk to you." Mr. Wilson cornered me one Sunday in the churchyard. He moved under a big oak and out of earshot of people passing by.

"Okay." I leaned against the tree.

He was swelled up like he was going to bust. "That nigger gal of Roy's, is she staying at your place all the time?" He started shaking his finger at my face. "I warned you about getting mixed up with her. Folks around the community are starting to talk, saying your grandma would be rolling over in her grave if she knew what you were doing."

If he touched me with that finger I'd leave his ass on the ground. "Why don't you tell me what I'm doing so I know what you're talking about, and you best be leaving Grandma out of it."

Veins in his neck bulged. "Folks think she's being a common whore."

I glanced at the sky. This was the day I knew might come. "Folks need to worry about their own business and leave mine alone."

He got a smirk on his face. "Junebug, my cousin's girl works in Apex at the courthouse. You know what she does?"

At that moment I knew exactly what she did. "Can't say as I do."

"She's in charge of recording deeds and wills and such; that give you some idea?"

I was sick of him. "Why don't you just make clear what you got to say?"

"Says she recorded a will for you; says you're leaving the farm to Fancy Stroud."

"How's it any of your business what I do with what's mine?"

"You're leaving the farm to a nigger? Boy, ain't ever going to be no niggers owning property in this community."

"Not that it's any of your business, but I'll tell you what I told the lawyer. I don't have any more family. If something happened to me, the state would sell my land at auction, so I'd just as soon leave it to somebody who deserved it. Fancy and me growed up together, and she's been there to help me all this time, and I'd want her to have it."

Mr. Wilson went from red to blue, like he was about to choke. "If you wanted to sell it, why didn't you come to me?"

"Don't want to sell it, ain't going to sell it. Mr. Stern told me it could be changed any time, like if I got married, and had some kids. Besides, why would I want to sell it to you?" I moved closer, forcing him to step back.

Mrs. Wilson started waving at him to come on. He turned toward her, then looked back. "I hope nothing happens to you, Junebug. Things might get ugly around here."

I spit on the ground at his feet. "Appreciate your concern." I hoped he could feel my eyes as he walked away. After that Sunday, I didn't have to worry about any more visits from Mr. Wilson to be neighborly.

When I got home, I sat Fancy down. "Mr. Wilson cornered me at church. Said the community suspects about you and me, and he was mad as hell."

"What did you say to him?"

"Told him what I did wasn't none of his or the community's business."

"Do you think he would kick Momma and Daddy off his

place?" Fancy covered her mouth. "What have we done, June-bug?"

"He didn't say it, but you should talk to them in case it happens."

"I got to go tell them. If he does, it will be all my fault, and I wouldn't blame them if they never wanted to see me again." She started to cry.

"Not your fault, mine. If it happens, they can come live with me until they figure out what to do."

Roy and Clemmy decided they would wait and see. All that happened was Roy got a good cussing from Mr. Wilson, but he didn't throw them out. It being tobacco season, I guess their cheap labor meant more to him than the way he felt about me. Or maybe he had something else in mind. I wouldn't let Fancy walk home by herself anymore.

I heard nothing else from Mr. Wilson over the next month, and neither did Roy. By the end of September, putting-in-tobacco season had come and gone. Roy and Clemmy had helped me when Mr. Wilson's work was caught up, but he piled on plenty of extra, so we had to work late in the afternoons and on Saturdays. I had to let one acre rot in the field because there just wasn't enough time to do it all.

It was October and my tobacco was cured and ready for market. Fancy was cooking supper. "Let's take a load to Durham tomorrow."

She grinned big. "Absolutely. I'm ready to get away from this place for a day. Maybe we could stop at a grocery store and get something different to eat for a change." It had been a tough season, and that night we went to bed early, excited for a day off. I was sleeping sound when Fancy shook me.

"Junebug! Junebug, get up. Somebody's outside."

I put on some pants and reached under the bed for the shotgun. I made my way to the back door and looked out. Immediately I saw the flames. "Fancy, get up! The pack house is burning!" I took off running.

At first I didn't notice the three pickup trucks at the edge of the yard. A group of men in white sheets stood beside them, watching my tobacco burn. One of them saw me coming. He raised a shotgun from under his sheet. "Stop right there, boy." The rest of them pulled their guns. I recognized the one talking from his size and the sound of his voice. It was Luther, the man with the KKK tattoo.

I screamed at him. "You going to let my house and barns burn too?"

"Rest easy, son," said Luther. "We're here to teach you a lesson, not kill you. Decent folks ain't going to tolerate you laying up with that nigger whore. You want to live amongst white folks, you're going to act like white folks. You need to get your mind straight."

I jacked a round into the gun. "You cross-eyed son of a bitch, how the hell do you think I can live with you burning my crop? I've never bothered one soul! All I've been trying to do is survive, and now you think you're going to run me off? I'd rather die right here."

"Well, that's what is fixing to happen if you don't put down the shotgun." I recognized Bull Jones's voice.

Fancy came running out the back door. "Junebug put the gun down." She got between them and me.

I kept yelling. "Shoot me, you chickenshit bastards. You're real brave hiding under your sheets."

Luther spoke again. "If any killing gets started, boy, she's going to be right after you."

"Let it go, Junebug, let it go," Fancy pleaded, tears running down her face. "Tobacco ain't worth dying for." She jerked the gun from me. "Come on." She grabbed my arm, trying to pull me.

"That's a right smart gal, boy. Let her get her ass back home where she belongs, and you start acting like you got some sense."

The bitter odor of burning tobacco settled over the yard, stinging my eyes. I studied every one of the men, settling on one standing in the back like he was hiding. The sheet couldn't disguise his potbelly.

"Go on in the house now." Luther motioned with his shotgun. I framed the picture in my brain before I walked away.

Fancy waited in the kitchen. She put her arms around me, and we stood that way until we heard the trucks crank up and leave. As soon as they rounded the curve, we ran for the pack house. The fire had charred most of the upper level, but the packed dirt and heavy timbers on the cellar ceiling had kept the fire from burning through. I hoped I had time to get to the jars that were buried in the dirt. There was no choice except to try. I crawled inside to stay close to the floor, Fancy right behind me. When I moved the barrel, I went to my knees, hands and fingernails raking into the dirt like a dog digging a hole. As the top of each jar showed, I handed it to Fancy and she tossed them through the door. Fortunately, since they'd been underground, the glass wasn't hot and hadn't broken. I counted as I dug, and when I got to the last one we crawled out, choking and coughing.

CHAPTER 41

We sat at the kitchen table, exhausted, soot smeared across our face and clothes. "I'm going to kill them, Fancy, every last one."

"No, you're not. This is my fault. I should have kept staying at home and nobody would have known."

I pounded my fist on the table. "It's nobody's fault except Mr. Wilson's; he's the one who turned them on us. That bastard caused this and he's going to pay."

Fancy's voice was resigned. "Just be glad they didn't decide to burn the whole place. There's no way to fight them."

"We worked hard for that tobacco, Fancy. They don't give a damn if we live or die."

She sat bent over, arms wrapped around her middle. "We got enough money to make it through the winter."

"And what, sit here while they burn us out again?" I felt like a snake full of chicken eggs that discovered the hole he crawled in was now too little to crawl back out. "How the hell do you live like this, Fancy?"

Fire shot from her eyes. "Junebug, one of these days black folk gonna get sick of this shit, and the blood's going to run the other way." She slammed the back door on the way out. I watched her walk in circles in the yard, talking to herself. In a few minutes, Fancy came back inside. "I'm going home, Junebug."

"You're going to leave me?"

"I ain't leaving you, Junebug. I love you, but I won't be responsible for something awful happening."

"I'm asking you not to." I reached for her hand.

She moved a step backward, her bottom lip trembling. "You'll find a white woman one of these days and make a life. These people won't ever let us live in peace."

"Look at me and say that's what you really want."

Her eyes were fixed with a stubbornness I'd seen before. "It's not what I want, but it's the way it's going to be."

I sat, not knowing what else to say. "I see. Well, guess you better get moving then."

She went out the back door and headed toward the woods. I grabbed an ax from the woodshed and headed behind her. Each time the sharp blade sliced a deep cut into a tree trunk, I imagined Mr. Wilson's neck.

The next two months were so sorry lonesome even I got sick of me. I began to prowl the night, sometimes sleeping next to a tree or waiting for the sun to come up before going home. On a night with a first moon, I walked through the woods, crossed the clover field, eased to the side of Mr. Wilson's house, and stood in the shadows outside his bedroom window. I watched him pull off his clothes and change to a nightshirt. I fingered the shotgun. It would be easy. I raised the gun to my shoulder. Just then, Mrs. Wilson walked into the room. She was the only reason he lived that night.

I put new tin on the tobacco barn roof even though it didn't need it. I pounded nails and worked out a plan to kill Bull Jones, Luther, and Mr. Wilson. At night I got out paper and a pencil and wrote down details, like who I should shoot first, then second. The problem was how to get them together in the same place at the same time. It got to be all I thought about.

In December I went to Apex to settle up with Lawyer Stern. I told him about Mr. Wilson's kinfolk telling him what was in my will. He got very angry.

"What's done is done," I said. "Just let it go." I didn't bring up the Klan, figuring he probably already knew.

Late in the afternoon on Christmas Eve, dark, heavy clouds scooted quickly from north to south, bringing a cold, stinging wind. I sat on the porch wondering if snow was coming. Out of the corner of my eye, I spotted Fancy come 'round the curve in the road. She walked slow, head down. A stab of pain went through my chest. I'd missed her so much.

I waited on the steps. When she got close, her face broke out in a big smile and her eyes glistened wet in the fading light. "Hey, Junebug."

"Hey, Fancy." When she got to me, I held out my hand. "Missed you awful bad."

She nestled into me. "Missed you too." She arched her head backward. "Do you care if I do something?"

"What?"

"Kiss you."

"I ain't had much practice lately."

She laughed. "Let's see if we can work on that." The kiss was long and warming. "Not bad for a redneck."

I put my lips to her ear, breathing in her scent. "I've been practicing on my hand."

She pushed my forehead back and play-slapped me. "I figured you were starving by now, so thought I'd fix you some supper. Come on." She started up the steps.

"I'm willing to do without the food."

Fancy stopped and put her hand on the back of my neck. "We got all night, Junebug, just you and me."

I sat at the kitchen table while Fancy cooked. "Had any trouble from the Wilsons?"

"Mostly tried to stay away from them as much as possible, but I let Mr. Wilson see me a lot, to know I'm at home."

"What are we going to do?"

Fancy didn't turn around. "Maybe we can talk after a while."

We finished supper and went to sit on the porch. Clouds hid the stars. When heavy drops of icy rain started to hit the tin roof, we went to bed. The lovemaking was wonderful, but had a desperate feeling to it.

Fancy lay under a heavy quilt; the only things visible were her big black eyes and her nose. The room was quiet except for the tap of raindrops. We lay still and listened.

She broke the silence. "I need to ask you a favor, Junebug."

"Whatever it is, I'll do it." I tried to move, but she held me in place with her arm.

"You need to hear it first."

I pulled loose. "Go ahead and say it."

She let out a deep breath. "I need you to let me go."

I was scared to ask. "Go where?"

"From here." Fancy sat up, back against the headboard, and covered herself with the sheet. "I can't take this life no more, Junebug. Living every day scared to do something that might piss off some white person, knowing there'll never be a way we can be together. I'd rather die than believe this is the way I'll spend the rest of my life."

I'd never heard Fancy in such pain. As bad as things had been for me, it was only a small part of what she had to go through. "Where will you go?"

"If you'll carry me to Durham, I'm going to take the bus to New York. Folks say coloreds can make out okay up north. I want to find a job and live like a real person."

"What kind of job?"

"Have to figure it out when I get there."

I stared at the ceiling, remembering how happy I'd been with the two of us working the farm, laughing and playing even when we were exhausted, daring to let myself daydream about a life together. "When you plan on leaving?"

"Day after tomorrow. That would give me Christmas with Momma and Daddy one last time for a while."

"That quick? You can't wait a little longer?"

"Momma's got some relatives in New York, and she already wrote a letter telling them to expect me. I'll stay with them until I can get on my feet."

The rain had quit, and the clouds lifted enough to let some light come through the windows. I concentrated on her face. What I saw was the skinny little eight-year-old girl who took my hand on that first day we met, the one who felt my hurt. "Fancy, as bad as I don't want you to go, I ain't going to be selfish enough to ask you not to."

She laid her forehead on mine. "I know you love me, Junebug. If the day ever comes when things change, I'll be right back here if you would still want me. Until then, we just have to know what we know, and hope."

CHAPTER 42

Fancy went home before daylight on Christmas morning. I pulled the drug money from the back of Grandma's closet and counted out Lightning's half, ten thousand dollars. As I stacked the money, I remembered the shock on his face in the pack house cellar, and the sound his body made when it hit the bottom of the well.

The money rightfully belonged to Fancy. She had paid a price for it, and it would give her a fighting chance. Still, it was painful knowing once she left I'd probably never see her again. I was the only thing I had left to lose.

It was pretty miserable sitting alone in the house all Christmas Day. Fancy came in the porch after dark, toting one suitcase that was tied together with tobacco twine. I lifted it onto the kitchen table. She ran her hand across the worn brown cloth. "Don't seem much to show for a life, does it, Junebug?" She grabbed around my waist. "What am I going to do without you?"

I held on to her. "You're going to get a chance to have a new life, Fancy, one you get to make for yourself. My granddaddy used to tell me, 'Don't stand in the back of the boat to see where you've been, stand in the front to decide where you're headed."

She searched my eyes. "Come with me, Junebug."

"I can't, Fancy, this place and this life is all I know." The real reason was fifty yards away and fifty feet down. "I can survive here, but don't know if I could there."

She laid her head against my chest. "I know."

That night we clung to each other. "Do you want me to stay, Junebug?"

"No." I sat up and looked her in the eyes, stroking the face I was going to miss terribly. "You remember those dreams you told me about that night at Mr. Wilson's?"

She rubbed at the wetness on her cheeks. "Yes."

"That's what I want you to think about, Fancy." As much as I was going to miss her, I refused to argue for her to stay because I knew she would if I asked. "You'll never find them here, and you'd never have a chance to chase them down with somebody like me holding you back."

With the morning came hard rain, sounding like a drummer gone mad on the tin roof. I slipped out of bed to fix breakfast. In a few minutes, Fancy walked in the kitchen, wearing a freshly ironed blue dress. "Morning," I said. I set the food on the table.

She came behind me and coiled her arms around my waist. "I'm scared."

"You'll handle whatever you need to, Fancy, just like you told me when Grandma died." I pulled out a chair for her. "Try to eat something." We pushed food around on the plates until I got up. "Wait here."

I came back with the money wrapped in a paper sack. I opened it and showed her. "This is so you can get on your feet. You keep some in your pocket, but the rest you hide."

"How much is it, Junebug?"

"Ten thousand dollars."

Her hand went to her mouth. "I'm not taking all that. What will you live on without money coming in?"

I wanted to tell Fancy what I'd done. Maybe someday I would. "It's my share plus yours. I ain't going to starve." I faked a grin. "Besides, if you make it big in New York, you can lend me some."

She came around the table, gripped my neck, and laid her face against my head. "Junebug, you're the best man I'll ever know."

I closed my eyes, ashamed.

The loneliest steps I'd ever walked was carrying her bag to the truck. Daylight forced its way through the heavy clouds, but it didn't stop the rain. The only sound on the ride to Durham was the slapping of windshield wipers. They sounded like a sad heartbeat. "Expect you'll have some wondrous things to see in New York."

"I won't know how to act around big-city folks." She pushed on her dress, drying her hands over and over. "What if I can't find a job?"

I reached across the suitcase to calm her bouncing knee. "You're a good person, Fancy. Folks will see that right off." She pulled my hand up and kissed the back of it.

The bus station was big and square, framed in dirty red brick. A streetlight on the corner was still burning because of the dark morning. Large glass panes across the front of the building had the blinds open to get what little light there was. The stink of diesel from the large buses was strong as they pulled onto the street, headed for some far-off place. My forearm dangled over the steering wheel. I laid my head against it, talking to the horn. "I can't go in with you, Fancy. I don't think I can watch you leave." I reached out and ran my fingers over her face, touching like a blind man.

"I'll always love you, Junebug, no matter what." She kissed me on the cheek, grabbed her suitcase, and pushed open the door. "You take care of yourself." She ran up the steps to the glass doors. I waited, but she didn't come back.

CHAPTER 43

It was the middle of January when a not very long letter came from Fancy.

> Dear Junebug:
> I arrived in New York safe and sound. I'm staying with Momma's cousin, and you can write me at this address. As soon as the weather lets up, I'm going to try and find a job. I've never seen such an amount of snow; it's piled up everywhere and freezing cold. I can hardly walk without slipping down. I miss you so much, it's hard to get through the days. It seems all I do is sit around and think about you. That's all for now. I'll write again soon and hope you will send me a letter.
> Love,
> Fancy

Reading her words made my heart hurt. The paper smelled flowery, and that night I stuck it under my pillow. From then on,

I got a letter about every other week to let me know how things were going, and I tried to send one right back.

The time to kill hogs came and went, but I'd had enough killing to last me a lifetime. If I wanted some meat, I'd buy it. When the weather warmed, farming work kept me busy most days. But a lot of the time, I sat on the porch staring into space, smoking and thinking about Fancy. They were some awful lonesome times. Once in a while Roy and Clemmy would walk down, and Clemmy would bring enough supper for all of us. We would sit on the porch and talk for an hour or two. They were a real comfort. Roy said Mr. Wilson had calmed down once he found out Fancy had moved to New York. Clemmy called Mr. Wilson a fat piece of shit, and we got a good laugh. Roy wondered why he hadn't heard from Lightning.

I got a letter in April from Fancy.

> *Dear Junebug:*
> *I finally got a job! I'm working for this lady who lives in a big fine apartment downtown. I take the bus every morning and spend the day cleaning the place, ironing, and fixing her supper. It was scary at first traveling on my own, afraid somebody would rob or hurt me, but it didn't take long to get used to it. The lady is paying me enough that I can afford to move into my own room at a boardinghouse not far from Momma's cousin. I can't wait. I haven't spent very much of the money you gave me and opened myself an account at the bank. There's so much to see in this city, and black folk are mostly friendly and watch out for each other. I'll send you the new address when I get moved in. I still love you more than anything and wish you were here with me.*
> *Love,*
> *Fancy*

She wasn't coming back; I could read the pleasure of living on her own. The first week of July, I got a late birthday card. It had a big heart on it and was signed *"Happy eighteen. Wish you were here. I love you, Fancy."* It felt as if she was getting farther and farther away.

Two mornings later I did my chores and headed to Durham, thinking I might try to find a job of some sort. I went to both of the big tobacco factories, Liggett-Myers and Lucky Strike, and filled out applications. They weren't hiring at the time but said they'd be in touch if something changed. Maybe I should have stayed in school like Grandma wanted. I sat waiting on a red light when my eye caught a blue and white sign on a corner building, MILITARY RECRUITING OFFICE. There was a big poster in the window, UNCLE SAM WANTS YOU! He was pointing his finger right at me. I had plenty of time to kill, so I pulled into a parking space at the curb in front, curious to see what the military was about. Inside was a long hallway and tables covered with magazines and pamphlets on the marines, army, navy, and air force. I picked out a few to take home.

A big man dressed in a tan uniform with red stripes on the sleeves stepped out of a nearby office. The sign over the door read UNITED STATES MARINE CORPS. "Can I help you, young fellow?"

"Reckon not, just looking."

He motioned with his arm. "Come on in and let's sit down a minute." He seemed friendly enough. The room was spare, with bright white walls and no leather chairs like Lawyer Stern's. He stretched out his hand. "Sergeant Howard."

"Raeford Hurley." It was like sticking my hand inside a ham. No use getting familiar with him by using my nickname. I studied the mountain of ribbons on his chest. He was a good cut of a man, strong cheekbones set high over a square jaw, broad across the shoulders, close-shaved, and had a clean smell about him.

"You live in Durham, Raeford?"

Sergeant Howard made me nervous. "Chatham County, near Apex." I felt a need to sit up straight.

"Live with your momma and daddy?"

"I stay by myself. All my folks are dead."

Sergeant Howard's eyebrows arched in surprise. "How come you to be living alone at your age?" He leaned forward when he talked, his dirt-brown eyes laying right into mine, like he expected an answer anytime he asked a question. I was sorta scared not to answer, and ended up telling him all about my family.

"You've had some troubles, that's for sure." His tone became friendlier. "I was freezing my ass off in Korea when I was your age. Intended to go home after that, but wasn't a lot to go home to, and I figured I was happier in the marine corps than I would be working some nine-to-five dead-end job."

I asked and he answered my questions about what war was like. He said no soldier liked killing other people but that was the job, and you had to be better at it than the other guy who was trying to kill you. Before I realized it, an hour had passed. "I got to get going, Sergeant Howard."

He walked me to the door. "If you want to talk some more, I'll be right here. We'd like to have you in our family if you think you might want to join up. From the way things sound, could do you some good."

"Appreciate it. Just might come back to see you," I said, not really believing I would.

On the ride home, I played around with a picture of myself in a marine uniform. At home I threw away the other magazines and read the marines ones from cover to cover. Late that afternoon, I walked down to the edge of the woods and sat. "Grandma, I feel like I'm truly lost right now. You said in the hospital that sometimes we got to take some new reins and head in a different direction. I believe it's time for me to do that. Hope you think it's all right."

Two days later, I was back in the recruiting office. Sergeant Howard and I got down to talking seriously about joining the marine corps. I had some questions. "How long is the boot camp?"

"Sixteen weeks, and I'll tell you right now, it'll be the hardest thing you've ever done for the first fifteen, and the greatest feeling of accomplishment you'll ever have in the sixteenth."

"You know I didn't graduate high school."

"Me either, but the marine corps taught me more than I could have ever learned in a book. You'll do fine; you've had a tough life and the corps will give you a family you'll have forever." Sergeant Howard had a way that made a person think he couldn't fail.

I stood up and shook hands with him. "I'll be back the first of August. That'll give me time to settle my affairs with the farm."

"You're making a good decision, Raeford."

I grinned like I'd been keeping a secret. "People call me Junebug."

Sergeant Howard squeezed my hand hard. "You keep it, but I prefer Raeford."

The first thing I did was write to Fancy.

> *Dear Fancy:*
>
> *I've got news. I'm joining the marine corps. Can you believe that? It's time for me to stop moping, and find some purpose that don't include grubbing dirt and sniffing mule shit. I just can't stand to stay around here anymore. I met a real nice sergeant at the recruiting office and agreed to join up. Guess I sort of feel like you did when you headed to New York, scared some but ready for a new life. I'll write you when I get to the boot camp in South Carolina. I'm going to see Mr. Wilson in the morning and ask if he will buy Sally Mule and the pigs. I'll give your daddy my truck. Think about me because I sure will you. We can still love each other no matter where we might be, so nothing will change that. Who knows, we might run across each other in one of those countries you always wanted to see.*
>
> *I love you,*
> *Junebug*

I went to visit Lawyer Stern and took a bag filled with all but two hundred dollars of my money. We talked about what I was intending to do. "They won't need to make a man out of you, Raeford, because you already are one. But it'll do you good to understand how the rest of the world lives."

"Yessir. It feels like time for me to take another path in my life. There's got to be more out there than what I've been living." He walked down to the bank with me to open a savings account.

The man at the bank counted out the money in the bag, and his desktop was full when he finished. "Where did all this cash come from, Mr. Hurley?" He looked at Mr. Stern.

"My grandma, granddaddy, and the ones before them saved up and buried it around the house. No disrespect, but Granddaddy used to say 'keep skunks and bankers at a distance'."

He laughed. On the banker's suggestion, I gave Lawyer Stern power of attorney so he would be able to get to the cash if need be.

We went back to Mr. Stern's office. "What about the farm, Raeford? You're eighteen now and can do whatever you want."

"I don't have any inclination to sell it. I agreed with Mr. Jackson to rent him the tobacco acreage, and told him to bring the money to you after he sold his crops. He promised me he would, and I had him sign this paper." I handed the envelope to Mr. Stern. "I'll make sure to write so you know where I'm at, and when it's time for taxes and such, you can draw out what you need to pay them, including your charges."

He stood up. "Good luck, Raeford. Take care of yourself. I'm proud of you for serving our country." He never had taken to calling me Junebug.

At home I walked around, wondering what the hell was keeping me here until August. The next afternoon I went to Sergeant Howard's office and signed the papers to enlist for three years. He told me to be in Raleigh the following Monday to have the physical and take the oath.

It galled me, but I went to see Mr. Wilson to tell him I was leaving and wanted to sell off the animals. He acted surprised about my decision, but I got the feeling he was relieved. "What about your truck?" he asked.

"Giving it to Roy." I walked out the door.

I stopped a few minutes at Roy and Clemmy's, told them my intentions, and let Roy know I was going to give him the truck. They were tickled to death about having a vehicle. "Clemmy, you and Roy and Fancy are the only family I got now. I want you to know how much I appreciate what you mean to me. If for any reason Mr. Wilson were to make you move, my house is there and you're welcome to live in it."

Roy got a little overcome, and turned his head. "I always said you was a good man, Junebug."

"And if anything was to happen to me, you get in touch with Lawyer Stern in Apex." They didn't need to know why.

That night I put extra ears of corn in Sally Mule's box. "Guess I'm going to be leaving you, girl." She batted the long lashes over her big, sorrowful-looking brown eyes. Gray was beginning to color her muzzle. "You've been a good friend. I wish I could just turn you out to pasture and let you loaf the rest of your life. If the bastard mistreats you, kick him in the nuts." I hugged her and gave her neck a good long rub. She bobbed her head up and down the side of my face. The next morning when Mr. Wilson and Roy came to get her, she watched me as they tied her to the truck.

On Sunday, I put all the tools in the feed barn to be out of the weather, cut off the propane, cleaned and unplugged the refrigerator. I went to the chicken house and opened the gate. "Watch out for the foxes, and run like hell." I clapped my hands to scatter them into the woods.

Monday morning I walked around in the yard, trying to plant every memory in my head, feeling like it might be a long time before I saw the place again. I pictured past days, the faces of Grandma and Granddaddy and my parents. I walked down by the well, and imagined my childhood friend's body in that deep, dark hole, remembering the fact that he and Fancy had taken me as a friend when I needed one the worst. I paid him back by not even giving him a decent burial.

I stood staring at a long sky, remembering the other secret I kept. I wasn't really sorry about killing Lightning or Twin. It was a dark place that I'd tried hard to ignore. I thought about the dream of God and the devil, and the devil screaming he was the God of Truth.

Roy pulled up right on time. "You sure you're ready for this, Junebug?" He put his arm across my shoulders. "You can change your mind, you know."

"It feels like the right thing to do, Roy." After an hour's drive and a couple of wrong turns, we found the three-story stone building in Raleigh. I grabbed the paper sack that had clean underwear, a razor, and a toothbrush, remembering what Fancy had said about not having much to show for a life.

PART 3

CHAPTER 44

Inside the building was a large open lobby. I could see a crowd of men down the way standing in one line or another, fat guys, skinny guys, black guys, white guys, a bit of everything. I gave my name and paperwork to an army lieutenant, and he directed me to the medical check line. The army, air force, and marine recruits all processed in the same place. We went behind a screen to undress, waited in line to drop our drawers, get our nuts checked, and make sure our feet weren't flat. At the end of the line, the doc asked if I was a homosexual. When I said no, he gave me a stamp of approval.

On Monday, July 20, 1965, I took the oath for the United States Marine Corps. A marine sergeant kept us in the room after the swearing-in. "You're about to get a chance to become part of the finest fighting force in the world, a brotherhood you'll treasure for the rest of your life. But you're going to have to earn it. When you get to Parris Island, listen, learn, and work your ass off. You won't know yourself in just a few weeks." We walked out of that room with a swelled chest and fire in our eyes. Late that afternoon, thirty of us loaded onto an old Greyhound bus bound for Parris Island, excited, looking forward to being marines. I felt tougher already.

We spent a long day inhaling diesel fumes, shooting the shit about where we were from and the latest rumors about the war. I'd read about Vietnam, not paying it much attention, but some of the guys seemed to be experts. The consensus was that marines would be invading the place any day now. I'd only ever seen one John Wayne movie and I looked forward to becoming the marine he was.

It was the middle of the night when the bus pulled up to a checkpoint in front of a sign that read: WELCOME TO PARRIS IS- LAND, WE MAKE MARINES. The bus was waved through and wound around the street, stopping in front of a set of buildings. A marine, wearing a single stripe over crossed rifles on his sleeves and a round, wide-brimmed hat, boarded. His face was thin, and the edges of his jawline looked like they could cut paper. His voice sounded like a bugle, deep, loud, and bouncing on the low notes.

"Listen up, you maggots. I am Drill Instructor Lance Corpo- ral Cook. From now on, understand your momma and daddy don't live here, and I'll personally kick the shit out of you any- time I feel like it. You will speak only when spoken to, move when I say so, and sleep when I say so. If you so much as act like you're stupid, I'll put a boot so far up your ass you'll shit leather for a week. When I ask a question, you answer with 'sir, yes sir.' Do you understand?"

Evidently the response wasn't loud enough for him. He grabbed the first guy in the front seat, dragged him up, and mashed their noses together. "Did you hear me, faggot?" He slammed his forehead into the recruit's. I was glad I'd decided to sit in the back.

The kid made a mistake. "Yes, sir."

The drill instructor screamed, "You fucking dipshit, what did I just tell you!" He yanked the recruit off the bus by his shirt collar. We heard more yelling outside, then the sound of a body being slammed against the side of the bus. The rest of us sat deathly silent. We all wanted to look but were afraid to. My asshole was drawn up so tight a crowbar couldn't pry it loose. I tried to figure my chances of getting out the back door of the bus and finding my way home.

The drill instructor guy got back on. "Anybody else not remember how I said to answer?"

A thirty-person cry went up. "Sir, no sir."

"Good, now get your asses off this bus, single file, and I better not hear a word. You understand me, maggots?"

"Sir, yes sir."

Such was my introduction into the corps. From there it got worse. I got to know the flavor of Lance Corporal Cook's toothpaste he was in my face so much, spit flying. Screw up and he didn't hesitate to kick you in the ass or punch you in the nuts. The physical training was hard, push-ups, pull-ups, over walls, under fences, all the while that bugle voice screaming in your ear.

But it worked. In three weeks, what started out as a bunch of dumb-ass, raggedy boys became a unit, a slick-marching group of men who began to accomplish things they had no idea they could, all with a common motivation—undying hatred for Lance Corporal Cook. If a man was fat, he slimmed down; if he was skinny, he bulked up; if he was weak, he got stronger. We learned to vent our frustrations in the training. Hand-to-hand combat classes got ugly.

I seemed to catch on pretty good, finding the most satisfaction on the shooting range. We learned to fire M-1 rifles, M-14's on full automatic, and to strip and reassemble them blindfolded. We learned to use mortars. The first time I fired a .50-caliber machine gun, I understood what true power over life and death felt like.

In our fifth week, a recruit killed himself by slicing his wrist with a razor one morning in the bathroom. The medics carried him out, and the rest of us weren't allowed time to be sorry about him. If anything, the instructors worked us harder.

The biggest emphasis in marine boot camp was on how to kill another man with whatever weapon you might have: a bayonet, a rifle, or your bare hands. My mind got conditioned to stay calm in the middle of chaos, and understand that a marine's job in combat was to protect his fellow marines first, and kill every son of a bitch trying to kill you. It was like I'd been born again; they tore me down and rebuilt me with discipline and structure, all the while instilling a sense of pride and a willingness to die for the marine corps.

I wrote Fancy around the middle of September.

> *Dear Fancy:*
> *Sorry I haven't written before now, but they have kept us going from sunup until sundown seven days a week. It's the toughest thing I've ever done by a long shot. The first two weeks were the worst, having somebody screaming in your face every time you moved, learning to march and the right way to eat your chow, that's what they call meals in here. Remember how I never liked a lot of rules? Well, that's out the window; took some doing to learn to eat somebody else's shit with both hands and like it, but it's not so bad now that I'm used to it. I did make expert on the shooting range, so I guess hunting squirrels and rabbits had some benefit. You won't believe it, but I've gained almost twenty pounds. At first I didn't think I'd make it, but I'm feeling good about it at this point. I'm proud of what the marine corps stands for and can't wait for graduation. I'll write again as soon as I get a chance. I hope you continue to like your job. I just hate you're still having to work for some white woman. I'd appreciate any mail you can send. It would make it not quite so lonesome.*
> *Love,*
> *Junebug*

At the end of sixteen weeks, all but twelve who started together marched in the graduation parade. Every chest stuck out, filled with the pride of being a part of something much bigger than ourselves. The day I pinned on the Eagle, Globe, and Anchor was the proudest day of my life. I watched as the other guys hugged, laughed, and took pictures with their families.

After graduation in December, most of our unit deployed to Camp Pendleton in California for jungle training to get in "Vietnam shape." It was no secret we were going. Soon. The surprise was there wasn't a jungle within a thousand miles of Camp Pendleton. The jungle training consisted of humping rolling, scrub-brush hills day after day for almost six months. Instructors taught us how to set up and detonate anti-personnel mines called "toe-poppers," and how to look for booby traps in the jungles. The rest, they told us, we'd learn on the job. At the end of May 1966, almost a thousand of us were transported to San Diego Naval Base and loaded on ships.

CHAPTER 45

The boat was nose to neck with marines, a few I knew, but the most I didn't. During the thirty-day trip, we were forced to sleep so close to each other you didn't dare move for fear the guy next to you would misinterpret it. It was nasty, hot, and miserable. There was nothing to do but sit around and tell lies or play cards. Plenty of fistfights broke out; nothing like a crowd of bad-tempered marines in a foul mood. It seemed every time the ship rolled, my stomach followed. I dirtied the ocean with vomit almost daily. Hell of a way to spend my nineteenth birthday.

When we waded ashore on the beaches of DaNang, Vietnam, the humidity was so thick it felt like walking through a jar of honey. The mob of us new boots were organized and moved onto the grounds of the air base. I recognized the froggy, deep-throated voices and figured this must be the place old drill instructors had gone to die. From the smell of the place, a lot of them must have been lying dead somewhere close by. I didn't see anybody who looked like John Wayne; not surprising, because back at Camp Pendleton, I'd read in a magazine he'd never served a single day in the military, much less the marine corps.

After being assigned to squads and platoons, we were shown to temporary barracks, instructed to get some rest and fall out with packs when the bugle blew at six the next morning. Nothing like a good night's sleep on wooden cots trying to breathe stifling air, waiting for your brain to catch up and realize it's not rolling on the waves anymore. We cussed the cruel bastards who built wooden hootches and topped them with tin roofs so we could be slow-roasted like hogs at a barbecue. The consensus was it had to be the Navy Seabees, and we vowed to kick the shit out of any navy puke we saw. Off in the distance, we could hear the sounds of artillery exploding and bombs dropping. I figured we'd be hearing them up close real soon.

The next morning we mustered, standing at attention in the unbelievable heat, smelling the overpowering stink of rotting fish and sewage. A lieutenant assured us he had the list of where each of us was headed, and we'd be departing that day or the next. When the lieutenant finished, a short, stocky gunny followed.

"My name is Gunnery Sergeant Phillips. Raise your hand if you qualified expert on the rifle range."

Nobody moved.

That upset the gunny just a bit. "Now, I know some of you dipshits qualified. Don't make me go to the trouble of looking up your records." He walked up and down the rows. "Do that and I'll find a nice hellhole deep in the jungle where you won't see daylight for the next year."

Even though I'd learned never to raise my hand for anything in the marine corps, I stuck it in the air. Fifteen others did as well. "Thank you for volunteering for the marine scout sniper unit. Fall out and follow me." I was the only one I knew.

He led us to a deserted corner of the base. "Take a load off," Gunny instructed. We sprawled under a shade tree. He paced up and down in front of the group. Gunny was built like an oil lamp, wore a pencil mustache that curled at the ends, and had a voice loud enough to peel paint. "I've been in the corps longer than you're old, cut my teeth in the Chosin Reservoir in Korea, and I couldn't wait to get here and kill little gook bastards. My beloved corps said they needed snipers and it's my job to provide them. If I think you got what it takes, you'll become one. If I take you, write your momma good-bye, because it ain't likely you'll see her again. It's an honor for all marines to die in battle, and you'll get a free military funeral. Any questions?"

There was dead silence.

"I know a few of you are asking yourself, 'Gunny, what's it like killing a live person?' Am I right?"

Several nodded.

"I'll tell you what it's like. Killing an enemy soldier is like getting laid and shooting your wad that first time. Anybody remember how good that felt?"

More enthusiastic nodding this time; Gunny had a laugh that sounded like a guinea fowl hollering.

"Tomorrow I'm going to sit down with each one of you and evaluate whether or not I think you got what it takes to do this job. If you can look another man in the eye and blow it out, watch his head turn to mush and enjoy it, you might have what it takes. If not, you can go flop-and-slop in the boonies with the regular grunts. Sniping is an up-close-and-personal job. It ain't for everybody." He told us how to find his hootch and to be in front of it right after chow the next morning.

The group split up and we went our different ways. I fell in with four other guys, and we walked the grounds outside the base. Street booths packed the area just beyond the guard gate. I thought I'd seen nasty before, but this place was unbelievable. Ragged, dirty-faced kids swarmed us like gnats. "You got cigarette, GI? Gimme money. I take you to my sister, she boom-boom you good." A couple of kids tried to distract us while another one would stick his hand in our pockets. We had to slap a couple of them on the head to run them off. They cussed us like we would a sailor. Old women or scrawny men sat under umbrellas selling everything from switchblades to canned fruit. The men didn't look like much, and I had a hard time getting a picture of them with a machine gun.

We stopped at one stand that displayed about every kind of bladed weapon you could imagine. I hefted an ugly-looking machete. "How much?" I motioned to the old woman sitting in the sun. When she opened her mouth to smile, what few teeth she had were black as old walnuts. She held up five fingers. "500 P." I had no idea how much that was. I reached in my pocket, came out with a five-dollar greenback, and looked at her. She snatched it from my hand before I could close it. "Okay." She grinned.

One of the guys, a kid with jet-black hair, skin as brown as an oatmeal cookie, and a body square as a stable stall door, bought a tomahawk. "You know how to use that thing?" I asked.

He waved the tomahawk around and balanced it for weight. "I've been playing with one of these since I could walk. I'm half-Sioux." His name strip said Jones, but he told me his Indian name was Hotah, which meant "strong." He looked it.

"Your folks same as Crazy Horse?" I'd read his name in a book in school.

"Yep, him and Sitting Bull. And that's no bullshit." He cackled.

Another Vietnamese kid ran up to me. "Give me smoke, marine." He was taller than the others, badly pock-faced, and skinny as a rail. I felt sorry for him and reached in my pocket to give him one. He tried to snatch the whole pack.

Hotah caught him by the arm before he could run, bent down, and set the edge of the tomahawk under the kid's chin. "I'm gonna do my best to kill your daddy while I'm here." The boy spit on his shoes. Hotah kicked him in the ass, sending him sprawling in the dust. The kid walked backward, flipping us the finger with both hands.

The next morning we met at Gunny's tent. While one of us went in, the rest sat around telling lies until the guy coming out pointed to the next one to go in. I was close to last.

Gunny sat at a small desk with an electric fan blowing wet air. "Hurley, tell me about yourself, how'd you grow up, what's life been like for you, shit like that."

I explained what I thought was necessary, and left out what

wasn't his business. I'd been imagining all night long what it would be like to be a sniper, picturing myself roaming the jungle in the dark, hanging out in the treetops, invisible to the rest of the world. I wanted to be one.

"Hurley, you think you can look a man in the eye and kill him?"

"I expect I could."

He studied me for a minute or two. He had black-flecked nut brown eyes. Like Lawyer Stern, he seemed to look inside your head. "You ever killed anybody, Hurley?"

That pushed me back in my chair. I took time to retie a bootlace. "Can't say as I have."

He scribbled some notes, then sat looking at me while he rubbed his chin. "I think you'll do. Send in the next man."

The following morning I counted a dozen men at Gunny's tent. Evidently three hadn't measured up, Hotah being one of them. "Men, you can be proud of yourselves for being a part of this unit. You're going to be important to the war effort; the last time marines had sniper outfits was in Korea. Make no mistake; what you're going to be doing will get you killed. Look at the guy beside you." He waited. "One of you will probably be going home in a box. Consider yourself dead right now, and the rest won't seem so bad. Before you die, I want you to make sure a lot more of them go home in boxes. You're United States Marines, the toughest sons of bitches on the planet. Don't let me down." He reached into his tent and pulled out a rifle. "Gentlemen, meet the Remington 30.06 sniper rifle. Learn it, kiss it every night, and rub it like a pretty woman's ass. When you get to your destination, you'll be trained to use it by a senior sniper. Grab your sea bag and be back here at eleven hundred hours. It's time to do what you came for."

CHAPTER 46

I got a quiver of excitement in my gut; my war was fixing to start. I thought back to the Vietnamese men in the village yesterday, and wondered how they could even imagine beating us. But the flatbed truck stacked with silver body boxes I'd passed yesterday proved guns don't care how big or tough you are. I hoped if they killed me, it would be by blowing my body into a hundred pieces. I didn't want to travel home in a box to nobody.

When we reassembled, everyone was issued a brand-new rifle, ammo, and a Unertl scope. Gunny loaded us on a six-by truck and we headed to the airstrip. The Flight Line was full of helicopters. Gunny dropped six guys off at one chopper headed to Phu Bai and five more at another headed to Chu Lai. I wondered what made me special.

Gunny and me pulled up to a Huey, the rotor blades already turning. He leaned toward me, spinning one end of his mustache with two fingers, like he wanted to ask me a question. "Hurley, I got a strange feeling there's something in that head of yours I probably don't want to know. Don't make me regret taking you. You're going to Hill 283. It's so close to the DMZ you'll be able to smell the gooks take a shit. When you get there, look up a mean-ass sergeant that goes by the name of Snake. Tell him I don't want this chopper bringing your ugly face back in a body bag."

I climbed aboard. Since there were no seats and the only thing between my ass and bullets was a thin metal floor, I shoved my duffel into a corner and sat on it. The pilot looked back and said it would be about an hour and a half in the air. A wild-eyed kid manning the M-60 checked and rechecked the gun, hands and fingers flying like he'd eaten a handful of speed pills, all the while singing "Blowin' in the Wind" at the top of his lungs. As soon as the chopper lifted off, he flipped off his steel pot and let the red bandanna tied around his blond head flap in the wind. When he looked back at me, there was a peace sign drawn in black on the cloth. He searched the ground in hopes of getting a chance to cut loose on something.

I liked that the bad smell dissipated when we gained altitude. The sun was low on the horizon behind us. I looked out the door at patches of green and brown intersected by the watery reflection off of flooded rice paddies. Farmers walked behind their water buffalo the same way I'd done with Sally Mule. It was hard to believe a war was going on somewhere down there.

The roar of the overhead engine dulled my senses, and the bounce of turbulence was soothing. I closed my eyes and dozed. Fancy was on my bed; sweat glistened off her brown skin and teeth clamped her bottom lip as we made love. I could feel my own pleasure as we moved against each other.

A sudden, hard right-hand bank caused me to slide into the door gunner. He slapped me on the head. "Get your cherry ass out of my way." When I looked out, the ground was coming up fast.

I could see an open space of red dirt, and could pick out a couple of huge tents, a variety of trucks and jeeps, and two big 105-artillery pieces flanking either side of the compound. The firebase sat on a hill that looked like it'd had the top sheared off and flattened. Green hills and mountains, like a desert in the middle of an oasis, surrounded it.

The chopper slammed hard on the ground. I grabbed my pack, hopped off, and squatted to duck the blades, using my soft boonie hat to block the flying dirt. I waved at the gunner as they lifted off. He flipped me the finger.

When the air cleared, I surveyed the camp. It was a small, fortified combat base, surrounded by triple concertina wire and heavily sandbagged guard posts spaced about five hundred feet apart around the circle. The two big tents that used to be green but were now brownish red from layers of dust sat in the center. Mounds of double-stacked sandbags bulged like yard-mole trails, and identified underground bunkers. Beyond the wire, Seabees and daisy cutter bombs had cleared a three-hundred-yard kill zone between the camp and the jungle.

I made my way toward the largest tent, figuring it was the HQ. A flag flying outside the tent identified the base as First Force Recon. A hand-painted sign was tacked on a post in front: NORTH VIETNAM 2 MILES, LAST GAS STATION BEFORE ENTERING. I told a marine standing nearby I was supposed to see a Sergeant Snake. He pointed to my right. "Go down to the fourth bunker. I think he's in the bush today, but you can wait for him there."

A bleached skull with a string looped through its eye and a bullet hole in the forehead hung over the entrance to the bunker. The ladder leading down was built from wooden pallet skids. It was about six feet deep and dark at the bottom. When my eyes adjusted, I could make out two wood-framed bunks, one on either side, and extra gear stored in the far end of the eight-foot length. I dropped my stuff on the bunk without anything on it, then sat in the cool shadows, ate some c-rat peaches, and smoked a cigarette. I pulled an extra uniform from my pack to use for a pillow, lay down, and went to sleep.

Something jolted my rack. "What the hell you doing in my house?"

I jerked up to find a green-and-black-camouflaged face staring down at me. A lantern gave enough light to see.

I pushed into a sitting position. "Well, if you're not Snake, I guess I'm in the wrong place."

"I'm Snake. Who're you?"

"Hurley. Gunny Phillips said I was to report to you."

He took a seat across from me. "Old Gunny, huh? I suppose that old fart's still at DaNang pulling out dumb-ass boots and telling them what a wonderful thing it is to be a sniper."

"Guess I'm one of them."

"What do they call you, other than stupid?" He was a rangy, tall, big-jawed man, and his drawl was definitely southern, but not South southern, more like Texas southern.

"Junebug."

He laughed. "That's a dumb-ass name to leave on a headstone." He fluffed his pillow and stretched out. "I'm tired. We'll talk more in the morning." He doused the light.

I noticed he had stacked two weapons against the wall: a Remington like mine and an M-14. I pulled off down to my boxers and T-shirt, lay down on the hard cot, and covered my genitals with my shirt.

"Put your pants back on," came from the dark. "And your boots."

"Why?"

"You'll find out."

I was dreaming about Fancy, seeing the blood on her face after she was shot, when rockets and mortars started slamming into the ground above. Dirt showered my face. Snake had his M-14 and was headed up the steps before I knew what was going on. I grabbed my Remington and followed. The moonlight glinted off his bare back as he sprinted to a reinforced position close to the wire. I could see marines falling behind anything that gave cover and pouring fire outward from the camp. Snake and I went in behind some sandbags. He stuck his head up and let go with a burst on full automatic. He looked over at me. "You going to use that rifle or lay there and piss in your pants?"

Gooks screamed like wild animals as they attacked the wire with satchel charges and bodies. Whistles and bugles were blowing, and incoming rounds sounded like bees as they spit into the sandbags and ground around us. I wanted to scream myself, but no sound would come when I opened my mouth. I couldn't stop my hands from shaking, fumbling as I loaded. I couldn't see shit in the pitch-black dark at first, but when the flares started popping, targets were everywhere. I aimed the Remington and fired.

"Come lower," said Snake. "Exhale out, let your finger relax, then squeeze when you go from one heartbeat to the next." He sounded like he was sitting in his living room having a glass of tea. Then he demonstrated what he'd just told me, and one of the attackers flew backward. They were so close it would have been hard to miss. My next shot caught one in the upper right of his chest and Snake filled him with four more rounds before he could hit the ground. The gooks trying to get to the wire began to trip over dead bodies.

It was over in half an hour. I'd never felt such a rush in my life. I sat still and sucked air like a man who'd almost drowned. All I could think was: "*Oh God, oh God, oh God,*" not believing I'd actually survived. When my heart rate dropped to normal, I thought I might faint. This was intensity and terror on a level no man can be prepared for.

Snake's white teeth were shining in the dark. "Now we can get some sleep."

I'd killed my first NVA, not from a treetop the way I'd imagined, but up close and personal. "They do this every night?" I couldn't help the little swagger in my step.

"Just on the days we get new guys." He lay down on his bunk and was snoring in five minutes.

I lay awake most of the night, listening for the whistle of incoming rockets. The hypervigilance in my head wore down after a while and I drifted off.

Sounds of people and vehicles outside woke me up. I could see a wedge of daylight at the open end of the bunker. My brain was fuzzy as it tried to get up-to-date on where I was and why.

Snake's bunk was empty. It hurt my feelings a little that he didn't give me a shake.

When I got outside I could smell coffee, so I went back and grabbed my canteen cup. A dozen or so guys were hanging around the smaller of the two tents.

Snake was sitting on a sandbag. He pointed to the tent flap. "Go get some marine oil." The coffee was so thick a spoon could stand at attention, but it was hot and strong and I was in need of something to kick-start my brain. "Sleep good?" Snake asked.

"Yeah, you?" A marine never admits weakness.

"Like a baby on a momma's tit."

"What's the schedule today?" I was hoping we'd get down to learning this sniping thing.

"I'm going to rest up. You, on the other hand, have the new guy's privilege of shit-burning detail. Latrines are right over yonder. They're expecting you." He pointed to the far end of the camp, slapped me on the shoulder, and pulled himself up. "When you get done, pack a ruck good for about three days, plenty of c-rats and water, and make sure your ammo sack's full. Tomorrow we'll see how you like the bush."

Smelling fuel oil and burning shit in hundred-degree heat and 98 percent humidity is enough to break anybody down. It was misery and it didn't have any company. Snake wouldn't let me back in the house until I found a water truck and washed off the stink. Before sundown he headed up the ladder. "Come on, son, let's go get some grub." I flipped him the finger.

CHAPTER 47

It was still dark when my cot rattled. Snake was standing over me. "Off your ass and on your feet, sonny boy. It's time to play war." He tossed a tiger stripe camo shirt to me. "Put that on."

"What time is it?" The shirt smelled like shit, and had no name or rank or any other military insignia. Snake was wearing one just like it.

"Time to get your ass up, we got a long walk. Let's go." He started for the ladder.

I rolled out, grabbed my rucksack, strapped the machete on the back, and slung my rifle. By the time I got outside, Snake was already at the guard post, and I had to run to catch up. The dim glow of early morning showed in the sky beyond the mountains. "Where we headed?"

"To teach you how to use that killing machine you're carrying."

Snake moved at a steady clip, following a track he obviously knew well. After an hour we came to a rice paddy and started across the dike. We'd got most of the way when a kid who looked to be about ten years old came running to meet us. He had on a boonie hat that was way too big and a wide, gap-toothed grin. "*Chao anh*, Sergeant Snake. *Chao anh*."

Snake picked him up and swung him around. "Hello, Huy, how you doing, boy?" Snake sat down in the dirt, and the kid plopped on his lap. They chatted back and forth in broken Vietnamese and hand gestures. Finally, Snake reached in his ruck and handed the boy a c-rat box. "You go home now." Snake patted him on the butt and pushed him back toward the village. The kid waved with one hand; he had a death grip on the rat box with the other.

"Making friends with the population, huh?"

"Come by here every chance I get on the way out. These are basically good people who are caught in a shit storm they didn't make."

It surprised me to hear a grizzled man like Snake talk that way. After seeing his fierceness in the firefight when the camp was attacked, it would have never occurred to me he could sit in the mud and play with a kid like a kind uncle. I liked this side of him, but wondered how he kept the two separate.

At the end of the dike we veered left, skirted the village, and headed into the jungle. Snake found a small path and worked up a high hill, slowing his pace and walking more cautiously. His head moved constantly. I could swear his nose twitched, like he was smelling the air. After crossing the crest, he took us in a southwest direction leading down to a wide valley. There were bomb craters everywhere, and the vegetation was dead as a winter cornfield. When we got to a cleared spot, Snake swept the area with his binoculars.

He dropped his ruck. We sat and wiped sweat while he talked. "I want you to pay full attention for the next couple of days. You either learn and live, or stay stupid and die. This ain't a practice game." He waved at the mountains around us. "There are little brown people out here that want to kill you. If they catch you and know you're a sniper, they'll make you suffer a long time before letting you die. First thing, take off one of your dog tags and stick it in your bootlaces so if you get blown up somebody can ID you." He waited while I did what he said. "From this minute on, forget everything about the world back home, because if you're going to survive in this work, you've got to learn to focus on nothing but the work, to become part of what's here, and understand your job is to kill people, plain and simple. There ain't nothing back there that'll help you out here. Understand Uncle Charles is one tough little bastard, and he's fighting for a purpose. We're just fighting 'cause they tell us to." Snake's jaw was set hard, and his words were almost angry. "Any questions?"

If he was trying to scare me, he succeeded. The serious expression on his face caused my butt to pucker. "No."

He handed me the binoculars. "You see that piece of steel hanging off that banyan limb?" I followed the direction of his arm. "That's your four-hundred-yard target. Now, imagine in your mind a hundred-yard football field behind it, and at the end of that you'll see the five-hundred-yard target. Flip the field over and you'll have the six-hundred-yard target. There's no yardsticks out here, so that's the way you adjust your distances. I hung these things out here almost a year ago to sight my rifle."

"I see them."

"We're going to concentrate on the five-hundred-yard target so you can learn to allow if the shot is shorter or longer. To get a feel for the wind, watch the tops of the elephant grass, see how much it's moving and from what direction. If you're somewhere you don't have grass, watch the treetops. You have to learn this good because you're usually only going to get one shot and it has to count. You miss and some very pissed-off folks will be on your ass."

"Aren't you afraid somebody out here will hear us?"

"You know the kid on the dike?"

"Yeah?"

"He's up in the bush at the top of this hill. If somebody's coming, we'll know."

I took a prone position and chambered rounds, getting the hang of it after thirty or so, and began pinging the first target

regularly. Snake watched with his binoculars and kept correct-
ing, telling me to feel the target and let the natural settings help
me adjust my sight. By the time we moved to the second, I was
starting to understand and didn't waste near as much ammo.
Six hundred yards was a long way, and, while I got so I hit it,
most of the shots weren't center mass, the sure kill zone. We
practiced until dusk, then rolled out ponchos for sleeping. Night
fell, and we found a soft spot in the grass, used C-4 for heating
ham and lima beans, then wrapped into ponchos and lay down.
The air got chilly, and the sky clouded over. The dull boom of
artillery sounded in the distance and occasionally we heard the
roar of jets and saw flashes from bombs being dropped. Eventually things got quiet. "Dark out here, ain't it, Sarge?" It was like
the blackness was stuck to you.

"Like a shantytown at midnight, son. You'll get used to seeing with your ears as much as your eyes. The jungle will teach
you its sounds, and you'll learn to recognize what ain't natural.
Your eyes will get to be like a cat's. Them and your brain are all
the tools you got to work with out here."

"What about snakes? No offense."

He laughed. "None taken. They might crawl in with you, but
all they're doing is trying to stay warm. Nights up here can get
cold. Try not to do too much rolling over in case one climbs in,
it tends to piss 'em off. Tigers are what you got to be careful of,
them and Rock Apes walking up on you."

"Rock Apes? What the hell are they?"

"Oversized monkeys or undersized gorillas, take your choice.
They'll throw rocks at you, or run up and scream and holler.
Saw one on a night mission with the recon boys last year. The
guy on watch started yelling like somebody was killing him, and
when we got there one of them apes was beating the dog shit
out of him. Funniest thing I ever saw." He rolled over. "Try not
to snore, it attracts attention."

CHAPTER 48

In the predawn dark the next morning, we sat eating canned peaches and drinking c-rat coffee. I pulled out a pack of smokes.

"Don't light that."

"Why?"

Snake reached over and clipped it from my mouth. "Charlie will sniff an American cigarette from half a mile, same with aftershave or smelly soap. You need to smell like the ground, the mud, and the shit water in the paddies. These boys are at home in the jungle, know what's supposed to be here and what ain't, and if you want to live you got to learn the same way."

We spent most of that day practice shooting until my shoulder was sore. I started to feel like the rifle was an extension of my arm. In the afternoon Snake took me on a walk across the valley and along a small creek that threaded between the hills. He taught me the telltale signs of booby traps. We went over hand signs for when we would be "creeping" as he called it, things like cupping a hand to your ear if you heard voices or making a circle over your eye if you could see a trip wire, the silent language of a sniper.

This world suited me, my mind recognizing it as a true place I could be invisible and watch the world. I remembered the feeling from my time in Grandma's woods. This was where I was supposed to be.

We lay back at camp and watched the stars light up like a million little lamps coming on at once. Snake took off his boonie hat and rubbed his head. I'd noticed he had a good amount of gray in his "high and tight" cut. "How long you been in the corps?"

"This is my twentieth year. Went in right after the big war and learned the trade in Korea."

"How was that? Compared to this, I mean."

"Cold." Fighter jets screamed to the east of us, followed by several giant fireballs of napalm. We watched until it died down. "The ground froze so hard you couldn't dig a hole to hide in; so cold you couldn't feel your fingers to adjust your sights. We killed all we could, but the Chinks kept coming." He stretched his head back and rubbed his neck. "They'd start screaming, and charge at you like a pack of rabid dogs. At times it got down to hand-to-hand, using rifle butts and shovels. I was about your age then. Never thought I'd live to be this age. I saw boys do stuff no man should be capable of." Snake's voice struggled some on that last part. He looked at me. "That's all war is, Junebug: survival. It ain't about flag and country. Hell, fifty years from now, nobody will give a shit you were even here." He got quiet. "We didn't win that one and we ain't going to win this one." He pulled his boonie hat over his eyes and lay down; the talking was over.

Snake shook me out of my sleep. The moon had journeyed beyond the mountains, but the sun wasn't up yet. "Let's go put some meat on the ground."

Without conversation, we moved back across the valley and onto the hill we worked yesterday. This morning, Snake walked with a purpose, heading due north. By the time daylight began

to peep over the horizon, we had crossed the top and were looking down on scrub brush and more craters. Across the way was
another small village. We circled toward it, but stayed high
enough to move among the heavy foliage. We pushed through
five-foot-high, brownish yellow elephant grass that had blades
sharp enough to cut skin. Snake came across a worn foot track,
and pointed it out. We backed ourselves higher up the side of
the hill to have a better view.

"What are we doing?" I whispered.

"Gooks are like fish, you have a better chance of catching
them early or late. Let's see what might be stirring out of that
ville. You see that big area of flat ground out there about two
miles?"

I could just make it out. "Yeah."

"That's North Vietnam." Snake swept his 7x30 binoculars
from the village northward. "Maybe we can find you something
to do."

The top rim of a red sun edged into the sky to our right, and
the warm light made my eyes want to close. Snake tapped my
shoulder and handed me the glasses. "He's headed from the last
hootch, the one closest to us."

I located the round straw hat bobbing up and down. He was
dressed in a black shirt, and pants rolled up to his knees.

"Picture football fields in your mind, and tell me how far you
think he is."

I began to flip goalposts. I got to four and the man kept
coming toward us. "Figure he's around four hundred yards
and closing."

"Keep watching. When you think he's about two fifty, he's
yours."

My palms were damp as I pulled the Remington to my shoulder. When the man crossed the goalposts at three hundred, I no
longer needed the binoculars. I sighted him in the scope, checked
the grass tops for wind, and adjusted. He looked down as he
walked, making it hard to see the face below the hat. Gently, I

put pressure on the trigger, let my breath out, and waited for the next heartbeat to end. At that moment, he lifted his head and looked right at me. I could see his black eyes staring, like he knew what was coming but couldn't turn away. I squeezed. His face exploded. He pitched backward. I couldn't move the scope off him, fascinated by the sight. The spit in my mouth got a strange sweet taste.

Snake slapped the back of my head. "Good job. Let's go. Now!"

We headed back almost in a trot. Snake didn't take the trail to the valley, instead moving south by west. I was giddy. This was not at all like killing Twin; this was doing my duty, no need for remorse.

It took all day to get back to the firebase. We humped through the guard post with enough light left so they could identify us. Our house had a new hole in the ground beside the top, and a bunch of our sandbags were busted open. "Guess we missed the fun last night," said Snake. The inside wasn't damaged, just a little extra pile of dirt at the bottom of the ladder. We dropped our packs and stretched out on the bunks.

"I was thinking about something, Snake."

"Not a good idea, but I'll bite. What?"

I put my feet on the floor and sat up. "I didn't see that gook carrying a weapon."

He looked over at me with a grin on his face. "Yeah, I noticed that. Must have been a collaborator. Still felt good, didn't it?"

I turned my face to the ceiling. It hadn't been like killing Twin or Lightning; they had been trying to hurt me. Maybe I'd just killed some poor farmer who happened to be in the wrong place. I couldn't get those eyes out of my head.

I'd been on the hill two months when a resupply chopper came in loaded down with food, ammo, and mail. There was a letter from Fancy. I put it to my nose and inhaled, then slid my fingernail under the flap to slowly ease it open. It was like a piece of candy not meant to be chewed, but rolled on your tongue to make the sweetness last. I pulled out the white paper.

Dear Junebug:

I hope this finds you well and making out all right in the marines. I've been struggling along here in New York, and have come to realize things aren't really that much different than they were back home. Like you said, all I'm doing is still cleaning white folks' mess. They don't put us coloreds down to our face, but I sense their real feelings.

I wanted you to know I'm thinking about moving on. I work for this white lady who is rich and travels all over, and she wants me to hire on as her girl and go along to take care of things. She's headed to France in a month, so I have to make up my mind soon. I'm pretty sure I'm going. It's still working for a white woman, but if nothing else, maybe I'll have a chance to see some of them places I read about in books. I'll write to you when we get settled. We'll probably be gone six months or more, and she said we might keep on to Italy. I think about you all the time, Junebug, and you're still the best man I'll ever know. Don't you get yourself hurt over there.

Love,

Fancy

I pictured Fancy's smile. It made me happy she might get to visit places she'd always dreamed of. I sat in the bunker and wrote a three-page letter, telling her Vietnam was a very strange place. I didn't tell her what I was doing, just that it was hot, smelled awful, and the story about having shit detail. When I licked the seal on the envelope, sadness settled over me. It felt like Fancy and me were on two different planets. Life pulled the plug on us, and I had no idea if we could ever reconnect it. I encouraged her to go with the lady to France, and if she moved on somewhere else, to go there too.

CHAPTER 49

Snake and I started to work missions regularly, in the bush for a few days and back to recoup for a couple. We would set up in places Snake knew should have traffic crossing from the north. He taught me how to read grids on a map and how to call in artillery. It wasn't unusual to come across big groups of NVA troops, too big for the two of us to take on, so we'd plot the position and call in the heavy guns. After passing on the coordinates, we'd ask them to "fire for effect," then adjust and watch the results. When the soldiers scattered, we'd usually manage to catch a couple away from the main force and pop them. Other times we worked with the long-range reconnaissance boys, getting out ahead of them and scouting, which is where the "scout sniper" name came from. Generally we had six or seven days in the bush on those missions.

Snake and I were drinking coffee at the firebase one morning after working along the border three days. He looked over his canteen cup. "Son, you're about as natural at this job as I've ever seen."

That was rare praise coming from him. "Why you say that?"

"You got that ability to adapt to circumstances without getting rattled. That's a good trait for a shooter, and not a bad way to live your life. Most cherries out here in the jungle in the dark are pissing-in-their-pants scared. You like this shit."

I poured the rest of the bitter, strong coffee over the dirt and lit a smoke. The memory of standing outside Mr. Wilson's window with my finger on the trigger came to mind. "Shit, Snake, I think I've been training for this all my life."

Monsoon season started in late October, and rain came daily, cold rain that made "creeping" miserable. It was almost impossible to see much with clouds and no moon. We started using a small starlight scope, what snipers called the "green eye," for seeing in the dark.

The week before Thanksgiving, the recon captain sent Snake and me to work around Con Thien, a place that nudged the DMZ. Marines called it "The Hill of Angels" because so many were getting killed in the place. We walked four days to get there and scout the situation.

The open ground around Con Thien looked like a red, muddy mess. The North Vietnamese desperately wanted to take out that base and the one at Gio Linh so they'd have a free run south. Marine camps at Con Thien, Gio Linh, Dong Ha, and Cam Lo made up Leatherneck Square, and their job was to block the movement. There was a lot of killing going on in that square. The NVA were getting a lesson on what a crowd of mean-ass marines were capable of.

Due to the lousy weather and heavy clouds, dark came early. We eased down closer and north of the marine outpost. I was nose to ass with Snake because it was black as gunpowder moving along a footpath through the middle of the elephant grass. Suddenly Snake's right hand shot out behind and hit me in the face. I stopped. He reached until I gave him my hand, then inched me forward. He squeezed me to stop. I didn't move my feet but lifted up to get my head next to his. He whispered into my ear. "Something's caught on my boot." He moved my hand down his right leg. "Use your fingertips and see if you can touch it, but whatever you do, don't pull."

I did as he said. I didn't feel anything at first, but as I came back up the laces, very gently easing along, I felt the wire. "Got it."

"I want you to lift it gently with your finger, just enough so I can back my foot out. Can you do that, Junebug?"

I let out my breath to keep my hands from shaking. "I'll try."

Snake had the balls to snicker. "If it doesn't work, I'll see you in hell."

I held the wire steady as he slowly inched his boot backward. "Doing good, son. Just a bit more." He whispered. "Relax and you'll be fine." The pressure on the wire eased when his boot came clear. He moved away and lay back in the grass. "God almighty. If you smell anything, don't worry, it's just the shit in my britches."

I held the wire with my finger, not knowing if I could let go. "What now?"

"Stay right here while I get about a hundred yards. When I yell, you run like a jackass in a rodeo."

I started to panic. "You son of a bitch, you're going to leave me here!"

Snake bent over on his knees, holding his stomach with one hand and stifling his mouth with the other.

"Goddammit, Snake, this ain't funny."

He finally was able to quit laughing. "Just ease your finger down until you feel it stop. And hurry up, we got stuff to do."

I relaxed the wire little by little until I felt space between my finger and the wire. As Snake rose to his feet, I kicked him right in the ass.

We moved off the path and worked farther toward the base. At daylight, we could see the NVA dug in beyond Con Thien. They had trenches full of soldiers facing the marines. "Damn," said Snake, "got to be battalion strength. They want this place bad."

We continued to circle, trying to find a place closer to the NVA but not in a crossfire spot between them and the marines. Finally, we decided on a giant deserted ant mound; it offered us cover before the cleared open space around the fire zone. Snake moved the glasses slowly along where the NVA were grouped.

"Well, look at that," he said. "They're setting up a recoilless. Damn thing must be an antique, but it'll blow some serious holes in shit." He handed me the glasses to look.

"What can we do?"

"I want you to plot that grid and call anybody you can raise on the radio who can throw some heavy stuff in there."

I got a call out, and we waited for the white phosphorus target shell to arrive. It landed long and I adjusted with the artillery boys. The next one landed right in the middle of them.

"That did it. They're scrambling, trying to move the recoilless," said Snake. "How far you guess that thing is?"

I looked again. "I'm guessing about seven hundred yards."

"About what I think too. You keep watching that bastard on the saddle. Let's see if I can discourage them a little." Snake focused his scope. I watched through the binoculars. The NVA soldier directing the towing of the big gun never heard the shot before it tore into his jaw and his head snapped sideways.

"You got him. Hell of a shot, Snake, hell of a shot."

"Thanks, Junebug. Tell them boys on the radio to blow their asses to hell. Let's see how many we can get before we got to go." We chambered round after round, taking our time as the artillery poured in, and NVA scattered away from the big gun. By the time they turned their attention our way, seven lay on the ground. It was time for us to get out of Dodge.

CHAPTER 50

On Valentine's Day 1967, Snake and me sat under a banyan tree beside the HQ tent. He looked over. "Junebug, I've put in my retirement papers; time to leave this war stuff to you young bucks."

I spit out the coffee in my mouth. "You're shitting me!" I felt sick to my stomach. "When you leaving?" Snake had become the nearest thing to a daddy I'd ever had.

"Day after tomorrow." I'd never seen his hands shake before.

"Son of a bitch. I would a thrown you a party if you'd told me sooner."

"Scared to, figured you'd get so excited you'd get me killed out there in the bush." His big jaw crooked in a smile. "We'll save the party until you get home."

Two days later, I went with him to the chopper. He passed me his M-14. "Use it in good health." When we shook he kept a grip on my hand. "Son, you're on a road that's got a lot of ruts and low shoulders, and there's going to come a time you'll wish you'd taken another one. This shit ain't real, Junebug, it's a nightmare that some will wake up from and some won't. When your time is over, get your ass home and do something else. This ain't no life for a man." He gripped his hand behind my neck, and held my eyes. "Be good at what you do because you have to be, not because you like it." Snake let go and smacked me on the back. "Come find me in Texas, son, and we'll have a real throw-down. I'll keep the beer cold and the stories warm."

There were very few secrets between men living with each other twenty-four hours a day, and Snake knew all of mine. I threw him a salute as the chopper lifted off. I was on my own again.

I worked the bush alone, and got better and better at killing. The night was my friend. I was able to dissolve into the shadows, to smell the air and listen to the wind and let them tell me their secrets. I'd swallowed pain and fear in the other life, but the jungle was a place no man could hurt me. I no longer feared my soul going to hell; let the ones I hunted worry about it. I was God in this place. If I died, they could just leave my body to rot until the earth took me back piece by piece.

I broke the news of Snake leaving to Huy. Fat tears fell out of his eyes and rolled down his cheeks. "Don't cry. He wanted me to visit you and make sure to bring you a box." I handed him the carton of c-rats.

He smudged the tears with his dirty hands. "Sergeant Snake my friend." He took off a little braided water-buffalo-hair bracelet he wore on his arm. "You send him this for me?"

I took it and stuck it in my pocket. "You bet I will. He would want you to be a brave boy. I'll stop and see you whenever I come this way." Huy hugged my neck and I patted his behind, sending him home. He was the only semblance of sanity in this place of insanity.

In May of 1967, my year was up. I went to the captain and told him I wanted to extend for another six months. "You're due for some R&R, Hurley, so take it and get out of here for a few days." I did just that, caught a chopper to Phu Bai, hitched a ride on a convoy to DaNang, and got a plane to Hong Kong.

I'd never been much of a drinking man, but I tried real hard to become one that week. I stumbled into a street bar one night and heard a loud voice cussing and raising hell. It sounded familiar. I weaved along the bodies until I got to the source. It was Hotah. "Man, what the hell are you doing here?" I slapped him on the back.

He spun around on his stool, let out an Indian war whoop, and leaped up to hug me. "You ain't dead yet, white man?"

"Can't kill a redneck, or evidently a red man. Where you been hiding in the jungle?"

"They stuck me up on a little hill around Hue. Plenty of action, though, killing a lot of those little slants. You creeping and peeping?"

"Yeah, up by the DMZ."

"What are you collecting?"

"Collecting what?"

"Souvenirs, man. I'm collecting eyeballs, got a sack full."

I'd heard of ears, but never eyes. "Why?"

"Old Indian custom. If you take your enemy's eyes, he won't be able to find you in the next life. They used to take feet and hands too, but I ain't got room for all that."

Hotah and I drank until he passed out in a booth. I managed to fall into a cab and get back to my hotel. It was the last time I saw him.

I bought Fancy several gold jewelry trinkets and mailed them to her, hoping they'd catch up to wherever she was. I sent a letter with them, telling her I'd extended my time in Vietnam because I'd rather be here than in some boring base stateside. I didn't tell her I stayed because I loved it.

When I got back to the hill, there was mail waiting and a letter from Fancy.

April 24, 1967
Dear Junebug:
I arrived in France this spring and it's such a beau-
tiful place. Folks here don't seem to care what color a
person is, and I'm making friends. The lady I'm with
said we'd be moving on to Italy in a few months. I
believe I'd rather stay here. I think about you all the
time and wish you were with me, especially now. We
could be happy in this place. I watch the stars every
night and wonder which one you might be under.
Please don't get hurt over there, because after seeing
this part of the world I know there's a chance for us
to be together.
I love you as always,
Fancy

She included a small picture. I sat and stared at it. She had changed her hair, lightened it and cut it short. I could see a much happier look than I remembered, and something was different about her expression, the direct way she stared at the camera. Fancy's beauty as a grown woman was starting to show itself. I wondered if any of the new friends were men. The part about a chance for us to be together creeped into my mind, but I shoved it out. Death was too close in this place for daydreaming.

The captain said most of the recon boys were out on a big operation and wouldn't be back for a week, so I could occupy myself however I felt I could do some good. I packed a ruck and walked north the next morning to see what might be happening. Huy spotted me crossing the dike and came running. I was in no hurry, so we sat and gibberished at each other for a while. I reached in my pocket and surprised him with a little gold wristwatch from Hong Kong. He hopped up and down, laughing and hugging my neck. I gave him a rat box and headed into the heavy bush, crossing the valley to a favorite spot Snake and I had used to catch folks crossing the DMZ. There wasn't a day that went by I didn't miss the security of having him with me. I stayed out three days, getting two kills, which brought my total to twenty-six for the year.

It was so humid and hot my sweat was sweating when I dragged by the guard post the afternoon I returned. I was paying a high price for all the whiskey I'd drunk in Hong Kong. Two steps down the bunker ladder I stopped. There was a funny smell. It hit me that it was aftershave lotion. At the bottom, I saw a black guy sitting on Snake's cot.

"What're you doing in my house?"

The kid got to his feet. "Came in today. Gunny Phillips said you needed a replacement. Moses Lane, folks call me Mo." He was black as coal, big-eyed, and had giant hands.

"How you doin', Mo. I'm Junebug. Consider yourself a substitute, 'cause nobody's capable of replacing the man whose rack you're sitting on." He had big arms and his hair was shaved down to the skin. "I'll drop this stuff and we'll visit awhile."

We walked up to the medic tent where the coffee was always hot. I introduced Mo around and we took a load off on a couple of sandbags in the shade. I don't know why it surprised me to see a black man as a sniper, but it did. "Where you from, Mo?"

"Mississippi." He had an easy smile.

"You get confused and stand in the wrong line?"

Mo dipped his head and laughed. "My brother was a marine. When he got killed, I decided I needed to come see what he went through."

"If you came here for payback, let me be the first to tell you that you messed up."

"Not that. I was studying to be a preacher at Biloxi Seminary College. My brother's dying hurt my folks real bad, and I had a hard time with it too. We lost three from our little community in a year, and I decided if I was going to be a comfort to people in pain, I needed to understand what the war was like." His eyes were calm and steady, like he was fixed on what he had to do.

"A lot of folks would say a black man fighting for a white man's country ain't too smart."

He nodded his head slowly. "That's true. And a lot of them are angry they ain't good enough to be treated equal except when it comes to going to war. The way I see things, it won't always be the white man's country." He smiled innocently, but it was clear Mo wasn't the type to shy away from straight talk, or be intimidated. I hoped that would translate to the bush.

Back at our house, we ate some c-rats while Mo told me about the new sniper school they'd sent him through back in Camp Pendleton. "Is it as bad out here as they said it would be?"

"How bad did they say it would be?"

"That I probably wouldn't live through it."

"Yep." I fluffed my pillow and blew out the lantern. "I'm going to rest up tomorrow, but you need to report to the latrine officer first thing in the morning. He's got some new guy work for you." I lay back on the bunk and closed my eyes. I heard him undressing. When he was down to his skivvies, I said, "Put your clothes back on."

It was important for me to get a feel for what motivated Mo and how he thought about things. Once we started in the work for real, I had to feel comfortable he would have my back. Was I being more cautious because he was black? Maybe. After several days, I came to believe he was a man I could trust. Besides, the captain in charge of the recon unit started pushing me to get back in the field. It was time to quit yakking and start packing.

"In the morning we're going creeping."

I opted for Snake's M-14 and Mo carried his Remington when we headed past the guard post in the early morning dark. I said to Mo, "Always make sure they see you go out so they'll be expecting you to come back in a few days. If they don't, somebody will come looking."

I decided to take him along the same route Snake had taken me the first day. It was hard to believe that was over a year ago. Sure enough, when we started across the dike, I spotted the boonie hat coming out of the village. At first Huy was shy around Mo. He touched the skin on Mo's face. "*Mi dang,*" he said, and I figured it meant "black man." We messed around a bit, and Huy began to warm up to Mo. I gave him his rat box and a pat on the butt for him to go home. We headed over the hill.

When we'd made our way into the valley where Snake's targets still hung in the trees, we stopped. I wanted to see what kind of training Mo had gotten stateside. I pointed out the steel plates. "Let's see what you got."

Mo was dead center on almost every shot. He moved easily between the targets from four hundred to six and back again. In a couple of hours, I'd seen enough. "You're good. Let's go."

It was nightfall by the time we had worked our way four miles up and along the DMZ. I hacked a clear place in the middle of a bamboo thicket. Once the ponchos were unrolled, we ate cold beans and fruit and chased them with water. "I'm going to get some z's. If you hear anything don't tell me; I'll know you did if you ain't here in the morning."

"Very funny." He yawned and lay back. "Stars seem mighty close this high up. Pretty amazing what God created, ain't it?"

I thought about the conversation Fancy and me had about God so long ago. "You're a religious man, Mo. Tell me if you really think somebody sat around for a week magically sticking all those stars up there, making oceans and animals, not to mention creating people."

"Start out with the hard questions, don't you?" He rolled to his side. "When I was a kid, an old man down the road from us kept bees, you know, in hives he tended. I used to love to talk to him. He was a deacon at the church, and I considered him a wise man. We talked about this very thing one day, me having some doubts about God. I followed him to his backyard. 'Moses, you see them bees?' he said. 'I don't mess with them too much except to keep wasps away, little stuff like that, but I'm always watching out for their well-being. Who do you imagine them bees think I am?' I thought about that for a long time, Junebug."

That was a curveball. I lay there thinking about it for a few minutes. "Sounds like a pretty wise man, all right. Tell me something, Mo. If there's a God-plan, why would He let shit like this happen, us running around in a hellhole killing each other?"

He yawned. "You surely are a man in need of answers, ain't you? If I was to decide to kill you while you are asleep, is it because there's no God, or did I just make up my mind to do it? Junebug, folks still got free will. God ain't going to stop the world from doing evil; He's just going to be sure you pay for it when the time comes. What makes you such a bitter man, Junebug, like you don't have a lot of hope in your life?"

"Oh, I got hope. I hope I wake up one of these days and this has all been a dream. But you and me both know that's not going to happen. I went to church when I was a kid, but, Mo, the next time you see some eighteen-year-old boy crying for his momma because his face is half shot off, tell me why it happened and where was God when he needed him."

Sounds of bombs and heavy firing reverberated in the distance.

"And another thing, how do you square being a preacher man with coming out here to kill people?"

He sighed. "I made the mistake of being the best shot in my basic training outfit. Next thing I knew I was in California at sniper school. Guess I could have objected to it, but I have a strong belief in destiny. God must want me out here for a reason, to teach me something. All I can do is have faith."

I rolled to one elbow and fixed on him. He was genuine, a gentle guy. "What you going to do when you get home, Mo?"

"Try to finish school, I hope, then find me a little church that needs a preacher. What about you?"

I raised my hand in front of my face and folded and unfolded my fingers. "Hell, I don't know. Might go to France."

"You know somebody in France?"

"A girl."

"How'd you meet her?"

"In a tobacco patch."

"Can't wait to hear that story."

"Her momma and daddy were sharecroppers."

"Now, wait a minute. Her momma and daddy were French sharecroppers?"

"They're black as you are."

The pause was long. "Junebug, my man, you are full of surprises. The two of y'all get to courting?"

"Grew up together, then it just seemed to come natural. Crazy, ain't it?"

"Why's she in France?"

"Went after the Klan threatened to kill us."

"I'm surprised they didn't. How'd she get there?"

"She went to New York, then hired on with a lady who travels."

"And you're still carrying the torch for her?" He sounded disbelieving, like I'd told him there really was a Santa Claus. "I'm beginning to understand what's got you so bitter, Junebug. Being a good Southern boy, you think what you did is a sin, don't you?"

The night critters went silent, or at least I wasn't able to hear them. "No. She's not a sin. But the fact I killed her brother is." I watched a streak of light flash high in the sky. "And she don't know I did it."

Mo's voice became serious. "I see your troubles." He didn't ask me why I killed Lightning. "Do you need forgiveness, Junebug?"

"No."

"Then what do you need?"

"Peace."

I heard Mo scratching his face. "Junebug, in the Bible, Romans 7, verse 21, Paul says that, as mere men, we cannot always control the evil that lives in us, and sometimes we sin because we're not strong enough to fight it off, that we're all subject to the power of the devil. But even when we fail, Junebug, God will forgive us if we ask. Do you want me to pray with you?"

"No. But you can pray for me."

Chapter 51

I shook Mo awake before sunup. "Time to go hunting." I took the point and moved beyond the bamboo onto a small walking path leading downhill toward a stream. We got cover in some elephant grass. With the binoculars I could see a trail on the other side of the creek. It came out of the heavy bush and led toward where the water was just a trickle, a good crossing point. The sun had just started its climb in the east when I spotted movement at the edge of the trees.

One came out, then another. Both were wearing the ragged clothes of a farmer, but each carried a pack strapped to his back. I knew they were satchel charges. The little bastards were sappers looking to fade into a village, then surprise some marine base in the middle of the night. I pointed them out to Mo and handed him the glasses. "Use your football fields and watch the tops of the grass."

Mo stared through the binoculars longer than he needed to. He was sucking up the reality that he was expected to kill a live human being. In this moment he would decide. Just like I had been, Mo was scared. It was hard the first time.

He lowered the binoculars and picked up the Remington, sighting and adjusting. I got ready with the M-14 in case he changed his mind. I was focused on the targets, and the boom of his rifle startled me. The man in front jerked sideways. Mo chambered another round. The second one was crouching, trying to figure out where we were when his head exploded. Mo dropped his forehead on his rifle.

I slapped him on the back. "Good job." I lifted the M-14. Taking aim at the backpack of the lead guy, I punched a round. The charge blew up, setting off the second one as well. When I looked through the glasses again, there were body pieces scattered here and there. I grabbed Mo by the scruff of his shirt. "Let's get the hell out of here."

We moved steadily, stopping for water breaks every two or three hours. By sundown, we were halfway home. We shimmied up a big banyan tree and tied ourselves in the crook of branches to wait out the night. It took all the next day to make it back to the hill leading to Huy's village and the rice paddy dike.

The sun was fading, and I didn't want to be walking up to the guard post in the dark, so we hurried down the hillside and came out of the jungle a hundred yards from the crossing. I squatted in the dusky light and watched through the fog lifting off the paddy water for a minute to make sure the way was clear.

I was surprised to see Huy's boonie hat at the far end of the dike. We started across and I called his name. "Huy, *chao anh*." He didn't move. When we got within fifty feet, I saw why. I began to run. The boy was tied to a stake; the rope strapped from his neck to his waist. His skinny arms lay on the ground at his feet. They had been cut off just below the shoulders. He had been left to bleed to death. Streaks of tears had dried on his dirty face. Flies and insects crawled all over him. I puked.

"God almighty," said Mo. "God almighty."

I was on my knees heaving my guts. "Cut him down, Mo." He did and gently lowered Huy to the ground. The gold wristwatch was stuffed in his mouth. I should have left him alone. I couldn't stand up. This was my fault. All I could do was kneel on the ground and cover my head with my arms.

I felt Mo's hand on my shoulder. "There's nothing we can do for him, Junebug. We got to get out of here. We can come back in the morning."

I struggled to stand up. Anger so dark it filled everything in the universe took me over. I saw the devil standing on that mountain, fire shooting from his hand. My mind calmed. "You go on back, Mo."

"I'm not leaving you." He tried to pull my arm.

I moved the barrel of the M-14 to his chest. "You go on back, Mo. I'll be along directly. Don't argue now, just get moving."

Mo stepped closer to stare me down, and I could see the edge of his jaw twitch. When he stretched out his hand, I took it. Mo closed his eyes and bowed his head. After a minute, he released me and headed across the berm without looking back.

I dragged my finger in the blood from Huy's clothes, streaked it along the sides of my face, then across my forehead. I took the poncho from my rucksack and covered him. I sat with the boy while I waited for complete darkness before walking toward the village. There was no hurry.

My head started to throb. I circled behind the village, staying in the shadows. The smell of rice and vegetables cooking drifted on the air, and I could hear the singsong chatter of women. I eased to a place that had a good view of the common area. Whoever did this to Huy was here somewhere.

I squatted and watched for half an hour before three men, dressed in the black garb of VC cadre, strapped with bandoliers and carrying AK-47s, appeared from trees behind the hootches across from me. They stacked their weapons like a tripod and chose a log at the edge of the gathering place to sit. A couple of women brought bowls of food for them.

I heard a clatter from the other end of the village, and a woman came running up to the three men. She screamed in their faces, then threw something one of them had to dodge. He got to his feet and knocked her flat with his fist. I figured her to be

Huy's momma. They'd murdered her child, and she had to leave the boy where he was or risk punishment for everyone in the village. This way, they would only kill her. Before he could hit the woman again, I stood and walked into the light of the cooking fires, raking a single burst above their heads. Everything went silent, chopsticks frozen in place between bowl and mouth.

I made a direct line to the VC. Only their eyes moved: They were wondering if they could get to the AK-47s behind them. I motioned up with the M-14. After they stood, I shoved them shoulder-to-shoulder, took a step back, and stitched 7.62 rounds across their legs. They fell, grabbing and crying out in pain, attempting to drag themselves by their elbows in some futile escape attempt. One by one, I kicked and shoved each of the three men along the ground to where everyone could see, then picked up Huy's momma.

I rolled the log they'd been sitting on to where they lay in the dirt. When I stretched the first one's arm over the wood and unhooked the machete from my pack, he began to slobber and beg. It took two hard strokes to cut all the way through the bone. The villagers began wailing and waving their hands. The other two men were squirming, trying to crawl. The second man got his turn to suffer what they had done to Huy.

When I extended the last man's arm over the log, Momma grabbed my shoulder and gently pulled the machete from my hand. "*Lam uhhu, Lam uhhu.*" She bent down to the last man. He was just a teenager. She rubbed his young face gently, stood up, and then, screaming Vietnamese words I couldn't understand, the old woman hacked him to pieces.

All three lay facedown in the bloody dirt. I took the machete and walked out of the village. When I reached Huy's body, I knelt down and stroked his head. All he was guilty of was being a kid who liked c-rat peaches.

CHAPTER 52

Sixteen months in the jungle had taught me to feel what I couldn't see. I turned around to look toward the village. At that moment I realized I should have searched for any other VC. The sudden impact felt like a baseball bat slamming into my chest, knocking me backward. There was no pain, just a sense of falling, of being sucked down a pitch-black, silent hole. Eventually, I emerged into a soft, calming white light. I could see my body lying face-up in the water at the bottom of the dike and the hole ripped into my chest, but felt nothing. This was a peaceful and warm place, and I no longer cared about that body. Dying wasn't so bad. I wondered if Fancy would miss me.

It felt like time was passing, but it didn't seem important. When the abrupt noise of guns and shouting erupted, it destroyed the white light, and I was pulled back through the tunnel. "Here he is! Junebug, Junebug, can you hear me?" Strong hands dragged me out of the water. "He's got a sucking chest. I think he's dead." I became aware of the hot burning in my chest, but couldn't move my hand to touch it. I screamed at them to leave me alone, but realized they couldn't hear me. I wanted to go back to the other place.

"I got a pulse. Hold that compression tight and let me get this jelly gauze on. It'll seal the hole." Seconds later I felt a rushing sensation, and a great gush of air sucked in and stayed. "Get him on the stretcher and haul ass. Call for a dust-off and tell 'em to hurry."

I heard myself moan. "Hold on, Junebug, we got you. Can you hit him with the morphine, Doc?" I felt the jab of the strettes in my leg. "Hang in there." I could barely make out Mo's face. I wanted to raise my arm, but didn't have the strength. The pain eased and I floated toward the light again.

The next time I woke up, I could hear but not see. Maybe I had died after all. I started to panic, thinking I was in a death box. Then the downdraft from rotating blades blew the towel off my face, and I was being shoved into the belly of a chopper. "They're going to get you fixed up, Junebug. Time for you to go home." Mo gripped my palm and grinned at me. "I'll be doing that praying for you, count on that. You're a good man, brother. Tell that gal of yours hello for me." I tried to smile. When the chopper lifted off, my head flopped to one side. I wasn't on the ride alone. There was a body bag beside me.

I saw hands with gloves and faces with masks, and I slept without dreaming for what seemed like a very long time. When my eyes opened, the stark brightness hurt and I had to blink several times to be able to focus. White walls, white ceilings, white lights, white sheets, not at all like the peaceful place from before. Only the floor was different, a blue linoleum. I turned my head to the right, and in the bed next to me was a guy with his head totally wrapped in white gauze except for his nose, one ear, and a small opening for his mouth. He lifted his hand to touch his face, and I could see the skin had been burned off in some places below the wrist. I checked my own head, but all the handiwork was on the left side of my chest and extended below my rib cage.

I tried to turn to my right side to get a better view, but pain shot through me so bad it took my breath. I looked up and could see medicine lines running from my left arm to bags over my head, the same way they'd done on Grandma. The tube poking from my chest ran toward the floor.

I did my best to lie absolutely still and put my mind somewhere else. I closed my eyes and pictured Fancy in her pigtails when she was little, and us talking under the tobacco barn shelter, and kissing that first time. I thought about collecting bottles and eating blackberries. Lying there that night listening to the moans of pain and the screams of nightmares playing out in the minds of those around me caused my own dream horrors, like the sound of Lightning's body hitting the bottom of the well. And Huy tied to that stake.

A nurse made rounds the next morning and brought me pills and water. "Ma'am, where am I and how long have I been here?"

She was an older, strong-faced, motherly type, and I could tell she didn't take any crap. But there was kindness in her hazel green eyes. "You're in the Naval Support Activity Station Hospital in DaNang. Today makes a week."

I swallowed the pills and water. "Any idea how long I'll be laid up?"

"As long as it takes to make sure you don't have any infection. That's what this tube"—she touched the one in my chest—"is for, to drain your damaged side." She leaned over and brushed hair off my forehead. "Your war is over, sonny boy, so don't get any ideas that you're going back to the field. You're lucky you aren't in the morgue, so don't give me any trouble, you got it?" She gave me a smile and a pat on my good shoulder.

When she came that night, she talked while taking my temperature and checking my bandages. "The docs are saying about a week to let your strength build up. They need to make sure your upper body doesn't blow up with air on one side since you only got one lung working."

A couple of times my blood pressure dropped and they had to lift the seal on the hole in my chest to let some air out. It was actually two weeks before the doctors decided I was stable enough for the ride to Japan. When the airplane lifted off, I gave a salute to Mo, and Gunny Phillips, and Hotah, and a place I knew would never leave me.

The navy hospital in Yokosuka, Japan, was a much bigger and livelier place, as modern as the hospital back home where Grandma stayed. They asked me if I wanted to make a phone call. Who the hell was I going to call? We got a lot of TLC from the docs and nurses, and the little Japanese aides were cute.

In addition to the chest wound, the skin on my feet peeled off in layers and smelled awful from jungle rot. They treated me with medicines for that and the leech bites on my ankles. My main doc came to see me early one morning after I'd been there a month. He was a tall, fairly young navy officer. His name tag said Dr. Halperin. "I know you understand your lung is collapsed, and so far, we've been fortunate that there's been no serious side effects from the bullet, like lead poisoning, or some other nasty infectious stuff that guys get in the jungle. With time, your lung might possibly reinflate, but probably not. Either way, any ideas you had about playing professional football, forget them." He was a nice guy for a navy puke.

Some days I'd read newspapers that showed white kids protesting or running off to Canada so they wouldn't have to go to Vietnam. I thought about Mo. What kind of appreciation would he get fighting for a country that would rather see him back picking cotton?

When I was strong enough, rehabilitation folks began to work with me to try and bring my body back into shape. I'd lost over twenty pounds and looked more like a scarecrow than a marine. First it was simple things like moving my arms in a circle, knee bends, and agility tests with my hands. Over the next several weeks, it progressed to more strenuous stuff like walking short distances. The place in my back where my bad lung was would burn like forty hells. Understanding what bad shape I was in humbled me. It took three months before I learned that making do with one lung required me to think differently, and practice patience.

Mental issues were another can of worms entirely. I would dream about trying to cover the bullet hole in my chest, but it kept growing bigger and bigger until it was huge, then Huy's head would pop out from it. I saw Lightning and Twin, and the first Vietnamese man I'd killed while he looked me in the eyes. I would dream I was drowning in water, then realize it was an ocean of blood, so thick it choked me, so heavy it pulled me under. I swam for all I was worth, desperate for a log that would save me. Some nights I would take my pillow and blanket and lie underneath the bed, afraid to sleep.

In October mail caught up with me. There were three letters from Fancy and one from a life insurance company wanting me to continue my coverage when I was discharged. The last one from Fancy was dated in May.

> *Dear Junebug:*
> *I am so worried. I'm praying to God this letter will find you and you will write back to let me know you are okay. I don't know what I'll do if some harm has happened, or worse. I wrote Momma to ask her to get in touch with that Lawyer Stern to see if he had heard anything, and she said she did and he hadn't heard anything either. I look at the stars every night and send you all the love I've got.*
>
> *I decided to stay in France when Mrs. Francetti moved on. This is a place where I've found comfort and peace. The people here only judge you by who you are. I've got a job that for once doesn't include cleaning up for white folks, have made some good friends, and am learning so much I would never ever*

have had the chance to at home. Please let me hear
from you because my mind will not rest until I do.
  I love you as always,
  Fancy

Immediately I sat down and wrote.

  Dear Fancy:
  I'm very sorry I haven't written. I got hurt a little
and have been in the hospital in Japan. Don't go to
worrying because I'll be fine. They are treating me
very good and I hope to be recovered by the first of
the year. I'm so glad you sound happy and have
found good friends and, most of all, a job you like
that don't involve saying "Yes'um" to nobody. You
deserve what you're getting, and knowing you are at
peace makes me feel so much better. Tell Roy and
Clemmy I hope to see them sometime next year when
my enlistment is up. There have been many times
when I was at my worst and could feel you around
me. It never failed to keep me going. I'll watch that
last star in the handle of the Big Dipper every night
it's shining, and if you do the same, we'll know we're
thinking of each other.
  Love you back,
  Junebug

CHAPTER 53

One morning after physical therapy, the nurse gave me a note for an appointment with a new doctor. When I found the office, it was in the Mental Health Ward. I had to force myself to knock.

"Enter," came a female voice.

When I opened the door, a dark-haired, blue-eyed lady navy officer sat facing me. The nameplate on the desk read Lieutenant Heaney. Not knowing if I was supposed to salute or not, I raised my right hand to my brow. "Corporal Hurley reporting, ma'am."

She smiled. "No formalities necessary in my office, Corporal. Have a seat." She nodded toward the chair. A file was open on her desk. She opened it and looked at me. "My name is Lieutenant Heaney, and I'm a psychologist. I see you were in a scout sniper unit. That must have been pretty dangerous duty." Her voice had a scratch to it.

I eased into the chair, suspicious. "Sometimes."

"How are you doing with your recovery? I understand you have a chest wound. Are you in pain?"

My hand moved to my left side. "You know what the marine corps says, ma'am: Pain is just weakness leaving the body."

She smiled. "I also know marines can be full of shit on occasion." She was a little bit of a woman from what I could see; her face, nose, cheekbones, and chin were sharp, accented by the way the sides of her brown hair swept behind her ears. I guessed her to be in her early thirties. "How about your mental recovery? Combat troops don't often come home without bringing some of it with them. How are you doing with that?"

I didn't say anything.

She waited until the silence got uncomfortable. Lieutenant Heaney closed the file and pushed back in her chair. "How about we go get a cup of coffee?" We walked to the twenty-four-hour canteen on the lower floor of the hospital. She paid for the coffee. I held a plastic red chair for her at one of the blue Formica-topped tables. "Your file says you're from North Carolina, Corporal. How'd you come to be in the marine corps?" While her lips smiled, her eyes searched.

"It's Lance Corporal."

"Sorry. Why the marine corps?"

"Wanted to meet John Wayne."

She chuckled. "Still want to meet him?"

I watched as a marine private cleaned a tall window along the far wall. He used a long stick and spray. "Not so much." The private had only one arm.

"In your file, nurses say they've found you sleeping under your bed. Any particular reason you do that?"

"Need a vacation sometimes."

"From what?"

I spread my fingers on the tabletop, then flexed them into fists. "Everything."

Lieutenant Heaney sat back. "What kind of everything?"

"Seeing faces in my sleep, hearing stuff that isn't there. You know, everything."

"Soldiers often don't get to see the faces of the enemy. I guess it must have been different in your work, huh? I would imagine being a sniper is more personal."

"Some." Huy's face appeared in my mind.

"Why did you become a sniper? I'm pretty sure you had to volunteer for it."

"Extra pay." I set the coffee cup down too hard.

"Did you like it?"

I stared at her. Was there something in that file from Snake? "It was a job."

"So is shoveling horse shit. You're not answering my question."

"Sometimes." I pushed my chair back from the table.

She laid her hands out flat. "You always talk so much?"

I sipped the last of my coffee. "Not always."

She waited for more, holding my eyes, then let out a breath. "Listen, Ray, I can try to help. But all I can do is help you help yourself. You've got to want to come back from where you were." She started to fold her arms, but stopped and leaned across the table. "Let me put it to you this way, Corporal Hurley—sorry, Lance Corporal. War doesn't end with a period, just a comma. When you survive, demons often come to live with you, and it's possible many won't go away. You can learn to put them in their proper place, find a way to cope when they haunt you, and if you'll give me a chance, I'll try my best to help you."

This little woman had no idea what she was asking. But maybe she was the log I had been waiting for. We met every morning at eleven o'clock. I told her about Snake and Mo. I told her the story about Snake getting his boot caught on the trip wire. I told her all kinds of stories.

After a week, she held up her hand. "Enough with the bullshit, Ray. It's not that I don't enjoy your little war adventures, but they aren't why we're here. We've got to get down to what's in your head, what scares the shit out of you so much you want to sleep under your bed, what makes you wake up screaming. So, stop with all the extraneous crap. Horror doesn't like the light of day, Ray, and if you're going to get better, we need to put some sun on it."

I felt like a kid whose momma had spanked his ass good. It made me mad. If she wanted it, I'd see how she liked it. I intentionally tried to shake her calmness. I put it all out there: the gore of up-close killing, what a man's face looked like when you shot his eye out, what a rush I got hunting other men. I even told her about Huy, and what a child looks like with his arms severed and insects are crawling in his mouth and eye sockets. I expected her to curl up and cry. But she never budged. She wanted it all and she wanted it out loud, refusing to let me have any silent gaps, even when I needed them worse than she did. Lieutenant Heaney insisted it was important that I speak the words. When the ice started to thaw, the spigot opened, and it poured out.

A few weeks later, she surprised me. "Your file says you have no next of kin. How come?"

The war was one thing, but my before life was something else. "Just worked out that way."

Lieutenant Heaney picked up an orange ball she kept on her desk and threw it at me. "Don't even try it. We're done with that Silent Sam stuff. I want to know what happened to your family."

I got up and left. It was two days before I went back.

She folded her hands on the desk, the look on her face unsympathetic. "Are you ready to talk to me, Ray?"

I glared at her. "My granddaddy's dog, Grady, got run over when I was six. Grady was crying from the pain, so my daddy shot him in the head while I watched. That was the last time I cried around my daddy."

Her face scrunched, but she quickly caught herself. "I'm sorry, Ray, but what's that got to do with your next of kin?"

"I ain't finished. When I was eight, my parents were killed in a car wreck while my daddy was hauling a load of moonshine whiskey. The car caught fire and burned him and my momma alive. I guess he wasn't satisfied with just killing the dog."

I could see a hint of color change in her eyes. She blinked a couple of times.

"Then, when I was fourteen, my granddaddy died, and I was left to look after Grandma." I let the silence sit between us. "Two years later, my grandma died because I didn't have sense enough to understand how sick she was."

Harder blinking. She intertwined her fingers. "Is that it?"

"No. I killed two men in a drug deal when I was sixteen."

Lieutenant Heaney made no move to say anything. I wondered how she liked me now.

"The only other person I've ever cared about is a black girl. I can't be with her because of the hate it'd bring. Plus, I killed her brother and she don't know it. That's why I don't have any next of kin." I got up and left.

I went to Lieutenant Heaney's office on the last Friday in December. When I entered, I sensed something. "What's wrong?"

"Lance Corporal Hurley, I'm sorry to tell you this, but I've been transferred."

"When?"

"I leave Monday." She was all military business. "You've done so well, Lance Corporal, I'm sure you won't let this stop your progress."

This was the person I'd trusted with my soul. "So now it's 'Lance Corporal'?" The window slammed down; I'd seen this movie before. I stood up and saluted. "Well, good luck to you, Lieutenant Heaney." I turned to leave.

I heard her chair scrape. "Wait." She came behind and grabbed my elbow, pulled me around, and put her arms around my neck. "Don't let up, Ray. Make your peace." Her eyes were wet on my skin.

For three days, I refused to do anything but sit on my bunk. Once again, it was up to me to root hog or die. The flashbacks were regular. I found myself unable to stand in long lines or be in the middle of any kind of crowd. Certain smells, like wet ground or fishy food, could put me right back in the jungle. Anger was quick to come, and when it did, my first reaction was to punish the offender. I trained myself to, instead of wanting to hurt somebody, go to the physical therapy lab, work myself into a sweat, and drive out the poison. Peace was a hard place to find.

CHAPTER 54

In January of 1969, the medical staff felt I was sufficiently recovered to return to duty. I sat on an airplane in Yokota, Japan,
and watched snow swirl outside the window, wondering what it
would feel like to be in the States again. Fourteen hours later, I
landed in Chicago, where it was also snowing, but more like a
blizzard. Flights were grounded the rest of the day, and I spent
an uncomfortable night in O'Hare Airport slouched in a plastic
chair, watching the people around me. Some were dressed nor-
mally, and usually nodded a greeting at my marine uniform.
Others wore an assortment of flowered shirts and dirty jeans,
and stared at me like I'd killed their child. None of them offered
a "thank you."

After a two-hour flight and a three-hour bus ride the next
day, I was in Camp Lejeune, North Carolina, on a cold, sunny
afternoon. I reported in and was assigned to live in a common
barracks, given desk duty, and ordered to have weekly follow-
up medical evaluations. After a couple of visits to the docs, this
major suggested I go over to the VA, said I could probably get
some benefits since I only had one lung. "No disrespect, sir, but

I'd rather eat something that came out of another man's ass than bother with those people." He scratched his marine-cut gray hair and let out a chuckle.

After six months, the marine corps concluded I was unsuitable for regular duty and discharged me on June 19, 1969. Nobody said thank you then either. They gave me a check for two thousand dollars to cover back pay and unused leave. I cashed it at the bank, bought a used Chevrolet truck from a car dealer, a Remington 30.06 rifle from a pawn shop, a fifth of Jack Daniel's, and headed home.

It was close to midnight when I pulled into the yard. I shut off the engine and took a pull from the half-empty whiskey bottle. I waited for the parade and marching band to welcome me home. They never showed. Instead, a familiar loneliness waited, like a shadow hiding behind the house. I was scared to death to open the truck door.

I sipped on the bourbon. The old house seemed so much smaller than I remembered. Grandma waved from the porch and I could smell frying chicken and biscuits in the air. Fancy was sitting on the steps in her red dress, constantly tucking it under her legs, and Sally Mule was in the barn. Things had come full circle. I'd hoped coming back here would let me find that beginning and somehow change it. I took a deep breath, flipped the door handle, and stepped to the ground.

Grass and weeds were grown up everywhere. One of the porch steps broke when I put my weight on it, and a hinge on the screen door pulled loose. I sat down on a straw-bottomed chair, and remembered other nights spent sitting in this very spot.

Inside, the house smelled musty, the odor of longtime emptiness mixed with a dose of sadness. I found a candle in the sewing machine drawer, lit it, and walked around. It was still the same as it was when I'd left, Grandma's bed covered with the quilt I'd laid across it four years ago, the kitchen table that had been privy to so many conversations still protected by the red-and-white-checked oilcloth. I listened for voices, but the only sounds came from little critters scurrying across the floor. I stood in my bedroom, the place where Fancy and I made love the first time, and the room I'd spent so many nights trying to make sense of my life. This house should have been where the world was safe and peaceful and things always worked out for the best.

I pulled some jeans and a T-shirt from my duffel bag, then carried my marine uniform to the trash barrel out back, dropped it in, soaked it with the remainder of the liquor, and held my lighter until the green clothes caught fire. I watched the last four years disappear.

The mesh screen on the porch suffered from neglect, the wire rusting and corners pulled away from missing nails. I gazed out above the dark treetops at a yellow summer moon, remembering days when my biggest concern was the weather. People had come home to this land from wars before. I hoped I would be the last.

I walked across the road to the edge of the woods where I first learned to become invisible. The stars winked a welcome home. "I thought for a while I was going to be with you, Grandma. In a lot of ways, I wish I was. I'm not sure I can do this life alone."

When the sun came up, I made an inspection. I stood by the dry well. "Wish it was me down there, Lightning, instead of you." I waited like I expected him to answer. The chicken house had fallen down, and the pack house was a pile of burnt rubble. The tobacco barn still stood, but honeysuckle vines and wisteria covered its sides and roof. I walked up the old horse path toward the Wilson farm. Kudzu and briars had reclaimed a lot of the trail, but the stumps Lightning, Fancy, and me sat on to tell ghost stories, and the place I got my first kiss, were still there. At the clearing, I could see Fancy running home across the clover field. Our childhood had been too short.

The fact that I'd killed three people before I was eighteen felt unreal even now. It was more unreal that I hadn't stopped there. I would have settled for that. It was a destiny I never wanted but seemed to want me. I'd just turned twenty-three, but felt so much older. I looked up and talked to the sky, hoping my words would make it all the way to Texas. "Is this what you meant by 'you won't ever be the same,' Snake?"

I piddled until the sun was up full, then got in the Chevy and drove to Apex. It didn't appear a lot had changed through the countryside, but closer to town there were a couple of new gas stations and a 7-Eleven store where before there'd been just open fields. A café I'd never seen advertised a country breakfast, good ham, eggs, grits and biscuits, a thing I missed. Some of the voices at the other tables had a Yankee twang, another surprise. I sipped through four cups of coffee and read about Joe Frazier's upcoming fight with Jerry Quarry in the newspaper. By then, I figured Lawyer Stern's office would be open.

He stared like he was trying to place me at first, but after a couple of seconds he broke into a big smile. "Raeford Hurley! Good God, son, you've grown up. Look at you." He grabbed my hand and shook hard. He'd got a little heavier. His bald head had wrinkles that started over his eyebrows and folded backward. "When did you get home?"

I smiled, embarrassed by his goings-on. "Last night. Figured to visit you first thing." The only new item in his office was a picture of Governor Moore.

"Clemmy Stroud came to visit me last year, seemed to be worried that nobody had heard from you. She's the one that told me you were in Vietnam. How'd you make out over there?"

"Fine. The only hard part was keeping all that equipment running in the mud and jungle. I worked in the motor pool, and got hurt when a jack handle flew back and hit me in the chest. I was laid up awhile, and just forgot to write. No big deal."

"I'm real happy you're home in one piece. From what I see on the news, a lot of boys aren't so lucky." I didn't take the bait. We went to sit down. He offered a cup of coffee, but I passed on it. "What's on your mind this morning, Raeford?"

"I figure we're all up-to-date on our business, but wanted to make sure."

"We are. You don't owe anything to anybody as far as I know."

"That's good. If I decided to sell the farm, how would it work?"

He explained the process. "But I'm going to give you this piece of advice, Raeford. Folks are starting to move in here from all over. All of a sudden everybody wants to live out in the sticks. Couldn't hardly give land away a few years ago, but now it's getting to be right valuable. You might consider holding on to the place awhile to get the best price, or maybe sell part and keep the house."

"I'll think about that. Would you mind going to the bank with me?"

We took our time walking down Main Street on a beautiful early warm morning. I enjoyed the noise of storekeepers opening their shops, cars moving up and down the street, folks standing and talking. Smells coming from a donut place we passed were much better than the stink of shit-fertilized paddy water and rotted vegetation imprinted on my brain. My ears still wanted to listen to the wind, and I cut my eyes around every blind corner.

At the bank, the man printed a statement of my account. I asked to take out a thousand. Mr. Stern reminded me to stop at the post office and let them know they could deliver mail.

The drugstore hadn't changed, and neither had the saleslady. She stared at me like she might be trying to remember my face, but then went about her business. It seemed a lifetime ago Fancy and me had sat on the curb outside eating ice cream. I wandered to the back where they still had comic books, and picked up a couple to sniff the paper. On the way out, I considered asking for a pack of Trojans just to watch her reaction, but got a chocolate cone instead.

CHAPTER 55

I stocked up on new towels and sheets at Salem's General Store, got home early in the afternoon, and fixed up the bed. After sweeping out four years' worth of dust and dirt and wet-mopping the floors, I decided to ride to the Wilsons.

Mrs. Wilson answered my knock. She looked thinner, her face pale and drawn. Time had not been kind to her. Her mouth gaped open. "Well, Lord have mercy." She yelled toward the back of the house. "Clyde, come see who's here!" She took my arm and pulled me inside, giving me a big hug. "I'm so glad to see you, Junebug."

Mr. Wilson came through the kitchen door, his gut drooped over his belt like a fat woman's butt. He walked with a cane for support, hadn't shaved, and blotched red patches crisscrossed his nose and sagging cheeks. "Junebug Hurley! Well, ain't you a sight for sore eyes."

I was glad he looked bad. "Came home last night and thought to drop over, so if you noticed somebody at the house you wouldn't worry." Didn't want him to think he had any black folks for neighbors.

"Where in the world have you been these long years? Sit down here and tell us about it." He motioned to a chair. "You want some iced tea?"

"No, I appreciate it. What's with the cane?"

"Hurt my back a while ago, ain't been able to do much of anything since. Then Lila got sick, so we just been living like two wore-out mules."

I looked at Mrs. Wilson. "What caused your sickness?"

She dry-washed her hands. "Got to feeling real poorly one day, went to the doctor, and he sent me to the hospital to run some tests. They think I've had a couple of little strokes. I'm better now, though."

She must not have been looking in the mirror. "You need to take care of yourself, slow down some." We spent a while catching up.

"Did you have to go to Vieet Naam?" Mr. Wilson asked.

"Yep. Spent a little over a year there."

"What did you do? Was it bad? Did you get to kill any of the little chink bastards?"

"Never fired a shot. Worked in the motor pool." I could see the letdown on his face. "Mostly it was like living through a year of late Julys, hot as hell, and the place smelled like Fido's ass. How's the farming business been?"

"Ah, you can't hardly make much of a living no more. Can't get help. All the niggers"—his eyes made a quick cut at me—"is moving to town and getting public jobs. Plus, Roy's got too damn old to do much of anything. Hard to farm tobacco without good labor."

That was enough for me. I got up to leave.

"We sure are glad you're home, Junebug. A lot of boys are being killed over there. We're real proud of you."

Heat rose up my face. Him saying he was proud of me was like spitting in my face. But I let it pass. "Appreciate it, happy to be home." I paused at the door. "By the way, whatever happened to my old mule, Sally?"

Mr. Wilson shook his head. "That was the craziest thing. She didn't live a month after you left, just lay down one day and died. I could swear she was grieving."

"To tell you the truth, she was what I missed most." His face wrinkled, like his feelings were hurt.

Mr. Wilson walked as far as my truck. When we were out of earshot, I turned around to face him. "I know it was you." I held his gaze until he looked away. "You should know I ain't forgot." My face flushed red as that night came back to me. "If you or any of your sheet-wearing sons a bitches ever show up around my place again, I'll kill you. You understand?"

He nodded and quick-limped back to his house.

I stopped at Roy and Clemmy's. I ran my hand over the fender on Granddaddy's old truck. Clemmy answered the door. She didn't say anything, just grabbed me around the neck, held tight, and started crying. She took my hand and led me to a chair. "I was worried we might not see you again. Fancy said you got hurt."

"I was worried a bit myself there for a while, but the docs fixed me up, so no worse for wear." The little house had good cooking smells, a hominess unlike the Wilson place. There was a line of pictures on one wall, a few of Fancy and Lightning as they grew up, and a big black-and-white framed one of Fancy. I walked over to it. "Is this recent?" It showed her from the waist up. She wore a white shirt with a collar that stood up against her neck. I could see a river behind her, and it must have been spring because her sleeves were short. Seeing that face never failed to stab me in the heart.

"She sent it about a year ago. That girl has sure grown up, ain't she?"

Fancy was far from a girl anymore. She was a beautiful woman. Her hair was cut and fashioned around her face like I'd seen in magazines. She looked stylish, but I could still see my Fancy, the one with bowed teeth, skinny legs, and that fire in her eyes. I could almost feel her saying, "I dare you."

Roy was out in the backyard and came shuffling as fast as he could when Clemmy hollered to him. We hugged each other. I was truly happy to see the closest thing I had to a family. Roy was showing his years. His hair had turned completely white, and a lifetime of hard labor was catching up with his once-powerful body. We sat down and I teased him about being gray-headed. "Weren't you and Grandma about the same age, Roy?" I asked.

"I expect so. I'll be seventy-one next month." He said it proudly. I looked at his eyes. When you're young, all grown-ups look old, and by the time you are a grown-up, they are old. Only pictures assure you they were young once. I wondered if this was the way Roy thought his life would turn out, what his dreams might have been when he was young.

When we settled down, Clemmy wanted to talk about Fancy. "She decided she would stay and live in France, did you know that?"

"Got a letter from her a while back that said she was. I sure have thought about her a lot, hoping she would make out good. She sounded happy."

Clemmy smiled. "I think she's doing fine; homesick some I can tell, but don't expect she'll ever come back here after what them Klan people did. That scared her down deep."

Roy spoke up. "Things are changing, Junebug. Black folk about had a bellyful of being on the bottom. These young bucks ain't going to take shit no more." Fancy's words rang in my head, "*One day the blood's going to run the other way.*" "What are you aiming to do now that you're back? If you're considering farming, I'll help you."

I shook my head. Roy was fooling himself if he thought he'd ever prime another row of tobacco. "About had enough of ruining my back growing up. I'm going to take some time and wind down, figure things out as I go along."

Clemmy rubbed her hand down the side of my face, the same way Fancy used to do. She'd always had knowing eyes. "I'm guessing you got some stuff that's going to take a bit to get out of your system."

I pulled up from the chair. "If you hear from Fancy, tell her I'm home." I hugged Clemmy and Roy. "Y'all come down anytime. I expect I'll be around."

Roy held on to my arm for an extra minute. "You know, Junebug, we ain't heard nothing from Lightning since before you and Fancy left. I can't help wondering if one of these redneck sumbitches didn't kill him and never let on."

I gripped his shoulder. "Maybe he'll just show up one of these days like he did before." It galled me pretty bad to lie to such a good man, but what could I tell him? That Lightning tried to kill me and I'd just been lucky to kill him first? I believed if I could sit down with Roy in the right circumstance I could tell him the truth, because I felt like he'd always known the truth about Lightning. But at this point it would just cause more hurt, and I figured Roy had suffered enough pain in his life.

CHAPTER 56

I pulled all the machinery and tools from the barn, tinkered, oiled, rubbed the rust off, but had no urge to use them. My farming days were over. I went to Durham, bought a television, and would sit watching it for hours, turning it off when there was news about the war.

I dreaded the nights and my dreams. I began to roam the woods in the dark again, slipping in and out of the shadows, reliving the jungle. Other times, I'd just sit and talk to Grandma. "You always knew more than you said. I need the comfort right now to know I'm not completely lost." I never sensed her around me.

I was still haunted by the rush of war. Lieutenant Heaney had warned the taste for that feeling of living on the edge caused many soldiers not to be able to adjust to regular life. It drove many to risk everything to feel it again, others to drugs to dull their minds, and some simply disappeared. I would see Huy over and over, asking me why. I still didn't have an answer. Many times I considered sticking the rifle in my mouth, but was never brave enough, or maybe desperate enough, to do it.

At the end of October, Roy had a heart attack sitting at the supper table. I did as much as I could for Clemmy, paying for the funeral in a way she wouldn't know it had come from me. As long as Roy had lived in the community, and had at some time or other worked for about everybody in it, I was the only white person at the church. "Glory be to God for letting us have such a fine man all these years," said the preacher. "Amen," echoed the congregation. I listened to Clemmy cry. The choir sang beautiful hymns, and I couldn't help but think it would have been a big comfort if Fancy had been there for her momma. I sat in the pew and confessed silently to Roy about what happened to Lightning. Maybe he could forgive me. In the graveyard, I watched another box lower into a hole in the ground.

Mr. and Mrs. Wilson assured Clemmy she could stay on in the house as long as she helped Mrs. Wilson. Mr. Wilson said he'd plant her a garden so she could make do. It turned out to be a blessing. Mrs. Wilson had a major stroke the first of January 1970, and was bedridden. Clemmy looked after her because Mr. Wilson was too frail to do it. He fixed up a room so Clemmy could stay in the big house at night. I wondered what the neighbors thought.

In late spring, May I think, an old dog wandered up in the yard. He was bowlegged and ratty-looking. I chased him off. "You need to get your behind somewhere else, mutt, ain't nothing for you here."

For the next couple of days, I would see the dog hiding behind the barn or lying at the edge of the trees. I couldn't figure out why he didn't just move on. One morning he was under the woodshed.

"Dog, I thought I told you to stay away from here." He lay looking at me, wagging his tail. "Dogs don't make out too good around this place."

He didn't make any effort to get up, and I wondered if he was hurt. I squatted and looked him over. He stumbled to his feet and licked me in the face. It didn't look like he had any injuries. "Are you just hungry? I've been hungry." I went in the house and got a bowl for water and some leftover chicken. "When you finish this, move on down the road. Go find somebody else to mooch off." That night when I looked, the dog was gone.

The next morning, I went out the porch door and almost shit in my pants when the dog ran out from under the steps. "You son of a bitch, git your ass away from here!" He took off across the road and into the woods.

That night I found him in the woodshed again. I sat down on a peach basket. "Persistent cuss, ain't you." He got up and shyly walked over to me, head down, looking up with sad brown eyes. "Think you've found a home, do you? Two old lost souls wandering around in this world." By the time I fed him for a month, he turned out to be right good-sized, and younger than he looked when he first come around.

The dog got so he followed me everywhere. Pretty soon, he was sleeping in the house, and rode in the truck like a person. We got in the habit of riding over to a little country store a few miles away every day after supper to get us a five-cent ice cream cup. I'd eat mine with a wooden spoon and he'd lick his clean.

I named him Grady. We had many long conversations, him being almost as good a listener as Sally Mule. "What makes a man take pleasure in killing other men, Grady? I didn't start out like that, just seemed to happen." He would sit and watch as though he was interested, then give me a sloppy cheek kiss when I was through. Grady showed up just when I needed him.

Thanksgiving Day that year came in cold. The sky was a deep cobalt blue, but the bright sun didn't offer much warmth. Since there was only Grady and me, I didn't want any big meal, just some chicken and dumplings from a can. After dinner, I went for a walk in the sunshine. At the edge of the yard, I remembered Momma and Daddy driving off the last time I ever saw them, her blowing kisses and laughing. Grady followed me behind the house to the old iron pot, and I thought about the time Grandma and me sat plucking a chicken, seeing her patient smile when I asked questions, and the way her nose wrinkled when her glasses slipped down. In the woodshed, I sat on the kindling stump and relistened to Granddaddy's stories of the old days, and what he intended to be life lessons for my future days. And I remembered the funerals for all of them.

I thought about Fancy when she was a little girl, scared of anything that went bump in the night, and how she'd become my partner, willing to stand with me and face the world. I missed her a lot.

Thanksgiving night the temperature dropped low, and Grady decided he wanted to snuggle under the quilt. I slept deep and dreamed I was walking in fields of clover. The day turned to night and I lay down in the sweet-smelling grass. Huy was lying next to me, the watch I gave him stuffed in his mouth. The air filled with fireflies; they began to attack me like a swarm of angry bees. Lightning was speaking some Vietnamese gibberish to the fireflies while he struggled to pull bullets from his chest. "I'm sorry," I said. "I'm sorry."

Grady woke me licking my face. In the darkness I got up, put on clothes, grabbed the gun on the way out the door, and headed to the woods. Grady wanted to follow, but I chased him back to the house. At the edge of the field, I slid to the ground beside an oak tree. The butt of the Remington went between my knees, and the barrel under my chin. I closed my eyes. "God forgive me for what I've done. I ask for mercy." I thought about Mo and hoped he had prayed for me.

I lifted my eyes to a sky lit bright with stars and a winter white moon, and located the Big Dipper. I wanted to keep that vision as I passed from this world. I wondered if it would hurt. My finger tightened on the trigger.

Something touched my leg. I opened my eyes. It was Grady. "Git, dog! Get your ass out of here!" I needed to get this over with. I shifted the rifle and slapped at him. He ran a few feet and stopped.

I moved the barrel back beneath my chin. Grady came again, whining and pawing. I moved the gun. It was my intention to hit and run him off, but things got mixed up. Instead, I pulled him to my lap and buried my face in his fur. Grady lay in my arms, his nose against my neck. After a while, we went back to the house and the bed. Grady slipped under the covers, and I slept without dreaming for the first time in months.

CHAPTER 57

We got back home after getting ice cream on a warm, cloudy night in the middle of December. Grady sat with me on the couch while I watched television and dozed. His head was in my lap when I felt him stiffen. He jumped to the floor. "What's the matter?" Grady stared out the front window and growled, the first time I'd ever heard him make an angry sound. I thought back to another night when men in white sheets were perfectly willing to kill me, and picked up the rifle that leaned against the wall in the corner. I eased around the doorway, sliding against the wall, staying in the dark. The hair on Grady's back bristled and he stayed between the door and me. I could make out a shadow just beyond the porch steps. "You best be making some noise." I clicked off the safety.

"So, I come to visit and you want to shoot me, Junebug?"

I froze. It couldn't be. I switched on the outside light. "Fancy? Is that you, Fancy?" I pushed Grady aside, jerked open the screen door, leaped over the steps, grabbed her in my arms, and swung her around, laughing. Grady followed me, barking and running in circles. I set Fancy down and put my hands on both sides of her face. "Please, God, don't let this be a dream."

She laughed. "I've missed you too, Junebug." She pulled my hands down. "I promise I'm real."

"When did you get home? I didn't think I'd ever see you again."

"Got here this morning, needed to make sure Momma was all right since Daddy died. She about pushed me out the door after supper."

"You don't know how happy I am to see you, Fancy." I stuttered like some country bumpkin, trying to think of the right things to say. "How long are you staying?"

"A couple of weeks maybe."

I took her hand. "Come in here. I've got to get a good look at you." I noticed her palm and fingers had lost their calluses.

Fancy slipped her arm into the crook of my elbow. "Since it's not too cool, why don't we sit on the porch awhile." She leaned her head against my shoulder and pointed at the sky. "You have any idea how many times I've looked up there and wondered where you were and if you were all right?"

She held herself different, the way she sat, even the way she crossed her legs. This was a new, self-assured, refined, and worldly-looking Fancy. Her hair was cut straight and softened with light red streaks. The bell-bottom jeans and paisley shirt were a big change from the flour-sack dresses her momma used to make. I couldn't help wondering how much she might have changed on the inside. "So, tell me what you're doing to get by in France." We held hands like two teenagers. I couldn't stop smiling.

"Before Mrs. Francetti left for Italy, she introduced me to a friend who ran a café concert, it's like a restaurant with music, and the lady gave me a job as a hostess. I've been doing it ever since. The French don't like Americans very much, but seem to like black Americans. They have this idea we're all jazz singers." She giggled. "Makes me feel bad that I can't sing." As soon as she rolled those playful blackberry eyes, the years started to peel away.

"You've done good for yourself. I can see it in you, Fancy." What I saw was that butterfly that had broken from her cocoon, stretched her wings, and was no longer afraid of the world.

"You look some older, Junebug, them blue eyes are harder than I remember." She ran her fingers along the side of my temple.

"War can change a person, Fancy." The weight of the last four years hit me all of a sudden. I realized this was the moment that had kept me going. I would tell her all of it if she asked.

She reached under my chin and pulled my head around to meet her eyes. "That's over now." Just like always, Fancy knew how to make the world seem not so desperate. We talked into the night about her adventures getting to where she was now. "If you hadn't helped me with the money, Junebug, I'd still be saying 'yes'um' to all the white ladies in this community."

I passed on the truth. "It was only a little push for you, Fancy. You did the rest on your own. I'm really proud of you."

We went inside and sat next to each other on the couch. "Want to thumb-wrestle?" Fancy grinned.

Both of us laughed, remembering the beauty of innocence that belonged to another lifetime. I reached my arm around her and pulled close, searching for some way to find the time we'd lost. The laughing was what I'd missed the most. The more we talked, the more the strangeness and awkwardness began to fall away like snow off a warm roof. I pulled her up and she followed me to the bedroom.

We lay facing each other on the bed. I kissed her. Fancy laid her hand against my chest. "Tonight can you hold me and we just talk, Junebug? Four years is a long time. I want us to know each other again. Do you understand?"

There was that seemingly constant question in my life. "Is there somebody else?"

"It's not that at all. I've just spent so many years keeping my heart covered against the pain of being alone and scared, it's not easy to let go. I need to know you're Junebug, the Junebug I remember."

I let out a deep breath. We lay across the bed, and I moved my arm beneath Fancy's neck and pulled her head to my chest. It was a relief. I'd been scared to death too. "Where do you want to start?"

She curled into me, her arm across my stomach. "Tell me about the war. What did you do?"

"Are you sure you want to hear about that?"

"Yes."

There in the darkness, I told Fancy everything: about being a sniper, what it was like to hunt and kill other men, about Snake, about Moses, and the hardest part—about Huy. By the end, the tears flowed. It wasn't sorry-crying, more like emptying a bucket I'd been toting for a long time. It felt like freedom, like I'd crossed the last road home.

I thought I would be embarrassed, but Fancy wouldn't let me. She simply held on, not asking questions. "Thank you for trusting me, Junebug. Your heart was always good. I know God will give you the peace you need."

We spent an amazing night discovering each other again, replaying childhood things, laughing, sitting in the kitchen at three in the morning while she fixed what she called crepes and I called craps. "Make me some biscuits, woman." And she did. In the morning, I drove her home. Mr. Wilson was standing in his yard, but wouldn't look at me.

When she came the next night, we sat on the couch. Grady snuggled between us, and we talked over how concerned she was about her momma being alone now. "Will you check on her for me, Junebug?"

"You know I will, and I promise won't no harm come to her."

Fancy told me stories about the odd habits of French people, laughing about her trying to get used to the food. "I haven't had any pig tails or turnip greens in a long time, but I did eat some snails." After a while, she got to her feet and took my hand. "Come on."

"Where we going?"

"To find some memories." I followed her outside and past the tobacco barn. We turned up the path toward the stumps. The night woods were cold, quiet except for the crunch of brittle oak leaves under our shoes. Winter limbs stretched like bony fingers, and there was a frown on the face of the full moon. I heard the hoot owl call.

Fancy ran her hand over the letters I carved in the oak tree that first Christmas. "This was when we didn't think the world would hurt us on purpose, wasn't it, Junebug?"

"I remember your momma saying we'd find out what an ugly face the devil had, and I guess we did." I looked up through the treetops. "You remember when we stood right here one night and tried to figure out how folks got to heaven?"

"I thought then we'd ride on the backs of angels."

"What do you think now?"

"I don't know. I'd like to believe my daddy's up there, and your grandma. Maybe she was able to help him." She put her arms around my neck and drew me to her. "I love you, Junebug, and always have. You were strong when I needed it, and you showed me a real man is gentle and kind. Even when it got bad, I knew you'd stand by me and protect me. I'll always be grateful for that."

Just like in the jungle, I felt what I couldn't see. I was afraid to move.

"I need to ask you something." Fancy leaned her head back, watching my eyes. "Lightning's not coming back, is he?"

The words I'd intended to say changed from the time they left my head to when they reached my mouth. I pushed her to arm's length. "Why would you think I have any idea about that?"

She held my face, not letting me look away. "After all these years not hearing from him, I considered something might have happened you never told me."

You lying bastard, tell her the truth. "Do you really think if I knew anything, I wouldn't have told you?"

Fancy's shoulders sank. She started to cry, sobs choking in her voice. "I just thought maybe . . ." Her words trailed off.

All these years I'd tortured myself when the only thing I'd done was keep myself from getting killed. I wanted to scream at her, "*Would you have felt better if he had killed me? I did everything but beg him to let it go, just leave, but he wouldn't. So, you want to hate me, go ahead. Your brother was a murderer and I'm sick of feeling bad about saving my own life.*" But I didn't. "The only thing I know about Lightning is what I told you. I took him to the bus station and that's the last time I saw him."

Fancy didn't come back the next day. She knew. At least I was pretty sure she knew.

Two nights later, Grady started wiggling and barking. Fancy was standing on the steps. I opened the door. "Thought maybe something was wrong."

"Just needed some time with Momma."

We went to the living room. "Fancy, I need you to believe I don't have any idea where Lightning is." As far as I could remember, it was the only lie I had ever told her.

She held up her hand. "It's okay, Junebug. He's probably right not to get in touch with us. At least he won't give these white sons of bitches the pleasure of hanging him."

The rest of the two weeks, Fancy and I were together as much as possible. Lightning was always there, like an invisible witness, but he didn't interfere, maybe understanding his truth was gone forever. I believe Fancy understood that whatever happened to Lightning was for the best.

On our last night together, she asked if I would take her to the airport. "Why don't you stay, Fancy?"

We lay facing each other. She kissed my forehead, running her hand down the side of my face. "I can't, Junebug. To me this place represents nothing but hate. I've worked hard to find where it feels I belong, and don't want to give that up. Every step along the way I was scared, but I'm not scared anymore." Fancy kissed me. "You could sell the farm and come with me. It's peaceful there, you'd like it."

I knew I'd never be able to sleep beside Fancy night after night knowing I'd betrayed her. "It is a temptation, but, like you said, it's a place *you* found where it feels *you* belong. The only way to be completely free of this life is to be away from everything that reminds you of it, and that includes me."

That night our lovemaking was gentle, giving, and forgiving.

We sat holding hands until her flight to New York was called. Fancy started crying, and I wanted to. We stood and hugged. I looked into her beautiful eyes. "We've had quite a time, haven't we, Fancy?"

She stepped back, and, despite the tears, gave me that amazing smile. "You're the best man I've ever known, Junebug Hurley." She turned and walked toward the entrance to the airplane, stopped, looked back, and pointed toward the sky.

EPILOGUE

Lawyer Stern's predictions came true. Folks were all over looking for land to build new houses. A real estate man visited me one morning and offered ten thousand dollars an acre for the farm. I could sell forty of the fifty acres; that much money should do me nicely for the future, so I decided to take it. Mr. Stern separated the deed and put the house and ten acres of land in Clemmy Stroud's name. She cried when I carried her the title. "Clemmy, you don't ever have to be beholden to anybody again." It would never repay what I had done to her child, but it was something. A week later, Clemmy told Mr. Wilson to look after his own wife, and I helped her move in. We shared the house, some of the best days I ever spent; I could almost feel Grandma smiling. It felt good knowing Clemmy would be living so close to Lightning. Maybe his spirit would know she was there.

Fancy and I continued to exchange letters on and off over the next few years until the spring of 1974, when I received a large envelope from her. Inside were a big picture and a short note. The picture showed Fancy dressed in a long white gown, flowers in her hair, her face as beautiful as I could ever have imagined, and on the back she wrote: "*To Junebug: On clear nights I still watch the sky.*" The note said she had met someone and was getting married. I was happy for her, but have to admit it hurt a fair amount. The hardest thing to miss is love, and I missed it mighty bad.

The flashbacks still troubled me from time to time, so one day I piled Grady in the truck and decided we'd drive out to Texas, see if Snake had any of that cold beer he talked about. He had plenty, and we spent a couple of weeks reminiscing about our time in hell. He always did have a way of helping keep my head straight.

When we got back home, Grady and me bought a little cabin deep in the high mountains of North Carolina near the Cherokee Reservation. My ghosts will still come occasionally and I invite them in, but they never stay very long. I've been down that road of ruts and low shoulders, and know this is where I need to be. I feel safe here.

The only thing I kept from the old house was the cigar box. I pull it out once in a while, roll Grady's collar in my hand, stare at Momma's gum wrapper necklace, squeeze the little braided bracelet I never did give to Snake, and clean Grandma's gold-rimmed glasses.

Sometimes folks camping along the Appalachian Trail will tell the forest rangers about seeing a dog sitting in the darkness and watching. They all swear there is a shadow of a man with him, but they can never be sure.

ACKNOWLEDGMENTS

A writer spends innumerable lonely hours of thought, frustration, and self-doubt before a novel is completed. But the absolute joy of accomplishment is like no other. The tendency is to sit back and say to yourself, "I did it. I did it when nobody thought I could, and I did it all myself." Nothing could be farther from the truth.

The accomplishment belongs to so many who have loved and supported you while you ignored them, slammed doors in frustration, and withdrew from life in general. There are many fingerprints on this novel, and my biggest fear is I will leave out someone who has provoked a thought, an idea, an unusual facial expression, or simply allowed me to sit and talk my way through issues I was having. You are many, and any I fail to publicly recognize, know I am grateful and will not forget.

My heartfelt thanks to my wife, Sandra, who has put up with my follies for forty-five years. My personal hero, my son Eric. The one person who never let me give up, encouraged me, and even threatened me on occasion, my best friend and fantastic southern writer, Jan Parker.

To Laurel Goldman, the best mentor an idiot like me could have. She had a temporary lapse of good sense when she allowed me into her writer's group, but it was the luckiest day of my life. Laurel is the most insightful and caring person I've ever had the pleasure of knowing; she is determined for each of her writers to

succeed, and gives her utmost to that end. I treasure every minute I am in her presence. To our writer's group: David Halperin,
Chrys Bullard, Martha Pentecost, Kathleen O'Keeffe, Linda
Hanley Finigan, and Alice Kaplan: They taught me the difference
between telling a story and writing a story.

To my amazing agent, Renee Fountain, who took a giant leap
of faith on a first novel. Italia Gandolfo of Gandolfo, Helin, and
Fountain Literary Agency, who is proof you never know who
you are talking to on FB.

A particular thanks to wonderful poet and songwriter Jules
Riley, who allowed me to use his words "put some meat on the
ground" from his poem "Waist Deep in Winter Water." To all
the wonderful instructors, friends, and participants at WildAcres,
where I learned to love the writing community.

Many years ago a little group of hope-to-be-writers came together to begin an Open Mic night in a wine store in Fuquay-
Varina, North Carolina, and yes, it's a real city. We were all
naïve and without a bucket full of talent between us, but we
practiced, embarrassed ourselves, and got better. I am proud to
say we are all still dear friends, still root for each other's success,
and still drink a lot of wine. That special group is made up of
Jan Parker, Laura Towne, Jack Lloyd, and Robin Miura.
Thanks to all of you for helping make my dream come true.

To my warrior brothers from Japan and Vietnam. A special
nod to my great friend Mike McBride, with whom I flew so
many missions. We will always stand faithful.

Lastly, I want to pay tribute to the writers who have most influenced me. They represent the best of southern literary fiction:
Ron Rash, Rick Bragg, Harry Crews, and the great William
Gay. Through their work they have set the bar high, and stand
as an example of how far the rest of us must reach.

**Please turn the page
for a very special Q&A
with Danny Johnson!**

What inspired you to write your first novel?

Like most folks in this business, I simply wanted to write, and the only thing I knew to write was a novel. By that I mean I knew very little about short stories or flash fiction, and hated poetry, so I just dove in and hoped for the best, which, of course, was awful. I knew I had a lot of stories to tell, but soon discovered I knew absolutely nothing about how to actually write them.

Do you have a specific writing style?

As much as it surprises me, I am now addicted to the literary genre. I say surprised because all I read growing up were comic books, John D. MacDonald, Harold Robbins, books of that nature. I had no idea what "literary" fiction meant.

How did you come up with the title?

It was purely by accident. The initial title was *Junebug and Fancy,* then as I was doing my last major revision, and in the scene when Fancy comes home for the visit from France, there is the line when Junebug is relating the horrors of his war experiences to her and he says, "It felt like I was crossing *the last road home,*" and I thought, *That's it!!* That was the title I'd been looking for during the whole process.

Is there a message in your novel that you want readers to grasp?

There is more than one, I hope. The first being the fact that children only begin to see racism when it is taught to them, the example being when Lightning is run off the neighbor farm when he asked to collect Coke bottles; racism does not occur naturally in our DNA. The other is about the power of love and how folks will sacrifice almost anything to hold on to it, and I think that is demonstrated by the relationship between Junebug and Fancy. The next is the horror of war and how men in desperate situations will revert to almost an animal state in order to survive, and most never fully recover from it. The final one I think is that veterans of such horrors sometimes spend the rest of their lives in some form of apology, an example of which is Junebug giving Fancy's mother the house so she could be near her son.

How much of the book is realistic?

I think all of it is realistic in as far as fiction represents reality without identifying real people, but there's nothing in it that I would consider fantasy. I think most literary fiction is based on truths of one kind or another, and the magic for the reader is to figure out what they are. I believe it is the responsibility of literary fiction writers to present the reader with something new each time, i.e., a new idea, a new thought, a new reality about something they are not familiar with.

Are experiences based on someone you know, or events in your own life?

Some of them I do, or have known. I do have some experience with some of the events, but not to the extent described in the story.

What books have most influenced your life?

Wow, tough question. I've read hundreds of books of all kinds in my life, but, as a writer, I think the one that influenced me the most was *Serena* by Ron Rash. I don't think it would have been such an "aha" moment had I not been moving forward with my understanding of literary fiction. I group *Serena* with William Gay's *The Long Home* as the two most influential books in my pursuit as a southern writer. And that's not to fail to acknowledge the many greats, Rick Bragg, Harry Crews, Flannery O'Connor, Harper Lee, Jill McCorkle, Lee Smith, and so many more who are fixtures in southern literature.

If you had to choose, which writer would you consider a mentor?

That's an easy one—Ron Rash, he's a friend and the absolute best "place" writer I've ever read. If he would just pick up a tab once in a while, I would like him even better. ☺

What book are you reading now?

I just finished Rick Bragg's biography about Jerry Lee Lewis, and it is a masterpiece.

Are there any new authors that have grasped your interest?

Yes, one comes to mind, and that is James Scott and his debut novel, *The Kept.*

What are your current projects?

I am working on a novel with the working title of *A Time of War, The Journey of Billy Cole,* which I'm sure will not be the final title.

Name one entity that you feel supported you outside of family members.

Easy, my writers' group has been the most amazing support group I could have ever hoped for.

Do you see writing as a career?

Well, at this point and at my age, if I don't I'm pretty well screwed. ☺

If you had to do it all over again, would you change anything in your book?

Like most writers, if I went through the manuscript a hundred times, I'd change something, or many somethings, every time;

some small, some major . . . as you grow as a writer, you are better able to see bigger ideas.

Do you recall how your interest in writing originated?

I was pretty much a loner as a kid, and books gave me an outlet for my imagination, whether it was comic books or adventure stories or magazines, I just simply loved reading. It let me go anywhere, visit any country, live any lifestyle, all vicariously through the characters, and they still do to this day. My tastes in literature have changed, but that magic in a well-written book has no equal, regardless of the genre.

Is there anything you find particularly challenging in your writing?

Never being satisfied with the work. I wish I could simply get to a point and say, "That's the best it can be," but I don't think any writer ever reaches that point. I heard Ron Rash tell the story about his latest book, and this is a guy who could write the dictionary and sell a million copies, that he was 100 pages deep into the manuscript when he looked at it one night and said, "This isn't working," chucked it and started over. Now, if a guy like him is willing to do that, how can I not face up to my work in the same way?

What was the hardest part of writing your book?

Hearing criticism from my writers' group, and believe me, it got downright ugly at times and I took it personally, my feelings were hurt, and I would walk out of class and say, "I'm never going back to that damn place again," but I stuck it out. Each time when I went back to the manuscript and compared what I had to what they suggested, they were right every time. I'm sure if Laurel knew beforehand what a lousy writer I was, she would have never let me in the group. I will forever be grateful she did, and I will forever be grateful for the amazing feedback of our group. Writers owe other writers only one thing: the truth. I always tell folks who want me to read their work that I don't mind, but if they don't want the hard truth, they need to find someone else. It's the only way one can improve his ability.

Did you learn anything from writing your book and, if so, what was it?

I learned the value of constant learning through reevaluation, being able to look at your work with a critical eye, and being willing to change what needs to be changed, no matter how big it might be or how brilliant you thought it was.

What were the challenges (research, literary, psychological, and logistical) in bringing it to life?

My biggest challenge was learning my craft. As I said earlier, I knew I had stories to tell, but no idea how to write at a level anybody else would want to read them. Once I was embarrassed enough, once I had been kicked in the ass enough, there was no workshop, no class, no writers' conference, no open-mic opportunity I missed. And I listened. And I learned. And I practiced. To me, fiction writing is total imagination, it must come solely from your mind, and while I might read Jung or look up facts to base the fiction on, by which I mean things like what actually happened on a particular date, etc., I find little need to do a lot of formal research. The biggest fear I have is I will begin, or by accident, take on another writer's phrases or point of view or character or descriptions or style. It is absolutely important to me that I provide my own everything by thinking about my characters and who they are, imagining their surroundings in my own unique style and voice, being able to bring at least one single new thought to the world of readers, because that is the beauty of writing, that is the honesty of the craft, and it's one of the few honest professions left in this world, I think.

Do you have any advice for other writers?

Learn your craft, practice your craft, develop a thick skin, appreciate the talents of other writers and figure out what makes them successful, and take every opportunity to embarrass yourself.

THE LAST ROAD HOME

Danny Johnson

ABOUT THIS GUIDE

The suggested questions are included to enhance
your group's reading of Danny Johnson's
The Last Road Home.

DISCUSSION QUESTIONS

1. When and how do Junebug and Fancy become aware that their feelings for each other are more than friendship? Do you think their elders—Roy, Clemmy, and Junebug's grandmother—realize this before Junebug and Fancy do?

2. In what ways did Junebug being an orphan, then a soldier in Vietnam, lead him to identify more with African American sharecroppers and the soldiers he served with than the privileged whites living in his community? Did his economic status and service in an unpopular war do more to classify him than race in a part of the United States where race determines everything? Has it done more to determine whom he feels closest to?

3. What were the two or three most pivotal events in Junebug's life and how did he change as a result of those events? If his grandmother had lived, how might that have changed his relationship with Fancy?

4. How does the violence that Junebug experienced as a young man influence his seemingly natural immersion in combat? How are they different?

5. What are the themes in the book?

6. Why does Junebug so intensely dislike Mr. Wilson? Why does Fancy? Is it possible he's not quite as bad a man as they imagine?

7. How does the author's depiction of life as a soldier in Vietnam differ from other/similar sources on the subject?

8. What are the comparisons and/or contrasts of Fancy's female role models in the novel, i.e., Fancy to her mother, to Junebug's grandmother, and even to the woman she travels with to Paris?

9. Were you happy with the ending of the book? How did you envision the future for Junebug and Fancy?